Across the Pacific

Western Samoa

American Samoa

Tonga

Cook Islands

Fiji

The Captain's Cook

THE CAPTAIN'S COOK

A Novel

Victoria Vanransom

BROWN BOOKS

PUBLISHING GROUP

The Captain's Cook: A Novel

Brown Books Publishing Group
Dallas, TX / New York, NY
www.BrownBooks.com
(972) 381-0009

A New Era in Publishing®

Publisher's Cataloging-In-Publication Data

Names: Vanransom, Victoria, author.
Title: The captain's cook : a novel / Victoria Vanransom.
Description: Dallas, TX ; New York, NY : Brown Books Publishing Group, [2025]
Identifiers: LCCN: 2025936863 | ISBN: 9781612547336 (hardcover) | 9781612547343 (ePub)
Subjects: LCSH: Women cooks--Fiction. | Divorced women--Fiction. | Yachts--Fiction. | Ship captains--Fiction. | Man-woman relationships--Fiction. | Self-realization--Fiction. | Courage--Fiction. | LCGFT: Romance fiction. | Action and adventure fiction. | BISAC: FICTION / Women. | FICTION / Romance / Contemporary. | FICTION / Action & Adventure.
Classification: LCC: PS3622.A6745 C36 2025 | DDC: 813/.6--dc23

ISBN 978-1-61254-733-6
EISBN 978-1-61254-734-3
LCCN 2025936863

Printed in Canada
10 9 8 7 6 5 4 3 2 1

For more information or to contact the author, please go to
www.CaptainsCookNovel.com.

Dedication

This book is dedicated to my beloved husband, a tribute to our journey, and to the love that will forever anchor my heart. You navigated the seas of life with unwavering courage and a heart full of adventure.

Sunset against blue on the horizon: you have set sail on your final journey, but your spirit lives on in every gust of wind, in every swell of the sea, and in the quiet moments beneath starlit skies.

And to my beloved son, whose stories lit up the world around him. Your time with us was far too brief. Countless adventures left unwritten.

For the ones we love who leave us with a profound hole in our hearts, they live on in every tale told, every dream spun, and in every moment cherished.

Prologue

Two Weeks at Sea

The voice of a woman came over the radio, faint and zombielike.

"Mayday, mayday, mayday. . . . Please, *please* someone hear me. . . . Dear God, please don't let me die. My husband is dead on the mast of our boat, and I can't get to him. Oh God. . . . I am sorry, I can't get him down . . . please—"The voice made a choking, crackling sound and was gone.

Captain Reed immediately radioed Captain Mendoza of the fishing vessel. "Whiskey, Echo, Charlie, Victor. *Slow Dance* here, do you copy?"

"*Slow Dance, Slow Dance, Maria Atun* copies you."

Captain Reed asked, "Have you tuned to CH 16?"

Captain Mendoza replied, "That is affirmative. Channel 16. Have not heard a thing but we spotted a boat eight miles south. Seems to be drifting out there. Not even the mainsail is up. We picked up the DSC bling two days ago. The boat's radar had to be switched on because we have detailed latitude and longitude. Whatever their situation is, it has been going on for two days. We will report back. Stand by, *Slow Dance. Maria Atun* out."

Jess cuddled Trinidad against her chest like a child squeezing a stuffed animal. The little pooch had over a hundred sea miles to her credit, making her a stout four-legged sailor.

"Jesus, sounds bad," said Cheri.

Lou moved next to where Captain Reed was standing at the radio.

Sydney added, "Super bad. The woman's voice seriously creeped me out." She began stroking Trini to calm herself.

It was the first time Jess experienced *Slow Dance* taking water over her bow. "Digging into the trough," sailors called it. The squalls were not what unnerved her. It was the woman's voice on the radio.

1

Quantum Leap

Chef needed for 92-foot Don Brooks monohull ketch, sailing from Marina del Rey, Los Angeles, December 28, 2023, for Tahiti.

Jessica Kline wanted to be as far away from the current ex-boyfriend and her second career in real estate as she could get.

Closing her eyes, she recalled the places in the books she shared with her mother: blue seas, white sandy beaches, palm trees, romance, and adventure. A lovely, distracting daydream, shattered by the reality of her immediate basic need for food and shelter.

She was flat broke and in all kinds of trouble, again.

Jess had been offered a chance to barter her real estate services for some therapy sessions, and it seemed like a promising idea. After all, nothing in her life was working; she felt desperate. The Malibu therapist was quirky, eccentric, weird, and unconventional. "Nothing is going your way, darling, because you force it," she'd said. "You need to learn to trust your intuition. The seven-year relationship, well, just shit on it. Shit all over it! You need to let go; let all the balls drop; just let it all fall apart."

Had that been good advice? It felt right at the time. Everything else felt wrong and self-destructive. To deliberately allow everything in her life to fall apart seemed impossible. She was ready for a shift into something out of character, and it would take courage. A chef position on a super yacht bound for the South Pacific sounded like the perfect start to a new chapter.

Mr. Shit had been Jess's partner for seven years. Jess had thought this would be her least controlling relationship, but, in truth, the man turned out to be the most controlling person she had ever selected as her tormentor. She took another chance on love without understanding her role in the dynamics, which made it difficult to break the cycle of her past mistakes. Presently, she was willing to make changes and determined to do the work necessary to navigate those triggers differently. It was herself with whom she needed to fall in love. Sailing the seven seas sounded like an effective way to make this shift, but was she getting more than she bargained for?

October 2023
California Yacht Club

Jess stood outside her apartment, gazing at the bustling street as she waited for her ex-boyfriend to pull up. The sun glinting off the sleek cars driving by a stark contrast to her situation. Her car was in the shop, and now she was relying on her ex, of all people, for a ride to her big interview on the yacht.

She felt a knot in her stomach. The yacht was a dream opportunity, a chance to showcase her culinary skills in a luxurious setting but being in a confined space with her ex made her uneasy. He had a way of veering into sarcasm or bluntness that could ruin her mood. She needed to be at her best today, not dealing with his unpredictable attitude.

The drive to the marina felt longer than it was.

"Are you even excited about this?" he asked abruptly, breaking her concentration.

"Yeah, I am," she replied.

"Is the captain interviewing you alone on this yacht?"

"No, his assistant, Kari, is taking care of that."

"What else does assistant Kari do for the captain?" he asked, his tone judgmental.

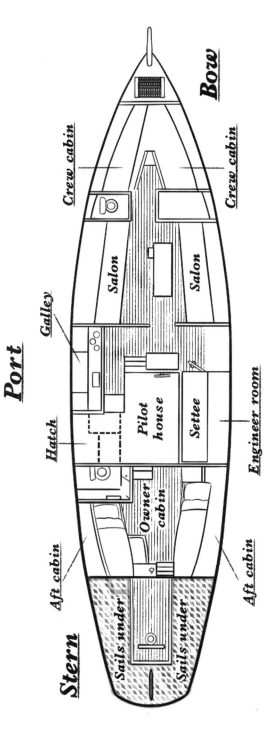

Victoria Vanransom

Slow Dance: floor plan

Bow

Stern

Port

Starboard

Crew cabin

Crew cabin

Salon

Salon

Galley

Pilot house

Settee

Engineer room

Hatch

Owner cabin

Aft cabin

Aft cabin

Sails under

Sails under

Jess bit her tongue to suppress a negative retort. "When we chatted on the phone, she mentioned that she's a masseuse."

Mr. Shit parked the car, and Jess took a moment to gather herself. "Thanks for the ride," she said and quickly exited the car.

Shaking off her ex, Jess concentrated on the gentle October breeze that carried a promise of adventure as she hurried toward the docks for her interview. Clutching the folder containing her résumé, she meandered through a flotilla of super yachts, dreaming of a future that included both the challenges of the job and the freedom of the open sea. The sound of the waves lapping against the dock turned her thoughts to the realization that she had zero experience on boats, and she felt a sudden lack of confidence. Jess told herself that even if she did not get the job, this would remain etched in her memory as a perfect Southern California day, filled with possibility and beauty. Arriving at gate 6, where the sailboat berthed, curiosity replaced her chaotic thoughts, and she dialed the number for Kari, the woman who arranged the interview, to announce she was waiting at the gate. Jess chanted *Tahiti* over and over in her head. She couldn't remember the boat's name, only that it meant escaping to adventure.

As Jess hurried toward the gate, Mr. Shit beat her to the entrance, and in his unmitigated, unflinching way, he talked his way onto the dock to have a look at the boat.

"What a life. The boats are impressive, but it's intimidating to think how small they look out in the middle of the ocean. I would be scared." Mr. Shit pushed past Kari, squeezing himself between her and the gate to access the private dock.

"One peek, and I'll be on my way."

Before Jess could speak, Kari said, "A very quick peek. Captain Reed does not appreciate lookie-loos."

"Copy that," Mr. Shit replied. "I'm going to walk the dock. If that is okay with you."

Kari waved him off, and Jess followed her down the dock toward the yacht.

Centering herself, Jess took a deep breath, the scent of the ocean mingling with the aroma of fresh herbs and spices lingering in her memory. She was reminded of her father standing over the stove, his large hands chopping vegetables, transforming simple ingredients into something magical.

Her father had been her anchor, and the kitchen a place of refuge from her mother's illness. She had spent countless hours at his side creating dishes that evoke joy in the darkest of times. As she prepared mentally for the interview, the weight of her father's lessons felt comforting. Jess heard his words in her head. "Cooking is about intuition." Now, as she walked toward the yacht, she wondered if she would feel that same intuition on the open water. Would she be able to translate her culinary skills into the rhythm of the sea? Sailing was uncharted territory.

Just think of it as a new recipe, she told herself, trying to quell the anxiety bubbling inside. *You got this.* She could almost hear her father's voice.

As she stepped aboard the *Slow Dance* yacht, Jess was taken by the beauty of her surroundings. The deck of polished wood, warm under her feet, and the sleek lines of the boat spoke of past adventures and new possibilities. The spacious deck provided ample room for relaxation and entertainment. The interior of the sailboat was equally impressive. The walls were solid sheets of teak, polished to a rich golden hue. The sofas and pillows created a luxurious and inviting atmosphere. The open-plan layout maximized space and allowed for easy movement throughout the yacht. Large windows encircled the pilothouse, offering a panoramic view of the surrounding marina. It was magnificent and completely foreign to her. Jess had grown up surrounded by the comforting embrace of the forest, where the rustling of leaves and changing seasons were familiar and predictable. The thought of venturing into the vastness of the ocean filled her with a mix of excitement and dread. Jess was suddenly terrified she might get the job.

As she stepped into the pilothouse, the strong scent of the sea mingled with the ocean breeze caused her heart to race. She sat quietly on one of the sofas opposite Kari, admiring a painting of a mermaid that hung on the pilothouse wall.

Jess had prepared for the interview, but nothing could quite prepare her for the sight of the captain. Emerging from the shadows of the saloon, he stepped into the light, revealing a weathered, handsome face that spoke of years spent navigating the seas and the intricacies of life. His hair, a dark and silvery mane, caught the sunlight, giving him an almost ethereal glow. His piercing blue eyes regarded Jess with a mix of curiosity and authority.

Kari was about to start the introduction when the uninvited boyfriend entered the pilothouse, flashing his charismatic smile-like mask that hid a more aggressive nature. Interrupting the conversation, eager to dominate the discussion, his voice filled with charm that felt rehearsed rather than genuine, he blurted out, "So, Kari, you're a masseuse, I hear? Me too. I ran the spa at Murrieta Hot Springs. I could come along on the voyage to keep everyone relaxed."

He was the only one chuckling. Jess was glaring at him in discomfort. His pushiness manifesting in persistent offers of help came off as self-serving. He had a knack for making others feel obligated, as if refusing him was personal.

"Who are you, and why are you on my boat without permission to board?" Captain Reed demanded, addressing the uninvited Mr. Shit.

Jess stood up; her cheeks hot with anger. "I accepted a ride because you were coming this way. Suddenly, you are part of my interview?"

Kari rose and extended her hand to Mr. Shit while looking at Captain Reed. "I gave the okay to look at the boat from the dock, not the interior. Thank you for bringing Jess to the interview."

Taking the hint, shit boyfriend stood up, shook Kari's hand, and gave Captain Reed a ridiculously awkward salute before exiting the boat.

Kari began a formal introduction. "Captain Cliff Reed, this is Jessica Kline."

Jess extended her hand and said, "You can call me Jess." Captain Reed took her hand, holding on to it long enough to make her uncomfortable. Jess sat back on the sofa, and Captain Reed settled into his captain's chair, the leather creaking softly beneath him, a throne of sorts for this seasoned mariner. Jess felt a rush of intimidation that made her feel uneasy. As the light danced across the captain's features, accentuating the strong jawline and soft wrinkles around his eyes, she could not help but think that the complexity of the man was both formidable and inviting.

Jess's palms were sweaty as she fidgeted with the edge of her résumé. The captain sat in his imposing leather chair, a silent sentinel. His presence loomed large, but he remained still except for his fingers, which he kept interlaced whilst twiddling his thumbs. Kari, a poised woman with an air of confidence, took the lead. "Let us get started. Can you tell us about your culinary experience?"

Jess took a breath. "Two years of college in Boulder, Colorado; completed eighteen months at the Culinary Institute of America in Hyde Park, New York, and jumped on a plane to the Netherlands."

"Go on," he said.

"I was unable to obtain a work permit, so I placed an ad in the international newspaper *De Telegraaf* and landed a job as the head chef at the Iranian Embassy in Wassenaar. I had to master Persia's culinary culture, historically intertwined with neighboring regions, including Turkish, Greek, Central Asian, and Russian cuisines. The ambassador and his wife liked American food, thank goodness. Diplomatic dinners were required twice per month, and the wives of the embassy were enlisted to teach me the art of Persian food. It was a terrific learning experience. The Persians are experts in combinations of rice, meat, vegetables, fruits, and nuts. They utilize herbs, along with fruits such as plums, pomegranates, and raisins. I learned to incorporate their flavorings such as saffron, dried lime, cinnamon, and parsley into various dishes."

It was an adventurous time in Jess's young life. In the coffee houses of The Hague, she met a young man from New Jersey who wrote poems and played guitar in a band.

She fell in love and followed him to India, where they lived in an ashram to avoid the war and the disapproval of his wealthy family. Leaving India, they traveled to Sri Lanka, where they lived with a family in the mountainous region of Kandy. While Edan filled his notebook with poems and lyrics, Jess embarked on a culinary odyssey, immersing herself in the heritage of India and Sri Lankan curry. She loved the bustling markets and humble street-food stalls. She absorbed herself in the regional cuisines and techniques that would shape her future creations.

Despite their best efforts, Jess and Edan broke up but remained friends. Jess returned to New York on her own, and over the next three decades she embarked on a remarkable culinary journey working at renowned restaurants, where she impressed customers and colleagues with her unique preparations.

Jess continued diving into her background years spent in bustling kitchens, honing her craft in fine dining, and delving into healthy menus. She could feel the captain's gaze scrutinizing her every word as she spoke. The silence from him was deafening, amplifying her nervousness. After a series of questions about her cooking style, adaptability, and willingness to cook on a ship at sea, Kari paused, looking to the captain for his input. He finally shifted in his chair, but instead of speaking, he simply regarded Jess with those piercing eyes as if weighing her worth in a single glance.

"Is there anything you would like to ask Captain Reed?" Kari prompted, breaking the tension.

Jess turned to the captain, feeling the weight of the moment.

"What do you expect from your onboard cook?" she ventured, her voice steady despite the knot in her stomach.

The captain leaned forward as if to speak, but then simply leaned back, his gaze locked onto hers. "I don't have expectations. That way, there are no disappointments." His comment left Jess with a sense of both dread and curiosity.

Finally, Kari thanked Jess and dismissed her, but as Jess rose to leave, she couldn't shake the feeling that the captain's silence had been more revealing than any words could have been. Kari offered to call Jess an Uber and walk her to the gate. Jess exited the boat, her mind racing with questions about the enigmatic man who had watched her so intently, leaving her wondering what lay beneath his stoic exterior.

As they walked to the gate, Kari turned to Jess. "One hundred people applied, and we only chose thirty-five to be interviewed, so give me a couple of weeks to get back to you."

One week later, to Jess's shock, surprise, and every other emotion, Kari called to offer her the job. She informed Jess that the reason the captain selected her was because he needed a healthy diet. Though she had experience with healthy menus, Jess wondered if that was the only reason Captain Reed hired her.

2

Seaward Peril

March 2024
Pacific Ocean

Jess stared at the radar screen, watching the straight line as it made its way around the screen, lighting up with red flashes every time it passed over the storms ahead. Captain Reed gently placed his hand on her shoulder.

"Don't worry; the squalls will be short bursts of rain with a bit of wind. We have been consuming fuel in these windless waters. The closer we get to the equator, the worse the doldrums, so the wind is a good thing. I don't want to think about being out here with no fuel and no wind. You know what the doldrums are?"

Jess smiled. "Yes, my last marriage."

Captain Reed laughed. "Very funny. Can you make a pot of coffee? I am going out on deck to join the crew and get the storm sails up before the squalls hit."

Jess was concerned. "Captain, I am worried about the mayday signal. What do you think could be happening?"

Captain Reed gave her a reassuring look. "Don't be; it's probably a boat out here that's having engine problems."

Despite his answer, Jess felt an overwhelming sense of dread regarding the mayday. It meant someone was in trouble. *Slow Dance* began heeling—over-tipping to one side—due to the increased wind in the sail. Jess grasped the railing with one hand as she descended the steps to the galley, the lowest level on the boat and a never-ending trigger for her seasickness.

To maintain balance, she wedged herself between the cupboards and prepared the coffee pot. After pressing the brew button, she hurried back up to the pilothouse. The anti-nausea patches Captain Reed had given her worked, but she had been rationing them by wearing half a patch at a time. Given that she was new to sailing, she figured it best to save a few in case of rough seas.

The boat mascot, a cute, gray poodle named Trinidad, Trini for short, appeared on deck. Her little legs were swaying in unison to accommodate the motion of the boat. Jess patted the cushion, and the dog jumped up alongside her.

"Trinidad, even you have sea legs. Me . . . well, I'm destined to be a landlubber."

Captain Reed returned to the pilothouse and secured the door. Crew members Harrison and Chaz checked to ensure all portholes and hatches were dogged down tightly to prevent seawater from seeping into the boat. Jess suddenly realized Captain Reed was speaking to her.

"How about that coffee? Stow the pot. The next squall is just ahead." Jess reluctantly made her way back down to the galley, where the gratuitously female crew, Cheri, Lou, and Sydney, were sitting in the salon playing cards.

Cheri collected the deck and placed it back in the box. "What's going on up there?"

Jess answered, "Captain Mendoza from a nearby fishing boat hailed us because of a boat that's in some kind of trouble." After she prepared the captain's cup, the girls followed Jess up to the pilothouse.

Jess handed Captain Reed his coffee and he took it from her while holding onto the chart table. The seas had come up, and, due to the increased swells rocking the boat, Jess sat on the sofa with Trinidad, her feet against the chart table to keep from rolling off portside. Cheri and Lou sat across from Jess on the opposite sofa, holding onto the side cabinets for stability. It was not the first time the women crossed the ocean, so they remained calm, if a bit concerned. Sydney sat next to Jess, her feet also braced against the base of the chart table. Sydney and Jess both wore the same anxious expression. As Captain Reed said, the storms were quick microbursts of wind and rain with a bit of calm in-between. During a calm stretch, Captain Reed turned the radio to CH 16, a channel reserved for sailors in trouble.

3

Consternation

March 2024
Pacific Ocean

"When I crossed here years ago, you never saw another boat. Just a wide-open ocean and a million stars. Now, here we are with a boat in trouble and *Slow Dance* close enough to investigate." Captain Reed was speaking to Harrison when Chaz added his two cents:

"Sailors should cross in a group. Safety in numbers."

Captain Reed turned to Chaz. "I am not a rescuer, and as soon as the situation is under control, *Slow Dance* resumes course."

Chaz gave Captain Reed an annoyed look. "God knows what we'll find when we approach."

Harrison, who had been looking out the pilothouse window with binoculars, announced, "Hey, I see the fishing boat."

Chaz and Harrison ventured out of the pilothouse, and Jess followed with Trini on her heels. Trinidad was trained to do her business in the scuppers, which ran along the outside deck, and she took the opportunity to relieve herself. The wind was still gusting, but not enough to justify the storm sail. Chaz and Harrison furled the small sail, and Captain Reed positioned himself at the outside helm. The three men stood at the stern.

As Captain Reed steered *Slow Dance* toward the two boats, he addressed Chaz and Harrison. "I heard the woman on CH 16 a while ago. She sounded in trouble, big trouble. Says her husband is dead on their mast and she cannot get him down. I'll support as possible, but I am not equipped to take on injured people, dead bodies, or boats that need a tow. I am counting on the fishing boat *Maria Atun* and Mendoza to manage the situation. He should be in a better position to get this woman to safety. The *Maria Atun* most likely has medical personnel on board."

Chaz took the binoculars from Harrison. "Good God, it's the *Calypso*, Brian and Mary's boat."

Slow Dance reduced her speed, and Jess joined the group at the outside helm. She was trembling as *Slow Dance* approached the distressed boat. Jess could see someone at the bow frantically waving their arms.

"What's that smell?" Jess covered her nose with her hand. The wind was causing a tumult. The halyard lines used to hoist the sails were clanging against *Slow Dance*'s mast, and the incessant noise was contributing to Jess's angst. Captain Reed utilized the bow thrusters to bring *Slow Dance* closer to the *Calypso*, and Trini began barking wildly as they flanked the boat. The person who had been waving their arms was now slumped over on the deck near the boat's mast. Jess could see it was a woman. Her head was hanging on her chest, and she was clawing at the mast in a repetitive motion, first slow and then fast, screaming, "I can't get him! I can't get him!"

Jess turned her gaze from the woman to the body hanging from the mast. The face was unrecognizable, shriveled from the sun, and the eyes were hollow sockets from the pecking of seabirds. The wind carried the smell of his death into Jess's nostrils, and she raced below deck with Trini close behind.

Mortified, distressed, and nauseated, Jess thought if there was ever a time she needed something to calm her, this was it! After lighting the joint she was given in Yelapa, Mexico, she took several puffs until the effects of the smoke ceased her shaking and quieted her nerves. She took another puff, but before she could exhale, she lost her footing and landed on the commode.

"Shoot! Well, that is that." Jess steadied herself, carefully wrapping the remaining joint in plastic and stowing it under the sofa cushion. She figured it was safe there, just below the wooden panel where Captain Reed hid his money and gun. Stepping into the bathroom, she lifted the toilet seat and gave in to her nausea.

Hours passed, but the clanging had not. Jess pressed her hands tightly against her ears, hoping to shut out the sounds of the halyards. She had been hiding below the deck in Captain Reed's cabin with Trinidad for what seemed like days. The engine had stopped hours ago, and she heard several voices but could not make out what they were saying due to the clanging noise. *Slow Dance* was bouncing from side to side, rekindling Jess's nausea, and the putrid smell of decaying flesh made it even worse. Jess was gifted with an uncanny sense of smell, and she hoped it hadn't been compromised. The little poodle tilted her head and perked up her ears as if she understood the way Jess felt.

"What do you think, Trini? Good of them to leave us to our meltdown."

Trinidad laid her head on Jess's lap.

"Jess, are you okay?" Captain Reed was knocking on the door. "You cannot stay in there forever. Anyway, it is over."

Reluctantly, Jess acknowledged his knocking. How pleasant it had been to hide from the man decaying on the mast of his boat, seagulls pecking at him until his gaping eye sockets were the only feature left of his face. She shuddered at the memory.

Taking a deep breath, and with a cottony mouth, she replied, "I will come out when things calm down and the boats are gone. Sorry."

"It's done." He coaxed, "*Maria Atun* is helping the poor woman. The crew removed him from the mast. Thankfully, the poor fellow kept the boat's radar on so someone could pick up the signal. His wife knew enough to activate the distress signal but couldn't receive calls or didn't know how the receiver on her radio functioned; I do not know which. She thought she would die at sea. Terrible as it is, dreadful things can happen out here. It is over and we need to be underway. *Maria Atun* took them aboard their ship. Captain Mendoza headed back to the coast and the Mexican authorities will come for the *Calypso*. It is all worked out. Now, come on up. We are hungry."

"How can you even think about food?" Jess opened the door, and Captain Reed gave her a sympathetic look.

"Forty-eight years at sea, and I've seen a lot worse. I nearly died out here; every man for himself. Now, come up top, look at the horizon, and take in the fresh air. Once the engine starts, you will feel better."

Although the situation was under control, Jess was scared. The *Calypso* was a wake-up call to the dangers of sailing across the open sea. She trusted Captain Reed but not Chaz, the boat's amateurish second-in-command. She liked Chaz until the night in Marina del Rey when he totaled the company SUV. He had been drinking with some old yacht friends but somehow escaped DUI. She considered quitting because she no longer trusted him, but she did trust Captain Reed and felt he would keep her safe. She needed this adventure.

Jess wondered why Captain Reed tolerated Chaz. Their relationship had become strained after the three women gratuitously joined the boat in Mexico. They were in the middle of the Pacific Ocean, and every day, Chaz became increasingly hostile toward everyone except Harrison.

Dabbing a bit of toothpaste onto her tongue and rubbing it over her teeth, she worked at quieting her emotions. She tried to push away the thoughts of what could go wrong. She was brave when she boarded *Slow Dance*, but now, she utterly understood how ignorance is bliss.

Slow Dance had been at sea for twenty days, putting the ship three thousand miles out from land—with five strangers as crew members and an owner who seemed to believe that in times of crisis, it was every man for himself. There was no escape, only vast miles of ocean. Jess could not push the memory of Brian or Mary from her mind, and she prayed it wouldn't haunt her for the rest of her life.

Trini gave Jess a nuzzle. The poodle was her only comfort now. The animal attached herself to Jess the first night she slept on the boat. She was a woman's dog. She loved Jess, and the feeling was mutual.

"Thanks for hanging with me Trini, you're a real pal." Gently scooping the little dog up into her arms, Jess gave her nose a kiss. "Come on girl, time to go up top."

Jess climbed the steps to the pilothouse, where she encountered Captain Reed.

"Feel better?" he asked in an inscrutable tone.

Jess hated that confusing attitude of his. Was he joking or admonishing her? She had been feeling an incipient urge to like him, despite his sometimes-injurious behavior. Setting aside the time Jess spent in Mexico aboard *Slow Dance*, she still could not tell if he was a shallow, immoral wizard behind the curtain, or if he even knew how to sail. Meanwhile, she was in the middle of the Pacific Ocean with no feasible way to leave the ship.

Suddenly, the engines started, and Jess's thoughts were fully interrupted when Chaz appeared from the engine room, wearing his mechanic's overalls as if they enabled him to perform actual, necessary mechanical tasks. His boyish face was drawn, and he was looking all his sixty-two years.

"The seas are calming, Captain. The storm passed. Poor Mary was in bad shape, being out here alone with him up there on the mast and no way to get him down. Birds pecking at him. She almost didn't make it. Awful. I am shaken from helping the *Atun* crew get him down and then roll him up in the tarp. If only he had not been such a pompous know-it-all bastard and traveled with a group, he would still be alive."

Captain Reed shot Chaz an annoyed look. "He had a heart attack, Chaz. It's a shame they didn't carry a defibrillator with them; we have one."

Chaz continued, "We can expect some large swells every twenty minutes or so, coming south from New Zealand."

Chaz waited for an acknowledgment. He desperately wanted to show he knew something regarding sailing and the ocean, but as usual, Captain Reed ignored him. Getting a poker face from the real captain, Chaz turned his attention to Jess and the poodle. Giving Trini a rub, he said, "You seasick, too, you little wooly monster? We can't have a seasick pup or a seasick cook. It does not seem like either of you two are cut out for sailing."

Jess answered him sarcastically, "No, Chaz, it has more to do with finding dead people on their boat out here in the doldrums. Is there meaning to finding dead people at sea? Are we jinxed? Thank you, though, for managing it; and please, no details." Jess put her hand up to ward off Chaz.

4

Sound Off

March 2024
Pacific Ocean

"Why don't they help you more?"

Chaz was gesturing toward the three women in the saloon sipping wine to soothe them from the drama of the *Calypso*.

Giving Chaz her biggest eye roll on hand, Jess answered, "Doesn't some oil or hydraulic fluid need your attention?"

Chaz mumbled under his breath, "Damn bitches need to open a can of harden up," and he huffed back to the engine room.

Jess decided to lodge a formal complaint with Captain Reed.

"He has a point, you know," she said. "Your Gratuitous Three are getting on my nerves. They leave their dirty cups and glasses anywhere they please. Lou does not do dishes because she is allergic to soap, the sponge, and the rubber gloves. Sydney does every domestic job poorly *on purpose*, so I no longer ask. And Cheri, although the best sailor on the boat—except for you, of course—wastes precious food supplies. Harrison is the only one who respects me."

Captain Reed looked at her in a way that made most people uncomfortable. Not Jess. She knew he was forming a plan.

"Quit."

"What?" she said, the power of her rant suddenly dissolving before her.

"I am telling you. *Quit*," he said tersely, as if directing a film.

Jess answered, "Um, we are in the middle of the ocean. How does that work?"

Jess wondered if Captain Reed was more aware of her inner struggles than she realized.

"Call them all up here and quit," he replied. "It is simple: just quit. Plus, this will be entertaining for me."

"What about lunch?" Jess asked.

Captain Reed settled back in his director's chair at the helm.

"Is that even a proper chair to have at a helm?" Jess said, regretting her complaint and trying to change the subject.

"Not really. The chair was gifted to me by Robin Williams when the boat chartered for the film *Old Dogs*."

"This boat was in movies?" Jess asked.

"Yeah," Captain Reed replied. "She worked in films for five years while she docked in Marina del Rey. I had a marine coordinator and open-heart surgery."

"Right," Jess said. She recalled seeing the scar when she became the captain's unwilling nurse after he fell off a ladder—*or jumped off, because who knows with him?*—and shattered his arm during her first week living aboard *Slow Dance*. And later Captain Reed hobbling back from the hospital with his girlfriend, Sophia. He was helpless, she had realized. Sophia made it clear she was not going to take care of him.

Her thoughts dug deeper into that fateful day. How she tended to his needs, with a mixture of trepidation and care. As she bandaged his arm and prepared meals, their conversations deepened. It was during these moments that their friendship blossomed, and Jess realized the accident had brought them together in a way she never could have anticipated. They had come a long way from her second encounter with the captain when he watched her place the cushions back onto the saloon sofa. It was her first day aboard *Slow Dance*.

"You put the cushion back wrong," Captain Reed told her, pointing at the sofa. "The zipper part goes the other way."

Looking at the cushion, Jess saw he was right and turned the zipper to the back. *Good grief,* she had thought. *He makes me nervous. I hope I have not made a huge mistake; I don't know a damn thing about boats.*

But with his arm in a sling after his mishap, their dynamic shifted. He was no longer the stern, aloof captain that made her palms sweat every time he entered her galley. Jess found herself juggling the roles of both cook and reluctant nurse. She saw a man grappling with both vulnerability and frustration. Their conversations, once silted and formal, began to flow more freely, filled with laughter and shared stories that bridged the gap between them. Jess discovered not only her resilience but also a deeper connection with the man she once regarded with trepidation.

Captain Reed removed his hat and, giving a little bow, replied, "Cookie, you are my savior. Without you, I would be landlocked."

"Cookie?" Jess tilted her head. "I assume that name is meant to be endearing? Never mind, and anyway, you would have another babe in a nanosecond to take care of you, Captain. What other movies?"

Half smiling, he said, "One of the *Meet the Fockers* films, a photo shoot with Jessica Simpson, an Arab sultan's birthday . . . I am bad with names."

Captain Reed snatched the microphone from its holder, and his voice boomed over the intercom outside and below deck.

"All hands to the pilothouse! Our cook has an announcement!"

"Jesus-Mother-Mary-and-Joseph," Jess muttered under her breath.

The three women came up to the pilothouse and plopped themselves down on the sofas.

Chaz appeared from the engine room and Harrison from the top deck where he had opened the hatches now that the Brian-and-Mary ordeal had passed along with the rain. They were all looking at Jess. The fresh air flowed in from the hatches, and Jess took a deep breath.

"You look tired, Jess," said Lou. "Terrible what happened to Brian and Mary, and we know how freaked out you were, but it's taken care of now and we need you."

"Okay, thank you," Jess replied. "I am good, and I quit!"

They all stared at her. Sydney broke the uncomfortable silence by bursting into laughter. Then Jess started laughing, and soon they were all laughing, except Chaz, who looked disgusted. Although his intention was to mumble under his breath, they all heard him.

"Bunch of cackling idiot hens, be a wonder if I make it to land alive."

Jess ignored Chaz's comment.

"I've asked you three women to lend a hand, but you don't," Captain Reed put in. "You continue to drink from glasses which inevitably end up broken on the deck every time. None of us wear shoes on deck, except Chaz, so please just drink from plastic wineglasses. You are supposed to be experienced sailors and should be picking up your cups and glasses before they smash in rough seas. All of you are guilty of leaving your personal belongings cluttering the communal areas. There were rules clearly laid out before we set sail. Your mother is not on the boat."

Cheri said, "You don't take your dog out on deck for her business and this morning she peed on my pillow!"

Jess sighed. "I do not feel the least bit bad about that, Cheri. I have cautioned you to keep your cabin door closed. That used to be my cabin. Trinidad is trying to tell you something."

Cheri stood up, placing her hands at her hips, "Okay, whatever you say; and from now on, I'll keep my door closed to keep the dogs out . . . all of you!"

Captain Reed intervened. "Okay, meeting is over. In less than three hours we cross the equator. Jess has a bottle of Dom Pérignon on ice to celebrate, and we all need a little calming down."

Jess recalled the first time she saw her cabin; it smelled like the sea. It was snug, but the drawers under the bed provided ample space for her clothes. There was also a closet with hangers and a nice bathroom. She put her things away and opened the portholes to let in the fresh air; she heard seals barking outside on the docks. She liked the sound of them. Seal of approval, she had thought.

Jess thought back to that first Sunday aboard the yacht in Marina del Rey when Chaz received a phone call from Kari that the captain had fallen off a ladder and shattered all the bones in his upper right arm. Jess and Chaz drove to St. John's Hospital near the marina to inquire about Captain Reed. An aid directed them to a room on the fourth floor, but when they got there, the nurse informed them Captain Reed had checked himself out. The nurse looked annoyed. "Honestly, the man is crazy to think he is going to deal with that arm on a boat," she commented. "The idiot left with a blond woman and pain medication."

Arriving back to *Slow Dance*, Chaz and Jess had found the captain lying in bed, his arm in a sling, and a petite, attractive blond standing by his bedside. Chaz had extended his hand to her. "You must be Captain Reed's sister, Phyllis."

The woman recoiled from him, "No," she said twisting her lip into a sneer of disdain, "I am *Sophia*."

Jess recalled breaking the tension by asking if the captain needed anything, and Sophia answering, "He is heavily medicated and needs to sleep. Check on him later; I must run."

Jess had consulted Chaz regarding the captain's accident and how it would affect them.

Chaz was at a loss. "I honestly couldn't say."

5

Zero Degrees Latitude

March 2024
The Equator

"The Shellback Ceremony," said Lou, placing her hand on Captain Reed's shoulder.

"Oh, you know about that, do you?" said Captain Reed.

"Yes, as a matter of fact, I do," Lou said in her ultra-sexy voice. "King Neptune comes aboard to exercise his right as King of the Sea. He judges charges brought against pollywogs who pretend to be sailors and have not paid respect to him and his domain."

Captain Reed raised an eyebrow. "Impressive, Lou."

Four hours after Jess served lunch, Sydney and Cheri returned to the pilothouse carrying a bag.

"We have a surprise for you, Captain Reed," said Sydney.

Lou and Sydney spent weeks working to surprise Captain Reed at the crossing of the equator. Sydney wove a Rasta wig entirely from sail line braided into long knots to resemble Johnny Depp's character in the *Pirates of the Caribbean*. She had been secretly working on it during the crossing. Lou rummaged through a bin in the salon that contained celebratory banners for any occasion, as well as wigs, novelties, and other party favorites stored there by the captain's deceased wife, Angie. Captain Reed shared stories about her with Jess when she addressed his arm; nothing personal, mostly factual, and the amusing antics she pulled. Angie sold her famous party-planning store and transferred party favorites, fine linen, and catering wares to the storage bins on the boat. Lou found a couple of tassels and fixed double-sided tape to each tassel. Sydney giggled as she crowned Captain Reed's head with her impressive wig. Lou pulled off Captain Reed's T-shirt and placed one tassel on each of his nipples. Jess noted how Captain Reed was enjoying the ladies dressing him up as King of the Sea. Cheri put on a striped pirate shirt, hat, and eye patch from the party bin, and Sydney draped her purple sarong around her head and shoulders like an exotic dancer and did a sort of hula dance. Jess went below to fetch the champagne, glasses, silly eyewear from the bin, and her camera.

Jess thought she would have liked Angie. She sounded like a lot of fun. The bin and the stories were all that remained of her. The captain said Angie would put her wigs on the heads of foreign government officials who came aboard to clear *Slow Dance* into their country and pour shots of fine tequila after the paperwork and sometimes prior. The captain fondly recanted amusing stories of Angie roaming the streets of Puerto Vallarta wearing a nun's habit, a scotch in one hand and a cigarette in the other. He told Jess a story about Angie trading clothes in the airport bathroom with the female attendant during a boring layover and then pranking him by sweeping the floors, pushing the broom into his feet as he walked to the men's room. He said he turned around, annoyed, and when he noticed the rude woman wearing a head scarf and Chanel shoes, he realized it was his wife.

One afternoon, while cleaning out a drawer in Captain Reed's cabin, she found Angie's phone. Captain Reed teared up when she presented it to him. Recovering quickly, he handed the phone back to Jess and commented, "My wife bought me this boat, and then I killed her. I killed my wife, you know."

Crossing the equator was important and a much-needed mood changer. Sydney called Chaz and Harrison to join the ceremony. Cheri handed them each a glass of bubbly as they stood in the doorway leading to the engine room. Sydney stood on the steps that led to the main deck, and holding her glass of bubbly in the air, she made the toast.

"Behold, King Neptune. We toast and honor you and beg for your protection to guide us to land with fair winds and following seas. We drink in your honor and ask that all pollywogs be delt with according to the laws of the sea."

They all took a drink from their glasses.

Jess was filming when Chaz appeared in the frame, his face red and twisted in disgust at the sight of Captain Reed as Neptune, tassels on his nipples.

"Goddamn idiots."

No one heard Chaz over the laughter except Jess. Lou was behind Captain Reed, and, as the camera panned their way, Lou pulled down his shorts. The women erupted in hysterical laughter. Trinidad was barking with excitement. Captain Reed stepped out of his shorts and held his arms out.

"Oh, my girls, my girls."

The four women surrounded him in a group hug. Chaz shot a disapproving look and retreated to the engine room, with Harrison following closely behind.

Jess wondered how Captain Reed tolerated Chaz. The tension between the two men manifested in many ways, ranging from subtle, underlying animosity to overt conflict. A dynamic influenced by their beliefs, values, past experiences, and external circumstances. Whether the tension would spiral into open hostility or eventually dissipate remained uncertain.

Chaz spent his time at the yacht club in Vallarta, attending meetings with other novice sailors crossing the Pacific Ocean for the first time. First-timers cross in a group, keeping a distance from one another but close enough to lend aid in the event a boat has trouble. Chaz had been busy making plans with the other boats to form a buddy system for their crossing.

It would be Captain Reed's second crossing to the Society Islands of French Polynesia. He crossed before the age of GPS, using paper charts, a timepiece, and a sextant. He sailed by the sun, moon, and stars, and he had no intention of crossing as a "cluster of problems," as he put it. This upset Chaz, who was determined to change Captain Reed's mind by requesting him to attend one of the yacht club's meetings.

"What possible objection could you have to safety in numbers?" Chaz asked.

To placate Chaz, Captain Reed agreed to attend one of the meetings.

Somewhere between the map of routes, GPS coordinates, and the question-and-answer period, Captain Reed dozed off out of extreme boredom. The captain was annoyed when Chaz shook him by the shoulder to awaken him to ask why he objected to sailing in a group.

The captain said, "Look, Chaz, this is going to be my last adventure at sea. I have been waiting decades to return to Tahiti, and the thought of rescuing boats out in East Jesus—who know fuck all from apple butter—is unappealing. *Slow Dance* is five times the size of all the other boats and ten times as fast. Even under full sail, they will not keep up, and I will not slow down to maintain any grouping. Never was and never will be a groupie-type guy. Before *Slow Dance*, my boat was *Lone Wolf*."

Captain Reed and Chaz's disagreement had originated from opposite ends of a spectrum, their views clashing like opposing forces. Chaz was a man driven by his passion and convictions. In stark contrast, Captain Reed exuded an air of calculated composure. His eyes, though guarded, harbored a steely resolve. His body language, while composed, hinted at a restrained readiness to take on any provocation.

One week prior to *Slow Dance* leaving for sea, Chaz gathered the crew together for a meeting to discuss cabin space.

"Cheri and Sydney are sharing the aft cabin across from our cook's cabin; I am in the forward boson cabin and Harrison has the crew cabin. So, Captain Reed, you have invited Lou. Will she be sharing the cabin with you?"

Captain Reed shook his head. "No. Lou will bunk with Sydney, and Cheri will take our cook's cabin."

Chaz was visibly upset, coming to Jess's defense. "And where exactly is Jess supposed to sleep? On deck?"

Captain Reed remained calm. "Of course not, Chaz. Our cook will bunk with me. I am still convalescing and need her assistance. The sofa in the primary cabin turns into a comfortable single bed, and there are further options where she could sleep comfortably, on deck, or in the salon. My habit is to sleep in the pilothouse when the boat is at sea, so Jess will have the cabin all to herself."

Chaz looked to Jess. "How do you feel about this?"

Jess was trying to decide if she was upset and remarkably, she was not. She had gotten to know Captain Reed well while mending his broken arm and they had developed a kind of symbiotic relationship.

Chaz made it clear he was not okay with the arrangement, nor was he okay with Lou joining their adventure. The atmosphere grew heavy, charged with an energy that crackled between the two men. The air was suffocating.

After a long pause, Jess spoke up. "I have to admit, I'm okay with it; and having slept on the outside deck a few times, I rather enjoy it out there when it's not raining, of course."

Captain Reed smiled. "See, Chaz, everything's cool."

Chaz had no more comments regarding Captain Reed's decision, but he would take it out on Lou during the crossing. Lou would become the main target of Chaz's disapproval of Captain Reed's decision to invite the women aboard *Slow Dance*.

During the first two months in Mexico where *Slow Dance* waited for the trade winds and Jess addressed Captain Reed's injured arm, the captain expressed to her his intention to add two more crew to assist in crossing the Pacific; however, he insisted on women. Captain Reed directed Jess to a site called *Find a Crew*, and Jess realized quickly the site was for horny male boat owners seeking naïve females with sailing fantasies. Jess scrutinized the ads, pointing out featured photos of attractive women who possessed earnest credentials.

"It will be nice to have other females aboard, so I am not the only one. I like this one." Jess pointed to a twenty-something girl with a round moon face and lovely smile. "She has a coastal captain's license."

Captain Reed looked at the ad. "Yes, but she lives in Wisconsin and sails on a lake."

Jess responded, "Most of these women are clueless."

"Yes, and so are you," he said.

Jess wrinkled her nose. "More reason to get experienced females. And besides, you did not hire me to sail; you hired me to cook. How about her?" Jess pointed to a very fit and attractive woman in her sixties. "A sailboat racer and fitness trainer from San Francisco. She crossed the Pacific twice! This woman is coming for the adventure."

Captain Reed nodded. "Hmm, attractive for her age. Oh, how about her?" He pointed to a shapely young Mexican girl striking a sexy pose in her photo.

"Valentina, nineteen, and lists her job as babysitting." Jess gave Captain Reed a look. "Perfect for you. Valentina can take care of your arm, and I can be released to the galley."

"Okay," he said, "reach out to the girl with a captain's license and the fitness trainer. I am getting hungry for lunch."

The Gratuitous Three

Sydney: The Girl with a Coastal Captain's License

Sydney was originally from Wisconsin, had a coastal captain's license and a small boat on Lake Superior. She accepted the offer, and Captain Reed sent her a ticket to fly to Vallarta the following week. Sydney arrived in Mexico with a duffle bag, waist-long dreadlocks, and quarter- sized holes in her ear lobes plugged with wooden gauges, looking much like a character who once ventured with or at least crossed paths with Captain Jack Sparrow. The only thing true to the picture she posted on the website was her beautiful smile. Captain Reed complained afterward regarding her unshaven body parts.

Cheri: Sailboat Racer & Fitness Trainer

Cheri jumped at the chance to sail on *Slow Dance*, agreeing to help Captain Reed rehab his arm. The day after Sydney arrived Captain Reed and Jess waited at the gate to greet Cheri. She looked like her photo. She was fit and sexy, with curly white hair, a lovely singing voice, abundant confidence, and a lot of sea miles to her credit. Cheri was—in Jess's opinion—Cliff Reed's type. Cheri had experience sailing both the Pacific and the Atlantic Oceans. This would be her second crossing to the Society Islands.

Lou: The Chick Captain Reed Finds in a Bar

Lou was fifty-eight, a quiet little slip of a woman from Canada, and part of the notorious Barra de Navidad party scene. These vivacious women were a group of fifty-somethings known affectionately as cougars, living their best lives in the picturesque coastline town of Barra. They were determined to embrace the joys of life, spending their days on the beach, soaking up the sun. By night, donning vibrant dresses and dancing under the stars at beachfront clubs, they hoped to catch the eyes of wealthy suitors. The cougars were all about enjoying the moment, living inexpensively, and reveling in the thrill of romantic possibilities, proving that life truly begins at fifty.

Captain Reed did not find Lou on the horny sailor website. He met Lou in one of those Mexican bars where the tequila flows like water, the mariachi band plays Beatles songs, and local patrons tie their live donkeys to the outside rail. Captain Reed was in a competition for Lou with an old sailor friend, Ernie. Lou set her sights on the captain, determined to convince him to invite her onto the boat and into his bed, which he did on Lou's first night aboard *Slow Dance*.

6

Phosphorescence

April 2024
At Sea, South Pacific Ocean

Jess was standing at the rail thinking how losing all her possessions seemed insignificant out in the middle of the Pacific Ocean. She hoped her things would become useful to others. She thought, *Nothing I have is truly mine anyway. We move through life, never truly owning anything. My townhouse in Malibu overlooking Paradise Cove went into foreclosure and now someone else is enjoying it. Hopefully, not the banksters. My furniture is a treasure to someone who needed it, and the bulk of my clothes appreciated by some women in need. I have absolutely no use for leather jackets and designer jeans. Bathing suits, sarongs, little dresses, and flip-flop sandals should do it.*

Suddenly, Captain Reed appeared on deck with Trinidad in tow and walked over to her to ask how she liked sailing out in the big blue.

"The sunsets are amazing. I cannot tell where the ocean ends and the sky begins. They blend to infinity."

Running his hand along the rail, Captain Reed gathered the dry salt into his palm, then opening it, he showed her the salt crystals.

"Beautiful, mysterious, and dangerous, Mother Ocean. Vast, mesmerizing, calm, until she is not. You can get into trouble out here as you saw with the *Calypso*, and I should know; I sailed *Slow Dance* through a ten-day hurricane from the Bahamas to the Portuguese Azores. Sixty-foot waves, pushed by fierce winds, ripped every sail apart on this boat. The sea became an angry mass of white foam, incredibly angry. Scared me. I called Angie and told her I am finished; I was selling the boat."

Jess looked up at Captain Reed from where she was leaning on the rail. "I hear the strongest storms make the best sailors."

Captain Reed continued, conscious of her compliment. "Angie told me no, you're not selling the boat; it defines you and you'd be lost without her. She knew me so well. At least the sailor part of me. The other parts she tolerated, and the worst parts killed her. I killed my wife, you know."

Captain Reed put his hand over Jess's hand. The salt was still in his palm, and it made her hand itch.

"Are you listening?"

Jess pulled away, scratching her fingers.

"Yes, you killed your wife. You keep saying that, but I am not clear what you mean. Sounds like you've been grieving all this time in an unhealthy way." Jess stared at the waves that were darkening in the fading light. "I feel free—from what, I am not sure, but it feels great. Life always fills with new possessions. I always land on my feet, and here I am on *Slow Dance* sailing to Tahiti. Long sea voyages make you introspective, don't they?"

"I don't know," he answered. "I hate sailing, and I hate the ocean."

Jess contemplated his contradictory statements about sailing and about his wife. She thought that the ocean could be a way to mask deeper feelings. The captain's complexities intrigued her, even as they confused her. She considered addressing her feelings directly by questioning him to open up a door for deeper conversation that might reveal more about his character and motivation. It would also be a chance for her to express her feelings and confusion, which could help them connect in a more meaningful way.

"Forty-eight years doing something you hate. Really?"

"Yup," he said, "but at least it hasn't been boring."

Jess looked down. "My life's been very boring. I made mistakes that reduced me to mediocrity. Hopefully, I am turning it into wisdom."

As the last light dipped below the horizon casting a final glow across the sea, Jess leaned back holding the rail for support, the salty breeze playing with her hair, making it dance around her shoulders. The captain leaned against the railing, his gaze lingering on her with an intensity that sent a flutter through her chest. Their conversation flowed, light and teasing, but something new was brewing beneath the surface. An unspoken tension, a shared longing that neither dared fully acknowledge.

"You're kind of cute, and you can cook, too. I didn't know if you could cook when I hired you. I took Kari's word for it."

Jess lifted one shoulder in a sexy pose and spoke in a phony French accent. "So you hired me for my sexy self. Hey?"

Captain Reed was about to answer when Lou appeared and slipped her arms around his waist. Winking at Jess, he said, "Stick with me, and you'll never be bored."

Then he disappeared below with Lou, leaving Jess with Trinidad and her thoughts. She had been enjoying her conversation with the captain when Lou interrupted. Jess's cheerful mood turned introspective. She felt caught in a web of thoughts about the captain. His flirtatious banter ignited a spark of excitement within her. She admired his confidence, the way he carried himself. When his blue eyes had shimmered with mischief, she felt a twinge of caution. Behind his facade lay subtle red flags that whispered warnings in her mind. Her instincts told her to tread carefully, to keep their interaction light, despite the undeniable chemistry pulling at her. Her conversations with the captain flowed easily, but Jess was determined to avoid vulnerability. She would flirt lightly but hold back emotionally. She was determined to never give her power away. She accepted the job to reclaim her independence, not to get tangled up in a romance. "Just keep it casual," she whispered to herself, the sound of the waves swallowing her words.

Trini pawed at Jess's leg, making little whining sounds to gain her attention. Turning away from her thoughts, she was astonished to see thousands of lights in the water.

"Wow!"

"It's phosphorescence, bioluminescence—"

Jess jumped slightly, startled by Sydney. Lost in her thoughts about the captain, she hadn't noticed her on deck.

"—living organisms, made by algae suspended in the water. Stars in the sea."

Jess moved closer to Sydney and they both leaned over the rail gazing into the water.

"Magical," said Jess, "like catching fireflies on summer nights. How do you know so much about it, Sydney?"

Sydney pulled her dreads away from her face. "Marine Biology classes, University of Wisconsin–Eau Claire. This is my first time experiencing it, much better than reading about it."

The two women stood at the rail, watching the multicolored lights sparkle in the darkness of the waves.

Sydney broke their silence. "I saw Captain Sexy up here with you having a moment. You two looked cozy."

Jess turned toward Sydney. "Yeah, sort of, until the cougar came to eat him."

Sydney laughed. "He's way more interested in you than her."

Jess shook her head side to side. "Cheri doesn't want a thing to do with him romantically, nor do you, and his only interest in me is to keep feeding him and rehabbing his arm. Lucky for him, Lou's a nympho."

Sydney chuckled. "You got that right; but I am telling you, he thinks more of you as a dish than the food on his plate, and after Lou took him below, he sent her packing to her cabin."

Jess mulled over Sydney's observation. "I doubt that, Syd. The captain and I were thrown together by circumstance when he broke his arm. We developed a friendship, nothing more. When I traveled with him to L.A. to see his doctors, he stayed with his girlfriend Sophia, and I stayed with my son and daughter-in-law. The day he returned to the boat from the hospital I checked on him during the night in case he needed anything, but he was out cold from the pain medication. In the morning, I found him sitting on the edge of his bed, shirtless, with his left arm in the sling. He was helpless," Jess continued, her voice full of frustration. "With his arm shattered he couldn't do anything, not even tying his shoes, let alone manage the boat. He asked me to drive him to an appointment in the afternoon and to help him take a shower."

"So, you gave him a shower?" Sydney asked suggestively.

Jess grimaced. "I told him, 'You do not expect me to be your nurse, I hope. I am here to cook.' Then the captain put his head in his good hand, begging"—Jess imitated him—"'Pretty please, with sugar on top, will you help me? I only have one good arm. You can hold the shower head with the curtain closed. I am sure it is nothing you have not seen.' He was so swollen and helpless that I succumbed to his predicament. It was beyond awkward. I had to remove his underwear and wrap a towel around him. He was a mess."

Sydney put her hand to her mouth. "So that's how you came to share the captain's cabin."

Jess sighed. "Yep, that's how it happened."

Sydney shook her head. "Sounds like a meet-cute; and on that note, I am off to bed."

Jess closed her eyes, searching her emotions for clarity. Was she having feelings for Captain Reed, or was she about to repeat a past mistake? She thought about the dead man on his boat, and suddenly, it all seemed unimportant, fading away with each wave full of lights passing gently under the boat. Speaking softly to Trinidad, she recited a mantra someone once taught her. "My worth increases every day, and as my spirit grows, so does my love, health, and wealth." Cuddling the poodle, she thought, *My life seems like a series of extraordinary mistakes that have brought me to where I am supposed to be.' Whoever said that is brilliant.*

7

Laws of Attraction

April 2024
Pacific Ocean

"What a spectacular morning. Red sky at night, sailors delight."

Captain Reed was in the pilothouse studying the charts when Jess joined him with her coffee.

"Delight for you maybe, but Trini and I had to sleep on deck, which was spectacular, by the way, due to the lights in the waves."

Captain Reed turned his attention to Jess. "Yes, looks like a skyful of stars fell into the sea. My cabin door was open all night; and about our conversation, it sounds like you read that book, *The Secret*? Law of Attraction, positive thinking, dream-board manifestation stuff. Do you think any of that really works? Kari was into numerology. She was always using it to explain why I'm such an ass. Sounds like poppycock."

Jess laughed. "Poppycock? Who even says that anymore?"

"I do," he replied. "So, you think you're on my boat because of fate?"

Jess set her coffee on the chart table and, matching his energy, replied, "I am not a fatalist. I am on your boat because I kept my thoughts positive, knowing from experience I would find my way out of my dire situation. I made a dream board, and there was a boat on it. So there."

Captain Reed picked up Jess's coffee and took a sip.

"Well, truth is, you were not the first choice from the ad."

Jess gave him a puzzled look. She wanted to be upset but could not muster any ire. She decided to act nonchalant and not give him the satisfaction of upsetting her. "That is me, always second. Who, then, and what happened?"

Captain Reed handed Jess her coffee cup.

"My choice was a pretty young lady who wanted exact sailing dates, planned destinations, and paid vacation time." Jess looked at him, and they laughed in unison.

Turning to go to the galley, Jess looked back at Captain Reed. "You get more bang for your buck with me. You got lucky."

Captain Reed winked. "We both got lucky. Now, can you bring coffee?"

Jess returned to the pilothouse with two cups of her brew and handed one to the captain.

He cradled his cup in both his hands.

"This boat is a lifeline for me," Jess continued the conversation. "Life was smothering me. I needed something amazing; I needed a new story. I deserve it. I've had enough of deferred satisfaction and heavy responsibility. I am taking control of my life now, as opposed to life controlling me."

Captain Reed took a sip of his coffee. "Life isn't about your chances, Jess, it's about your choices."

"I never thought I had a choice."

The captain looked up from the chart he had been studying. "You always have a choice," he said.

Jess was not sure what role Captain Reed was playing in her new story. There was a dangerous component to him. She was still figuring the man out. It was apparent his erratic actions were guided by a compulsion to keep his true feelings at bay. This voyage of his was to breathe life back into himself—or die; the same as her, but for different reasons. Jess thought of the Fool card in a tarot deck: a man merrily and carelessly about to walk off a . . . cliff he never saw coming.

Yet Captain Reed would prove her wrong. At first landfall, Jess would be amazed to find out he knew exactly what he wanted and how to manifest it. The man's mind was an aggravation to himself, never unarmed with plan

A, B, and C. Everyone underestimated him and Jess wondered if Captain Reed consciously portrayed himself as an incompetent, foolish man, while he carefully assessed those around him with laser precision.

Jess turned her attention back to the captain, who was staring at her.

"Yes, my boat is a lifeline, if only I could figure out when and where to grab the line. Speaking of lifelines, it reminds me of when I sailed my boat, *Lucio*, to Hawaii; I tied a rope to the bow with knots five feet apart on the line, then jumped off the bow into twenty-foot seas and grabbed the line as it went by. If I missed . . . well, goodbye boat, hello death . . . because they would never find me. I did stupid things in my youth. I took chances with women, with money, and with death. I saved all my money from working in my father's ice cream business. At twenty-two, I flew to New Zealand with my girlfriend, June, and her sister. I bought my first sailboat—the most expensive one because I figured it would be the best. I didn't know a thing about sailing or the ocean. I had never sailed."

"Your parents must have been frantic," she said.

"They were. I was the only son, a Jewish boy, born in Hollywood. The folks in South Island wrote about me in the newspaper: 'American Boy Sure To Die.' The locals convinced a one-armed man to sail with us long enough to teach me how to use the sextant, paper charts, and timepiece. No fancy GPS back then. They also sent a native Maori girl to assist. I cast off from the South Island to sail the boat back to Los Angeles against the good advice of the Kiwis. The weather was not in my favor; we were sailing uphill into the waves. We were vomiting in a bucket and hand-steering the boat. Autopilot wasn't invented yet. I woke up on our third day at sea and when I put my feet on the floor, the carpet was floating; we were sinking."

"Good lord," Jess replied. "What did you do?"

"I crawled around in the bilge until I found the problem. Prior to casting off, I had replaced a drain in the bathroom with a two-way plug—the wrong kind—and it was letting seawater flow into the boat. I fixed the problem, but we had to pump the seawater out using a foot pump."

Jess was looking at him with respect. "Your parents must have been relieved when you arrived in Los Angeles. How long did it take you?"

He shook his head no. "I never made it."

Jess gave him a puzzled look. "Well, you didn't die, because here you are."

"Nope, did not die," he said. "I was blown off in Fiji; at that time, the damn natives had never seen white people. After our short stop there, we limped into American Samoa, where I left the boat and flew back to Los Angeles. My girlfriend, June, stayed behind to sell the boat for me."

Jess added more cream to her coffee. "What happened to the one-armed man and the Māori girl?"

He shook his head. "The Māori girl nearly died in a storm when the boom swung around and knocked her out cold. She lay on the pilothouse sofa for days, moaning until we got her to American Samoa. As for the one-armed guy, I cannot recall his departure."

Jess frowned. "I am glad you are more experienced now. Did June sell the boat?"

Captain Reed gave off a low whistle. "That is another story. I flew back to American Samoa to surprise June and found her in the act of screwing the guy buying the boat."

"Goodness, what did she say?" asked Jess, suppressing a giggle.

Captain Reed let out a laugh. "She said, 'Out of sight, out of mind.' That was June. We are still friends to this day. I took chances. Hopefully, I am wiser now, and my chances are based on good choices when I get the chance."

Jess let out a sigh. "Jeesh, you are hard to understand on so many levels. You speak your own language!"

Jess found herself in this moment trying to define her feelings for Captain Reed but found it impossible. She liked spending time with him. He was interesting, and although he had begun to speak about himself openly, he remained an enigma to her. He certainly wasn't boring, and Jess didn't have time for boring people. Life was moving too fast to waste time. She wasn't sure about Captain Reed, but she was certain she loved sailing on *Slow Dance*. Living aboard made her feel special. The boat was magnificent. An eighty-four-foot Don Brooks ketch, built in New Zealand. It boasted over-the-top features: teak decks, flawlessly varnished rails, five bedrooms, five bathrooms, a laundry room with a stacking Bosch washer/dryer, a spacious galley equipped with double dishwashers, a Viking Range, large freezer, and ginormous refrigerator. The ship's interior walls boasted solid sheets of teak. The saloon had an amazing entertainment system, an outstanding bar, and a small U-line fridge with an ice maker. The doors on the cabinets were crafted from fine Italian wood, beveled glass, and brass edging. A partition that walled off the galley from the saloon and folded out from the wall was etched with a ship on a turbulent sea. The outer cabinets were stocked with Baccarat crystal wine glasses that had been wrapped in Pampers diapers to avoid breakage during their crossing—obviously, something Lou did not appreciate as she was doing an excellent job of unwrapping glassware and letting it break in rough seas.

Harrison was teaching Sydney to master a bowline knot, and the other girls were lending a hand by polishing the teak in the saloon. Jess chose to polish the teak in the pilothouse, where Captain Reed was adjusting the Furuno radar. Standing on the sofa to reach the upper part of the wall, she asked him, "How did you come by this boat?"

The captain continued fiddling with the radar system. "I purchased her in '95. After twenty years of lusting for a Don Brooks, there she was, tied to a dock piling in San Pedro, seized and repossessed. I took a frigate out to *Slow Dance* and paid cash for her to avoid state tax."

Jess interrupted. "Wait, isn't a frigate a warship?"

Captain Reed smiled. "Uh, very astute, but not exactly. Frigates were full-rigged ships in the seventeenth and eighteenth century, built for speed, and utilized for scouting. In modern times, they can be warships or simply merchant marines' boats. I often wish I had been a sailor back in those days. Exciting times."

"Maybe you were in a past life," said Jess as she continued her polishing.

Captain Reed stopped fidgeting with the radar. "I have enough trouble in this life without thinking about a past life. Angie sold her luxury home in Santa Monica to help buy *Slow Dance*."

Jess acknowledged him. "Is that why you tell people your wife bought you the boat?"

"Well, she did buy the boat, and then she ended up not enjoying it."

Jess worried her question caused Captain Reed to turn melancholy. She ceased polishing and jumped down from the sofa. "That might have something to do with going through the Panama Canal backwards and withstanding ten-day hurricanes, yes?"

"Probably," he said. "I told you about sailing her to the Mediterranean and going through the Panama Canal backwards?"

Jess nodded. "Yes. You babbled in your sleep after taking the pain meds the doctor prescribed for your arm."

Captain Reed stared out the pilothouse window. "There were close calls. The Panama Canal incident rattled Angie, and rightly so. Despite that incident, she sailed with me a second time to Panama but couldn't tolerate rough seas. She was so cute; she would put her life jacket on and then put a mini life vest on Trini. They would sit on the bed in the cabin, waiting to get into the dinghy. It made me laugh every time. I have had four boats in my lifetime; one sank at sea, hit by a tanker. I thought I was dead at that time, but here I am. It must be angels because people have told me I am dumb as a block and do not know the first thing about sailing."

Jess was weighing his words and calculating her risks.

"It sounds like you have used up your nine lives, which means we are going to have to rely on the few lives I have left. My adventures were not on the high seas but dangerous in other ways. I didn't set eyes on the sea until I was in my twenties, and twice I nearly drowned when I found the courage to take a swim. Forging through jungles, backpacking mountain trails, and banging on pots to chase bears away, yes, but never a thought of crossing an ocean thousands of miles from land. Surprisingly, I have not had any panic attacks, and . . . *so far*, find the experience awe inspiring. That is . . . until your stories. I'm going to be worried now until we hit landfall." Jess had apprehensions, but in no way could she anticipate the adversity they were sailing toward.

Captain Reed let out a huge sigh. "I think about what I want, not what I don't want, so I get what I want, at least most of the time."

"What did you just say?" Jess answered, shaking her head at Captain Reed's comment.

8

Shoreward

April 2024
Nuku Hiva Island (French Marquesas Islands)

"Land ho, sailors!"

Sydney was standing on top of the pilothouse roof, shouting excellent news. The tiny spot in the distance was Nuku Hiva, one of the islands in the French Marquesas Islands chain.

"Lower the main."

Captain Reed was not speaking directly to anyone, and Jess thought it curious Chaz remained below deck, while Harrison hurried to lower the sail. The girls had it nearly cradled before Harrison arrived, and Jess realized Cheri and Lou had anticipated taking it down before

Captain Reed gave the order. She liked that.

Jess stood at the bow of *Slow Dance*, watching as the captain made his approach through the entrance leading into the wide bay of Nuku Hiva Island. The bay, surrounded by lush tropical mountains, palm trees, and horses grazing on green grass by the shore, was a welcome site. Sydney joined Jess at the bow, watching as the boat approached the interior of the bay. Jess filled with excitement as she scrutinized the shoreline. She had expected the islands to be comprised of flat land, sand, and palm trees. Instead, there were rugged, mist-shrouded peaks reaching up dramatically toward the sky. The lower mountains were a rich tapestry of greenery, with cascading waterfalls adding to the mystique and beauty of the island.

Jess followed Sydney atop the pilothouse.

"It's breathtaking," Jess commented. "I want to paint it. Look at those hundred different shades of green against the blue sky with white clouds."

Sydney smirked. "You are such a romantic, Jess. I'm going to snap pictures with my iPhone."

The water in the bay was a gorgeous cerulean blue and beyond inviting. As soon as the anchor dropped and the boat settled, everyone but Captain Reed and Harrison jumped in for a swim. Chaz, who was still noticeably absent, suddenly appeared in his Speedo, showing off by doing a perfect swan dive from atop the pilothouse.

Floating on her back, Jess looked up at the clouds drifting overhead and felt relief at being off the boat for the first time in thirty-five days. She was certain the other swimmers must feel the same. She wondered if their laughter and playful splashing were because they had arrived in one piece.

Drying off from their swim, the cruisers dressed for shore leave while Harrison lowered the dinghy into the bay. Jess gathered all the necessary paperwork to clear into the French Marquesas, and one by one the crew climbed down the ladder into the tender boat.

"Come on, you wooly monster, down you go," Chaz addressed Trini as he handed her down to Jess. Trini had been a gift to Angie when *Slow Dance* anchored in Trinidad, and that is how she got her name. Angie trained Trinidad to never get off the boat. The pooch would climb the portable steps to jump aboard and never attempt to jump off.

Lou was holding the line. "Hey, where is Sydney? I hope she didn't drown. Did anyone see her get back onto the boat?"

Captain Reed looked annoyed, as did Chaz.

"She probably swam to shore and is drinking beer in a seedy pirate bar," said Cheri. "We can look there first."

Jess had worried about Sydney during their time in Puerto Vallarta. The girl liked her beer but not paying the tab. Sydney had mastered the art of getting guys to pay for her food and drinks without indulging them in so much as a reach-around. Jess liked this about her blue-eyed crewmate with

-Nuka-Hiva-
Marquesas Islands

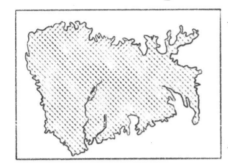
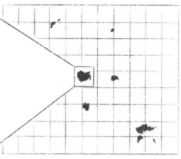

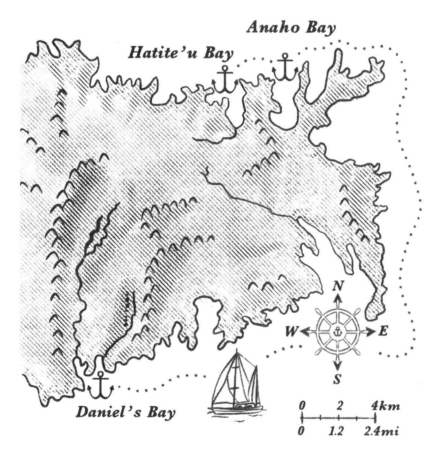

Anaho Bay

Hatite'u Bay

Daniel's Bay

N
W — E
S

0   2   4km
0   1.2   2.4mi

waist-long dreadlocks. Sydney was an adventurous woman who cultivated a perfect blend of Kama Sutra charm and priestess aloofness. She could create a sort of pleasant tension with men, releasing either persona depending on the situation. Jess thought if only she had such power at twenty-seven, she could have avoided the inappropriate men of her generation.

With that thought, Jess glanced at Captain Reed driving the dinghy. She recalled how helpless he was after breaking his arm, how she unbuttoned his shirt, pulled his pants off, and held the detachable shower head while he washed his lanky body with his one good hand. Seeing him naked, admitting to herself that the image—not at all interesting at the time—was currently arousing. The situation was absurd at best but worth it, she thought as she gazed out at the beautiful island of Nuku Hiva.

Captain Reed's interest lay with Lou, and when he went to Los Angeles, it was Sophia. Jess decided to lock away her feelings for him in a mental box. For all she knew, this was another case of her wrong-guy syndrome. All her past relationships had been with eccentric, quirky men, Captain Reed being no exception. Only this time, there was an adventure, a great adventure.

"Are you okay, Jess?" Captain Reed was looking at her.

"Yes, Captain, just hunky-dory."

While Harrison remained on the boat to keep watch, Captain Reed, Chaz, and Jess went to the magistrate for clearance into the French Marquesas Islands. Trinidad followed along, and it amazed Jess how she never needed a leash. They strolled at a slow pace toward the offices because Trini had so many new things to sniff and fifty pee breaks to mark her trail. Like the rest of the crew, she was excited to be on land.

A large man behind the desk greeted them with a smile as he took the passports and ship documents for inspection. Suddenly, his smile turned to shock, and he rattled off something in French that sounded serious, judging by his tone. The man pointed at Trinidad and spoke in English. "Animals are forbidden on these islands. I am covering for my boss, but if he were here, he would take your animal and have it immediately destroyed. This is a serious matter; please take the animal directly back to your vessel and please do not let it back on the island."

Captain Reed turned to Chaz. "Take her and get her back to the boat."

Chaz tucked the little gray poodle under his arm. "Come on, you troublemaker, let's hit it."

Cheri and Lou found Sydney, as expected, in a local café, still in her bathing suit, enjoying a cold beer with a handsome local artist. Sydney's disappearing acts would become more troublesome as *Slow Dance* sailed west.

9

The Mutiny

April 2024
Nuku Hiva Island

Fatigued from the long sea voyage and consumed with heavy thoughts regarding Captain Reed, Jess slept in until late morning. Carrying her coffee cup to the upper deck, she encountered Chaz, who appeared to be waiting for her.

"Harrison and I want to take you on shore for breakfast; we have something important to discuss with you."

"Where is everyone?" Jess asked.

Chaz told her, "The girls left early for the morning market, and Captain Reed went with them. We agreed to meet up with them at noon."

Traveling in silence, Jess wondered what Chaz was up to as Harrison steered the dinghy toward the shore. After securing the boat the three sailors walked along the sandy street to a small funky outside café.

Seating herself with the others at one of the three available tables, Jess asked, "Why are you being so cryptic? What's this all about, Chaz?"

Leaning across the table, Chaz put his mouth next to her ear. "He wants to die, and he doesn't care if he takes us all with him! He never planned on returning. It's a miracle that the boat is still afloat; there are so many problems. If you want to live, I suggest you come with me and Harrison."

Jess raised her eyebrows. "Um, where are you going?"

Chaz continued, "Whether you realize it or not, we were sinking the entire way across the Pacific. Reed knew full well the boat was not seaworthy to make this trip."

Jess looked over at Harrison, who was struggling to avoid eye contact.

Chaz had a pleasant face and a boyish look for his sixty-two years, but the three-week crossing from Mexico to the French Marquesas Islands had changed him. When Jess first met Chaz, he looked like a real seafarer in his blue jacket, sailor cap, snow white hair, topsiders, and book of knots. During their voyage, Chaz had grown progressively hostile, distancing himself from the others and skulking about the boat's engine room in his mechanic's overalls, looking increasingly like a prisoner.

Chaz leaned in on Jess. "By the grace of God, we didn't die out there like poor Brian."

Jess looked down at the breakfast her soon-to-be ex-shipmates had ordered for her: hot Nescafé, hard eggs, greasy bacon, and white toast with visible insect larva embedded into the slice.

"Are you serious?" Jess exclaimed, a mix of anger and disappointment flooding her voice. She crossed her arms, glaring at them. "So, where are you *going*? This sounds more like mutiny to me. Leave Captain Reed out here with the girls as crew. Have you sat down with the captain and expressed your concerns? If you knew the boat was in such bad shape, why are you here? You had four months in Mexico to determine *Slow Dance* wasn't seaworthy."

Rather than answering her question, Chaz gesticulated, pretending to hold a machine gun and pulling his mouth to one side, he imitated rapid automatic gunfire.

"That's how quickly things are going to go bad on that boat!"

The crew's long crossing had obviously gotten to him. Finding Brian dead in the doldrums, dealing with the girls, and the tension with Captain Reed, Jess could see Chaz was unraveling.

"Harrison and I already found another boat to get us to Tahiti. From there, we can get a flight back to Los Angeles."

As she listened to Chaz, Jess was thinking about the animosity he had shown toward the Gratuitous Three during the crossing. Even prior to sailing out of Marina del Rey, she could not understand how Captain Reed tolerated this man. There were so many things she did not understand about how Captain Reed's mind worked.

Jess pushed her plate away to the other side of the table. "You would think the French Marquesas would have decent coffee, for Christ's sake—a French press, a coffee maker, at least. Surely there is a café here that has something besides crappy instant Nescafé. . . . Back to the issue at hand. If I left with you, Captain Reed would be in trouble—and you know it, Chaz. Therefore, asking me to mutiny with you is not out of concern for me, but rather because you want to hurt him—*in the deepest way possible*—by taking his cook and caregiver. I don't need to think about it because I am staying with the captain on his beautiful sailboat, along with the sailor girls, and I suggest whatever arrangements you have made, you pack up and be ready to move off the boat, because as soon as I find Captain Reed, I will inform him of your intentions to mutiny."

Jess stood up defiantly and went to find the captain.

Passing another café, Jess decided she needed a break to think about what had just transpired. She was tired of the tension and the drama. Such a beautiful setting for so much angst. Would it never end, or was this just how life was?

"Cold beer, please."

The young man tending the café looked at his watch and back at Jess.

"Right, early morning drinking. You think you would be used to it with all the pirates anchored in your bay."

The expressionless young man popped the top of the bottle and handed the beer to Jess.

Finding a comfortable chair outside, Jess put her feet up and stared out over the bay toward *Slow Dance* bobbing on the hook, as Captain Reed described it. From her viewpoint, the yacht looked impressive, majestic—stunning, in fact. She let the sea breeze consume her along with the smell of the land, and it calmed her nerves. She remembered Chaz attempting to teach Cheri and Lou how to sail *Slow Dance* and how they demonstrated their superior ability to manage the boat—without a luff in the sails or the banging of a halyard. Jess would not consider abandoning ship, although she did acknowledge the fear in her gut. Her mind was swirling with a mix of anxiety and uncertainty. *What if Chaz is right?* she thought, picturing the vast ocean that lies ahead, full of unpredictable storms and hidden danger. She knew there was truth in what Chaz had said about Captain Reed and the boat.

Jess took a drink from her beer. *I need to think this through*, she thought to herself. *I need to balance my instincts against my fears.*

Right then she decided to face her fear, trust her intuition, and if she met with a watery grave, so be it; she was, in some ways, dead anyway. She gulped the beer down, realizing she had no money. At that moment, the captain walked into the bar.

"There you are."

Timing is everything, she thought.

10

Besieged

April 2024
Nuku Hiva Island

"What are you making? It smells wonderful, and I am starving."

Cheri stepped into the galley where Jess was preparing a last supper for the mutineers in an effort to ease the tense ambiance on the boat. Picking up a rolling pin, she shook it at Cheri.

"Get out, and stop stealing my Brie toasts—which, by the way, are not topped yet."

Jess slapped Cheri's hand away as she reached for a piece of sliced baguette brushed with garlic oil and browned in the oven. Jess was in the process of topping them with creamy slices of Brie cheese, sundried tomatoes, fresh basil, and pine nuts.

"Please, please? I will buy you a bottle of wine tomorrow at the café! Please, please?" Cheri made a begging gesture, and Jess playfully pushed the pan toward her.

"Jesus-Mother-Mary-and-Joseph, take one already and get out of my galley."

Lou's face suddenly appeared at the saloon's sliding pass-through window. "I smell garlic."

Lou and Cheri began to feign starvation, speaking fluent French. The girls put on a dramatic show convincing Jess she had made the right decision to remain on *Slow Dance*.

"Is that real French you're speaking?" Jess asked.

Lou had demonstrated her Spanish in Mexico. But French? A hidden talent that would come in handy in Nuku Hiva, as well as the Tahitian Islands.

"I want one, too. You are making me drool," said Lou. "Thank the lord for the froggies and their fabulous baguettes and Brie."

"Me wants one."

Jess looked up to see Sydney waving her hand from the pilothouse via the little sliding pass-through window to the galley.

"Oh, for God's sake. Here," Jess said, handing up an unfinished slice to Sydney.

Jess delivered her scrumptious Brie appetizers to the top deck, where Cheri was opening a chilled bottle of pinot grigio and then made her way to the pilothouse, where Captain Reed was sitting on the sofa. Jess sat next to him, her worry rising up in her.

"So, what's the plan regarding the boys? It is very tense around here. You look so calm and collected. The brawn is leaving you with a huge boat in need of repairs and an all-girl crew. How will we manage?"

Captain Reed uncrossed his legs. "When I sailed to the Galapagos, I missed it by five hundred nautical miles. I eventually got there. My crew lost faith in me and left the boat. Two days later, they showed up begging for food because their new boat had no food."

"What did you do?"

"I gave them a jar of peanut butter and a loaf of bread, found new crew, and went exploring. After two months, I cleared in with the authorities at the ranger station, and they gave me the customary two-week cruising permit."

Jess shook her head. "Have you always been a rebel?"

"What do you think? Chaz and Harrison need to come individually to speak to me regarding their plans to leave the boat. Can you please inform them I would like to meet with them now?"

"Of course," Jess said. "Would you like a Brie toast?"

"No, thank you. Maybe later."

Jess saw Captain Reed's mood was serious as he waited for Chaz and Harrison to confront him. Despite the gravity of the situation, however, the captain remained composed.

The Gratuitous Three were aware of the situation, so it was now official. Jess wondered how Captain Reed would manage it and how the mutiny would affect the three women. They might decide to leave *Slow Dance* when they arrived in Tahiti.

Captain Reed's reaction was not what anyone expected. Chaz went into the pilothouse first—feeling emboldened after consuming the captain's finest Caribbean Rum—and he was slurring his words.

"If you want to die out here, it's your damn business. But you are not taking me with you. You knew your boat was not ready for the sea. She sat at the dock in Los Angeles for five years, and you were willing to let all of us die with you. Harrison and I are jumping on another boat headed to Papeete. Screw you. You are one crazy, dumb son of a bitch. The whole situation is absurd and dangerous. I saw you when the hatch was open, in your underpants, wrapped around Lou sleeping. You lock Jess out and let Lou in. Good luck—you are going to need it. The mainsail doesn't hoist, you are low on fuel, the water tanks are empty, and your watermakers don't function in a place that has no fresh water for yachts. Then there are the dumb broads you brought aboard. Have fun, you horny bastard; you will get what you deserve."

Captain Reed calmly listened to the barrage of slurred insults Chaz hurled at him and his vessel. Chaz waited for a reply during what seemed an endless pause.

Captain Reed suddenly got up from the sofa, lifted the top of the chart table, and pulled something out. He extended his hand along with an envelope containing Chaz's final pay in cash.

"Thank you for all the assistance in getting us this far. Fair winds and following seas, Chaz."

The girls were listening from the top deck at the exchange between the two men. Then Chaz appeared on deck, his face red and contorted in a half smirk, half snarl.

"Go, Harrison, go down and tell that son of a bitch to his face that you are finished as well."

Harrison nervously got up from his seat where he had been working on one of the endless knots he was determined to master, as if perfecting them would somehow transform him into a true man of the sea. Harrison was mumbling about returning home to his sick mother who needed him. There were numerous apologies as he thanked Captain Reed, took his envelope, and disappeared to his cabin.

Lou was helping Jess, for a change, by exploring the linen drawer for a more festive table dressing. The linen drawer and bilge storage under the galley floor were all that remained of Angie's party store. With a sad fascination, Jess perused the fine china, silver service, banners for every celebratory occasion, wigs, props, fake teeth, strange eyeglasses, candles, and other amazing objects. Using the finest tablecloth, china, crystal, and cloth napkins accompanied by shell napkin rings, the girls went about setting the table.

"I am relieved Chaz is leaving," Lou admitted to the other girls as she twisted the napkins to make them fit into the rings. "He is such a toad. You don't think he would do something to the boat, do you? We should keep an eye on him tonight—he's drunk."

"Well, yes, I mean, I don't know," Jess answered. "I am nervous about what Chaz said. The boat is not seaworthy. He told me it's sinking. Captain Reed does not seem to have any real sail plan, and you and Cheri are the only ones who know anything about how to handle this boat."

Sydney poured herself a glass of wine. "Listen up, you sea wenches, I am learning, and I am not useless."

Jess and Lou laughed aloud at Sydney's reference to what Chaz thought of them.

Jess continued, "Captain Reed is the closest thing to a mechanic we have."

They did not see Chaz, who had been portside listening to their conversation while swigging more of Captain Reed's fine rum. Suddenly, he was upon them.

"That's right, Lou, dry your eyes, princess, 'cause you're going to be crying plenty without me and Harrison to oversee any real shit that happens on the boat, and there's going to be some bad shit. Everyone will find out just how incompetent and stupid you are."

Chaz loved to bully her, but this time, Lou stood her ground and did not cry. Disappointed by Lou's reaction, Chaz moved on to Cheri, who was climbing the stairs from the pilothouse onto the deck.

"You. You consider yourself a racer. I have participated in many regattas and sweetheart, you have a lot to learn."

Grabbing the handrail, Cheri completed her exit from the steps onto the deck and, nudging Chaz out of the doorway, she stopped briefly to place an exaggerated laugh in his face. Defeated, Chaz took another swig of rum from the bottle and went after Sydney, who was nibbling on a Brie toast. Before Chaz could speak, Sydney picked up the plate and offered Chaz one of the crispy garlic treats.

"You really should calm down, bro. You're a total douche."

Unable to elicit the desired response from the three women and spitting his words, Chaz turned his rage on Jess.

"I would never have you as cook on any ship I am captain of."

Jess stretched her face into her biggest fake smile as she removed one of the place settings from the table.

"Ditto, Chaz. I would not feel safe on any ship you captained or any SUV you drive for that matter; and, since you are no longer crew on this boat, I won't be feeding you tonight. Please take your drunken ass to your cabin or get off the boat."

The girls began to applaud Jess's remark as Chaz, being no match for the four women, staggered off to his cabin and was not seen or heard from for the remainder of the evening.

11

Collaboration

"The fish is delicious," Sydney said. "What is it?"

"Hammerhead shark," Jess replied. "Got it this morning at the fish market by the shore. The anglers bring it in fresh then cut it up for sale. They toss the unwanted parts into the bay, which draws more hammerheads, making them an easy catch. Big creatures, huge. I have eaten them in Sri Lanka. Delicious."

Cheri dropped her fork. "Oh my God, we were swimming off the boat, and at night, too! Jess, are you joking?"

"No."

Captain Reed stood up, placing his hands firmly on the table,

"I cannot have anything happen to my ladies, so please, no more swimming. There will be much better swimming where we are headed."

Sydney asked, "Where is that?"

Captain Reed put his hand on Sydney's shoulder. "I will show you my sail plan in the morning," he said, then sat back down at the table.

Jess passed the salad, adding, "No joking. We were lucky."

Surrounded by lush mountains, and under a thousand stars, the crew enjoyed Jess's delicious meal and each other's company. A tremendous shift was occurring, and they felt it. Satiated with food and wine, each retired to their cabin. Jess was just about finished with the galley chores as Harrison stepped in and placed his arms around her. Drawing Jess close, he whispered, "You are the sexiest woman I have ever known. When this is over, I will find you again, I promise."

Jess felt genuinely sorry for him. She could sense his distress.

"Harrison, we will never see each other after this moment, and that is all right. Let's be honest. Please do not feel the need to be a gentleman to ease some imagined wrong you have committed. It was New Year's, a beautiful night in Jalapa. The mood was right, and we had sex. I went a long time without any, and if I recall, I was the instigator. It was good. Now the time has come for goodbye."

Harrison took Jess's face into his hands and kissed her forehead. He looked like he was going to cry.

"The Aussie guy's boat we are sailing on is in bad shape. I hope I make it." This was the true reason, Jess realized, for his sudden gush of emotion.

"Me, too," she replied.

At first light, Jess slipped quietly off the couch bed in the captain's cabin and into her sarong. She wanted to be up early to enjoy the sunrise. Captain Reed lay sleeping, the first rays of light streaming in from the portholes illuminating his face. *He looks peaceful*, she thought, his tan body clad only in blue Calvin Kleins. Sharing his cabin evolved from a series of chaotic events, but chaos defined the adventure since she set foot on *Slow Dance*.

Jess covered the portholes with the screens to ensure the morning sunlight would not wake him. He almost never slept this peacefully. Nightmares interrupted his sleep and left him drained each morning. Perhaps making it to landfall would calm him. Whatever guilt and grief he felt was obviously detrimental to his well-being.

Jess was on deck watching the sunrise transform into a spectacular canvas of colors over the mountains surrounding Nuku Hiva Bay. The air smelled fresh, invigorating with the scent of salt, tropical flowers, and change. As the sun climbed higher the rocky cliffs and vibrant foliage revealed the island's natural beauty.

Jess's peaceful morning disappeared, though, when Chaz came up on deck carrying his duffle bag and looking very hung over. Uncomfortable at the memory of Chaz's atrocious behavior the previous night, Jess tried to push down her disappointment and remain cordial.

"Morning, Chaz. How about a cup of coffee before you go?"

Chaz's lips started to move but remained pasted together. He mumbled some words, followed by a sneer.

Harrison arrived on deck with his gear and coffee he had poured into a plastic cup.

"I am sure going to miss your coffee, Jess."

Before Jess could answer, the captain from their new sailboat arrived in his dinghy to take Chaz and Harrison to his boat. Chaz climbed down into the dinghy, grumbling under his breath, while Harrison hugged Jess before tossing his belongings into the boat and reluctantly climbing off *Slow Dance*.

The talk amongst the other yachties was not positive concerning the small, broken sailboat Chaz and Harrison were jumping aboard. Would they make it to the Tahitian Islands? Jess wondered if *she* would make it to Tahiti, recalling what Chaz had told her about *Slow Dance*.

She tried not to think about sailing on with only Lou, Cheri, and Captain Reed as experienced sailors. During the crossing, Captain Reed taught Sydney how to tie a few sailor's knots while Cheri assisted her with sheeting out the headsails, mainsail, mizzen sail, and the large genoa. Jess was also watching and learning but even so, this did not quiet her fears, and then there was Lou's concern about Chaz sabotaging the boat, which doubled her concerns.

Chaz had pointed out that the mainsail was not hoisting properly. In addition, the boat needed her bottom cleaned to remove the barnacles that attached themselves during their long ocean voyage. All this was on her mind when Cheri and Lou appeared on deck.

"Jess, you make the best coffee, bar none," Cheri said. "There is no good coffee on this island, and probably not until Tahiti. Those bags of coffee beans from Costco were a brilliant provisioning move, and so was the boxed milk."

Jess tilted her head to one side, imitating Bette Davis. "Thank you, darling. Anything to keep the new crew happy and our mutineers off the boat."

Lou was wearing a wet suit and handing a second suit to Cheri. Laughing, she said, "You shouldn't drink that much coffee, Cheri—you might puke in your regulator."

Cheri groaned at the sight of her wet suit.

"The barnacles won't clean themselves off," Lou insisted, "and if we don't do this, they're going to slow the speed of the boat."

Cheri put the cup down and pulled on the wet suit Lou had dug out of the dive locker.

"Perfect fit," commented Jess, amazed at the fact both women even knew how to dive.

"The diving gear and tanks are finally getting some use."

Jumping into the bay, Cheri and Lou set about wiping the barnacles from *Slow Dance*'s hull. It was fact: the bay was swarming with hammerhead sharks drawn to the fish parts tossed into the water by the local anglers. Jess marveled at the fearless sailor women. They were both certified divers, and fluent in French and Spanish as well. Smiling to herself, Jess wondered what other talents would surface from the all-female crew. Necessity *is* the mother of invention.

Sydney was on deck now, rubbing sleep from her eyes and holding her Big Gulp–sized cup from some fast-food establishment; she had it filled with Jess's awesome coffee.

"Whattup?"

"Your crewmates are cleaning off the bottom barnacles," said Jess.

Missing her mouth and spilling coffee down her shirt, Sydney remarked, "Good. You know that slows the boat down if they aren't scrubbed off. Horrible job. Did they plug their ears so the little microscopic crabs do not swim in? No shit. It's a real thing."

Jess raised her eyebrows and turned her lips down in disgust. "The ocean creeps me out."

Captain Reed appeared on deck, looking refreshed for a change, and Jess disappeared to the galley to brew another pot of her fabulous coffee.

"What's all this?" Captain Reed asked Sydney.

Sydney was sorting out the bosun's chair and safety lines for climbing the mast.

"When Cheri and Lou get out of the water, we are going up the mast to have a look at the problem with the mainsail. We need the main more than the other sails. Yes?"

"Why are Cheri and Lou in the damn shark-infested water?"

Just then, Lou appeared on the starboard side of the boat, pulling off her mask.

"Whoa, so many barnacles under the boat it's a wonder we were moving at all!"

Captain Reed laughed. "My God, my all-female crew."

Next, the sailor girls hoisted Sydney up the mainmast utilizing the safety line. She promptly discovered one of the cars was off the track and, under the captain's direction, popped it back into place, hence earning the nickname Beefcake.

"Sail problem solved!" Sydney added.

The following morning, Lou and Cheri returned from the Wednesday market in the kayaks.

"Jess, you should see the fabulous fruits and veggies we got you; and fresh garlic and weird avocados, too."

Jess was touched with appreciation. Lou stood in the kayak handing the bags up to her. Grabbing the last bag, she looked over the bay. Chaz, Harrison, and the Australian fellow with the broken boat were gone forever. It was a new day, with new energy and new adventures brewing.

12

The Cougar, the Mermaid, and the Siren

May 2024
Nuku Hiva Island

Boats arrived every day to Nuku Hiva Bay, regattas traveling together from the Galapagos Islands, Mexico, Australia, New Zealand, and one boat all the way across the Indian Ocean from Sri Lanka. There were even a few familiar boats. Jess felt a sense of relief and accomplishment wash over her. The tension that built up during the long and challenging passage began to subside now that they were on solid ground. At first sight of the lush island, the welcoming atmosphere of the locals, and the sailing community, Jess felt an elevated sense of peace and belonging to this new life on the water. A shift was occurring, and Jess's fears began to fade. And while the Gratuitous Three hiked and made friends with the new cruisers—their favorites being two handsome forty-something Australians—Captain Reed and his cook were colliding in unusual ways.

During the crossing, Sydney and Lou shared the third luxury cabin, which was aft of the boat and directly across from Cheri's cabin. Their cabin was built with bunk beds and a large bathroom. Chaz's forward captain cabin was up for grabs, and Sydney claimed it. Lou was overjoyed to be rid of Sydney, and, by all appearances, the feeling was mutual. The small double-bunk-bed crew cabin at the bow of the boat had been Harrison's, and Jess decided to move into this cabin for two reasons: it was close to the galley, and it provided a space away from Captain Reed.

Captain Reed was objecting as Jess was gathering her things. "What if I need help in the middle of the night? You are so far away up there in the crew cabin, and other than the worst cabin on the boat, the bathroom is in the laundry room."

Jess packed her toothbrush in a plastic bag. "I need my own space, and this way, if you lock me out, I have a private option."

Captain Reed gave her a boyish smile. "Please forgive me," he asked, making a pouty face. "You have taken good care of me, and honestly, I couldn't have made the trip without you."

The first weeks of the voyage, Lou would sneak into Captain Reed's cabin and lock the door, forcing Jess to sleep on the saloon couch or on the outside deck sofa. Jess did not mind so much because she had come to love the starry nights at sea. But Lou's behavior had inflamed Chaz, becoming the root of his bullying.

Jess replied. "Nothing to forgive; I am grateful for the adventure, and you are not such a bad bunkmate. It has been six months. Amazingly, your arm has healed without surgery, thanks to Cheri's physical therapy sessions and my devoted care. You are good as new."

Jess was thinking to herself: *The man seems more like a needy, lost boy than a gnarly sea captain.* She wondered about his demons, his fitful sleep, and the ladies of the night he paid to visit him when the boat was in the Puerto Vallarta marina. Captain Reed's hedonistic behavior had contributed to the taut relationship between himself and Chaz. Remarkably, it did not make Jess uncomfortable. She had experienced enough male debauchery in her past. She thought, *Here I am halfway around the world, on a less-than-safe vessel, with three strange women and a horny captain. What could go wrong?* Truth was, crossing an ocean was gutsy and helped her build new confidence in her choices. Not all the men in her life were corrupt and deceitful. Every one of them taught her lessons, and she was the sum of those experiences. If she learned anything, it was that the end is always visible in the beginning—if you choose to see it. The problem was, this grand adventure of hers had many endings, including death.

Cheri was a social butterfly, and one glorious day she and the girls invited twelve or so people from the other yachts to an evening party on *Slow Dance*. Being the largest yacht in the bay and designed for entertainment, it was the logical choice. Captain Reed loved a good gathering, and the party lasted well into the wee hours of the morning. Jess amazed the cruisers by producing platters of sautéed breadfruit (a very nutritious fruit from the tropical flowering jackfruit tree), barbecued steaks of wahoo fish, a tossed green salad, her fabulous Brie toasts, and a decadent flourless chocolate torte. Captain Reed's wine collection was reduced by several cases. New friendships formed that evening and *Slow Dance* would encounter them in countries throughout the South Pacific. They would spend months together in the same marinas, waiting for the weather windows to safely set sail. The new friends would circumvent the globe. Some would die in a horrific storm in the Tasman Sea between New Zealand and Australia. Not one item found to show they were there. They were gone . . . swallowed by the sea, which spares no one. Not the novice nor the man who knows the ocean better than any land.

"Lou, lend a hand, could you?" Captain Reed was moving the dinghy to *Slow Dance*'s stern, making room for the other small boats arriving for the party. "That is not how you tie a proper bowline knot."

Lou was attempting to teach Captain Reed about one of the most important knots a sailor must learn to execute flawlessly—*if he wants to secure his boat*. Captain Reed gave Lou an annoyed look.

"Yeah, right. Normally, the dinghy goes up on the platform at night, but we may need it to ferry these people to their boats."

It was Captain Reed's habit to place the dinghy up on the hydraulic platform every night for safety reasons. In the event the dinghy remained in the water, a bow and stern line must be tied to secure the dinghy to *Slow Dance*.

"Great party," Sydney told Jess as she helped her carry the remains of the party down to the galley. "Boat people are very cool. The food really makes or breaks a party, and you pulled that spread out of nowhere, Jess. It's amazing!"

"Dolly Dragonette, that's how," replied Jess.

"Who is that? An amazing celebrity chef?"

"No, she was my Italian godmother who was indeed a great cook and taught me how to pull a fabulous meal out of my butt cheeks."

Sydney leaned close to Jess. "Hey, want to know something hilarious that's going on right now?"

Jess was placing dishes in the dishwasher. Pausing and picking up her wine, she asked, "What's that?"

Sydney placed her arm around Jess. "People are leaving, but I just saw the good-looking Aussie disappear into Lou's cabin *for a massage.* Cheri and Lou have been in competition for him all day. This morning, he took the three of us in his jeep for a mountain hike. His boat is that crazy red racing boat."

Sydney was giggling. "Now the funniest thing . . . earlier, I saw him take Cheri into the crew cabin and close the door. After, like, five minutes, they came out. He was pulling his shorts up, and Cheri looked . . . *blissful.* Then, the two of them went back on deck to join the party. Cheri was talking a lot as usual and did not notice Lou slip away, taking the Aussie into her cabin. . . . They are still in there."

Jess was listening to Sydney, sipping from her wineglass when she erupted into laughter and a mouthful sprayed out over the sink.

Both were howling now. "What the *heck,* Sydney, are you stalking them?"

Suddenly Captain Reed appeared at the top of the stairs. "I am going to bed," he declared. "The people have left, and I am beat. Night, ladies."

"Night, Captain." Sydney followed Captain Reed up top to retrieve the candles and tablecloth.

Jess was washing the wineglasses when she felt two hands grasp her bottom. Spinning around, she was looking into the face of the Aussie, who had his arms about her waist.

"How did you learn to cook like that? Honestly, it is pure alchemy."

Jess wiggled out of his embrace and backed away. "Do you even know what that is?"

"Yes," he replied. "And I would like to have it with you. So sexy, and that apron, I just want to turn you around over your galley sink an—"

Jess smirked and shoving him even further away said, "Alchemy is the medieval forerunner of chemistry, based on a magical transformation. By magic, a simple base metal would turn into fabulous gold. Thank you for the compliment on my cooking, but no thank you for anything else you have to offer. My cooking is all you get from this apron. It's not my problem that my crewmates didn't generate enough heat to satisfy your desires. Now get out of my galley before I take a rolling pin to your overly handsome face."

The Aussie gave a hearty laugh. "You are one heck of a cook and feisty as hell. I hope that captain of yours has enough enthusiasm to manage you under the covers."

He exited her galley, and her thoughts turned to Captain Reed.

It was 3:30 in the morning, and Jess was drunk as a skunk, along with the Gratuitous Three and the Aussie. They were on deck playing a drinking game that required slapping the bottom of the loser as they drank a shot of tequila. Cheri was boasting about her ability as a great kisser, determined to demonstrate her talents on Jess, who was obliging. Captain Reed was awakened by their raucous behavior and shouted from below, "Party is over! Get the fuck off my boat and leave my ladies alone."

Jess pulled the Aussie to his feet, kissed him on each cheek and said, "You heard our captain. Get off his boat!"

Just before first light, Captain Reed was shaking Jess awake. He looked worried.

"What's wrong?" Jess asked, rubbing her head.

"The dinghy is missing. It's not tied to the boat. Please go and check the girls' cabins to see if they're aboard, and if they are, wake them up and bring them on deck."

Sleepy, hung over, and confused, the women gathered on deck.

"Where is my damn dinghy?" Captain Reed demanded. "Because it's not tied where I left it, nor is it on the platform."

Cheri spoke up. "I saw Lou moving the dinghy further to the stern as people were leaving."

"No, you did not!" said Lou, denying she ever touched the line. Lou pointed at the captain. "Your bowline knot was not correct. I tried to tell you that, and the dinghy must have pulled loose in the night."

If Captain Reed was upset by her answer, he wouldn't show it.

"Well, our dinghy is either far out in the open ocean, or we get lucky and find it in that cove over there." He pointed to the single inlet in the bay. "You realize without a dinghy there is no way to get to the shore. We are trapped on the boat, and buying another dinghy in East Jesus is not going to happen." Captain Reed abruptly walked to the pilothouse and picked up the radio receiver to call the local harbormaster for assistance. Before long, a patrol boat arrived to take him searching for his dinghy, along with Lou, who looked overly concerned and guilty.

Fortunately, the dinghy was indeed stuck on the rocks and not washed out to sea. The overly handsome Aussie atoned for his sins by lending a hand in returning the dinghy to its platform. Unfortunately, it sustained serious damage. Later in the day, the Aussie and his mate assisted Captain Reed in refueling *Slow Dance* at the service dock and making temporary repairs to the bottom of the dinghy. *Not such a bad fellow, after all*, thought Jess.

The next day, after bidding farewell to their fellow sailors, they readied the boat for an early morning departure. The women were coiling the lines and securing the swim ladder on deck while Captain Reed and Jess were in the pilothouse charting a course for the Tuamotu Archipelago.

"It has been more than forty years since I last sailed to these coral islands. I have sailed the world—granted, not everywhere—but Jess, I have never found water as blue as the Pacific that surrounds these islands. It is where all the fine black pearls are cultivated. Hopefully, in the last forty years, they have figured out how to cultivate a supply of fresh water."

Jess took a book off the bookshelf and showed it to Captain Reed. "I read Bernard Moitessier's book. He was quite a sailor and adventurer; he survived on these islands. There are no lakes or freshwater sources of any kind, only rainwater." Jess shifted her gaze to a chart on the monitor, imagining blue water, thatched huts, and naked brown children running on the beach to greet them.

"Bernard was half French and half Vietnamese," Captain Reed added. "His diary documented his solo, ten-month, nonstop sail, circling the globe one and a half times without his feet touching land. Sydney is reading his book about surviving on Ahe Island."

"Captain, is it possible we can anchor inside this reef here, on Ahe?" Jess pointed to a tiny dot on the chart.

"Indeed, we can, and we will. Look here, my plan is to take our time. We will stop at two bays on the leeward side of Nuku Hiva, spend a few days at each, and then sail on to the Tuamotus. We will anchor first at Manihi, then Ahe and lastly Rangiroa Island, before heading out into the open sea for Tahiti."

Jess followed along with Captain Reed's finger as he traced the route. She was excited yet apprehensive, knowing *Slow Dance* was low on fresh water—and Chaz had spoken correctly about there being no fresh water available in Nuku Hiva for a boat their size. The watermakers on the boat were nonfunctioning, another sign that *Slow Dance* was ill-prepared for their journey. Jess believed things happened for a reason, and Bernard Moitessier's book gave her the courage to believe they could manage whatever came their way. The man had sailed the world on his small sailboat with only the wind to carry him. His stories of seabirds, whales, and dolphins that saved his life on occasion reassured Jess they would somehow make port in Tahiti for water and necessary repairs.

Captain Reed stood at the bow, attaching a hose to the saltwater spigot on the front deck. "Girls, listen up. As you know, our freshwater tank is low, exceptionally low. Jess, use only salt water for washing dishes and a small amount of boiled fresh water to rinse and sterilize. Absolutely no washing of clothes, not even by hand, and if you must wash something, do it in saltwater. The shower attached here on the front deck is used with a special soap for saltwater body washing. Are we ready?"

In unison, the crew answered, "Aye-aye, captain."

With a sail plan, fresh provisions, and a clean boat, they lifted anchor in the early morning and set out for the lee side of the island.

Captain Reed had gotten his wish for an all-girl crew. *Please,* Jess thought, *don't let this be one of those careful-what-you-wish-for moments.*

13

Acute Stress

May 2024
Nuku Hiva Island

Captain Reed was navigating *Slow Dance* close to the rugged coastline of Nuku Hiva, seeking refuge from the turbulent waters farther out at sea. Cheri stood beside him, her voice rising above the howling wind as she berated him for what she claimed was a blatant disregard for maritime law. Her frustration was palpable, each accusation punctuated by the lurching of the boat.

"Captain, maritime law requires all vessels to navigate one mile from the coastline! You don't know if there's a shelf, coral bomb, rocks! Seriously! *You're too close!*"

Captain Reed remained stoic against Cheri's pleas, seemingly unfazed by her tirade, his eyes fixed on the horizon.

Jess wiped her sweaty palms on a dish towel, glancing nervously at the pair. *Slow Dance* sailed on, the coast looming closer, a stark contrast to the storm brewing in the pilothouse.

Slow Dance was surfing through small, choppy waters, causing the tops of the waves to break off, sending cascades of whitewater crashing over the bow. Lou was standing portside, leaning on the rail, when she let out a scream. Looking over, Jess immediately saw the reason for Lou's alarm. The dinghy hadn't been secured properly with the rear strap over the engine, and the rough waters were causing it to slide off the hydraulic platform. Although Captain Reed maneuvered close to the rocky shore, where the sea was a bit calmer, the boat was still heeling over and digging hard into the trough. Had they been farther out in rougher seas, the dinghy would have been lost, becoming what Captain Reed called a "sea anchor."

Lou was now pacing frantically. "What can we do?"

Cheri stared with her mouth open, and Jess looked around to see what could be done, but it was Sydney who sprang into action.

"Lou, get the line out of the locker over there, the one under the cushion. Now!"

Lou and Cheri awakened from their stupor and quickly fetched Sydney some line and tossed it to her. Sydney climbed out on the platform and into the dinghy and began securing it with the line. She twisted the line into one of the knots Captain Reed taught her and then tossed it up.

"Here, Cheri, take the line and securely cleat it portside."

Jess watched as Cheri wrapped the other end of the line to the cleat. As Cheri attempted to secure the rope, Jess saw the front dinghy strap begin to loosen. Acting quickly, she lifted the lid of the lazarette to grab the platform controller affixed to its underside and began frantically pushing the Down button to lower the platform. As the platform lowered, the front strap broke under the tension, and the dinghy slid off into the next wave, taking Sydney with it.

"Oh-God-oh-my-God-Jesus, help!" Sydney called out.

Cheri was screaming and Trinidad was standing on her back legs, barking wildly. Lou dashed immediately to the inside control panel and hit the MOB—Man Overboard—button. Captain Reed was struggling to turn *Slow Dance* around due to ground swells smashing into her starboard side. Jess held tightly onto the side rail, clutching the lifesaver ring in the event she spotted Sydney in the water. She remembered what Captain Reed said regarding the impossibility of finding a man overboard in rough seas—and she started to cry, salt spray misting into her eyes, mingling with her tears.

Captain Reed reversed, then, steering *Slow Dance* to the direction where the dinghy went into the sea. Suddenly, Jess's tears turned to joy as she spotted the dinghy over the crests of the waves.

"The dinghy!" she yelled. "There, over there!"

Lou had the binoculars and shouted, "It's moving toward us, and Sydney is in it!" Soaking wet, standing in the dinghy, Sydney called up, "I'm okay, it's all good." She was slapping her hands together as if dusting them off.

"Hang on!" Captain Reed yelled. "We must tow her, it's too damn rough to do anything else."

Captain Reed put *Slow Dance* back on course and slowed the engines. Then he turned his attention to Sydney.

"Toss that line up here to Cheri. Cheri, catch the line and secure it to the cleat. Good, now toss Sydney this other line so we can double-secure it. The seas are too bouncy, Beefcake; you're going to have to stay put until we get around to the leeward side of the island." Captain Reed looked worried.

Sydney called up to Captain Reed, "Have the girls pull the dinghy closer to the stern!"

Cheri, Lou, and Jess pulled the lines, and when the dinghy was near the platform, Sydney waited for the next wave to bounce her just high enough to grab the platform bars and climb aboard.

"Jeez, Beefcake." Captain Reed was smiling. "That was amazing. You're part monkey, and you've got the hairy body to prove it. Don't ever do anything like that again. I am not sure how we kept from losing you, but I am sure you nearly gave us all heart attacks. We must tow the dinghy behind. Not optimal, but no choice . . . too rough to get her back on the platform. I'm concentrating on driving the boat, so, Sydney and Cheri, secure the towlines to the platform and don't let Lou tie any of her knots."

Lou pretended not to hear Captain Reed's last remark.

"Dang, it happened so fast." Sydney rolled her shoulders back. "It was amazing that Jess was lowering the platform right as the front strap broke, sending me into the water with the dinghy. If that had happened from this height, I'd be fish food. I already tied the line to the dinghy's stern, and it was still in my hands when I went into the water, so it was easy to pull myself up and start the engine. Good thing you leave the key at the helm."

Captain Reed shook his head. "Damn, Sydney, you been hiding a set of balls in your pants?"

Sydney laughed. "No, Captain, just a pair of big ovaries."

14

Temperance

Slow Dance entered calm waters as she rounded the tip of the island, where Captain Reed sailed into a bay called Anaho. They dropped anchor and waited for the boat to settle, just beginning to relax from the terrifying moment of almost losing Sydney and the dinghy in rough seas. The shoreline was rimmed by deep white sand, lush palm groves, and visible trails leading up the mountain. *Slow Dance* swayed rhythmically in the protected blue lagoon. There were no other boats; they had it all to themselves.

Lou and Sydney untied the dinghy and brought it around to the swim ladder so they could disembark and have a look around on shore. Jess went below to the galley to open a bottle of chardonnay and prepare a cheese board with French baguettes. She figured they could all use a bit of refreshment to boost their resilience, but as she approached the upper deck, she heard Cheri continuing to voice her grievances with the captain.

"For a guy who has as many sea miles as you do, how is it you don't know much about maritime law?" she demanded. "We could have crashed sailing that close to the cliffs. You also didn't check the dinghy to make sure it was secure before putting us out for sea. As captain, it is your responsibility to check, check, and triple-check everything. Sydney could have died out there."

Feeling tension, Jess set the tray on the chart table and retreated to the galley. As she descended the steps, she heard Captain Reed say, "You're free to hop off at the next port." No response from Cheri.

By the second day, the beauty and serenity of their surroundings healed any residual trauma. The mutiny of Chaz and Harrison and the near loss of Sydney and their dinghy all faded after several days of blissful calm. The women were kayaking, hiking, swimming, and enjoying Jess's candlelit dinners under a million stars. Trinidad went for walks every day with Captain Reed and Jess, who had started spending more time together apart from the other three. Trini went for swims and began acting like a dog, as opposed to a groomed Beverly Hills poodle with ribbons in her hair. The Gratuitous Three were becoming more helpful, and an unspoken sisterhood was taking shape between them.

"Jess, look what we brought you." Lou was holding a sarong full of mangos and papayas. "We found them just lying on the path during our hike this morning. Manna from heaven; it falls from the trees. I love this place."

Jess placed the fruit into a wooden bowl. "Tomorrow morning I am going to make you all some scrumptious mango muffins, no sugar. The fruit is sweet enough, and I'll add some of the remaining walnuts to make them even better."

"No, add this to them." Sydney was holding a fresh coconut and a machete.

Cheri picked up one of the coconuts from the deck. "Yum, where did you find them?"

"While you and Lou were hiking this morning, Captain Reed and I went to the beach. Our captain has a talent for picking up perfect coconuts that fall from the palm trees."

"That's right," said Captain Reed, "and I am about to show Beefcake how to crack one open with the machete."

Sydney wielded the giant knife like a samurai sword, halving the coconut in one strike.

"Save the water," said Lou. "It's so good for us to drink."

Jess fetched a pitcher and was catching the liquid from the coconuts, trying not to think about depending on coconuts for survival.

Their evening supper consisted of the remaining wahoo steaks, roasted breadfruit, coconut water with a jigger of rum, and sliced papaya for dessert. Captain Reed was yawning as he pushed away from the table.

"Ladies, I feel a dark spell coming on, so I bid you all a good night. After breakfast, let's be on our way to Daniel's Bay . . . so no sleeping in, Sydney!" They all laughed. Trini followed along with Captain Reed as he headed to his cabin.

Jess was finishing up in the galley and Lou was drying the dishes and putting them away. When the last dish was in the cupboard, Lou said, "Come with me. I want to show you something awesome."

Jess raised an eyebrow. "There isn't sex involved, I hope."

Dubious, Jess followed Lou to the bow of *Slow Dance* and up the rungs to the top of the pilothouse.

"When the mainsail is cradled," Lou explained, "you can climb inside the cradle, and the sail becomes a comfy cushion. Come on, it's easy."

Jess climbed in after Lou, who was leaning against the mast inside the cradle. She stretched out with her head on Lou's chest, and it was more comfortable than she had imagined it would be.

"Hey, what are you two doing up there?"

Cheri and Sydney climbed up the rungs to the top of the pilothouse.

"Wouldn't you like to know," answered Lou.

Cheri and Sydney maneuvered themselves into the cradle. Sydney leaned against Jess, and Cheri leaned against Sydney. They were all in a row, lying there and gazing up at a billion stars with no lights to suppress the brilliance.

"Is that the Southern Cross?" asked Lou.

"Yup," said Sydney. "We are officially in the southern hemi."

Jess was speechless.

Gazing at the sky full of stars, she fell asleep as the boat gently swayed.

15

Jubilation

May 2024
Anaho Bay, Nuku Hiva

"Another fabulous morning in paradise."

Captain Reed was stretching his arms toward the cloudless blue sky when they heard Cheri holler, "Oh my God, gross! That's it, I've had it!"

Sydney was climbing the steps leading to the outside deck, carrying her large cup of coffee and looking mighty guilty. When she heard Cheri, she sprayed a mouthful of her coffee out over the deck. Jess grabbed Sydney to keep her from falling backward as she was laughing so hard.

"What have you done?" Jess asked.

Cheri and Lou arrived on deck at the same time and Lou was asking, "What's wrong, Cheri?"

"I'll tell you what's wrong, the dog took a crap on my pillow! My entire cabin smells like dog shit, dammit! *And even after Jess cleans it up*, I will continue to suffer with the smell."

Everyone was looking at Sydney, who could not control her laughter. Cheri was glaring at her.

"Did you do this? It's not funny."

Sydney regained her composure, "Okay, okay, wait here."

Sydney returned to the deck carrying a blob of what looked like dog doo in her hand.

Cheri made a face. "Oh my God, I am going to be sick. You are repulsive."

"It's plastic. It's fake poop from Angie's bag of tricks under the cushion in the saloon." Sydney began mimicking Cheri. "*Oh gross, I can smell it; my cabin is going to stink foreverrrr.*"

Cheri folded her arms and shook her head. "Well, you got me good, Marley girl, but be on your guard for a payback."

After a delicious breakfast of mango muffins, scrambled eggs, and organic coffee, *Slow Dance* prepared for sea. Captain Reed was at the inside helm, giving direction on the microphone.

"Okay girls, I am going to back off the anchor and when I say go, lift it, and keep an eye that it's coming up straight and not under the boat. Go!"

Jess watched the women working together. Sydney was down in the anchor locker with some crazy-looking crowbar, pushing the chain to either side as it came up from the ocean floor. Captain Reed taught her if the chain stacks on top of itself it becomes impossible to drop the anchor the next time. Lou was operating the controller that lifted the giant hunk of metal, and Cheri was watching to ensure it was coming up straight.

"I see it, Lou."

Cheri gave the hand signal to Captain Reed that the anchor was up.

"Easy now, Lou . . . let it swing into position, and when I say go, bring it up fast."

The anchor came barreling up and jumped perfectly into its cradle. Cheri and Lou locked the anchor in place with the snubber chain, just like Captain Reed taught them, to ensure the anchor wouldn't shift while the boat was underway. Jess was thinking they would make it after all—to where, she didn't know or care.

Slow Dance sailed out of Anaho Bay with enough wind for the girls to hoist the main and save on fuel. Lou was busy removing the American flag from the stern's flagpole and replacing it with something else. Jess was on deck relaxing with a book until distracted by Lou, who was fumbling with the lines on the flagpole.

"What are you doing?"

"I'm putting up our new flag so other boats can see who we are."

Jess held her book up, shielding her face from the sun. "Um, Lou, that is your animal-print leopard T-shirt."

"Right," said Lou, "and now it's our cougar flag!"

No one objected, so the cougar flag remained on the pole all the way to Tahiti.

The trip to their next anchorage, Daniel's Bay, was a calm six-hour sail from Anaho Bay.

Jess could already tell she preferred island-hopping to open-water sailing.

As *Slow Dance* approached the bay, Cheri was at the inside helm with Captain Reed, pointing at the chart on the Furuno radar screen. "Look here," she said. "The chart is showing the opening to the left of the rock wall." She tapped the spot on the chart. Leaning over the captain, she continued tapping on the screen, waiting for a response. *Slow Dance* was coming off the ocean and heading into Daniel's Bay on the southwest side of Nuku Hiva.

Captain Reed was displaying his uncanny ability to tune everything out around him as he remained laser-focused, his full concentration on the passage. He was not looking at the chart; he was assessing the situation from experience as he maneuvered the boat to the right of the ever-closer rock wall.

"What is the matter with you?" Cheri asked in a panicky tone. "Can't you see the opening here?" She pounded her finger on the chart. "You are about to crash us into the damn rock wall!"

Realizing Captain Reed was oblivious to her, Cheri sat on the pilothouse floor in a crash position, with her head tucked between her knees. It was obvious she had lost all faith in Captain Reed's ability to pilot the vessel. Lou and Sydney stood firm by Captain Reed, however, looking straight ahead at the oncoming rocks, while Jess remained on the sofa, holding Trinidad, eyes closed and picturing white light surrounding the boat.

After another tense few moments, Jess heard Sydney call out, "All right, O Captain, My Captain, you're the bomb." Jess opened her eyes to see Sydney hugging Captain Reed, out of relief or respect, it was hard to tell.

"How did you know to go right of the rocks?" asked Sydney.

Captain Reed scratched his head, "I didn't." Then he gave her a wink.

"I'll go up and ready the anchor," said Lou.

Cheri followed Lou to the bow, and if she was embarrassed by her freak-out, she didn't show it.

Jess, able to breathe again, asked Captain Reed, "How *did* you know, and why didn't you follow the chart?"

Captain Reed smiled. "First of all, I have two hundred thousand sea miles under my belt, and secondly, the charts in this part of the world are inaccurate. Over the course of my forty-eight years at sea, I experienced mounting tensions with various crew and passengers who doubted my abilities to navigate safely, especially in turbulent waters. As a young man growing up in Hollywood, I somehow managed to get myself accepted as crew on a sailboat, participating in the famous Transpacific Yacht Race from Los Angeles to Honolulu. Knowing absolutely nothing about sailing, I could only conclude the owner of the yacht must have been desperate. During the nonstop race of 2,225 nautical miles, I argued about the course set by the yacht's navigator. I had a love for the night sky and tried to alert the navigator that we were heading for Japan. When the guy went to sleep, I changed the set course and spared the yachtsmen total humiliation. I am immune to other people's opinions, and other people's panic"—he glanced briefly at Cheri—"regarding my ability to sail."

Captain Reed turned his attention to Jess. "Where should we anchor, Jess?" He had become impressed with his cook's ability to read charts and make use of the depth sounder for determining the amount of anchor chain needed to hold *Slow Dance* firm. Captain Reed had a way of pushing a round peg into a square hole without a person knowing. He found pleasure in the interest Jess showed in sailing. She'd made it clear she was the type of person who felt anything worth doing was worth doing right, especially when that something might cause her to die. Jess had been paying close attention for months, watching Chaz, Harrison, and the Gratuitous Three as they navigated *Slow Dance* across the Pacific to the islands. "When I signal," he directed her, "let me know if you approve of the spot to drop the hook."

Jess made her way to the bow and looked over the bay. Three other boats had anchored close to the shore, so Jess motioned for Captain Reed to head toward the middle of the bay, a quarter mile from the beach.

Captain Reed was on the microphone. "Good call, Jess, and the mosquitos will not find us this far out. Okay, ladies, remove the snubber and drop three lengths of chain fifty feet."

Cheri and Lou carefully dropped the anchor as Jess and Sydney leaned over the rail to watch it sink down, settling on the sandy bottom. Suddenly, Sydney's sunglasses slid off her face into the water.

"No!" she cried, and without thinking jumped overboard to grab them before they settled in the depths.

Captain Reed walked out to the bow. "What's Beefcake doing? Checking the anchor? . . . What's that in the water? I hope it's not a shark."

Cheri was leaning over the rail and pointing down. "Whoa! Huge rays."

Jess saw the winglike creatures and was glad to not be in the water. Trini added her two cents by barking from the rail. "They're not the barb-tailed kind that killed Steve Irwin, are they?" she asked, suddenly looking worried.

Captain Reed laughed. "Nah, they're the kind you pet at SeaWorld."

Sydney appeared by the side of the boat, treading water and wearing her sunglasses. "Hey, Lou, there're cool rays in the bay. I'm going to toss up my glasses. Can you toss me a snorkel with a mask, please?"

Jess marveled at the fearlessness of the Rasta girl from Wisconsin.

Captain Reed looked over the rail at her. "Check the anchor while you're down there, would you, Syd?"

Daniel's Bay was picturesque and remote, surrounded by lush greenery and towering cliffs, a testament to nature's untouched beauty, a paradise that offered an enchanting escape into a world where verdant greenery meets azure waters. Coconut palms swayed gently in the warm breeze, and Jess imagined she could hear their fronds whispering secrets of the island's past. In the distance, the rugged mountains rose, their peaks often shrouded in mist, adding to the mystical quality of the bay.

The tranquil waters created a sense of isolation and uninhibited freedom. A hidden gem offering a peaceful retreat from the modern world.

A small village was nestled in the interior of the island, and a half-hour hike over the mountain trail offered a grocery store, a bakery, and an outdoor bar that provided yachtie camaraderie over cold island beer. Cheri and Lou spent their days hiking, kayaking, and flirting in the pirate bar, and Sydney played with the rays. Captain Reed and Jess spent their time walking with Trinidad and charting a more detailed course for the Tuamotu coral islands.

—Tuamotu Coral Islands—

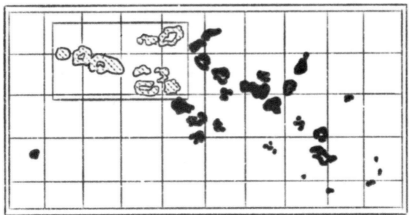

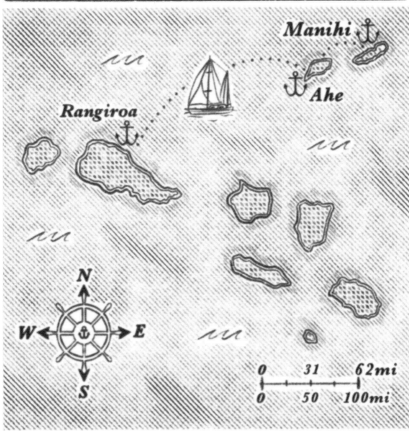

16

Precipitation

May 2024
The Tuamotu Coral Islands

Life on *Slow Dance* was taking on an entirely new vibration. Lou and Cheri cleaned the scuppers daily, swabbed the teak deck, and polished the walls inside the pilothouse. Sydney updated the maintenance log in the engine room after changing filters for the oil, fuel, and water pumps under Captain Reed's watchful eye. It amused Jess to see Sydney wearing Chaz's old mechanic's jumpsuit.

Cheri and Lou sunned themselves nude on the bow of the boat, utilizing the saltwater hose to cool off while listening to music over *Slow Dance*'s sound system. The sea was calm, the winds fair, and the mood significantly improved as they sailed toward the coral islands.

Jess prepared a tray of mai tais and carried them out to the sunbathers. Handing one to each of the women, she said, "There is something about being out here in the open sea that makes me feel free and a little bit crazy. Frankly, I did not know what it would be like. I worried I might hate it, but I love it, and not just a little." Then, deciding to embrace her newfound sense of freedom, stripped down to her panties and joined the two women.

"You love it now that it's calm." Captain Reed was standing at the bow, admiring the naked women, his eyes primarily on Jess. Clouds were gathering in the distance, and *Slow Dance* appeared to be heading straight into the darkening sky.

Pulling off his shirt, Captain Reed said. "I was going to join you, but we need to batten down the hatches, ladies. We're going to get much-needed rain."

Sydney was on deck now, wearing Chaz's old jumpsuit and wiping grease from her hands with a paper towel. "Rain? Did somebody say rain?"

Springing into action, Lou pulled on her sundress and retrieved eight one-gallon glass bottles that had once held Mexican red wine. During the crossing, she had rinsed the bottles out and, for an unknown reason, saved them. Jess was about to find out why. Lou had done weird, sneaky, unexplainable things over the past several months—the worst being when she emptied the garbage bag full of cut-up plastic into the sea. Harrison meticulously cut up all plastic items into tiny pieces to dispose of them properly when they reached land. One evening during Lou's watch, Jess caught her in the act of dumping the bag into the sea, and Lou made her promise not to tell the others. Lou could not explain to Jess why she had done it, but she cried, as usual. Jess let it go, but deep down, she had little trust or respect for Lou.

"Come give me a hand," Lou said, enlisting Sydney and Cheri's help with tying the canvas dinghy cover to the forward side rails, port and starboard.

"What's this for?" Cheri asked Lou.

"To catch rainwater and funnel it to these glass jugs."

"That is ingenious, Lou. You are redeeming yourself for losing my dinghy." Captain Reed was watching Lou capture the rain as it fell into the tarp and funneled into the glass jars when the sky suddenly cracked loudly, a bolt of lightning stabbing down at the surface of the water. Jess, visibly startled, bolted for the pilothouse, but Captain Reed caught her in his arms and pulled her close.

"You're shaking. Nothing to worry about. It will pass quickly. It's just a microburst." Still clad in only her panties, she shivered as Captain Reed continued to hold her firmly in his arms, her breasts pressing against his naked chest. Jess told herself the mai tai was responsible for her overwhelming feelings of arousal. She surmised Captain Reed was experiencing the same reaction by the expansion in his shorts. Did he desire her? Jess wiggled her half-naked body—along with her thoughts—out of Captain Reed's arms. They stood looking at each other. He gave her a mischievous half-smile.

"You know I like my dishes al dente, right?"

Jess snatched up her sarong, wrapped it around herself, and thought, *Yeah, some of your ideas are half-cooked, too.* She laughed to herself as she thought about saying that aloud.

The dark skies opened, and the rain poured down.

"I don't know about you, ladies, but I'm going to have a rain shower."

Captain Reed pulled off his shorts and his Calvin Klein briefs and headed butt naked for the soap on deck. Moments later, Cheri was on the opposite side of the deck with a bar of Dove soap. Both were showering naked in the rain, laughing like children. Watching them through the pilothouse window, Jess thought about pulling off her wet sarong, lathering herself with soap, and rubbing herself against Captain Reed's naked body. Erotic thoughts stabbed at her brain like the intermittent bolts of lightning. She went to the crew cabin to put on dry clothes and wait for the storm to pass, both above and below.

Lou busied herself with the water bottles now filled to the top with the precious life-sustaining liquid. Sydney was letting the rain fill four empty five-gallon buckets she fetched from the lazarette. Jess was chilling out in the pilothouse, doing nothing but wishing the rain could wash away her thoughts of Captain Reed soaping his naked body.

An hour later when the sun returned, the women strung a line between the forward shrouds to hang clothes, washed in the rainwater from Sydney's buckets.

"Arrrrgh mates, there be water for drinkin' with that rum." Sydney was wearing a pirate hat, eye patch, hook glove, and striped shirt.

"That's perfect for you," said Jess. "The dreadlocks make you look like a true pirate. This calls for a good supper." She disappeared below to her galley.

Slow Dance was approaching the Tuamotu coral island of Manihi. Its silhouette began cutting through the shimmering turquoise waters as the captain maneuvered the boat smoothly across the waves toward the pass to the interior of the island, leaving a frothy wake in her path.

Captain Reed was on the loudspeaker. "When I turn into the wind, drop the mainsail quickly."

Lou, Cheri, and Sydney were already on top of the pilothouse to pull the massive sail down into the cradle and secure it with the sail ties. The women managed the mass of canvas like pros, guiding it into the cradle and securing it.

Captain Reed stuck his head out of the pilothouse. "Well done, you salty dogs. Beefcake, I want you at the outside helm, steering us through the pass to the inside of the island. I will talk to you from inside the pilothouse. I'll be looking at the chart guiding you, but you are my eyes and helmsman. From the inside helm, I must stand on a stool, and that is not an option. The entrance is narrow. Because the ocean is rushing in, we're going to pick up speed and dig into the waves."

Sydney looked worried. "What if I lose control?"

"No worries, I can take over from inside but won't be able to see shit."

One of *Slow Dance*'s imperfections was visibility from the inside helm. The bow of the boat was forty feet from the pilothouse windows, and even at six-foot-two, the captain had to stand on his tiptoes to see over the top of the helm.

Jess carried Trini below and put her in Captain Reed's bathroom, the safest space for her in the event the boat lurched violently from any sudden thrust. The bathroom was small, and the carpet would keep her from sliding around. There was nothing in the bathroom that could endanger her.

Sydney stood at the outside helm gripping the wheel, and Jess sat on the raised captain's seat behind her. Cheri was sitting on top of the pilothouse, oblivious by choice. Jess figured Cheri knew involving herself in Captain Reed's plan would create further conflict between them.

Slow Dance was approaching the pass and Jess's heart went into her throat when she saw a man standing on the reef's edge, nonchalantly fishing. She stood up and went to the rail for a closer look.

"How narrow did he say the pass was? There's a guy standing on the reef, for God's sake."

Before Sydney could answer, *Slow Dance* violently pulled into the current, increasing her speed to ten knots. The boat dug into the waves, sending water cascading over the bow.

Sydney called out.

"Captain, I can't hold course, shit, shit, shit!"

Jess was holding tight to the rail and as they passed the man fishing; she could almost touch him.

"I got it," shouted Captain Reed. "How far from portside to the reef?"

"Looks ten feet or less," replied Sydney, "and there are some huge coral bombs starboard."

It took minutes to enter the pass, but to Jess, it seemed like hours. She began to relax again once *Slow Dance* hit calm waters inside the coral island.

Captain Reed took the outside helm from Sydney. "Good job, toots. That was a hell of a ride, eh?"

Lou was motioning for Captain Reed to come forward, where a man in a small boat had been waiting. In French, he said he would be their host and lead them to a good anchorage in front of a small resort. *Slow Dance* followed along, and the man waited for them to anchor. He offered Jess two fine-looking, freshly caught fish and informed them there was no fresh water on the island.

Manihi was a lush island born inside a protective coral reef in the middle of the Pacific Ocean. Naked brown children splashed playfully in the warm blue waters in front of thatched-roof houses situated in palm groves along the shore. Jess felt like she was in a dream.

"You were right, Captain; I have never seen water this blue. It is the color of robins' eggs we found in nests when I was a kid. This water is clear, like a mountain lake. The depth sounder reads sixty feet of water. Unbelievable! It looks so shallow."

Lou, Cheri, and Sydney sorted out the snorkel gear while Captain Reed went to the engine room to start the generator necessary for charging the boat's lights and electrical systems while *Slow Dance* was on anchor. Cheri put the swim ladder down, and Lou, inspired by the native children around her, stripped naked. Snorkel and flippers in hand, Lou leaped into the water. The others followed her lead, opting for their birthday suits. Together, they snorkeled naked toward a colorful wall of coral. Trinidad was doing her usual dance of running up and down the deck, barking wildly. She absolutely disliked any of her people jumping off the boat.

Jess watched from the surface as Captain Reed and Sydney glided effortlessly down a twenty-foot coral wall. The water surrounding Jess swarmed with colorful fish she had only seen in large public aquariums. Jess was impressed that Captain Reed could still free dive to that depth. Floating effortlessly, she felt the heaviness of life leave her, replaced with an incredible lightness of being in the moment. No past, no future, only the feeling of the sea on her naked skin. Free from her Catholic upbringing, her mother's illness, her poor choice of husbands, and the things in her life that wounded her spirit. Jess felt the sea was peeling away her old skin, revealing new skin, new life. Captain Reed offered her a second chance at life, a chance to be brave, free, and unburdened. Jess wondered if he could do the same for himself.

Cheri and Lou were already on the boat when Jess climbed up the swim ladder. Lou handed her a towel.

"Amazing, right? I spent five years sailing in the Caribbean, but the Pacific might be prettier."

"I am speechless," replied Jess.

A minute later, Captain Reed climbed back on the boat and dried himself with the damp towel Jess had used to dry herself. He suggested putting on clothes and taking the dinghy over to the Manihi Pearl Resort for cold beer and french fries, to which the women enthusiastically agreed. Pulling on shorts and T-shirts with Miss Trinidad in tow, they headed for shore.

The Manihi Pearl was an exotic, off-the-beaten-path type of place Jess had read about in fancy travel magazines. Remote, luxurious, and pricey. Captain Reed secured the dinghy while Cheri and Lou procured a table in the outside seating area. It amazed Jess how welcome Trinidad was on the island, a stark contrast from the French Marquesas. She noticed dogs onshore and wondered how they came to be in such a remote place. The waiter delivered their cold beers and inferior french fries, considering they were in French territory.

"Did you see Sydney come back on the boat?" Jess was suddenly aware that Sydney was missing. "Did she come back with you, Captain? I saw the two of you snorkeling together."

Lou shrugged. "She can take care of herself."

Cheri, not learning from past mistakes, began to lecture Captain Reed. "Don't you know about the buddy system? Remind me never to scuba dive with you. Are you even certified to dive or is it the same as with your captain certification?"

Jess burst into laughter.

"Did I say something funny?" asked Cheri.

Jess pointed to the entrance of the outdoor seating. Sydney was walking toward them. She had not made it back to *Slow Dance*, opting instead to swim to the dinghy naked, where she fashioned the soft leather Bimini cover into a wraparound skirt. She was topless, but her long dreadlocks concealed her perfect, twenty-seven-year-old breasts. Sydney sauntered toward their table and ordered a beer as she breezed by the waiter. Jess snapped a photo just before she fell off her chair laughing. (The notorious photo would later demand editing on Jess's blog after Sydney's mother discovered upon enlarging the picture that her daughter's nipples were exposed.)

That evening, Jess prepared the two fish from their Manihi host, barbecuing them whole with fresh garlic and herbs. She prepared breadfruit latkes for an appetizer.

"Too bad there's no sour cream in this part of the world. They do not know what they are missing, but it's amazing you had applesauce." Captain Reed was biting into another of Jess's latkes. "As a member of the tribe, I must ask, how did a shiksa learn to make such good latkes, and from breadfruit no less?"

Jess was dabbing applesauce on her latkes.

"I had a couple of Jewish boyfriends, and it was one of their Aunt Berthas who took me into her kitchen and would not let me escape until I mastered the most sacred of her recipes. I went to culinary school, but my talents are from Aunt Bertha types, or my Italian godmother, or from sitting on mud floors in Greece and India with local women teaching me about their cuisine. Sauces and spices determine the dish. Eggplant exists in many countries, but it is the sauce and spice that make the cuisine. When I get the right spices, I will make Indian food."

Lou was standing by the rail portside. "You want to see something neat?"

The others got up from the table and went to the rail where Lou was shining a flashlight on the water.

"We used to do this on the catamaran in the Caribbean."

Hundreds of fish came swimming toward the light, the same fish Jess observed during her earlier snorkel. Cheri pointed at one of the larger fish.

"That is a parrot fish. We will be seeing lots of those, but I am not sure what the blue or yellow ones are—clown fish, maybe?"

17

Indiscretions

May 2024
Manihi Island, Tuamotus

Taking a deep breath, Jess inhaled the intoxicating scent of tropical flowers carried by the warm breeze that wafted through the portholes. Opening her eyes, she was greeted by the soft glow of the sun rising on the horizon, painting the sky in hues of orange and pink. Sitting up in her cozy bunk, she felt a sense of peace and contentment wash over her. Stretching her limbs, she felt the gentle rocking of the boat beneath her, a soothing and familiar motion that spoke of the endless expanse of ocean surrounding her.

Pulling on shorts and a T-shirt, Jess headed up to the main deck. The new day held promise of adventure and discovery, and she felt a burst of energy and excitement at the prospect of exploring the island. The tranquil beauty filled Jess with a profound sense of gratitude for the opportunity to experience such a magical morning in such a remote place. In that moment Jess felt the freedom of the open sea and that she was ready to embrace whatever lay ahead with an open heart and sense of wonder.

In the late morning, their host came by and was gracious enough to offer the women use of his wife's washing machine—the only one on the island. After loading several bags into the dinghy, Cheri drove the women to the shore while Captain Reed remained on board, assigning his dirty laundry to Jess and admitting he had never done laundry himself.

The first load was on spin when Sydney and Lou disappeared, leaving Jess and Cheri to do the remainder of the washing. Before the second load was on rinse, Cheri vanished, and Jess was left to push the wet, soggy clothes into plastic trash bags and haul them back into the dinghy. Captain Reed had been teaching her to drive the dinghy, and Jess felt confident enough to drive the short distance back to *Slow Dance*.

"Where are the girls?" Captain Reed was at the ladder to secure the dinghy and help Jess haul up the heavy bags of wet clothes.

"Who knows," Jess said. "They're like cats. One minute they're right under your feet, the next minute, poof, gone. I should have put our clothes in the bag and left their clothes in the washer."

Captain Reed put the last bag on deck. "Why didn't you? Don't hang their stuff up for them either."

Jess began sorting their clothes from the women's clothes. "The thought wouldn't cross my mind. I'm not sure what water was being used in the washing machine, but the clothes smell good, so I'm guessing rainwater. None of these islands have a freshwater source. It's amazing their survival depends on rain and fish."

Captain Reed took her hand and pulled her away from the clothesline. "Have you ever seen a black pearl?"

"No," she replied.

"Come on, finish the clothes, and let's go explore this island, maybe catch a cold one."

Captain Reed pulled the dinghy alongside one of the floating farms inside the atoll that cultivated black pearls. Jess and Captain Reed were given an educational tour on the farming of the rare and costly black beauties. The man demonstrating the techniques of cultivation pulled up a long rope with the precious oysters clinging to it. Jess found it fascinating. Their next stop was a small local bar on the far side of the island, where they consumed more than a few beers, along with shots of a powerful local liquor made from coconuts.

"Jess, I must say, you're a good sail mate. I enjoy your company, and I didn't even know you could cook when I hired you!"

Captain Reed was lending a very tipsy Jess a hand into the dinghy.

"See," answered Jess, "you say stuff like that. You're confused. Why *did* you hire me?"

It was getting late as Captain Reed steered the dinghy toward *Slow Dance*. Suddenly, he turned off the engine and reached for Jess, who was feeling the coconut liquor and slurring her words.

"Oh, nooo ya don't. I am very bad at anything physical when I am inebriated, and boy oh boy am I hammered."

Captain Reed had his shorts halfway down. "I can hold my liquor, but obviously not my desire. . . . How about that pretty mouth of yours? Is that available?"

Jess, having lost all inhibition, began to oblige, but as she moved toward him, she grasped the edge of the boat and retched up the coconut concoction, thwarting Captain Reed's expectations of oral pleasure.

The captain had his hand on her back. "Poor baby, you going to be okay?"

Jess pushed his hand away. "Can it get any more embarrassing . . . Please, let's never speak of this again or drink whatever that poison was at the bar."

Captain Reed nodded, suppressing his urge to laugh.

Back on *Slow Dance*, Jess retreated to the crew cabin, not showing her face until nearly noon the next day. Searching for Tylenol in the galley, she encountered Sydney buttering some burnt toast.

"Jesus, Sydney, the smell is sickening."

Crossing one leg over the other and leaning against the cabinet, Sydney responded, "You look terrible. What kind of trouble did you and Captain Sexy get into last night? He's still in his cabin."

Jess swallowed two Tylenol. "Black pearls and shots of whiskey made from coconuts. Avoid it at all costs."

Sydney took a bite of her toast. "By the looks of it, you had too many shots. What else? Some long overdue nookies?"

Jess waved her away. "Mind your own business, Medusa."

It was late afternoon when Captain Reed stepped on deck to find Jess sitting with Trinidad on the sofa, sipping her third cup of coffee.

"Any coffee left in the galley?" he asked. "What was in that stuff we drank yesterday? My head still hurts."

Jess got up and started to make her way to the galley when Captain Reed grabbed her wrist.

"Listen, we were wasted, Jess. Don't let this ruin our friendship. I was out of line to take advantage of you in your condition"—his expression became serious—"and I am sorry I am such a horny ole sailor."

Jess took his hand from her wrist. "You took advantage of me? I was thinking it was the other way around. In which case, I am sorry."

Captain Reed was completely taken aback by her comment, and she enjoyed throwing him off guard.

"Want some Tylenol with that coffee?" she asked as she moved toward the galley, smiling to herself. As much as she didn't want to admit it, Jess desired Captain Reed, and if she had been tipsy, rather than drunk, she might have had the courage to act on those desires. She wanted more from him, but until she knew exactly what that was (besides sex), she told herself she would proceed cautiously. She wondered what he must think of her inebriated attempt at pleasuring him and then vomiting over the side of the dinghy. More importantly, what did she think about his low regard for women in general? Was there a shred of romance in the man? She was certain of what she wanted from him sexually—slow, erotic lovemaking.

Perhaps, the girl only got her romantic-hot-lover-guy in the movies. She hoped not.

18

Truth or Dare

May 2024
Ahe Atoll, Tuamotus

Captain Reed was eager to move on to Ahe Island, and Jess and Sydney were especially excited because of Bernard Moitessier's books.

Sydney was at the helm with Captain Reed, watching him steer *Slow Dance* out of the pass.

"I am going to dig down in the sand to see if I can find fresh water," said Sydney.

Jess was sitting behind Sydney on Captain Reed's chair, while Cheri and Lou snubbed the anchor.

Captain Reed turned to Sydney. "It was much smoother getting out of here than getting in. Only four hours to our next stop."

Sydney replied, "It's hard to imagine such awesome beauty. I swear, every anchorage is more stunning than the last. Nothing like this on Lake Superior."

Captain Reed was looking over the bow for a nice anchorage inside the Ahe atoll.

"Jess and Sydney, go out on the bow and tell me what you see. Here is a handheld radio. Guide me."

Jess took the radio reluctantly. "How do you work this thing?"

"Listen when I talk, then push this button *and hold it down* when you talk. Now get up to the bow."

Just as Jess reached the bow Captain Reed's voice emitted from her radio. "Check, radio check, can you hear me? Check."

Jess held the button down as instructed. "I hear you, Captain. Be advised, there is a minefield of coral bombs in front of us and you're heading straight toward them."

Captain Reed utilized *Slow Dance*'s bow thrusters to reverse the boat.

Jess pushed the button on her radio again. "Whew, that was close. I'm glad *Slow Dance* has a steel hull. To the left looks nice. What does the chart say?"

Captain Reed didn't answer, and Jess realized she was still holding the button down. Releasing her finger, she caught the tail end of what he said. ". . . besides, charts don't cover this part of the world. Instinct, baby, instinct, and experience, of course."

Ahe was like a chapter out of Robert Louis Stevenson's *Treasure Island*. Cheri and Lou spent a few days diving on the reef while Captain Reed snorkeled with Sydney and Jess, who insisted on bringing Trini on every outing. Sydney, much like Captain Reed, was fearless in the water. Jess could tell he admired that. What he didn't admire were her unshaven armpits and legs, which he constantly poked fun at without mercy.

Jess was floating on her stomach watching Captain Reed and Sydney swim with several large reef sharks.

Sydney swam toward Jess to surface for some air.

"Doesn't it make you nervous to swim so close to them?" asked Jess.

Sydney was blowing snot out of her nose. "No, totally amazing; and besides, reef sharks are shy unless you get uncomfortably close."

Jess was treading water. "So, what's too close?"

"I have no idea," Sydney said, placing her mask back on and taking a deep breath before returning to the reef.

Lou and Cheri were forming an exclusive bond. Lou hadn't visited Captain Reed's bed since the crossing, and Cheri, having lost respect for his competence as a sailor, was at odds with him. The personality shifts were exhausting, and Jess longed for continuous harmony even though she knew it wasn't coming.

Ahe, like Manihi, championed numerous black pearl farms, and Captain Reed took the women on several visits, which they found both educational and fascinating. Jess opted out of the excursions, choosing to stay behind to prep for dinner—and not be reminded of her black pearl adventure with Captain Reed.

Aside from the raw beauty of the island, there were only a few stores and no civilized bars and restaurants. After a few days of exploration, they decided to shove off to Rangiroa, their last stop before sailing on to Tahiti. Each of the women purchased black pearls at a good price, and the evening before pulling up anchor, Jess prepared eggplant involtini, a variation of eggplant parmesan. The aubergines (long, thin eggplants) and island tomatoes purchased in the village were perfect for the recipe. Jess was proud of her ability to replicate her Italian godmother's dish, working all day on the sauce the way Deloras Dragonette taught her: a long, slow simmer. Jess had been saving the last of the fresh parmesan and mozzarella for any eggplant she might find on these islands.

A commotion was taking place on deck as Jess carried her creation to the outside table. Cheri was hanging up her cute bikini with the little cherries on it.

"That's adorable. I bet it looks way better on me." Sydney snatched the top from Cheri's hands and ran behind Captain Reed's chair at the helm holding the top over her bare breasts,

"Look, see? What did I tell you? It looks better, right?" Sydney was now standing on the chair next to Captain Reed, out of Cheri's reach, waving the top to taunt Cheri. Both girls were bare breasted. Jess could see Captain Reed was thoroughly enjoying the show.

"Give it back, Sydney. Now!"

Sydney tossed the top back to Cheri, who went off in a huff.

Jess set the plate of eggplant on the table, taking note of a bottle of tequila, shot glasses, and eight island beers. *No wonder this is getting out of hand*, she thought.

"Yar pirate and ye wenches, you be needin' food in yer gullets so as not to be drunken sods."

Jess laughed at Sydney, who was putting on the striped pirate shirt and eye patch.

Lou, seemingly disinterested in what was going on between Cheri and Sydney, began dishing up Jess's green salad onto plates. "Wow, this looks wonderful!" she said. "And there's no pasta, so I can have as much as I want."

Sydney slid over the top of the sofa and sat next to Captain Reed. "Did you know the Tuamotu island group is shaped like a dolphin and constitutes the largest chain of atoll islands in the world?"

Captain Reed took a plate filled with salad from Lou. "No, and this is my second time sailing here."

Sydney put her arm around the captain. "Do you just point your boat in a general direction and let the winds of fate take you? How is it you're still alive and well, Captain Shark Bait?"

They all laughed at her comment, except Cheri.

"What did you call me?" asked Captain Reed.

Sydney put an entire rolled eggplant into her mouth.

"Captain Shark Bait! Your blood thinners make you bleed like a hemophiliac from the slightest cut, and then dripping blood, you jump in the ocean to check the anchor and stuff."

Captain Reed nodded.

"Thanks for the new title, Beefcake. Now we're even."

Dinner went well until Sydney suggested playing a drinking-game version of Truth or Dare.

Captain Reed reached for another rolled eggplant. "Are you sure you aren't a salty dog, Beefcake? You sure as hell drink like one, and if you were ever seasick, I never saw it."

Sydney was sitting on his lap pouring shots for everyone. Captain Reed took a shot. "Pour one for my dear departed wife, who loved tequila. These are her shot glasses from Mexico, where she used to dress in a nun habit and walk around with a glass of tequila in one hand, and a cigarette in the other. I killed her because I am a scoundrel and a cheat. She tried to love enough for both of us, but that, my girls, is impossible. Now, I spoke my truth, had my shot. Who's next?"

Jess could see Captain Reed was getting drunk, and the tequila was the equivalent of truth serum.

"What the heck," said Cheri, downing two shots in a row followed by a beer." I don't know how the hell you play this game, but I had sex with the handsome Australian guy in Nuku Hiva."

Jess and Sydney burst out laughing.

"How was it?" asked Lou.

Now Jess and Sydney were howling with laughter.

Cheri answered Lou, "Fast, from behind . . . but you know, it was good to get laid."

Lou managed one shot and continued nursing her beer.

"What, nothing from you? Nothing to tell, Lou?" said Sydney.

"Nothing. I don't like games," said Lou.

"But you're so good at them," said Sydney.

Lou got up from the table with her plate and attempted to leave for the galley, but Sydney blocked her exit.

"Remember the cute artist boy on Nuku Hiva? You invited yourself on the night he wanted to show me his sacred mountain. I went to have a look at the mountain view and when I got back to his truck, you were doing him in the front seat. Once a cougar, always a cougar."

Lou sat back down at the table and took a drink directly from the bottle of tequila.

"What are you doing, Beefcake?" asked Captain Reed.

Sydney was sitting on the rail with her butt hanging off. "Uh . . . peeing." Trini was barking at her for fear she was going into the water.

Shaking her head at Sydney, Cheri commented on Sydney's decision to relieve herself. "Jesus, the damn dog is better trained. We have bathrooms on the boat—you're disgusting!"

Lou turned to Jess. "What about you? What's your truth thing?"

They were all looking at Jess, who was feeling the tequila.

"Um . . . uh . . . I nearly gave Captain Reed oral pleasure but puked instead."

Everyone burst into hysterical laughter, except Captain Reed, who was clearly surprised his cook would share that information.

Jess disappeared below, which Captain Reed attributed to her embarrassment, but in a few moments, she returned with her half-smoked joint. Jess lit the end and passed it to Cheri. They all took a drag except the captain, who never smoked anything, and Sydney, who hated pot but clearly loved alcohol.

"Figures the one with the dreadlocks doesn't smoke weed," Lou said.

Sydney took the joint from Cheri, inhaled, and holding the smoke in her lungs, she climbed onto Captain Reed, who was reclining on the sofa with his eyes closed. Thinking he was getting a kiss from one of the women, he opened his mouth and received instead a mouthful of pot smoke. Gagging and coughing, he staggered to his feet, dumping Sydney onto the deck. Lou rushed to his side and protectively rubbed and patted his back.

"Totally uncool, Sydney," said Lou.

"Unbelievable. You're trying to kill him," Cheri followed, fuming at Sydney and looking at Jess for support.

Jess held up the bottle. "Tequila, anyone?"

The following day, the sun was high overhead before the sailors crawled out of bed bleary-eyed and disheveled.

"Coffee, please, great lord, is there coffee?" Cheri was in the galley looking pasty, her movements slow and uncoordinated.

"I am bringing it up top right now," answered Jess. "There's cream, sugar, and the last of the mango muffins. I thawed them out last night and they're as good as the day I baked them."

"How do you do it, Jess?"

"We all have our talents," Jess replied, carrying the fresh pot to the deck.

Cheri followed Jess, pretending to float after the aroma, sniffing loudly in the air.

Jess announced, "Coffee's here."

Captain Reed and his crew gathered on deck around the outside table sipping their coffee and passing a bottle of aspirin around. All was quiet as they tried to piece together the events of the previous night, fragmented memories of raucous laughter, spirited singing, an embarrassing drinking game, and endless shots of tequila. Jess remembered lying on the bed in the master cabin with Captain Reed and Lou, but she couldn't remember the circumstances of how she got on the bed with the two of them; however, she clearly remembered making a dash for the crew cabin when Lou tried to initiate a threesome.

What else happened? Jess wondered.

After a late lunch, Cheri and Lou prepared to lift anchor. Sydney was in the anchor locker with the weird tool pushing the chain from side to side. The women worked systematically, and Jess noticed how efficient they had become at anchoring the large vessel.

"Done and dusted," said Lou, "as fuck-face Chaz used to say!"

"Oh my God, Lou!" Sydney's mouth hung open. "You said the f-word. Chaz who?"

They all laughed in unison.

"Off we go." Captain Reed was on the loudspeaker driving *Slow Dance* out the north pass of Ahe and into the open ocean.

Cheri gestured to Jess. "Come sit on the rail with us, Jess."

Lou and Cheri were sitting on the lower rail of the forward bow. Holding onto the upper rail, they let their feet dangle off the edge, catching waves splashing against the side of the bow.

Jess joined them and immediately wondered why she hadn't been sitting on the rail all along.

"This is amazing. I need to get out of the galley more often."

Ten minutes out from the island, a pod of spinner dolphins began swimming with the boat, playing with the bow by crossing quickly in front and jumping out of the water. There were hundreds of them. Jess climbed off the rail and stood directly at the bow.

"I've never seen anything like this. I am so happy I am crying. They're so beautiful."

Trinidad was running up and down the length of the boat barking and playing with the pod.

"Shut up!" Sydney had the microphone. "Trinidad, you are going to give yourself a heart attack. Tea Bag, do you hear me?"

Jess intercepted the poodle as she ran from bow to stern and scooped the hysterical pup into her arms.

"Did you hear that, Trini? You were just given another new name, Tea Bag," Jess told the poodle before kissing her on the nose.

19

Undertow

May 2024
Pacific Ocean

Jess stood at the bow of *Slow Dance*, the gentle sway of the boat soothing her as they headed toward Rangiroa. The winds were fair, the seas calm, and the day hinted at new beginnings. Yet, beneath the surface of the promising day, a sense of unease gnawed at her.

The headsail snatched the continuous breeze that blew across the sea, increasing their speed but avoiding heeling over. Sydney trimmed the mainsail to steady the boat, while Lou sorted what was left of the collected rainwater. There had been no water available to fill their tank on either island, so Captain Reed was rationing what was left in the jugs. The dynamic on the boat once again shifted from amiable coping to progressive disharmony. If Captain Reed was aware of the shift, he didn't show it, except when he caught Lou washing her clothes with the remaining drinking water. His reaction was the first time Jess saw him get angry.

"*Jesus*, Lou, you really have a screw loose in that pretty head of yours. I'm still pissed you almost lost my dinghy. We can't be certain Rangiroa can provide us with drinking water, and you sneak around washing your clothes in what little fresh water we have left! Beefcake, take the remaining jugs of water to my cabin . . . all of them."

Captain Reed's state of mind was difficult for Jess to read. The past few days, he appeared to be disassociated, not connected to the boat, the other women, or Jess. After the Truth or Dare game, he became tense and silent during their sail to Rangiroa. He was avoiding them by napping in the pilothouse, withdrawing to his cabin, and declining to join them for dinner. Jess's prior conversations with the captain had given her some insight into his priorities and passions. They shared similar opinions, and often he would say, "Damn, Jess, we think so much alike."

Jess wondered if the cause of his current sour mood was apprehensiveness about their perilous crossing to Tahiti, the lack of fresh water, and the truth regarding his boat's mechanical soundness. She didn't know what was going on in the captain's head. Her feelings about him were a tangle of confusion. He had become more captivating and magnetic to her—alluring yet dangerous, transformative yet steadfast. The situation had become challenging, like the stormy seas to those who aren't prepared for the intensity. Jess had never met a man like captain Cliff Reed. There was a mystery about him, and she wanted to discover what was hidden underneath his cool, meticulously made exterior. There was also a sadness to him, though she could only see it dart back and forth under the surface. He was more vulnerable than she had first suspected.

Rangiroa was the main destination for tourists visiting the Tuamotus. There were two lovely resorts, nice island shops, decent restaurants, and lively international travelers. The white sand beach sported tropical outdoor bars with thatch roofs, live music, and dancing.

"Let's get the dinghy in the water," the captain said irritably. "I'm anxious for civilization."

Cheri was undoing the straps in preparation for lowering the boat into the water. Captain Reed stepped onto the platform and climbed in at the helm.

"Can I lower the platform?" Jess asked.

Jess had the cover of the lazarette lifted and was holding the controller. She had gotten quite good at lowering and raising the hydraulic lift. Once the platform went into the water and the boat was afloat, Captain Reed started the engine and drove it off the platform.

"Good job. Now bring the platform up. I'm not expecting any chop, but always best to keep it raised."

Jess handed Trinidad down to Sydney and was the last one in the boat.

"Holy cow, ladies," she said. "I am not used to seeing you in fancy clothes. Cute sundress, Cheri, and love that sexy top, Lou."

Sydney made a pouting face. "What about me?" Her hair was swept up with a Rasta scarf to hold her long dreadlocks in place.

Jess smiled. "I've seen the green camouflage shorts, but your hair is stunning."

Captain Reed aimed the dinghy toward the unpopulated side of the island. "Let's have a look around the bay before lunch at the restaurant."

As they approached the center of the bay, Cheri cried out in alarm, "You're about to hit some enormous coral heads!"

But the captain seemed deaf to her pleas, his eyes fixed on some unseen point in the distance. He kept his heading without acknowledging Cheri.

"What the hell is wrong with you?" Cheri said. "You're dangerous. Do you want to crash on the coral?"

"Maybe," he said.

Captain Reed veered off momentarily, then turned the boat back toward the coral heads as he looked over at Cheri. "I might want to, maybe I should. Should I?"

No one laughed. Jess was trying not to look in the water as Captain Reed continued playing his game of chicken. Sydney came to the rescue by standing up and holding onto the bar at the helm where he was steering the boat.

"Captain Shark Bait, this sailor needs a beer."

To all their relief, he abruptly turned the dinghy around and headed in the direction of the white sand beach. Jess was deeply alarmed at Captain Reed's way of expressing his feelings—she had to admit it was increasingly unstable.

The swanky resort had a dock with a nice bamboo bridge leading to the restaurant and bar. Captain Reed cleated the dinghy to the dock while the women stood on the bridge looking down at the incredible array of fish in the shallow water. Cheri was fumbling in her bag.

"I brought a radio. Lou and I are going to grab some food and hang out. We can call you for a ride when we're ready to come back to the boat."

Captain Reed nodded, and Jess felt that same tension she had experienced when Chaz was around.

"How about that beer?" Sydney asked, trying to lighten the mood.

Sydney headed to the bar and the captain followed her. Jess opted for a walk along the beach to clear her head and the twisting in her stomach. She admired the captain's bravado and she felt safe sailing with him, but his recent antics felt like a dangerous game she didn't want any part of. In that moment, he was no longer the authoritative figure she had known; he was a man lost in the thrill of his own recklessness. Jess wondered if Chaz was right when he said the captain didn't plan on returning from the journey.

With each step Jess took on the soft sand, she resolved to keep an eye on the captain. The sea was a fickle mistress, and the captain's restless spirit was a storm waiting to brew. Jess had to find a way to bring him back before the waves swallowed him whole.

Jess was reading a book on deck when Cheri arrived with an entourage. Captain Reed, awakened by her, was standing in the pilothouse, expressionless, when she entered from the top deck.

"Sorry, did I wake you? Captain Reed, this is Joseph, his wife Patty, their son Adam, and his wife, Carla; and this adorable little guy is their son, Oliver. We met at the resort today. They're from Michigan and have a boat on the lake. Oh, and this is our chef."

"Were you napping? You look confused." Cheri was smiling her way through the awkward moment that was reflected in the faces of the uninvited group.

Joe gave his hand to Captain Reed. "Nice to meet you, what a magnificent ship."

The captain reluctantly took his hand.

"Let me show you around," said Cheri. "She's really a beauty."

Cheri disappeared down the steps to the aft cabins and the five strangers followed.

Captain Reed wasn't confused; he was pissed, Jess knew.

After the tour they made small talk while Jess served fresh papaya juice. She didn't know what to expect, breathing a sigh of relief when she saw the captain participating in the conversation. He was either honestly enjoying their company or trying to be polite, which was unlikely as the captain never tried to be polite. One thing Jess knew for sure, when Captain Reed was silent, he was either angry, disappointed, or formulating a plan.

After an hour or so, Cheri held the dinghy steady for the intruders.

Joe was the last to climb down.

"Thank you, Captain Reed," he said, vigorously shaking the captain's hand. "People only dream about doing what you're doing, sailing the world on this awesome yacht and with four gorgeous ladies no less. This place is so remote, it took us three planes to get here. I can't imagine sailing here from Los Angeles. You're at the edge of the world, man."

Captain Reed seemed relieved when Joe finally released his hand.

"Ignorance is bliss, Joe; and if you knew the things that I know—stuff that can and will go wrong out here—it's not so romantic."

Joe stopped halfway down the ladder. "Then why do you do it?"

Captain Reed looked down at him. "I absolutely hate sailing and the ocean."

Joe looked perplexed. "That's a hell of a statement. Why would you continue to do something you hate?"

Captain Reed smiled. "I love to travel, Joe, but I like to sleep in my own bed every night."

Slow Dance anchored for three days inside atoll Rangiroa, giving the sailors ample time to retreat from one another. Cheri and Lou explored the island together, doing their own thing, never inviting Sydney or Jess. Most afternoons and evenings, Captain Reed entertained Sydney and Jess at the local establishments, a welcome break for Jess. The night before their departure, Captain Reed gathered the women in the pilothouse.

"We leave at first light, ladies. We will be at sea four days before approaching Papeete. I don't want to take us in at dark thirty, so according to my calculations, we should arrive by noon. We have two jugs of drinking water . . . plus the four plastic gallons we were allowed at the grocery store here in Rangiroa . . . that should hold us. No washing clothes"—Captain Reed looked at Lou—"and we will have enough for drinking—because Sydney still has beer."

-Society Islands-

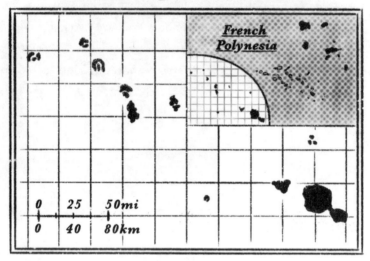

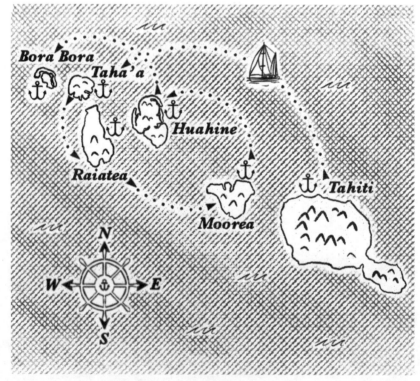

20

Self-Sabotage

May 2024
Sailing to Tahiti

Trinidad's paws were on the lower rail, her little tail wagging in anticipation of heading out to sea.

"Anchors away, Miss Tea Bag."

Sydney was closing the anchor locker hatch as Cheri and Lou secured the anchor with the snubber.

"Good to be moving this adventure along, hey mates?" Sydney said.

Jess was sitting in her new favorite spot, on the rail at the bow, when she pointed excitedly at the water.

"Dolphins! A huge pair."

Two gray dolphins were swimming with *Slow Dance* as if escorting them out the pass and into the open sea. Trini began barking and Lou came to have a look.

"The old sailors say, when dolphins playfully swim with your boat for a bit, it's a good omen. If they stay with your boat for a length of time, bad omen."

Cheri laughed. "You believe that superstitious stuff, Lou?" She wiggled her fingers in Lou's face as if putting a spell on her. "Ouk, ah, brew-ha-ha."

Two hours later, the dolphins were still swimming along with *Slow Dance*, and Trinidad was still barking at them. Jess pondered what Lou had said. She wondered if dolphins had the ability to sense danger the same way dogs sense cancer in a human body.

Jess looked over at Sydney. "In Bernard's book, he talks about dolphins alerting him to danger when he was asleep and his boat was headed for the reef."

Sydney was looking down at the dolphins, and she swore they were looking right up at her.

"Some heavy shit is going to come down on us girls."

Jess was holding Trinidad to quiet her barking.

"I feel it too, Sydney, and it always happens at night. I hope Chaz hasn't done something to the engine."

Cheri waved them off. "If Chaz messed with the engine, we would know it by now. Relax, girls, you're jinxing yourself."

The first two days at sea passed, one calm, the other turbulent. Dinner was being served in the saloon due to the latter, and Sydney was passing plates of Jess's Greek chicken through the galley window to Cheri and Lou. Jess was pleased Captain Reed joined them, and the women took their respective seats around the large wooden table.

"This is delicious."

Captain Reed was about to put another forkful of the roasted bird in his mouth when his plate nearly slid off the table. *Slow Dance* was moving side to side in the choppy seas, causing their plates to slide around. Each grabbed the other's plate before it slid onto the floor. Snatching Cheri's plate before it went off the table and onto the carpet, Jess replied to Captain Reed's comment.

"Thank you. The dish is a one-pot wonder and perfect for this weather. I toss it all together, place it in the oven, and sit down until it bakes. I roasted everything in my dad's cast-iron pot—the only thing I have left of his—with root vegetables and the last of the eggplant. It's nice to see you back," she added.

Captain Reed gave Jess a nod and held his plate while drinking wine with his free hand. "Reminds me of my cook on *Slow Dance* when I sailed through a ten-day hurricane from the Bahamas to the Portuguese Azores. Her name was Queeny, from Australia. The sea was white foam as far as the eye could see, and water was leaking in from every window in the pilothouse. I locked the doors after setting the storm sail, and no one was allowed outside. I heard Queeny from the galley, cursing like any good sailor, and I called down to her, 'What's the matter?' She was trying to make stuffed zucchini in sixty-foot seas and the pan kept flying out of the oven. Crazy woman. I yelled down at her, 'Just make a damn sandwich!'"

They all laughed at Captain Reed's story, but then no one spoke, they simply giggled their way through the rest of the meal, preventing plates from going overboard.

On day four, at two in the morning, Lou was on watch, and Jess was keeping her company because she didn't trust her.

"There's not a whole lot to watch out here," Jess said.

Looking serious, Lou nodded as she checked the radar and recorded the instrument reading into *Slow Dance*'s logbook. Suddenly she looked up attentively.

"Do you hear that?"

Jess was vaguely aware of a strange sound. Lou walked over, opened the door to the engine room, and confirmed there was an unfamiliar, ominous sound coming from the 6-71 Detroit Diesel engine.

Jess followed Lou over to the head of the steps leading down to the engine room. "Oh no, what is that? We should wake the captain," she suggested.

Lou closed the door, went to the helm, turned the engine off, and started down the stairs to the master cabin, but Captain Reed was already on his way up to the pilothouse when the engine stopped.

"What's going on?"

"The engine is making a weird sound," said Lou.

Captain Reed went to the controls and switched on the engine. Cheri and Sydney were in the pilothouse, also awakened when Lou turned the engine off. Over time, sailors become hyperaware of every sound and motion their boat makes. Jess determined it was something one develops after being at sea for long periods of time, where sound and motion can erupt into matters of life and death.

The engine was indeed making a troublesome noise, so the captain shut it back down.

"Lucky, we have calm seas. Sydney, go down in the engine room and have a look around."

Jess wondered why he wasn't going down himself to have a look. He started the engine, and after a few minutes Sydney returned to the pilothouse.

"Captain, there's water dripping into the bilge from a weird oblong hole, but it looks like this hole should be there. Funny thing, the hole is partially plugged up with metal. No leak in the steel. It looks like the engine is regurgitating the cooling water, but what do I know? Here, I snapped a few photos for you."

Captain Reed took her camera and flipped through the photos. What was apparent to Jess was becoming noticeable to the others—Captain Reed was stoned out of his mind and incapable of figuring out what was wrong with the engine, the hole, or the water dripping into the bilge.

"Beefcake, take this tube of liquid metal and go plug the hole the rest of the way."

It was as if he were sleepwalking, bordering on incoherent. Captain Reed turned off the engine and Sydney headed down to the engine room with the tube of liquid metal. Later he would confess he had taken three muscle relaxers with two sleeping pills due to his anxiety, relying on the women to sail *Slow Dance* in the open Pacific to the Tahitian islands—and although he didn't show it, that scared him.

"I did what you asked. The stuff hardened on contact, but it doesn't seem like that hole should be plugged up."

The captain ignored Sydney. "Okay, here we go." He started the engine, and the sound heard earlier was faint but still slightly audible.

"We'll have it looked at in Papeete."

That was all he said before going back to bed. Eighty nautical miles from Papeete, the engine failed completely.

At first light, Cheri sprang into action.

"Lou, help us get the jib sail out. I'll run the electric wench. You and Sydney work the line to let her out easy."

There was virtually no wind, and the mainsail was not sufficient to gain momentum. The women eased the line as Cheri slowly sheeted out the jib to catch even the slightest breeze, making the main more efficient and increasing *Slow Dance*'s speed from one knot to four. Jess was on deck when Captain Reed joined them, apparently recovered from his self-induced stupor.

"Cheri, do not pull the jib too tight or we're going to have problems."

Cheri shouted back, "I know, we don't want the boat to turn away from the wind."

Jess, feeling a sense of relief, went below to brew some coffee. Around ten minutes later, she reappeared, carefully balancing a tray of mugs.

"This boat has a lot of sails," Cheri said as Captain Reed grabbed a mug from Jess's tray.

The hot, black liquid began to act as an elixir on all the crew, refreshing and reviving them from the previous night's trials and tribulations.

"Some of the sails we have never used, I know from watching," Jess said, reappearing from another brief exit to dispose of her tray. "The main is used to steady the boat and the genoa is for catching bigger winds. I don't know about the jib, or the various directions the wind . . . it's called a broad reach or beam reach, right?"

"Ask me again—if we make it to Tahiti that is," replied the captain with a wink.

Jess wanted to trust that wink, but after watching him deal with last night's emergency, she was having trouble.

Cheri had mad sailing skills, and she handled *Slow Dance* like a pro. Utilizing the light wind to keep the jib full, Cheri sailed the huge boat within five miles of Papeete.

From the pilothouse, Captain Reed turned to VHF channel 14 for port control.

"I paid an agent to clear us in, and we will need her name and agency ID to give to the harbormaster."

Lou was handing the information to Captain Reed while he was on the radio.

"Shore patrol, this is *Slow Dance* yacht requesting assistance with a tow into port. Do you copy?"

A voice answered in French and Lou took the receiver from Captain Reed to explain their situation. "Get used to needing an interpreter," she said in aside to Reed. "French people want to speak French, and these islanders are no different."

Lou was making herself indispensable, just as she planned.

Captain Reed was now sitting on the sofa portside of the pilothouse, his legs crossed as usual, and he looked like a man in need of rest.

Sydney let out a long whistle. "This is going to cost you, Cappy."

Trini came running from the top deck and jumped up on the captains' lap, thinking he had whistled for her. Petting Trini, he said, "One of the nice things about being rich, Beefcake? I can afford to get the repairs we need, and Tahiti is just the place."

The sound of the tugboat interrupted their conversation.

"Our tow has arrived."

The tug maneuvered *Slow Dance* into the main port where she was side-tied at the commercial dock adjacent to a public park. A huge, open food market was located on the other side of the street, which ran alongside the docks, and the park was filled with homeless Tahitians.

"No way," said Captain Reed. "This can't be the same port as my trip here. There used to be a popular pirate bar over by the market. I had some good times there. Gone . . . just a bunch of unfortunate people hanging around."

Captain Reed's expectations were shattered, and it showed on his face.

That evening, Sydney stood watch to keep the unfortunates from boarding *Slow Dance*.

She tied her dreads up in a scarf, so they were sticking out like snakes protruding from her skull.

"How did you get those wooden plugs in your earlobes to stretch to the size of a quarter?" Jess was pointing to Sydney's enlarged tribal ear piercings.

"I don't remember, but there's effort involved to stretch the skin."

Sometime around two in the morning, unable to sleep, Jess walked to the bow and found Sydney in conversation with three men. The men were startled when she appeared behind Sydney.

"Everything all right? I don't think the captain would like these fellows being on his boat right now."

The men began speaking in French. The older man of the three was sitting on his haunches, grinning at Jess with his toothless mouth.

"You understand French?"

"No," Sydney answered. "They speak English."

Taking the cue from Jess, the three men stood up, thanked Sydney, and exited the boat.

"Au revoir." Sydney waited until the men were out of earshot.

"It was under control, but I am glad you showed up because I was tired, and it was turning weird."

Jess shrugged. "I worry about you, kiddo. I didn't care in Mexico, you were a stranger then, so when you wandered off for hours, I hardly noticed. But now, I've grown fond of you in a peculiar way."

Sydney rubbed catlike against Jess. "Ah, thanks, Mom."

Jess patted her head. "Right, not so much fond like kid-fond, but more like, stray-cat fond."

Sydney gave an ironic smile, then climbed to the top of the pilothouse to serve out the remainer of her watch.

"Good morning, Captain, I have fresh brew and fabulous French croissants with butter and loganberry jam. I love Tahiti already."

Jess was holding the breakfast tray with sliced watermelon, papaya, fresh red lychee nuts, and the smallest bananas she had ever seen. Trini was on Jess's heels waiting for another one of the small bananas.

"The market is amazing; there's even an Asian section selling Chinese vegetables, by Chinese vendors. Really fresh fish, too."

Captain Reed was stirring his coffee. "I don't think I've ever seen you this excited. You're acting like a chef or something. Where are the other two?"

"They got off the boat before you were up," Jess told him.

Captain Reed looked unhappy. "The rule is . . . before anyone leaves this boat, they must tell the rest of us and have a set time to return. They also need to carry a radio."

The captain was suddenly interrupted by their German agent Christina and her Hawaiian husband, Akamu.

"Bonjour, *Slow Dance*," Christina greeted. "Permission to come aboard?"

Christina was a beautiful thirty-something with black hair, green eyes, and a welcoming smile; and Akamu was handsome in his own right. They were living in Tahiti where she ran a lucrative agency for cruisers entering French Polynesia, and he operated the tugs.

"We are so sorry to hear of your troubles and happy you managed to arrive safe, despite having no engine," Akamu told Captain Reed as they shook hands. "I have all your cruising documents here in this folder, but most importantly, let's get you away from this dock."

The two men bonded instantly, and Jess thought there's nothing like two seamen working out a boat problem to turn them into a band of brothers. Akamu asked Captain Reed if he could have a look at the dinghy and the starboard side of *Slow Dance*.

"You need to be up the coast a few more miles in Marina Taina where you can have the necessary repairs completed. A tug will cost you another two thousand U.S. dollars, but if we tie your dinghy to the starboard side of the boat, I can drive you into the marina when the tide is right."

"You're my kind of guy," said Captain Reed as he began contemplating the maneuver. "Sounds incredibly dodgy. When do we go?"

Akamu smiled. "The tide is right, if you're up for going now."

Jess thought Akamu exuded manly confidence. He seemed like a solid guy. She especially liked his strong arms and tribal Hawaiian tattoos.

"What about Cheri and Lou?" Jess asked. "When they come back, the boat will be gone."

"Well," said Captain Reed, "maybe they shouldn't sneak off without telling anyone."

Christina left her husband with the task at hand while she went ahead by car to arrange a slip for *Slow Dance* in the marina.

Sydney assisted Akamu with the lines.

"I am getting into the tender boat now," said Akamu. "When I tell you, untie *Slow Dance* from the dock, starting with the spring line."

As Sydney was loosening the spring line, the toothless man from the previous night stood by the bow to watch them go.

"Hey, Captain, you got a few bucks?" Sydney asked.

"What for?"

"I want to give it to my new friend, so he can watch for Cheri and Lou and tell them we went to Marina Taina."

Captain Reed handed her three hundred Mexican pesos.

"What the hell is he supposed to do with *pesos*?"

21

Cast Out

Captain Reed was at the helm controlling *Slow Dance* as best he could, while Akamu was pushing the boat along the inside of the lagoon. Sydney stood portside ready to assist Akamu, should he need her. Jess was standing with Sydney, looking down into the water.

"It's so clear and colorful. We're in fifty feet of water and I could swear it's five feet."

Sydney was ogling Akamu and Jess gave her a nudge. "He's married, wench, and besides, there will be lots of sailor boys in the marina."

Within an hour, *Slow Dance* was approaching the marina where a side tie along the main dock had been arranged for them. Steering *Slow Dance* into the narrow waterway and parking her against the dock was not going to be easy. By the time the boat was secure, Jess was steeped in anxiety: sweaty palms, heart pounding, and waves of adrenaline were rushing to her head. Was she becoming a nervous Nellie or was the danger and carelessness of the past few weeks catching up to her?

Jess was just finishing up lunch when Cheri and Lou appeared on the dock.

"Thanks for leaving us, guys. It was fun figuring out where the hell you went."

Trinidad was barking at Cheri as she stepped onto the boat, bringing her attitude with her.

"Oh, be quiet, you yappy mut!" Cheri turned her attention to Sydney. "Why did you leave us?"

Sydney took a swig of her Hinano beer. "As I see it, you left *us*. No note, no radio, no nada. Right, Jess?"

Being a diplomat at heart, Jess answered, "Sorry. The tide was exactly right to move the boat away from that dreadful dock."

At that moment, Captain Reed and Akamu appeared on deck from the engine room where they had been examining the 6-71 diesel engine and discussing a plan to have repairs made.

Cheri's attitude faded instantly, and Lou asked in a sexy voice, "Who is *that*?"

Sydney made a face. "Dry your panties. The handsome lad is married to our agent, *and she is gorgeous*, so put your tongue back in your mouth."

With *Slow Dance* secure and tentative repair plans in place, Akamu left the boat, and Captain Reed turned his attention to Lou and Cheri.

"You will inform us of any plan to leave the boat for the day. You must take a radio and before you go anywhere, this boat needs the salt washed off, the scuppers cleaned out, and the teak rails polished. Sydney, you make a list and divide the work. Jess and I will do the shopping."

Lou was touching Captain Reed's arm. "Sorry, we had a chance to look around and Tahiti is amazing. There are fabulous restaurants and bars. We noticed the Australian we met in Nuku Hiva has his boat here as well."

Captain Reed gave her an empty stare. "I saw his boat, but unfortunately for you, he berthed the boat and went back to Australia."

The following morning, repairs began on the engine and the women went to work washing and polishing the boat. It was early June, and one day drifted into the next as they settled into life at Marina Taina. Sydney made friends with a group of young, hip international travelers, as well as a handsome local French boy whose heart she would break when *Slow Dance* departed for the Cook Islands. Cheri and Lou continued to leave the boat without a word or a radio. Jess spent her time with Captain Reed, looking at charts and assisting him with the repairs that were taking place. In addition to the engine repairs, Captain Reed decided to upgrade the galley refrigeration, so Jess was working closely with the lovely Frenchman in charge of the project. On weekends, Captain Reed and Jess took the dinghy into the bay and enjoyed snorkeling on the reef. In the evening, they dined out at one of the many seaside restaurants. They preferred each other's company, and Captain Reed began to rely heavily on Jess when making decisions for specific repairs on the boat.

While looking over the schematics for the new galley refrigeration, Captain Reed asked Jess, "How do you know so much about equipment maintenance?"

"All those years managing large restaurants made it a necessity. My job as executive chef at a large hospital was the worst job of my life. One time I had to crawl under the commercial dishwashing machine to pull forks and knives out of the impellor motor."

Captain Reed looked impressed. "You really are something."

Jess glanced up and her eyes met his, but he quickly looked away. She wasn't put off. She studied him, silhouetted against the light from the open porthole. He was a handsome man, rugged and strong, but there was a shadow, a lingering sadness born from a wound that had yet to heal. Jess sensed a flicker of something deeper in Captain Reed, a longing he was too afraid to express. Jess knew he needed to keep her at a distance because he told her he was lousy at love, and he had three unhappy ex-wives to prove it. Angie had deserved a man who would be faithful and love her the way she deserved to be loved, he told Jess. It was his big regret, he'd confessed one night after too many drinks, and he wasn't much on regrets. Angie's first husband, he'd said, took his own life, leaving her with two sons, a gorgeous home in Santa Monica, and a lot of money. The walls he built wavered as he opened to Jess that night. Angie was beautiful, cultured, funny, and rich, he said. It was love at first sight for her and complicated for him because she was in her forties, and he was dating an eighteen-year-old at the time. He told Jess he spent twenty years trying his best to be a good husband,

and, for the first five years of his marriage, they were happy. *Slow Dance* was his escape from the memory of her death, from his open-heart surgery, and from the hurt he caused. The captain masked it well, but Jess could see he was struggling internally with deep emotional pain. She attributed some of the captain's dangerous antics to the guilt and regret that ate away at him. *He set out to sea for his mental and emotional well-being*, she thought, *but I'm the one who's providing a safe space for him to untangle his mind, body, and soul.*

The captain was called to the upper deck, and Jess continued to mull over the night of his confessions. His words had tumbled out, fueled by alcohol but laced with a raw honesty that took her by surprise. "I am great at money, great at . . . well, other things," he said. "But when it comes to commitment? I run like a man from a hornet's nest. I thought I could keep my freedom while still being . . . whatever I was supposed to be for her."

Jess recalled the frustration on his face as he explained how he hurt Angie. Hoping to offer some solace, she had told him, "You can't change the past, Captain, and you're not that man anymore."

The captain was a puzzle she longed to dismantle, to draw him closer. She desired him but was acutely aware of her own emotional scars and insecurities, the damage she carried. The captain was not whole, but neither was she. Perhaps he was incapable of giving Jess what she deserved, or what most women deserved for that matter. Her heart ached with uncertainty. Would the captain's past struggles always hold him back? She sighed, contemplating the scars he bore, both visible and invisible, that seemed to create an impenetrable barrier between them. She longed for him to be whole again, able to embrace love without hesitation. For now, she wondered if her affection for him would remain unrequited, trapped in the shadow of his pain.

They had been in the marina ten days when Cheri and Lou returned to the boat late one afternoon with some new friends who owned a local restaurant. Jess prepared some appetizers to accompany the bottles of fine French wine the visitors brought aboard, and a spontaneous afternoon party lingered into the evening. Captain Reed, who interacted minimally, was now silent.

A bad sign. Jess was sitting with him at the outside helm, observing Cheri and her guests babbling in French.

"Damn rude," he said. "They spoke perfect English during the introductions. I am officially pissed right now. I am going to kick her off the boat."

He started to get up when Jess pulled him back into the chair.

"Please don't do that. Not now anyway. I agree it must be done, but it's not fair to the others."

Captain Reed reluctantly sat down. "You think I give a shit?"

Jess turned his face toward hers. "Please wait until tomorrow morning, and then tell her she's off the boat. Do that for me, okay? You know how much I hate conflict."

Captain Reed lightly pounded his fist on the chair.

"Okay, I am listening to you, but first thing in the morning, she's gone."

At eight in the morning, true to his word, Captain Reed was pounding on Cheri's cabin door. Opening the door, a crack, she asked, "What's going on?"

"I want you off my boat. Now! Pack and be gone in an hour."

An hour later they were on deck and Cheri came up carrying her backpack. Sydney was standing by the steps and gave Cheri a hug.

"Fair winds and following seas, sailor girl."

Lou was surprisingly cold to Cheri, giving her an I-told-you-so look with no verbal goodbye. Lou moved near Captain Reed and put her hand on his chair as if to say, *I am with you.*

"Maritime law says you buy me a ticket back to California. You probably never heard of it, but I will be back with the gendarme and make you buy me a ticket."

Captain Reed remained unrattled by Cheri.

"I have every intention of purchasing you a ticket . . . say one or two days from now?"

Cheri shrugged him off. "I saw it coming, and I am happy to not sail on with *Slow Dance*. It feels like eminent danger lies ahead for you guys. Rose from *Pinta*, the amazing wooden boat on dock four, is letting me stay with her until I leave. Good luck, you're going to need it, and I don't have to worry about dogs pissing on my bed anymore either!"

Jess felt sad and concerned that Cheri was leaving, but on the other hand, she would not miss the tension between her and the captain. Cheri was in her cabin packing up her gear when Jess knocked.

"I wanted to say fair winds and following seas, sailor girl."

Cheri ceased her packing to give Jess a hug.

"Thanks for all the fabulous food, Jess. You really are a great cook."

Jess sat on the edge of the bed. "I am sorry to see you go, and I do not approve of how the captain handled things."

Cheri gave a nod. "I am not the type to leave Tahiti without exploring the islands. After adjusting the return ticket Captain Reed purchases for me, I plan on spending several weeks exploring the Society Islands with a couple sailing on a nice Swan, called *Jewels*."

After Cheri exited *Slow Dance*, Jess went to Captain Reed to express her concerns about sailing on without Cheri.

"Cheri was the best sailor you had, so now what are you going to do?"

Jess was worried about sailing on through the islands once *Slow Dance* was repaired. Captain Reed put his feet up on the outside table and placed his hands behind his head.

"Well, what you don't realize is, Tahiti is a huge point for crew to jump off one ship and onto another. Once the word goes out, I will be turning potential captains away."

Captain Reed was right. Within days, three young men sought out *Slow Dance* to apply. Sydney and Lou were mostly off the boat after chores were finished. Sydney went with her new young friends, and surprisingly, Lou hung out with Cheri, who was aboard the wooden boat *Pinta*. Jess spent the days detailing the interior of the boat, restoring the luster after the long voyage. She was polishing the pilothouse walls when Captain Reed came to speak with her.

"I want you to sit in on my meeting today with the guy from New Zealand. He seems like the best candidate, but hell, I am terrible at picking people."

Jess ceased her polishing and gave him her biggest eyeroll. "Yeah, I know, because you didn't pick me first. Your girl Friday, sex slave, massage therapist—whatever you called Kari—picked me for you."

Captain Reed sighed breathily. "Sorry I told you. In case you haven't figured it out yet, I am a guy who needs a guy to tell the other guys what to do. I hate being out front."

Jess placed her hand on her hip. "Why does it feel like you're making me be that guy?"

Dismissing her comment, he replied, "Come on, it's time. Tell me what you think after meeting this guy."

In twenty minutes, the interview was over. Jess poured herself and Captain Reed a glass of the chilled French Rosé she had been hiding in the bar fridge.

Captain Reed sat across from Jess in the pilothouse.

"So, your thoughts?"

Jess took a sip of her delicious wine. "Love the Kiwi accent and I imagine he came out of his mother's womb trimming sails. The only thing is he has no sense of humor. He wasn't amused at your jokes, and I found him far too serious for this boat. But maybe that's a good thing?"

Captain Reed raised an eyebrow. "We certainly don't want to kill the fun, so I'll mull it over."

Slow Dance continued with the engine repairs, and Sydney had diagnosed it correctly: the engine was regurgitating water. Plugging the hole caused the water to go back into the engine and mix with the oil. A serious and costly problem. They wondered who plugged the hole to begin with. Sydney thought Chaz had sabotaged the boat, but Jess learned from Captain Reed such a problem would have surfaced long before they sailed to Tahiti.

Captain Reed asked Jess, "You don't think Lou would be smart enough to do such a thing—or crazy enough—do you? What possible motive would she have?"

Jess revealed to him how she saw Lou empty the bag of Harrison's cut-up plastic into the ocean.

"You know there are mothers who suffocate their infants to the point of death, then rush them to the hospital explaining how they saved the child's life, all for the attention. I wouldn't put anything past Lou. She's a nutball and I do not trust her."

Unlike the refrigeration repairman, Captain Reed did not care for the Frenchman conducting repairs to the 6-71 diesel engine. He was taking too long, and it was costing the captain time and money. The man was a pompous ass.

In the evenings during their walks around the marina, Captain Reed and Jess occasionally ran into Cheri and Lou or Sydney and her group of cool, eclectic Tahitian friends. The island mood had tempered any hard feelings among the group, so their encounters were relaxed and friendly. One evening, Jess and Captain Reed joined Sydney, her Frenchman, Mateo, Cheri, Lou, and other sailors at the same table to enjoy the music of a local band. Mateo was speaking with Captain Reed, and Jess was thinking his voice was as sexy as he was.

"*Capitan*, the larger yachts in the marina are planning a dock party for this Saturday evening and have asked if you would like to participate with some food and wine?"

Captain Reed looked toward Jess. "Yes, that is if that's okay with you, Jess."

Jess thought about the opportunity to participate in the dock party event and the chance to present some of her signature dishes.

"I'd love to contribute," she answered.

22

The Dock Party

June 2024
Marina Taina, Papeete, Tahiti

On a beautiful Sunday morning, after their coffee, Jess walked the outer docks of the marina with Captain Reed, and he pointed out the super yachts to her.

"That's the nice thing about my boat; she's large enough so the marinas give me a slip near the big boys."

Captain Reed spoke true. Tahiti was a haven. The boats were from faraway countries, some staying for years, and luxury yachts for a summer of cruising the Society Islands. In the evenings children from family boats played ball and rode bikes up and down the main dock. Young people with passports from around the world, crewing on the super yachts or hoping to be hired on a luxury yacht, partied in the bars at night and Captain Reed, along with Jess, partied with them.

"I don't care for the owners of the big yachts," Captain Reed told Jess. "But I love the crew. I would much rather mingle with them; they're more fun. Most owners visit their yacht a couple times a year and their crew deliver their yacht to whatever location they designate. Poor bastards work their ass off to maintain a boat they can only enjoy a few weeks a year."

It was the day of the dock party, and Jess was busy preparing a spectacular menu for the event. It would be her first dock party and a chance to demonstrate her culinary skills. Jess hadn't catered an event since *Slow Dance's* Bon Voyage party in Los Angeles.

Sydney finished cleaning the scuppers and came to see if Jess needed any help.

"Whoa, dude, where did you get all this stuff? It looks amazing."

Jess was putting white linen tablecloths over two eight-foot tables.

"Angie, of course! I found the most amazing things stashed in the aft bilges. There was an artificial Christmas tree, decorations, a thousand string lights, and twelve giant candy canes that light up. I can't wait until Christmas. The folding tables were stored in the lazarette, and the serving platters were under the galley bilges along with the silver."

"Wow, Jess, I've seen the effort by the super yachts and you're going to blow their shit away."

Jess turned to Sydney. "Well, I am a chef and catering's my gig. I owned my own catering company and catered some big-name concerts."

Sydney pinned down a corner of the tablecloth. "Anyone I heard of? Or was it before reggae?"

Jess tilted her head to one side and placed her hand on her hip. "I'll have you know, I saw Bob Marley live with just three hundred people at the University of San Diego, before you were born, little tenderloin. The original I-Threes were there as well."

"Why are you so awesome?" Sydney clipped down the other end of the white tablecloth. "By the way," Sydney added, "a couple of the guys will deliver the gas barbecue in an hour."

Jess was wearing her chef coat, the one with her name over the pocket and a double row of round black buttons, over a grass skirt, and her feet were bare.

"You look tres fab," said Captain Reed. "Now tell me what it is you turned the large grocery bill into? Smells great."

Jess took the roasted vegetables off the barbecue, and Captain Reed snatched a slice of zucchini and popped it in his mouth.

"Hmm, hot. What else did you make?"

Jess motioned toward the platters on the table. "Here we have grilled beef tenderloin, the skewers are chili lime chicken, the swordfish is grilled in lemon, garlic, and butter. On the next table go these balsamic grilled veggies, pasta salad, green salad, and Tahitian poisson cru."

"What is poisson cru?" Captain Reed asked.

Jess slapped his hand away from a grilled asparagus. "The French version of ceviche. For dessert we have a fresh tropical fruit plate and my famous flourless chocolate torte."

At dusk, the crowd naturally gathered around Jess's table. Sydney was putting more beer and wine into the metal tub and her French dreamboat was handling the ice bags. An attractive older gentleman wearing a Hawaiian shirt and pressed khaki shorts approached Jess. His accent sounded British.

"Absolutely no one is anywhere but at your dock, darling. The other chefs opted for hotdogs and hamburgers. Probably because the owners are cheap. Usually it's the other way around. The sailboat owners are the cheap ones, and the power yachts spare no expense. You know how to work your owner, don't you? Oh, I am Leonard, captain of *Noble House*."

The man extended his hand to Jess, and she thought it looked white and pasty. She accepted it reluctantly. Quickly retracting her hand she replied, "The food makes the party. I've seen *Nobel House* when I was walking the docks. Magnificent ship. How many to handle a boat that size?"

Leonard leaned in, uncomfortably close to Jess. "Nineteen, and I can show you around if you'd like."

Jess moved toward the empty salad bowl. "Maybe another time, Leonard. At the moment, I am host to a fabulous dock party."

Jess picked up the bowl and retreated to her galley, happy to get away and replenish the salad. When she returned, Captain Reed was fumbling with a piece of her cake.

"Hey, who's that kid working the barbecue for you, and who was the horndog trying to get under your grass skirt?"

Jess took the captain's cake and placed it on a paper plate.

"That's Dylan at the barbecue, from *Pinta*, Rose's son. Nice boy. She homeschools him. Her husband is a commercial sea captain. They own that beautiful restored wooden Swedish yacht, the one Cheri's staying on since you kicked her off *Slow Dance*. I think they're headed to Fiji. The man-pig is Captain Leonard from *Nobel House*, and I knew what he was up to. I was born at night but not last night, Captain."

Sydney's new friends were sitting on the dock playing music and people formed a circle around the performers. Jess joined in on her silver flute, one of the only possessions left of her former life, along with her father's cast-iron pot. When the music ended everyone cleared a space for a strikingly handsome young man lighting something on fire. Shirtless, he displayed six-pack abs and tribal tattoos that ran down the length of his side. He began twirling flaming fireballs in every direction, dancing and spinning so it appeared like a continuous ring of fire, then two twirling rings of fire, a spectacular show that had everyone cheering.

At the end of the fire-dancing display, the captain was waving at Jess. "Hey, come over here."

Jess went over to the captain, her curiosity piqued. As she approached, she could see a young woman standing with the captain, her energy lighting up the gathering, drawing people in like a moth to a flame.

"Let me introduce you," the captain said. "This is Laura Dekker, the youngest person to sail solo around the world." Jess took Laura's hand wondering how, as a young girl, she could have undertaken such a daunting feat. Laura had been barely sixteen when she circumnavigated the globe.

Laura placed both her hands over Jess's. "Great feast you put on. Made me homesick for mom's cooking. She makes excellent Indonesian food, but I am a terrible cook."

"I read about you," said Jess. "The Dutch court ordered you back in port when you attempted this at thirteen. They deemed you too young. I lived in the Netherlands for over a year. How about if you're still around day after tomorrow, you come to *Slow Dance* for my best attempt at Indonesian rijsttafel?"

Laura's face lit up. "You mean it? For sure I will come. Can I bring my boyfriend? He's from New Zealand and tells me I am the world's worst cook."

On Thursday evening, Laura arrived with her boyfriend and as promised, Jess produced an authentic Indonesian meal consisting of satay, bakso, nasi goreng, gado-gado, rice, and spicy sambal—a combination of rice, salad, veggie, and meat dishes.

"Oh my God," said Sydney pushing away from the table. "So good. Is it okay to burp? I hear that's a compliment to the chef in other countries."

Jess rolled her eyes at Sydney's remark and turned her attention to Laura. "I saw the documentary about your journey, called *Maidentrip*."

Laura's face lit up. "I was always messing the camera up on board while trying to film myself."

Jess studied the beautiful girl sitting across from her. Her thoughts went to all the possible danger, and she was worried about sailing on with the captain, Lou, and Sydney as their crew.

Jess was clearing the last of the dishes when she noticed Captain Reed and Sydney talking with the young man who wowed everyone with his fire dancing.

When they were back on the boat Jess asked Sydney, "Who was that handsome fire dancer?"

"That, my dear, is Don, the Don Juan of Marina Taina, a member of my wolf pack, and quite possibly, our new captain."

Captain Reed added, "I will be interviewing him in the morning, so make extra coffee. I am off to bed," and he disappeared below just as Lou was returning to the boat from her dinner out with Cheri.

"What's going on? How'd your dock party go, and who is that cute guy I just saw leaving?"

Sydney yawned. "The new captain, maybe."

"Yummy, we could use some deck candy," said Lou.

Sydney gave Jess a knowing glance. "You're way too old, Momma, so get the thought out of your mind. The man is surrounded with the most beautiful young girls this side of the southern hemi."

23

The Fire Dancer

June 2024
Marina Taina, Tahiti

Don was a thirty-five-year-old seasoned South African sailor whose very essence embodied confidence, daring, and a thirst for adventure—and he was on the lookout for the next one when Captain Reed decided to interview him. Whether braving stormy seas or exploring remote island chains, Don thrived on excitement of the unknown and the opportunity to test his skills to the limit. He presented himself as resourceful, able to think on his feet, adept at navigating through rough waters and unforeseen obstacles with a calm determination. He was a blend of courage, curiosity, and resilience. Jess thought the young man embodied the spirit that has driven sailors throughout history.

Don spent the past ten years in the Caribbean, working in his mother and stepfather's catamaran rental business. He sailed the Amazon, crossed the Atlantic and the Pacific, survived some gnarly situations on the high seas, and crewed for some unstable sea captains. He knew his way around boats, and according to the girl talk in Sydney's group, he also knew his way around a woman's body. He'd jumped off a boat named *Eighth Moon* that arrived in Tahiti from the Galapagos Islands. He described the owner as insane and recalled how the small sailboat limped into Marina Taina, sinking the entire way. Don and Captain Reed swapped sea stories that morning, and Jess could see a bond forming between the men.

From the moment Don stepped onto *Slow Dance*, he took command. Although Sydney was not a paid crew member, she saw an opportunity to increase her knowledge and quickly became Don's willing first mate. Together, they built a platform on the forward deck to make repairs to the damaged underside of the dinghy. Utilizing a harness attached to the main halyard, they lifted the dinghy onto the platform, which allowed access to her bottom. Each morning, Don went into the engine room to examine the work being completed on the 6-71 diesel engine, and unsatisfied with the French mechanic's progress *and attitude*, he took over the final process of flushing the engine with high-grade oil to eliminate any remaining water. Captain Reed seemingly had found his guy to tell the other guys what to do.

Don moved into the aft cabin across from Lou, the one Cheri had vacated. Lou didn't lift a finger to assist with any boat chores, opting to leave the boat each morning before work began and returning for dinner once work had stopped for the day. One morning Captain Reed requested Jess join him for lunch at a local restaurant. Lou, overhearing the offer, invited herself, and Captain Reed didn't object. Throughout the entire lunch, Lou ignored Jess, cozying up to the captain, and after ordering a second glass of sauvignon blanc, she put her hand on his, asking, "Do you trust Don?"

The new captain did not figure into Lou's plans.

"Why? Don't you?" Captain Reed answered.

"You're not supposed to answer a question with a question," she said, making flirty eyes at him.

Captain Reed pushed his chair back and stared at Lou. "Can you do what he's doing?"

Fluttering her eyelashes, Lou answered, "I could if you made me captain and I had a mechanic."

"It's a thought, Lou, but first you need to learn the correct way to tie a bowline knot. The reason my dinghy has a damaged bottom is because you do not tie a good knot."

Lou went silent. After paying the bill Captain Reed stood up and offered his hand to Jess. "Shall we head back?"

Jess took his hand. "Thank you for a lovely lunch, Captain."

He nodded. "You are most welcome."

Lou rose from the table and walked toward the marina without thanking Captain Reed for lunch. Judging by Captain Reed's attitude, Jess knew Lou would not be sailing on with *Slow Dance*.

Later that evening, Don called Lou to the upper deck where he and Captain Reed stood waiting for her. Don began the conversation.

"Lou, I am not sure what the arrangement was when you boarded this boat, but all that is changing now. You're not paid crew, so you have zero responsibility to the boat. Basically, you contribute nothing; therefore, you eat and sleep for free. I am having difficulty understanding why you're on board."

As usual, Lou started crying. "I am useful; just tell me what I can do to help."

"Okay," said Don. "First, you can move forward to the crew cabin. I want your aft cabin; it has more space. The other aft cabin goes to Jess, who is, in my opinion, the most important person on the boat—except for the owner. Starting tomorrow, we begin sanding the rails of *Slow Dance* to prepare for new varnish. Please be on deck at oh seven hundred."

Lou was staring at Captain Reed, waiting for him to come to her defense. But he said nothing, and Lou retreated to the soon-to-be Don's cabin.

In two short weeks, Don mended the dinghy, completed repairs on the engine, and kicked Lou off the boat. Lou tried everything from feigning sickness, crying jags, and seduction, all to no avail. She moved onto Rose's boat with Cheri and waited for her ticket back to Canada.

"This is Peter and Aga from Poland. They just arrived from the Galapagos on a boat with some crazy Mormon sailor who had ideas about sharing women."

Don had brought the young couple aboard to meet Captain Reed, Sydney, and Jess. Peter and Aga had been living in London where Peter helped upgrade the city to digital technology, and Aga worked as an astrophysicist. Aga spoke French, German, and English. They were not dumb kids.

Don continued, "They're hitchhiking around the world by working on boats. They want to sail around the islands with us, and to the Cook Islands afterwards. We need help finishing the teak rails, and I want to strip the deck and reseal it. These guys have done teak work. I figure we can anchor at each island and combine fun and work."

Captain Reed agreed. "Welcome aboard, Peter and Aga from Poland."

After the couple exited the boat, Jess turned to Don and Captain Reed. "So, where does the second most important person on the boat sleep now that her reclaimed cabin has been given away for the third time?"

Captain Reed placed his arm around her. "Mi casa, su casa."

Unhappy with his response, she replied, "That pertains to a home, not a bed."

"That's me, always second. Crew cabin, I am back."

Captain Reed put on a sad face. "Don't be upset. I hope you're still going to join me in my cabin for movie night."

Jess shrugged him off. "You know what's better than movie night? A raise, now that I have two more mouths to feed." And she abruptly left them to move her things from the aft cabin back to the crew cabin.

Captain Reed and Don stared after Jess in separate, silent contemplation.

But the purring of *Slow Dance*'s engine quickly wrestled the captain back to his immediate surroundings. His feet registered the engine's gentle hum, and he felt a warmth of appreciation for how well Don handled *Slow Dance*. He was also impressed with Don's expertise in managing the sails. He didn't have to instruct him on the use of the bow thrusters, appropriate sail, or anchoring.

It had been noticeable to Jess how much Don had impressed the captain; how confident he was that he had picked the right captain for his boat. But looks can be deceiving.

24

Aita Pe'ape'a (No Worries)

June 2024
Marina Taina, Tahiti

It was Sunday morning, and Jess was awakened by church bells ringing near the marina. She liked the sound of them. She was thinking about Cheri, and although she didn't miss the conflict between Cheri and Captain Reed, she missed her. It had been Jess who met her after she answered the ad on the horny-sailor website. Captain Reed was tending to boat business that day, so Jess conducted the interview. She had an immediate connection with Cheri as they chatted about yoga, hiking, sailing, and their travels abroad. It was disappointing the way things turned out. But Jess realized Cheri was off the boat long before Captain Reed asked her to leave.

Jess admired Cheri's confidence when taking charge of *Slow Dance*. It had reminded her of the way she took charge of a commercial kitchen. Jess had no doubt that Cheri's dreams of owning her own boat would come to fruition. Cheri knew what she wanted and how to make it happen. Jess admired those traits in a woman. Smiling to herself, she envisioned Cheri on her boat, sailing to the San Juan Islands, a destination she often talked about.

The church bells rang a second time as Jess wrapped her palms around her coffee cup. She had mixed feelings about Lou, who she considered a strange, secretive, and conniving woman. Lou never revealed anything about herself, where she grew up, her parents, or if she had any siblings, only that she sailed in the Caribbean for five years. Lou shared virtually nothing with Jess or the other crewmates, as far as she knew. Jess didn't hate Lou, she simply wondered what happened in her past to make her act the way she did. Cheri was gone but not forgotten, whereas Lou's presence would not be missed.

Jess felt herself being reshaped by change, both internal and external. She was missing her three closest girlfriends back home. The four of them had been friends for many years, through husbands, children, bad times and good. The kind of friends you may not see for several years, but when you are together, it's as if no time has passed. They followed her travel blog, but she was feeling the need to personally connect. She went inside to the computer to send them an email.

With the necessary repairs completed, *Slow Dance* motored out of Marina Taina, toward Cook's Bay, on the island of Moorea. Jess was excited to see more of the Tahitian islands. Don and Sydney anchored the yacht in between shorelines of deep white sand and lush palm tree forests. Peter and Aga, having traveled on several different boats over the past year, brought added skills to managing the large vessel. Jess stood on the bow as the crew settled the boat, thinking of the adventure books her mother used to read to her.

Her thoughts were distracted by a canoe approaching *Slow Dance*. A beautiful, young girl with long black hair and a wreath of flowers crowning her head was waving and speaking in French. Captain Reed called Aga to the bow to interpret what the girl was saying. Aga was a reserved, petite young woman with a short boyish cut to her blond hair, large intelligent blue eyes, and the intestinal fortitude of a gladiator. She leaned over the rail and began conversing in French with the young girl.

"She asks if we would come join the village this evening for a traditional Tahitian music and dance performance."

Captain Reed was looking down at the young girl. "Hell yes, if there's more of you on shore."

Jess felt a tinge of jealousy.

"This brings back memories," said Captain Reed. "My first encounter with Tahitian beauties—the last time I anchored in this bay. Naked girls swam up to my boat and wanted to make love with me."

Sydney shook her head. "Did you make love to any of these girls?"

Captain Reed answered, "Probably."

Jess was annoyed. "'Made love'? Ha!"

Sydney added her two cents. "Listen, gramps, while you were away, the locals were corrupted by Christian missionaries. So now they cover up feeling guilty for their natural urges, and the Europeans come here and want to get naked. Ironic, isn't it?"

Aga was amused at their banter. She had already told the girl they would be honored to attend. She found out the time and whether there would be food and drinks.

"The performance starts at eight, and they have a bar but no food."

"Thanks, Aga." Captain Reed suddenly looked sad. "You can never really go back. Tahiti was so raw the first time I sailed here. The old pirate bar in Papeete is gone. It was full of characters from around the world—the types of sailors who navigated by the stars. Today, any joker can take a boat across the sea. All the fancy radar, GPS, Windguru . . . and other stuff I find complicated. Honestly, I am disappointed by what I see here. Abandoned, broken-down resorts, graffiti literally on every wall around the island. This is the outcome when a place outprices itself and gets greedy. Tourists cease to come, and now we see these stunning resorts with the windows broken out. After Angie died, I wanted only to sail *Slow Dance* back to Tahiti, and now that I'm here, it's a huge disappointment."

Jess felt sorry for him.

"Captain, the world has changed a lot since you last sailed here. Even Tahiti, a place you think would stay pristine. I am seeing it for the first time, so it's beautiful to me. Was your plan to stay in French Polynesia? What if we just kept going? Maybe there's still a place out here untouched by civilization. Somewhere cut off from the world—wild, dangerous, and full of new adventures. In my early adventures, I hacked through the dense jungle in Sri Lanka in search of voodoo dolls handmade by some shaman. My guide was a local man named Hollyhinga, with missing teeth and a very sharp machete."

"What happened?" asked Captain Reed, suddenly distracted from his sadness. "Did you find the shaman and the dolls?"

Jess put her hand to her heart. "We found the shaman and his village. They darn near killed us when they heard I was looking for his voodoo dolls. Apparently, the dolls are used in deep magic and asking him to sell them was like asking him to cut off his arms or something. Scary moment, so we ran for our lives."

Captain Reed was looking at Jess admiringly. "Jeez, first I find out you can really cook, then you start looking cute, and now I find out you're a fearless explorer! I like your idea to just keep going and see how far we get. It's a big planet and all lands touch the sea. I finally have a good captain, so I can act like a rich owner and fly to my boat wherever my new captain sails her."

Jess gave him a wink. "Yes, you can, Captain, if there's an airport."

The Polynesian islanders had gone all out for *Slow Dance*. Tiki torches lined the jungle path to a clearing on the sand, where chairs had been set up by a makeshift bar serving fresh mango, pineapple, and coconut drinks. Don carried a bag full of cold beer, a bottle of spiced rum, and his fire-dancing chains to liven up the evening festivities. A gentle breeze was blowing across the islands, carrying that indescribable scent of the tropics, the one responsible for melting away one's inhibitions. Jess finally understood the true reason why Fletcher Christian mutinied against Captain Bligh. The nature of the islands released one from the taboos of the civilized world, and Jess wanted to shred her clothes and run naked across the soft sand, down to the blue lagoon, to swim in the moonlight. The drums began to play, and Jess's attention was turned to the lively Polynesian rhythms. Twelve dancers appeared on the sand wearing palm-leaf headdresses, grass skirts, and seashell bangles around their ankles and wrists. Their graceful, delicate hands moved with the purpose of telling stories of their ancient culture, as their hips gyrated, and their grass skirts swooshed with each beat. The combination of intricate hand movements, vibrant costumes, energetic music, and storytelling through dance was captivating.

Sydney was handing Jess another rum and pineapple.

"Amazing, hey, Jess? Not like in Hawaii."

"Right!"

After several performances, the dancers grabbed Captain Reed, Sydney, and Jess up on the sand for a dance. The two rum-and-pineapple drinks coupled with the Polynesian trade winds, tribal drumming, and the incredibly handsome tattooed man who was shaking his hips caused Jess to break out with some dance moves of her own. Aga and Sydney joined, and their dance became a sort of African dance, with a tinge of belly dancing. When the drumming ended, everyone was looking at the girls in total amusement, including their hosts.

"Whoa, Jess, that was a trip. You were totally into it."

Sydney handed her another pineapple and rum. Don was on the sand now with the other local fire dancers, fueling up their balls and chains. Thrilling displays of fire being tossed around in the air was the last thing Jess remembered.

"Rise and shine. Coffee's brewed. You look like you need this cup of joe, which I am leaving here on the table. Anchors up in fifteen minutes, and we all agree to never speak of last night."

Don put the cup down and Jess reluctantly opened one eye, rolled over, and fell off the outside cushion. She had apparently spent the night on deck. Her mouth was dry, and her head felt much too large for her neck to support. Groaning, she sat up and reached for the coffee.

"Damn, woman, you look frightful." Sydney was laughing. "Stick with me, I'll teach you how to hold your liquor. Your wet clothes are in the bucket over there."

Jess looked confused. "What did I do? Oh, I went for a swim, right?"

"Sort of," said Sydney. "More like a dive off the dinghy midstream. You swam back to the boat and Don slowed the dinghy down so we could make sure you didn't drown. That was after you performed a cool fusion of weird dance moves for the village people and tried to make out with the chief's son. What a show."

"Oh, God." Jess took a mouthful of the coffee and spit it out.

"Don, what the hell. You call this coffee?"

Don popped his head out of the pilothouse. "I like my coffee like I like my women: hot, black, and sweet. Now get your ass up, because we're sailing to Raiatea and Taha'a. Likely a seven-hour sail, and some breakfast would be nice."

Don retreated to the pilothouse chuckling to himself. Jess stood up, realizing she was naked. Wrapping the blanket around her body, she dragged herself toward her cabin with Trini following behind. The loyal poodle had slept by her the entire night.

"Come on, Trini," taking her first sluggish step toward the pilothouse, "you're the only one who loves and appreciates me."

Captain Reed was looking at the charts, plotting *Slow Dance*'s course toward the outer islands of French Polynesia. "You look like—"

Jess cut him off. "I know, I know, I don't want to know. Need a shower right now and my toothbrush. Talk later." And she hurried below deck.

Captain Reed had not seen this side of his cook. As he observed her playful antics the previous evening, he witnessed a new dimension of her personality, one that added depth and complexity to his feelings for her. Her actions revealed a spontaneity and abandon that surprised him.

Slow Dance sailed the islands for several weeks, anchoring in stunning bays where the crew combined work and play. Most days were spent varnishing teak rails and resealing the teak deck. The work was hard and tedious, and Jess could tell it was more than Aga and Peter had anticipated. Other days were spent exploring waterfalls and hiking on trails leading into the tropical jungle on the islands. They swam in pools of fresh water, then visited ancient burial grounds with large stone statues and other weird, tall, fork-like figures. They also took long walks into the forest in search of tribal burial grounds. Jess's favorite outings were on Bora Bora. They anchored in the Bay of Vaitape, the largest town on the island with a colorful, lively market full of abundant fruits, vegetables, beans, rice, and fresh fish. They spent two days provisioning the boat, and on their last day, the town was celebrating Heiva i Bora Bora, the biggest festival in Tahiti. There was singing, dancing, and crafts demonstrations, all featuring a colorful display of Polynesian costumes, tribal skills, and music; and there was even traditional sports competitions. Aga, Sydney, and Jess especially enjoyed the hunky tribal men in the rowing competition.

Bora Bora was stunning. *Slow Dance* spent four days anchoring around the island, and now that her rails were varnished and the deck sealed, everyone was in a party mood.

The island was a honeymoon destination home to world-class luxury resorts scattered around the land, where guests arrived either by helicopter or private boat. The shallow, sandy-bottom blue lagoons were set against huge tropical mountains, majestic and lush.

"This is magnificent. Thank you for bringing us aboard."

Peter was pointing his camera in every direction trying to capture all he could of Bora Bora. He liked to take candid shots and snaps when no one was posing. Jess once asked to see his photos from their dock party in Marina Taina and, out of hundreds of photos, only a few were worthy, and every unflattering photo of Jess was beyond hideous: mouth open to eat something, close side views of her face, and angles that made her look like the blimp with eye shadow. Afterwards, Jess became acutely aware of Peter and his camera, turning her back if she saw him pointing it in her direction.

"This place is sublime." Captain Reed was driving the dinghy onto a beach at what appeared to be the most exclusive resort on the island.

"Hmmm, we are for sure going to get booted out of here, Captain."

Jess was sitting on the pontoon holding Trini. He winked at her.

"Stick with me, kids, and just walk in like it's the natural thing to do."

Don jumped out to tie the line and secure the boat and surprisingly, Trini jumped out into the water and swam to the sand, not her usual clingy self. Trini trotted along behind as they sauntered right up to the outside bar and restaurant. They ordered food, drink, and towels for the pool and spent a lovely day just chilling. Three Polynesian employees approached their table at lunch and Jess thought for certain they were getting kicked out. Instead, they clustered around Jess's chair smiling and giggling at Trinidad. The women spoke in broken English.

"Nice dog."

Captain Reed stood up and called Trini over to where he was standing. He picked her up, and the three servers got a thrill out of patting her curly hair.

"We have no dog like this. We never see like her, like sheep."

It had in fact been a long time since the pup's last proper grooming and she did resemble a sheep. Captain Reed put Trini down and took a carrot from his salad.

"She loves carrots and will do tricks for them. Want to see?"

The three women clapped with excitement. Placing the carrot in his mouth, he bent down, and Trini stood on her hind legs dancing in circles before gently taking the carrot.

"Oh my God." The three women were thrilled, and the trick had to be repeated several times for all the staff.

Carefree and a little drunk, the sailors eventually climbed into the dinghy and headed home to *Slow Dance*. As they entered the bay where the boat was anchored, they saw a Paul Gauguin luxury cruise ship in the process of loading its passengers onto small boats for an afternoon outing. Don pulled up to *Slow Dance*, holding the dinghy steady while the others climbed aboard. Sydney suddenly asked Don to take her over for a closer look at the elegant ship.

"Pretty please? You know I am a hick from Wisconsin. Never going to see anything like that on Lake Superior."

Captain Reed shook his head. "Take her, but don't linger."

The last shore boat departed from the Gauguin and the platform remained down.

"Pull the dinghy up for a closer look inside," the captain suggested. "It's totally cool; no one is at the landing."

Don brought the dinghy even with the platform so Sydney could get a look inside.

"It's just a stairwell leading to the decks above. Forget this—" And Sydney jumped aboard the cruise ship.

"What? Sydney? *Get back in the boat.*" Don was furious.

"Come on, Don, just give me a few minutes to take a quick look." She turned, scurrying up the steps and was gone.

"Where are those two?" Captain Reed was looking over the bay with binoculars to see if he could spot his dinghy. The sun was near setting when Don arrived in the dinghy, alone.

"Where is Sydney?" Captain Reed seemed calm, but Jess could tell he was upset. Don was in the process of explaining when *Slow Dance* was hailed on the radio by the captain of the Paul Gauguin.

"It seems one of your crew has illegally boarded my vessel and I insist you retrieve her immediately. This is a serious offense. I hold my crew accountable for the breach, having left the platform unattended. I should charge you, sir, for the food and beverage your mate enjoyed during her romp through my ship."

Captain Reed pressed the button on his receiver. "I am truly apologetic, Captain. We are coming for her now. I hold myself responsible, and if you require payment, please don't hesitate to send over a bill."

The sun had disappeared into the Pacific as Don steered the dinghy toward the cruise ship. The guests were returning to the boat, and two men in security uniforms were on the far side of the platform standing with Sydney. Don pulled the dinghy next to the landing and Sydney jumped in quickly. Some people on the upper deck were whistling and yelling, "Goodbye, Sydney. We love you, Rasta pirate girl."

Don was laughing. "Damn, I am pissed, but at the same time I am amused. Do you have any idea how serious this is? Of course, you don't, 'cause you're drunk. What happened?"

Sydney puckered her lips. "Awww, don't be mad, Captain Don, it was fabulous. I intended to just run up and have a quick look but got sucked in. Everything I asked for at the bar they just gave me, and the food, oh the food. There were these people from San Francisco who didn't go to the beach, and I partied with them. That boat is amazing."

Don grumbled. "I am glad you enjoyed yourself, but as captain I am going to have to do my job and come down hard. You're basically in deep shit."

25

The Storm

July 2024
French Polynesia

It was late June, and by September, *Slow Dance* needed to be in Fiji to avoid getting caught in the open ocean during typhoon season. Sydney was on deck coiling lines, while Don and Peter were busy securing the dinghy onto the platform. Peter was having a difficult time latching the middle strap, which required him to lie on his plumpish stomach. Don was poking fun at him, and Peter was clearly annoyed. Jess wondered how or why a nerdy tech guy decided that hitchhiking on boats was somehow a good plan for seeing the world. Aga was surely the instigator and creator of their travel plans. An unlikely couple, in stark physical contrast to each other. It was intellect that bonded them. Don didn't hesitate to confide in Jess how he thought Aga could find a better match, and it became apparent that Peter disliked Don in more ways than one. They were total opposites. Peter was intelligent, sweet, and awkward, while Don was hard-drinking, overconfident, and bullish.

Jess felt uneasy as *Slow Dance* prepared to depart for the Cook Islands. Aga was with Captain Reed in the pilothouse reviewing the navigation system. She and Peter had crewed from the Galapagos Islands to Tahiti, so they were familiar with keeping watch and recording data in the logbook.

Slow Dance would take five days to cross to Rarotonga, the main port in the Cook Islands. Jess busied herself in the galley, preparing grab-and-go food items. She portioned her homemade vegetarian lasagna in microwaveable dishes and after the granola cooled from the oven, she put it in a large plastic Tupperware container. Next, she rolled twenty beef and bean burritos, wrapped them, and placed them in the refrigerator. Trinidad sat patiently underfoot waiting for a handout.

Slow Dance set sail for the Cook Islands leaving behind the stunning blue turquoise waters and lush green landscapes of French Polynesia. With the trade winds in their favor, the boat turned westward. Don demonstrated his superior sailing skills, as the sails caught the wind, and the boat cut through the waves at ten knots. Jess loved the swooshing sound of the boat pushing through the water.

Don poked his head into the galley. "Jess, darling, make some coffee and then come up top for a meeting."

Jess prepared the pot, pushed the brew button, and made her way to the pilothouse for the meeting. Don was standing at the helm, and Captain Reed was sitting in his chair. Peter, Aga, and Sydney were seated on the sofas.

Don looked serious. "This will be our first long crossing together, and it will probably get a little bumpy. I will take the first four-hour watch with Sydney. Peter and Aga will take the second four-hour watch, and then Sydney and I will start the cycle over. The ship's cook is never required to do watches; she's too important to our survival." He winked at Jess, and she winked back.

"The coffee is ready," she said, "and there is lasagna, granola, and bean burritos in the fridge. Just microwave and eat."

During the journey, the sailors would navigate through a series of open waters, islands, and atolls. The first two days were smooth and uneventful. On their third night Jess was not sleeping because the seas had come up and were thrashing the boat side to side, making it impossible to lie on the bed in the captain's cabin. When *Slow Dance* was at sea, Captain Reed's habit was to sleep on the sofa in the pilothouse. Abandoning all thoughts of sleeping, she climbed the stairs to the pilothouse, making certain to hold onto the side rails to keep from falling. Trini was at her heels whimpering. Jess was greeted by Don and the captain, and they looked concerned.

"Oh no, are we in a typhoon?" Jess asked.

Captain Reed helped her sit down on the sofa, and Trini jumped into her lap.

"No, just a storm, but we lost our autopilot, so we have to hand-steer to keep our heading."

Captain Reed turned to Don. "Better get the headsail down and set the mainsail to steady the boat."

Sydney, Aga, and Peter were also in the pilothouse, awakened by the rough seas.

Don and Sydney headed out on the foredeck to furl in the small head-sail and replace it with the storm sail.

Aga and Peter assisted Don in reefing the mainsail. Jess was watching and asked Captain Reed the purpose of folding the canvas of the mainsail to make it smaller.

"It's called reefing. They're folding and rolling one edge of the canvas in on itself and attaching the unused portion, to what is called 'the stay.' This helps with *Slow Dance's* stability in strong winds. Restoring the full sail is called 'shaking out the reef.'"

The winds came up, gusting at forty knots, and *Slow Dance* was digging into the sea, taking large waves over her bow and stern. Jess closed her eyes and held onto the chart table; it was the first time she was truly worried about dying at sea.

As Jess contemplated drowning at sea, Don called her over to the helm.

"Jess, take the wheel and keep our heading. Keep this point right here, in between these two numbers." He pointed to the large compass on the console, behind the helm. "The captain and I are going to try and fix the autopilot."

It had seemed so simple but proved very difficult. Fifteen minutes passed and Jess could not hold the heading.

"What is it I'm trying to do, Sydney? My arms are falling off."

Sydney took the wheel from Jess. "The compass has numbers from one to three-sixty, and our course to Rarotonga is set between these two numbers." She pointed to the numbers with her finger. "That's our heading. I'll give it a try; you take a break."

Jess dropped her useless arms to her sides in an exaggerated manner, then grabbed onto the chart table to keep from being thrown across the pilothouse.

"Ha, go ahead, show me up, but you can't compete in the kitchen."

Humor was inappropriate for their present situation, but it calmed her. Sydney held their heading for an impressive hour.

Don and Captain Reed returned from the engine room, where they had been unsuccessful at repairing the autopilot. To make matters worse, the inside steering controls also ceased functioning, leaving only one option—steering *Slow Dance* through the storm from the outside helm.

While they were discussing a plan, Aga was busy retrieving the foul-weather gear from the pilothouse locker. Pulling on the yellow overhauls with suspenders, and then yellow boots, a raincoat, and large hat with a chin strap to keep it from blowing away, she announced, "I will do it now."

They turned and when they saw Aga, they couldn't keep from laughing at the sight of her being swallowed up by her oversized gear.

"You look like a warning buoy," said Sydney.

Peter was trying to snap photos of her but needed his hands to hold on. Don stepped up to Aga holding two lines.

"You sure you want to do this? You're going to have to put the safety vest on and use the tether lines, in the event a wave tries to pull you overboard."

Aga replied, "Yes, I know. How do you say, 'Not my first rodeo'?"

Don shook his head. "My kind of girl."

It was obvious Aga had experienced rough seas in the past.

Peter put his camera down. "I will help you secure the lines."

"Okay, mate, and you keep an eye so we know when she's tired and needs someone to switch. I am going to try and get some sleep before my watch."

Jess looked at him amazed. "Sleep? How the hell can you sleep?"

"Been through much worse; this is just a little gale. Besides, I put my lee cloth up before the storm hit."

"What's that?" she asked.

"A piece of cloth in my cabin—a net, actually—to keep a sailor in his bunk in rough stuff."

Jess sighed. "All this time and Trini and I could have been snug in our bed."

"Sorry, luv. After we get past this, I will show you how to put yours up."

Jess felt her fears subside, and she was glad Don was with them, as opposed to those who came before him. She wondered why Captain Reed wasn't utilizing a lee cloth in his cabin, remembering he preferred the pilothouse when *Slow Dance* was at sea.

Jess had her arm around Trini, to keep her from sliding. She was in the saloon, attempting to sleep on the floor portside, the side that was heeling over. She wasn't sure if she had been sleeping or fading in and out of sleep—when she awoke to a loud crash and screams. She rushed into the galley to find the coffee pot shattered on the floor, with coffee and grounds everywhere.

"*What idiot left the damn coffee pot up on the counter of a boat you can't even bloody stand up in?*" She was angry, tired, and scared.

Then came the yelling and moaning from the pilothouse. Keeping her hands on the teak walls for balance, Jess went up to the pilothouse to find Peter lying on the floor, clawing at his left knee, with Captain Reed, who had been sleeping on the sofa cushions placed on the floor of the pilothouse, kneeling next to him. A closer look revealed a bone protruding just below Peter's kneecap.

"*Good God,*" she said, feeling bile rise in her throat.

Captain Reed was holding on to Peter's sweatshirt to keep him from sliding across the floor. Sydney and Don arrived simultaneously from their cabins and gasped at the sight of Peter. The pilothouse door was closed to keep the water out, but Jess could hear Aga yelling over the sound of the waves crashing over the stern.

Pushing down her need to vomit, Jess hurried to retrieve the first aid kit, and Don rushed to bring Aga in from the storm. A mug that once held coffee for Aga was spilled on the deck at the top of the steps. Peter must have fallen backwards down the steps, driving his knee into the base of the chart table. He had been bringing her coffee when he lost his balance. Peter was warned many times to have one hand free for holding steady. Aga began crying at the sight of Peter's leg. She rushed to him and placed a pillow under his head.

"I am going to the helm," said Sydney shakingly.

Aga pulled off the raincoat and hat and hastily handed it to Sydney.

"Don, hold his shoulders down," Captain Reed instructed. "Aga, cut his pant leg open."

Captain Reed handed Aga a pair of scissors from the drawer under the chart table. Jess returned with the first aid kit and handed it to Reed, before abruptly sitting down on the sofa holding on to the edge of the cabinet to stabilize herself. Captain Reed made certain *Slow Dance* stored the right items for this kind of an emergency, and Jess was impressed at the items inside the box.

"Hand me the morphine shots, Jess." Captain Reed swabbed Peter's arm with alcohol and gave him the shot.

The poor man was rocking back and forth, moaning, about to go into shock.

"Aga, steady his head."

Aga changed places with Don and began to rub Peter's head soothingly. Captain Reed unwrapped a splint and prepared to set the leg. The morphine was taking effect, so Captain Reed counted one, two, three, and straightened Peter's injured leg while Don kept his arms down. His screams were horrible, but after Don and Captain Reed got the splint on, he seemed to drift out of consciousness. The captain turned to Aga.

"Aga, go and get the cabin bed prepared. Don, help brace pillows around Peter. We need to leave him here on the floor until the seas calm down, and then we can carry him to his cabin. Why does this kind of thing always seem to happen at night and in rough seas?"

Jess was closing the first aid box. "I am going to clean up the galley now."

"No," commanded Captain Reed. "I do not want any of you doing anything, except steering this boat into port at Rarotonga. Wait until things calm down. We still have hours of storm and two more days until we reach the island. I will need to radio ahead for an ambulance."

As Aga was covering Peter with a blanket trying to make him as comfortable as possible, Jess was thinking to herself, *Will things on this boat ever calm down?*

Captain Reed let out a huge sigh. "Thank God my doctor is a friend and gave us some Dilantin, morphine, and oxycodone."

Don needed to get out to the helm to keep the boat's heading. Throwing on his rain gear, he rushed out holding on to the table before tethering himself to the strongest part of the stern.

Jess fumbled her way down from the pilothouse to the saloon bathroom and vomited. She found Trinidad whimpering under the saloon table.

"Poor Trini, come here and we can ride this out together." The poodle hunkered down on Jess's lap as she sat on the floor, braced against the sofa with a bucket nearby, and tried to get some sleep.

"Get up, lazy!"

Sydney was shaking Jess's foot. Jess sat up rubbing her eyes.

"I slept? I didn't think it possible . . . And please tell me last night was a dream. How is Peter?"

Don entered the saloon. "The route from Tahiti to the Cook Islands is known for sudden, intense storms. Lots of sailor stories about sailing this route." Don headed toward the galley.

"Hey, there is a mess in the galley, Don," Jess warned. "Glass and coffee grounds everywhere."

"Not anymore," Don said. "Sydney cleaned it up while you were sleeping. Even took the floor panels up and wiped the coffee and grinds off everything stowed underneath. I think you lost a few rolls of paper towels."

Jess looked at Sydney and put her hand to her mouth, feigning amazement. "No way. You performed a domestic task, and a difficult one at that? My respect and admiration grow daily, young Bodhisattva of the Lakes."

Don asked Jess, "Can you please make us some coffee and a bite; we're all weary as hell."

The seas were calm for the remaining two days and the drugs in the first aid kit kept Peter in a medicated trance. Aga left Peter's bedside only to fetch food and drinks. Captain Reed had done a great job at splinting the leg.

As *Slow Dance* approached the island, Captain Reed was on the radio arranging a slip in Rarotonga's harbor and making certain an ambulance would be waiting to take Peter to the nearest hospital. Don greeted the captain, who had just put the radio receiver back in place, and then shared a friendly wink with Jess, who'd been listening in on the captain's radio comms.

Looking at Don, the captain let out a huge sigh. "You're not going to like this: we have to med-moor *Slow Dance*."

"What's that mean exactly?" Jess asked.

Captain Reed explained, "Mediterranean mooring. I've done it plenty when driving boats in Europe. It's a technique for putting the boat to a pier at a perpendicular angle. In Europe they do it because the docks are crowded. The boat connects to a fixed length of the dock by width rather than length. The problem here is that it's not practical because of the deep water and large tide. *Slow Dance* is going against a cement wall, ten feet from the waterline, in a bouncy, rolling bay."

Don answered confidently, "After ten years crewing in the Mediterranean, it should be a piece of cake; but the bounce is concerning."

Don oozed confidence, yes, approaching every situation calmly—except for one: poop of any kind; then the man lost it, vomiting instantly. Jess and Sydney had great fun teasing Don, but quickly realized it brought out his dark side. He requested Trini's turds be tossed immediately overboard before he encountered them on deck. Sydney only got one chance with the fake dog doo, and he really got mad. It was clear the man couldn't take a joke at his expense and did not like to be criticized.

"What are we doing?" Sydney's voice was full of concern as she listened to Don's directions for getting *Slow Dance* to the pier. "This sounds bad."

Don demonstrated where to cleat the stern lines and Sydney stood by him.

"No worries," Don reassured. "I called for a couple of dock handlers to assist."

Captain Reed used the bow thrusters to reverse *Slow Dance*, maneuvering her stern six feet from the ten-foot wall, where two large men caught the lines tossed by Don and Sydney.

Don rolled his shoulders back. "Thank God for the monkey fist, otherwise I would never be able to toss the line that high."

"What's a monkey fist?" Jess was standing at the stern watching them.

Don explained. "It's a ball of rope wound tightly into a fist with a line attached to the ball. It's like a baseball, sort of, and makes it easier to toss a line over a distance or up to someone who needs to grab the line."

Jess shrugged. "I have so much to learn."

Aga appeared on deck carrying two backpacks, and her eyes were filled with concern for Peter.

"It doesn't look good for getting Peter off this boat."

Captain Reed addressed her concern. "Shore emergency should come any moment, Aga; they will bring a gurney and gently transport Peter by boat to meet the ambulance."

Aga sat down on the outside cushion to steady herself. "This bay is horrid. The boat is bouncing like crazy. How can Peter be placed in an emergency boat?"

She was about to continue when the emergency shuttle arrived.

Captain Reed put his hand on hers. "Aga, *Slow Dance* will be in port for at least a few weeks, please allow me to cover all medical costs, as well as your flights home."

Aga nodded. "Thank you. I will contact you when I have more information."

As Captain Reed assured her, the medical team took measures to place Peter on a board and lower him gently into their boat without incident. Aga handed down her bags and the men helped her climb down. Peter lay with his eyes closed and face drawn. Aga never turned around to say goodbye or give a wave off. Captain Reed stood on deck and watched them go.

Jess stood next to Captain Reed, her heart heavy as she watched the young couple leave. They came seeking adventure, and instead, they were leaving in a whirlwind of worry and fear. Her mind raced with thoughts of what could have been done differently, of the moments leading up to the accident. The emptiness of the moment lingered in the air around her.

Jess stood frozen, consumed by the gravity of it all.

26

Rarotonga

July 2024
The Cook Islands

Rarotonga maintained strict regulations regarding dogs, so Trinidad was not allowed to disembark the boat. The inspector from Quarantine checked the boat several times a day, and sometimes at night, to make certain the poor little poodle did not disembark. He apparently had nothing better to do with his time.

Cook Islanders were heavyset people with brown skin, much like the Polynesians in Tahiti, the difference being they spoke English with a cute Kiwi accent. They were also more friendly, offering fruit from their trees and invites to dinner. The Quarantine inspector, being no exception, arrived at the boat one afternoon, carrying a five-foot bunch of bananas cut from his tree as a gesture of goodwill.

"Did we get a monkey or something?" Sydney was breaking off a ripe banana from the enormous bunch.

"No, the Quarantine master brought them by to make up for his cruel and unusual punishment of a small defenseless poodle," said Jess.

Trini gave a bark, and Sydney offered her a piece of her banana.

"Damn, the dog eats everything. Too bad for Don she doesn't eat her own poop."

They both laughed heartily.

"What's so funny?" came Captain Reed's voice as he and Don came up on deck.

Sydney patted Don on his back. "Just a shitty joke that you wouldn't think was funny."

"Where did the banana tree come from?" asked Captain Reed.

Rarotonga was a beautiful coral island surrounded by a lagoon that sloped down into deeper water. Because of her size, *Slow Dance* was directed by the port captain to moor in the commercial harbor. Late in the evenings, Jess and Sydney would sneak Trini off the boat and walk her in between the massive shipping containers stacked up in the shipyard.

"I love the tropical breeze. It smells amazing." Sydney was squatting down by the side of a container.

Jess asked her, "What are you doing?"

"Peeing. I had a few beers prior to our nightly recon."

"Sydney, are you channeling the female pirate Anne Bonny?"

Sydney pulled her shorts up. "It's in my blood, woman. Bet you didn't know from 1830 to 1850, Rarotonga was a popular stop for whalers and trading schooners."

Jess replied, "They really messed things up here in paradise."

"Right," said Sydney. "John Williams was a famous missionary who single-handedly brought Jesus to the South Pacific and killed the islanders' libidos, destroyed their culture," Sydney went on as now Trini, apparently inspired by Sydney, engaged in her funny walking-while-pee-ing act. "They ate his white ass in Vanuatu. I would love to make it there one day."

"You're a beacon of information, Syd," Jess said, watching Trini complete her performance. "You go to college and study history or something?"

"Yes; and remember, I also have a captain's license."

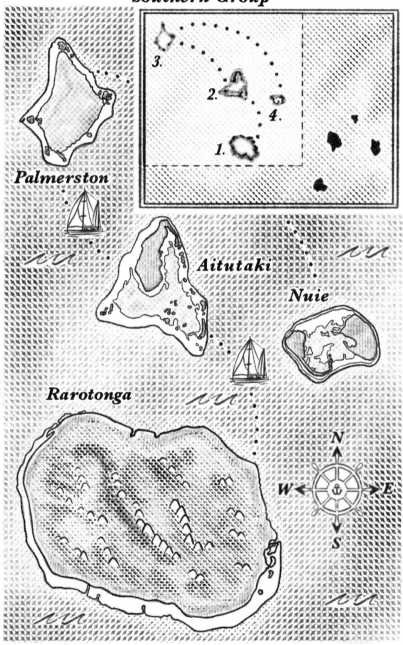

Cook Islands
Southern Group

Palmerston

Aitutaki

Nuie

Rarotonga

3.

2.

4.

1.

N

W E

S

The next few weeks were spent repairing the autopilot and correcting the steering problem at the inside helm. *Slow Dance* was the most impressive boat on the island, and it didn't take long for them to make new friends. Don and Sydney invited locals and fellow cruisers to gather aboard the yacht, which made for lively evenings of conversation over cocktails. Captain Reed seemed to enjoy these evenings. Jess could sense what he didn't say aloud. Although the captain was taking steps to address the repairs to *Slow Dance*, he lacked peace of mind knowing he would need to take precautions to keep his vessel safe and well maintained. He was worried about the repairs that could not be addressed until Fiji, and he worried about the approaching typhoon season. The ongoing mechanical problems plaguing *Slow Dance* were a reminder of what Chaz had said about the boat not being safe for sea, and this weighed on Jess's mind.

Jess immersed herself into the culture and the history of the South Pacific islanders, while Captain Reed and Don busied themselves with the repairs to *Slow Dance*. In the evenings they enjoyed their eclectic group of new friends. Jess's culinary additions to the gatherings were always a crowd-pleaser. However, not every gathering ended on a pleasant note.

One morning after a particularly fun night, Captain Reed was sitting outside buttering a piece of toast and discussing a sail plan with Don and Sydney when Jess came up the steps fuming mad.

"One of last night's guests went into the crew cabin and took a giant crap, stuffing the toilet full of paper towels. What idiot does that after being instructed to use toilet paper and toss it into the waste basket? The audacity to leave without saying anything. Man!" Jess put her hands on her hips.

"Sounds like a repair job for Don." Coffee flew out of Sydney's mouth before she finished saying "Don," she was laughing so uncontrollably. Jess was not amused.

"Screw you guys, we all know it's going to be me who takes care of it. You owe me big time."

Captain Reed was genuinely sympathetic. "Sorry, honey, I always say when people start to know me by name, it's time to leave, so that's exactly what we're going to do. Our repairs are complete, and there are some fascinating islands in this archipelago. When you are done with that nasty task, I'll take us all out for lunch."

Trini jumped up on the sofa trying to snatch one of the lower bananas hanging from the mast. Captain Reed broke one off and peeled it for her. "Poor Trinidad needs to get some freedom from this dog-banning island."

It was early afternoon, and the captain was looking at charts with Don. They were discussing where to go next. It was exciting for Jess not knowing the end destination, just continual sailing from island to island lined with palm trees, white sand beaches, and a mix of different cultures.

Captain Reed pushed his chair away from the chart table. "We pull out tomorrow for Aitutaki, Niue, and Palmerston Island. I'm looking forward to moving on from here. Like I said, too many people in town are calling me by name, a sure sign it's time to go! Ready to get some lunch?"

Jess sighed, pulling off her rubber gloves. "Yes, let's enjoy lunch, because we'll be eating banana bread for the next few weeks."

Captain Reed turned to Sydney. "I have a surprise planned for you this afternoon after lunch."

"Oh goody, I love surprises." Sydney clapped her hands. "What is it?"

"If I told you, it wouldn't be a surprise, would it? We're off the boat for lunch, and Sydney and I will take a few hours afterwards for my surprise."

Sydney frowned as if deep in thought. "Cryptic you are, Jedi."

Late in the afternoon, Sydney and Captain Reed stepped back onto the boat, clearly a bit tipsy. The captain's playful demeanor, the way he appeared at ease with Sydney, stirred up feelings Jess hadn't expected. She was a mix of amusement and jealousy.

"You look like the cat that swallowed the canary," said Don.

Sydney turned slowly around. "You don't notice anything different?"

She raised her arms up in the air. "No more hair! I am as smooth as a baby's bottom. The captain told the girls at the wax place to go for a Brazilian, and of course I thought he meant some kind of happy ending."

The captain had complained to Jess many times regarding Sydney's unshaven body parts, so Jess dismissed any thoughts of the captain and Sydney developing a thing other than being good pals and the captain getting his wish that Sydney loses the hair.

"You look good hairless; more shaggable," said Don.

Captain Reed interrupted the banter. "Tomorrow we sail to Niue."

Sail Positions

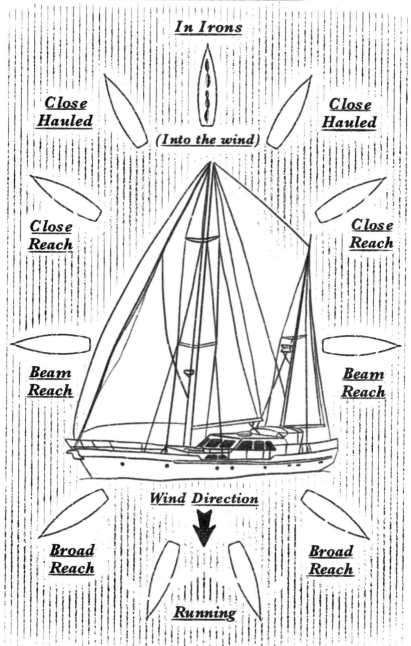

27

The Dark Sky Nation

July 2024
Island of Niue, South Pacific

Jess stood on deck as she listened to Don and Sydney engage in animated conversation following *Slow Dance*'s dropping anchor in the turquoise waters of Niue's pristine lagoon.

"Wow. Never in a million years would I imagine being on the Oceania continent," Sydney said.

"I bet you never thought you'd be first mate to a sexy South African captain, either. Have you forgotten about that boyfriend you left back on Lake Superior? Marlin. He sounds fishy."

"The only thing better about you, Don, is you don't hassle me about the number of beers I drink."

Don nodded. "Yes, you do drink like a sailor, and now I am going to teach you how to *be* a sailor—starting with the direction of the wind, which tells you what sails the boat needs."

Sydney answered, "A broad reach, beam reach, running downward, that stuff?" She flashed Don a cute smile. "I kind of get it but I know before you and Captain Reed are finished teaching me, I am going to be a great sailor. Don't forget, I have a coastal captain's license. Before the time of Columbus, nearly all sailing was coastal pilotage."

Jess joined Don and Sydney at the bow.

"I think Sydney is a natural, Don. She never experiences seasickness and has conducted repairs under the watchful eye of the captain. She's become proficient at handling the sails as well."

Sydney folded her arms against her chest. "I am halfway there, Don!"

Reaching into her shorts pocket, Sydney produced a pair of Aga's panties and tossed them to Don, who caught the lacy thong in his right hand.

"Aga left them in the dryer, I thought you should have them to sniff at night."

Don gave Sydney a sneering look. "Wise guy!"

Jess found herself genuinely enjoying the playful banter between Sydney and Don. The energy infused the boat with a sense of lightheartedness.

A blue sky stretched endlessly overhead, accompanied by the ever-present tropical breeze wisping lightly over the island, pushing puffy, cotton-like clouds off the mountain and out across the Pacific as Jess climbed down to join the others in the dinghy, telling Trinidad she had to stay on the boat. They were venturing out in search of the island's yacht club.

The water glistened under the bright sun, reflecting shades of turquoise and deep azure, as Don steered the dinghy toward the shore. Soon, he tied the dinghy to a dock where a long set of steps led to a café situated on the cliffs above.

The crew exited the dinghy and began the trek up the steps. The café eventually came into view, a charming structure with an inviting terrace overlooking the sea. The aroma of freshly baked goods wafted through the air, promising a delightful respite.

Settling at one of the tables, Jess began reading from her laptop. "Niue is a large atoll, a standalone island in the center of nations made up of the Cook Islands, Samoa, and Tonga. There are no rivers or lakes which keep the surrounding waters pristine and clear year-round. There are caves, coves, and beaches to explore. And it's nearly July, so there will be whales! Niue also has the biggest little yacht club in the world and amazingly, no one on the management committee owns a yacht."

Captain Reed looked confused. "Where the hell would that be?"

Jess gestured with her hands. "Right here, where you're sitting and eating. Behold, the Washaway Café, at the Niue Yacht Club."

Sydney was licking ketchup off her fingers from the messy burger she had ordered, when Don returned to the table carrying a tray of ice-cold beers.

"Got to love this place," Don said. "Everything is on the honor system: you write down your food and beers and then pay at the end. Anyone for a game of pool?"

Captain Reed stood up and nodded at Don in answer, and they headed for the pool table.

"I hope the captain is fairly good at the game, or he's about to be humiliated," Sydney said.

Jess looked puzzled. "Why's that?"

"Because Don is pretty much a pool shark. A regular Cool Hand Luke. I met him in a bar in Papeete, where he was hustling my Frenchman Mateo at pool trying to impress a Dutch girl named Katrina. Extremely gorgeous blond. You met her—at our dock party in Marina Taina. She's the reason Don was fire dancing shirtless, all hot and sweaty, because Katrina was watching. Unfortunately for Don, Katrina hooked up with the captain of a super yacht and sailed off to Papua New Guinea. Don beat poor Mateo every game they played, but I made it up to him." She winked. "He was a really nice guy, and his French accent—enough to drive a girl wild."

Jess handed Sydney another beer. "He *was* a nice guy, and he looked disappointed when we sailed out of there."

Sydney took a swig of her beer. "Isn't that the sailor's way: leave lovers in every port because the sea owns our heart? I intend to sail on and screw Marlin out of my head forever."

Captain Reed returned to the table. "You didn't warn me that Don is good at pool."

"He's good at drinking beer, too," said Sydney.

The four shipmates wiled away the afternoon at Niue's yacht club, eating, drinking, and swapping tales. Don was the main storyteller, but Captain Reed spun a few yarns of his own. Don crossed a few oceans, sailed around the Cape, the Horn, and survived a rogue wave where two oceans meet. He had stories of mad captains with rickety boats, life-and-death moments.

Don's younger brother also worked in their mother's catamaran business and within thirty days, he would join *Slow Dance* in Western Samoa. Captain Reed didn't need much convincing to realize he needed a full-time engineer on *Slow Dance*, so he paid for a one-way plane ticket for Don's brother, insisting on a thirty-day trial period. The two men decided to keep the news regarding Don's brother joining the crew between themselves for the time being.

The next few days were spent exploring Niue. They hiked in the rainforest, drove the dinghy into lagoons full of colorful coral, and snorkeled inside caves.

"I didn't think any coral this magnificent still existed on the planet," the captain had admitted on the second day as he, Sydney, and Jess returned from snorkeling.

Captain Reed pulled off his mask and tossed it to Jess, who had already climbed back into the dinghy. Sydney swam alongside, her long dreads spreading out in the water, making her look like a human octopus. Don remained in the dinghy while the others enjoyed the snorkel. It was apparent to Jess that Don had been well trained in customer service. He knew how to treat his owners. It was Don who took care of the dinghy before and after every outing, washing it down and checking fluids. Don made sure that certain drinks, towels, and snorkeling gear were prepared for each trip. He was a take-charge guy, assigning Sydney daily tasks, and a natural workflow began to develop between them.

Captain Reed's mood was tempered now that *Slow Dance's* autopilot and steering mechanism was operational. He had been absorbed in the malfunctions of his boat and Peter's accident. Between the repairs to *Slow Dance* and socializing on Rarotonga, he hadn't spent much personal time with Jess. Untroubled and relaxed, now, he renewed his interest, sharing wine and conversation with her late into the evening.

Jess was happy to see this side of Captain Reed return, but how long would it last?

They had been anchored in the bay for three days when the captain suggested they go explore some caves on the other side of the island. Sydney helped Don prepare the dinghy and Jess decided Trinidad should remain on the boat.

"That's a very large cave." Jess was leaning over the bow of the dinghy as Don maneuvered the boat through the arched opening. Bright sunlight filtered into the dark cavern, illuminating the surface of the water and sending beams of light penetrating into the depths until they disappeared into blackness. The light turned the water a deep blue, but everything past the light was pitch-black.

Jess wrinkled her nose. "I am going to sit this one out."

Don was prepared as usual. Pulling three waterproof headlamps out of his dry bag, he handed one each to Sydney and Captain Reed. They adjusted the lamps to their snorkel masks, placed their fins over their feet, and slipped into the water.

Jess watched as they descended deeper into the dark hole, their headlamps appearing dimmer and dimmer. She was amazed at how long they could hold their breath. She began counting, one-one-hundred, two-one-hundred . . . when something bumped the dinghy. She stood up to make sure the swim ladder was out when she saw what bumped the boat, and her heart stopped. A dorsal fin! A very large one. She let out a scream when the ten-foot oceanic whitetip shark swam through the sunlit part of the water.

"Oh no, no, no, no, no! What do I do?" Jess was trembling, wondering how to warn the others who were about to need air. Opening the locker, she pulled out the emergency paddles and extended the end of one paddle as far as it would go. Grabbing it firmly, her heart pounding as adrenaline rushed to her head, she began slapping the surface of the water on the opposite side of the swim ladder. Predictably, the shark swam to the commotion, expecting opportunity to pay off and for him to make a meal of whatever was wounded. Before Jess could drop the oar, the shark had it in his mouth and a tug of war ensued between them. As she let go, she lost her balance, falling into the water with the paddle and the shark.

There wasn't time to hold her breath and, in her panic, she swallowed water. Coming up to the surface, she was gasping for air and clutching at the lines on the dinghy—when Don pulled her back into the boat with one massive yank.

Jess lay on her stomach, unable to move, coughing and taking deep breaths to calm herself. Don started the engine while Sydney and Captain Reed helped Jess to recover.

"Almost lost my cook to a damn shark," the captain said, his arm around her while Sydney covered her with a towel.

"You in shock, Jess?" Sydney moved close to Jess to inspect her pupils.

"No, but I should be. What happened to you? How did you get back on the boat without being attacked?"

Captain Reed took his arm from around Jess. "I saw him first as I neared the surface, and he saw me. When I was young, I spent days spearfishing in the Pacific with my Hawaiian sling and faced off sharks on many occasions. This one was a big boy. He circled me and I kept him where I could look him in the eye. Then I made myself look bigger by waving my snorkel at him. I got the feeling he was going to come after me when the mad splashing on the surface drew him away."

"You saved the day," said Sydney.

Jess was still shaking but happy to be headed back to *Slow Dance*.

Calmed down and back in her galley, Jess prepared a meal of breadfruit curry over brown rice, with sliced papaya for dessert.

"Delicious as always," said Captain Reed, putting down his napkin.

Don made a face. "Yeah, but I have a request, I am at the top of the food chain and eating everything beneath me except fish. Some bangers and mash would be lovely one night, hint, hint."

Jess wrinkled her forehead. "What the heck is bangers and mash?"

Sydney pulled one of the bananas from the bunch tied to the mast. "It's sausages that look like dicks smothered in mash potatoes—a South African delicacy."

Captain Reed interrupted their banter and pointed toward the night sky. "I didn't like school very much, but if I was going to sail a boat back to Los Angeles, I had to learn astronomy. *Slow Dance* is sitting at nineteen degrees south in the tropics, an excellent spot for viewing the main Southern Cross, the Large and Small Magellanic Clouds, 47 TUC, and Omega Centauri. You can also expect to see a huge range of midlatitude constellations, including Orion, Taurus, Gemini, Cancer, Canis Major, Canis Minor, Scorpius, Sagittarius, and Libra."

Sydney stared at him in amazement. "Holy cow, I had no idea you were this smart."

Captain Reed winked. "Come on." He led her to the bow of *Slow Dance*. Don and Jess followed with Trini.

"I sailed this way from New Zealand, and in a few hours, there will be thousands of stars you can distinguish with your naked eye. Niue's skies have been observed for centuries. Star navigation, lunar cycles, and star positions have been passed down by tribal elders for generations. This is a 'dark sky nation' whose history bubbles up to the surface, refusing to lie dead in books. The islanders retell this knowledge before it is lost."

Captain Reed turned to Sydney. "Sailors today have GPS, but back when I started, you had to learn the constellations in the night sky if you didn't want to get lost at sea."

Jess loved and admired this part of Captain Reed. He continuously surprised her with his knowledge and understanding of things that were foreign to her. She never tired of their lengthy conversations about the trials and tribulations of living life on land and at sea.

Jess was climbing the rungs to the top of the pilothouse. "Come on, get in the cradle and let's have a proper stargazing love fest."

Captain Reed climbed into the sail cradle and leaned against Jess; Sydney was next, leaning against Captain Reed. Don picked up Trinidad who was barking to be included and placed her on the roof of the pilothouse.

He handed her up to Sydney and climbed into the cradle to join them. Don leaned against Sydney, with Trini in his lap. The night sea was flat and glassy. Captain Reed pointed out the midpoint of the setting Orion in the west, and they were treated to an outstanding view of the Sothern Cross. Hours later, it became impossible to tell the stars in the sky from their reflections in the water.

In the morning, *Slow Dance* lifted anchor from Niue and sailed toward the small island of Aitutaki, part of the Cook Islands chain. Aitutaki was encased in a triangular barrier reef with an incredible blue lagoon teeming with sea turtles, tropical fish, and other marine life. *Slow Dance* sailed past tiny uninhabited islands called *motus*, much like sandbars, fringed with swaying palm trees and lush white alabaster sand. Near the main village of Arutanga, they dropped anchor in Aitutaki's lagoon and rented a couple of motor bikes. Jess rode behind Don and Captain Reed behind Sydney, who insisted she drive because of the captain's story of how he crashed a motor bike in Panama and broke his jaw in two places. They spent the day exploring the island, motoring down single-lane roads through palm forests and villages that ended at white sand beaches. They stopped at an old church surrounded by gigantic Banyan trees and then continued to Ootu Beach for a late lunch at the Blue Lagoon Bar.

"Did you see that sign back on the main road?" Jess was talking to Sydney. "It said no flights on Sunday. The missionaries really did a number on these people."

Sydney was studying the menu. "Right, that guy Williams, who traveled all through these islands converting the islanders and somehow convincing them of his fairytale. They were already superstitious, so I guess it was easy until he got to Vanuatu, where the natives weren't having any of it. The first European to set foot here on this island was good ole Captain Bligh."

"How do you know so much?" Jess asked.

"It's right here on the back of the place mat!"

Jess grabbed the paper mat from Sydney. "Smart-ass."

Don and Captain Reed returned to the table with cold beer and a waitress. It had been a wonderful day, and a sort of bond was developing, although Jess could see the captain never truly let his guard down with Don. She had to admit to herself she instinctively felt the same. He was just too perfect.

The following morning Sydney was standing on the outside table cutting down what remained of the large banana stem. "We might need the mizzen during our sail to American Samoa."

She handed the shriveled stem to Don. "We'll chuck it over when we get out to sea. Before we pull anchor, I want to check all the sails, especially the headsails and the genoa. Also, we need to do a test on all the wenches."

Captain Reed stepped on deck with his coffee, and Jess followed behind carrying a tray full of fresh mango, papaya, coconut, crispy bacon, and homemade waffles with the pure Vermont maple syrup she had been rationing.

Sydney jumped over the sofa and slid into her seat. "Jess, will you marry me?"

Jess couldn't help but chuckle, but her gaze instinctively darted to Captain Reed, searching for his reaction. The question tugged at her. Would he ever consider committing to someone? Could she commit to someone?

28

Palmerston

July 2024
Palmerston, Cook Islands

Slow Dance set sail from Niue, navigating through azure waters, guided by rhythmic rising and falling swells, the autopilot pointing toward Palmerston Island. Seabirds soared overhead, their calls echoing across the blue water. The sail from Niue to Palmerston Island was not just a physical passage for Jess but a soul-stirring experience that was beginning to awaken her as she connected deeply to the beauty and vastness of Mother Ocean.

"My galley is secure, and the hatches tightened down."

"You're turning into a good little sailor, Jess."

"Why thank you, Captain." Jess tossed her dish towel over her shoulder and followed him to the outside helm.

"Come sit with me at the helm," the captain said, patting the cushion.

Jess climbed up onto the captain's chair beside him. They were sitting close, the warmth between them palpable, a silent tension mingling with the ocean breeze. The captain stole a glance at Jess, and she caught him. He was looking at her—this woman who had never sailed yet embraced the ocean with such enthusiasm. She knew he wanted to say something, but instead he let the silence stretch, filled with unspoken words.

Ten miles out at sea, they encountered a large pod of humpback whales. Jess had seen plenty of whales in Banderas Bay on Mexico's Pacific Coast, but this was *hundreds* of whales.

Captain Reed came and stood next to her. "The females usually travel in small groups with their calves, but we are in the southern hemisphere, so my guess is they're breeding. The males are breaching to warn off other males or to impress the girls."

"Do females breach?"

"Yes!" Sydney called down from the top of the pilothouse. "Females breach for a different reason: flirting, teaching calves, or when migrating. Look at all these whales!"

A whale surfaced next to the boat and rolled on its side, exposing its huge fin. "Wow, he's at least fifty feet," Sydney reported, "and probably checking us out to make sure we're not a danger to the pod."

"Hey guys, look, whales!" Don climbed up with Sydney to get a better look. "You don't see this on Lake Superior."

Sydney nodded. "No, you sure don't."

After *Slow Dance* was clear of the whales, Captain Reed prepared the fishing poles and positioned one on each side of the deck in the metal rod holders.

Jess was watching him. "You love to fish."

He turned to her. "And I love the way you prepare my catch."

Suddenly the reel made a whizzing sound and Trini began to bark. Don slowed the boat down so they could bring in their catch. Captain Reed was leaning over the rail with the gaffing hook and grabbing the fish in the gills, he pulled a large mahi up onto the deck. The poor thing was flopping about wildly, and Trini was barking, sensing the fish's torment.

"Give me some line from under the table there, Jess."

Jess handed the captain a short length of rope.

"What are you going to do, strangle it?"

"No, run down and put some vodka in a spray bottle."

When Jess returned with the vodka, the captain had tied the rope around the still-thrashing tail of the mahi and fastened the line to the helm.

He told Sydney to retrieve a five-gallon bucket from the lazarette and place it under the fish.

"This is how you kill the fish without clubbing it and getting blood and guts all over the deck."

Captain Reed took the bottle of vodka and sprayed it into the gills of the fish. Soon, the eyes bulged out and then it was dead.

"Well, I'll be damned," Don said. "All my years at sea and I never saw that trick, but then again, I hate fish so please don't ask me to clean it."

Sydney guffawed. "You're such a wuss. You puke at the sight of poop and wince at cleaning a fish. What kind of sailor are ye, mate?"

Captain Reed already had the fish on the cutting board, with the head gone and in the process of gutting it.

"I watched the old boy filet a few fish when we crossed to the Marquesas Islands," Sydney said. "He is a true master and a master baiter."

No one caught her joke, so Sydney gestured toward Captain Reed, and they all watched as he wielded the boning knife like a surgeon, cutting along the fish's body and peeling the skin off with his pliers. Next, he pulled the entire skeleton out in one tug and tossed it into the sea. Jess arrived with a stainless-steel bowl to hold the perfect filets Captain Reed cut from the mahi. That evening, they anchored off the island of Palmerston and enjoyed dinner on deck. Jess grilled the mahi on the outside barbecue, after marinating it in cumin, chili powder, cilantro, a touch of salt, and lime juice. She served it with baked breadfruit fries, black beans, and guacamole made from the large, weird avocados grown in the tropics.

"Not even a bite?" Sydney was waving a forkful of fish in Don's face. "What sailor doesn't eat fish?"

"This sailor. Now get that out of my face. No offense, Jess, I'm sure it's good. Thanks for making me the grilled chicken, it's delicious."

Sydney was still waving the fish at Don. "Tell me, Don, do you eat pussy?"

Jess and Captain Reed laughed out loud at Sydney's remark. "Ha. Very funny. Only if it's not fishy," Don replied.

Captain Reed was shaking his head. "Now children, what kind of talk is this at the dinner table?"

Jess was up before dawn. She wanted to have her coffee in solace and watch the sun rise over the tiny island. There were no cars on Palmerston, only the early morning sounds of roosters crowing and the smell of smoke from cooking fires drifting out to *Slow Dance* as the inhabitants of Palmerston awakened. The others had barely crawled out of bed when a small motorboat approached *Slow Dance*, and a voice called out for the captain of the vessel. Don and Captain Reed went portside to see who was hailing them.

"Hello, *Slow Dance*," called out a rotund man wearing a Nike T-shirt, his round belly protruding over the tops of his shorts. "I am Simon, and I'll be your host on Palmerston. Please come to the beach over there at noon." He pointed toward a spot on the white sand beach. "I invite you to lunch, Captain, my wife is preparing for you, and afterward I'll give you a tour of our island. You'll meet my family, and we also have a yacht club."

The man reached up and extended his hand and Captain Reed reached down and shook it. "Happy to meet you, Simon. Thank you, and yes, we will come for lunch."

"Good," Simon replied. "And how many shall join?"

"Myself and my cook. My other crew can settle the boat and then join us for the tour." Simon turned his boat toward the sandy beach and gave a wave as he pulled away from *Slow Dance*.

"This is going to be interesting," said Sydney. "Population here is thirty-five and quite possibly they are all inbreeds. In the 1860s, an English guy named William Marsters settled on this island. Lots of European missionaries and traders came to Polynesia in the 1900s. This guy married a chief's daughter on some other island and changed her name to Sarah because he couldn't pronounce her island name. How pathetic of him. He also brought Sarah's cousin along and bedded her as well. The horny Brit fathered children from a third wife, and between the three women, he sired twenty-three children. He left some kids in England before he split, and as of today, everyone on this island can be traced back to Billy Bob Marsters. Supposedly, they still refer to him, as 'Father.' UGH."

Don was listening while he coiled some line. "So, why didn't they name this island Marsterson or Williamson Island?"

Sydney answered, "Captain Cook landed here first in 1777 and found it uninhabited. He named the island Palmerston after Henry Temple, Viscount Palmerston."

"How do you know so much?" Don was grinning at Sydney, and she answered sarcastically.

"It's called the internet."

Thick strands of coconut and mahogany trees sheltered the home of their host. Pigs and chickens wandered freely under a canopy, supported by a large wooden mast from an ancient ship, most likely from the shipwreck they saw on the reef as they approached the island. Simon's wife was tending to the table, using one hand to secure the plastic tablecloth and the other to support the baby she carried on her hip. There were eight children of various ages assisting their mother with the dishes, silverware, and plastic cups. One of the girls looked to be about twenty or so. She was very pretty and not shy.

Simon appeared from the house wearing a new Budweiser T-shirt, also too small to accommodate his protruding belly, and clean khaki shorts.

"Sit, tell me all of your adventures and what brings you to Palmerston."

Captain Reed took a seat on one of the plastic chairs, ogling Simon's beautiful daughter who was pouring him a glass of what appeared to be lemonade.

"No, girl. Get our guests some cold beers."

The girl disappeared into the house and Captain Reed reluctantly turned his attention to Simon and his wife, who was placing platters of grilled fish, taro cakes, and steamed sweet peas on the table.

"So, Captain, why Palmerston?" Simon grabbed one of his wife's taro cakes and was stuffing it into his mouth while talking. Wiping his hands on his shirt, Simon waited for Captain Reed to answer.

"Because it was here, on my way elsewhere."

The pretty daughter giggled as she poured beer into Captain Reed's glass. She apparently liked the captain's sarcasm. Captain Reed took the young girl's hand as she placed his glass of beer in front of him. "What do they call you, and what do you do all day on this little island?" he asked her. "Do you have a boyfriend?"

Captain Reed's attention to the girl annoyed Jess and, in her opinion, he was behaving like a lecherous old man. Removing her hand from his, the girl folded her arms across her chest in a manner that said she could take care of herself. She was very articulate, and Jess thought she was far too savvy for Palmerston.

"I am Anna, and I am here visiting my family. There's a gathering in a few days for the descendants of our Father Marsters. There are thousands of us. Most of us live in New Zealand, so not many will make it for the celebration. I'm in my third year at the University of Auckland, and no, I do not have a boyfriend on the island because, sir, everyone is my cousin!"

Captain Reed chuckled along with Anna. Simon wiped some fish from his mouth with the end of the plastic tablecloth, and Anna retreated to the house, embarrassed by her uncouth father.

"I have an elder daughter who works on the big cruise ship," said Simon.

Captain Reed raised an eyebrow. "You have another kid?"

Simon answered, "Yes, and number ten in the oven. What else can you do here?" he said, as bits of chewed fish sprayed into the air. Jess was looking at Simon's wife and trying to force the revolting images out of her head. What the poor woman endured—she was basically pregnant since her first period. Jess was appeased that Anna had an alternative to her mother's life on Palmerston.

Two birds interrupted their lunch by landing on the side pole that held up the canopy.

"What kind of bird is that?" Jess wondered aloud. "They look so goofy with those bright blue feet. Are they friendly? They don't seem scared of us."

Simon's wife addressed Jess. "These are 'boobies.' They got the name because they are naturally drawn to humans, and because they're not afraid, sailors killed them easily. They are considered an unintelligent species of seabird. They fly high over the sea and when they see prey, they dive down, plunging into the deep water."

Jess listened to Simon's wife and thought she was more articulate than her husband. The older daughters were sent to New Zealand to find suitable mates and not suffer the same fate as their mother. Mrs. Simon was no dummy. Perhaps her mind was hers, even if her body was not.

Simon stood up from the table and rubbed the belly that protruded from his Budweiser shirt/napkin. "Thank you, wife. And now my American friends, it is time to show you our little village. Let's start at our yacht club."

They walked the sand path to the center of the small island. An inviting hammock was strung between two mahogany trees near the blue lagoon, and Jess could hear the gentle lapping of the sea as it touched the sand. She contemplated taking a nap in the hammock after Simon concluded the tour. The path veered away from the beach toward a large area covered by a massive, thatched roof. There were a few tables and chairs, a good-sized movie screen with a DVD player, a small cooking area, and a well-stocked bar of various liquor bottles. Simon was introducing them to another round man named Edward, who happened to be Palmerston's chief of police. The yacht club was the hub of the little island. Cruisers could eat, drink, have their laundry done, hang out on movie night, or gossip with the inhabitants of Palmerston.

Edward motioned for them to have a seat at one of the tables.

"We don't get many boats that stop here, Captain, and rarely such a grand sailboat as *Slow Dance*. I was given a tour by your Captain Don when I boarded to check all the ship documents. I especially liked your dog, Trinidad. It is a shame she cannot come and visit. The kids would be crazy for her because she looks more like a sheep than a dog." He laughed. "But we must obey the rules. Can I offer you a cold beer?"

"You can get me two beers."

It was Sydney, followed by Don. Edward gave Don an attaboy slap and went behind the bar to grab the beer.

"Your mates here were so kind to donate movies from your boat and some canned goods. Many cruisers contact me prior to arriving, and we send them a list of items the residents need from the grocery or pharmacy."

Captain Reed took a long draw off the cold beer. "I never quite know where the wind is going to take me, so planning something like that would be impossible for me. I'd most likely never make it with the goods and end up with stuff I don't need or want. But I'm happy we had some things on board we could donate to the community." He took another long swig and holding it aloft, gestured for Edward to bring him another one. The captain's mood soured, and Jess was trying to determine the cause. Most likely from boredom, but more likely because he wanted more time to talk with Simon's daughter.

The rest of the day was spent visiting some of Palmerston's residents, who survived by catching fish and placing them in freezers to sell to the ship that visited monthly. Some of the women also wove beautiful baskets, which were sent off for sale at market in Rarotonga. Simon's tour continued with a visit to William Marsters's gravesite, a visit to the church, and a walk of the circumference of the island.

In the late afternoon, Jess got her wish to lie in the hammock by the lagoon and do absolutely nothing. As she lay there looking up at the sky and listening to her iPod, Linda Ronstadt was singing, "When will I be loved . . . ?"

Me too, Linda. Me too.

Jess was awakened by Captain Reed gently shaking her. "You've been sleeping for two hours."

Looking up at him, she blinked to get her bearings and stretching her arms and legs, she said, "I dozed off; this place is so relaxing."

"Too relaxing, "he answered. "I am bored and wondered if you wanted to go back to the boat and eat some of your delicious leftovers. You know how much I like leftovers."

"Yes," she said, getting up from the hammock, "especially soggy salad."

The sun was setting when they returned to the island. Don had strung a slackline between two palm trees and was explaining a game to the group. A thick two-inch-wide line is strung taut between two poles or trees, and then people try to walk the length of the line without falling off. Currently, Sydney was having a go at it, balancing with one hand in the air while her other hand was holding a beer. Some of Marsters's descendants had arrived at the island for the gathering, and the men were cheering her on. Just short of a few feet, she lost her balance and fell into the soft sand. Several brawny, handsome brown men rushed to help her up. She was a vision in her fuchsia tank top, pink bathing suit bottom, and floral sarong tied at the waist. The dreadlocks alone were intriguing, but those big blue eyes and smile were driving the guys wild.

Don was watching Sydney with new interest that Jess perceived as alpha-male competition. A cute guy was brushing sand off Sydney's back when Don sauntered over to them. He put his arm around her waist. "Well done, Rasta girl. I'm up next, hold my beer."

Don practically ran across the slackline, not faltering once. Unfortunately for him, Sydney hadn't been watching, but instead put his beer in the sand and joined the others at the bar. No one had seen Don's remarkable dance across the slackline. Dejected, he plucked his beer from the sand and went to join the others.

Captain Reed motioned Don over. "I need you to take us back to the boat."

"Right now?"

"Yes."

As Jess was leaving, she looked back at the entire thirty-five inhabitants of Palmerston— plus eight descendants from New Zealand—sharing a wonderful evening. Naked children laughed as they chased each other in and out of the sea, returning to the fire to sit momentarily or fall asleep on their mother's lap. The air smelled of smoke, and a billion stars filled the sky overhead.

Captain Reed put his arm around Jess as they walked with Don toward the dinghy.

"This is a great place to visit, but I wouldn't want to live here."

"I wouldn't want to live here either," Jess admitted. "How do they do it?"

Jess strolled along with the captain, the remote beauty of Palmerston Island etched in her mind, a vivid contrast to the warmth of his arm wrapped around her. The waves caressed the shore, echoing her fluttering stomach, a mix of excitement and nervousness as they chatted about the charm of the remote paradise, yet how they preferred the comforts of *Slow Dance*. Though they both agreed that living on the island would be challenging, the moment felt perfect, leaving Jess with a yearning for more than just the picturesque scenery around them.

At midnight, Edward insisted he guide Don and Sydney back to *Slow Dance* with his boat because the reef was treacherous in the dark.

"All right, but it's not necessary," Don had said. "I can find my way around a bloody reef."

But after insisting a second time, Don acquiesced.

29

Boiling Over

July 2024
American Samoa

"Yes, American vessel, Whiskey, Echo, Charlie, Victor. We need shore power and a side tie: length eighty-four feet, beam twenty-four feet, mast sixty-seven feet. Last port Rarotonga, Cook Islands. Four aboard, sir."

Captain Reed was on the radio speaking to the port captain while Don and Sydney fastened large inflatable fenders to the starboard side of the boat to provide a cushion between *Slow Dance* and the dock. Jess was on the forward deck preparing the spring and stern lines to secure the boat to the dock. Her skillset now expanded beyond the galley.

Two smaller boats were already tied at the dilapidated, concrete dock, barely leaving enough space to position *Slow Dance* between them. There would be no wiggle room for a mistake.

Speaking into the microphone, Captain Reed called to Jess, "Tell me how close I'm getting to that damn wall."

Jess hastened to the bow and used hand signals Captain Reed taught her for denoting distance from a dock. She hated docking—almost as much as she hated anchoring near reefs.

She gestured, six feet, five feet, then a fist to warn him the bow was coming in too fast. Captain Reed applied the bow thrusters, and the boat straightened out. Four, three, two feet, and then an open hand signal to kill the engine. Don jumped off onto the dock with the spring line and two men from the other boats came over to assist. Captain Reed relied more on Jess to judge distance than the other shipmates.

When *Slow Dance* was secure, the crew of *Slow Dance* and other sailors introduced themselves.

"Hi, I'm Tim and this is my girl, Grace." Tim shook hands with Don and Sydney.

"Hello, fellow sailors, I'm Morgan, and this is my friend Libby, visiting from Hawaii." They were all American except for Grace, who was from Sweden. Don assisted Captain Reed with the heavy electrical cord used to connect *Slow Dance* to shore power while Jess and Sydney chatted with the cruisers.

The other sailors seemed genuinely excited to have new faces on the dock, and Captain Reed invited them all aboard for drinks. Morgan was an architect from San Francisco, living on his boat tied to the concrete wall for the past two years. Tim was from Texas and docked until a boat part arrived from California. Then, he and Grace would continue sailing on to New Caledonia to avoid typhoon season.

Sydney carried out an ice bucket filled with cold bottles of beer to the upper deck, and Jess followed with two bottles of pinot noir, real wine-glasses, a wheel of Brie cheese, crusty French bread, sliced pineapple, and the last of her delicious feta cheese and spinach turnovers.

"You sure know how to entertain. You have a freezer to carry ice?" Morgan asked Jess.

"We have two freezers and a bar with a U-line refrigerator that has an ice maker."

Morgan poured himself a glass of wine. "I would be honored if you would give me a tour, as long as it's okay. Captain?"

"Be my guest," Captain Reed replied, clearly aware of how flirty Morgan was toward Jess. Libby was cozying up to Don and it was apparent when Morgan introduced Libby as a friend that he truly meant just that.

Sydney went into the pilothouse and put on some music.

Libby had Trini in her arms. "Wow. This boat is a floating five-star hotel."

Captain Reed ignored Libby's compliment and turned to Sydney. "What's keeping Jess? Sydney, go below and ask Jess to come up. We need more wine."

Sydney went below deck to find Jess and after opening another bottle of red wine, she returned to the upper deck with Jess and the architect.

Jess filled Captain Reed's glass with wine and leaning in close so only he could hear, she whispered, "You sent Sydney to fetch me? What if I was getting it on down there? . . . I wasn't, but it was fun having someone to flirt with."

Captain Reed whispered back, "You are a free woman, Jess, as long as you feed me and keep my wineglass filled." Captain Reed turned his attention to Don. "We need to clear into port tomorrow. We're an American vessel, so it should be straightforward."

"You, Sydney, and Jess, can take the bus to immigration," Don said. "Tim mentioned there is a large market on the bus route for provisions. Would you like me to stay on the boat?"

"No," replied the captain. "We have other business, and Tim says the McDonald's up the street offers free internet to the yachties. He also said to be careful: here are wild packs of dogs roaming the streets at night and extremely dangerous. A woman was bitten last week."

Don chuckled. "No worries, I'll make a proper sjambok and show any mangy dog who is boss."

"What's a sjambok?" Sydney asked.

"It's a long whip usually made from rhinoceros hide. We use it in South Africa to drive off dingo dogs, hyenas, and lions. My dad lived in the bush and the wild dogs sometimes came around after my dog, Charlie. He was a great dog. I had him trained to sit in front of his food and not eat until I said so."

"You had a dog?" Sydney raised her eyebrows with an exaggerated look of shock. "Did you also train him not to poop?"

"Very funny, lake girl." Don grabbed Sydney and tried to tickle her under the arms.

"Not ticklish, boat boy. Now stop ignoring Libby."

Sharing drinks with the other boaters created a lively atmosphere filled with camaraderie. As the evening wore on, the captain suddenly announced he was retiring for the night. Disappointment washed over Jess as she watched him head below deck, leaving her feeling a little lonely among the bustling sailors.

As Jess lingered on deck, she caught the eye of Morgan, the handsome architect who had been flirting with her throughout the evening. His interested look was unmistakable, but Jess felt a pang of reluctance. While he seemed charming and engaging, her thoughts kept drifting back to the captain.

Don disappeared to his cabin with Libby, and Jess agreed to join the architect on his boat for another glass of wine. Sydney downed the last beer before she headed to her cabin.

Jess was on Morgan's boat sipping her wine, the soft lapping of the waves creating a soothing backdrop for her restless thoughts. The handsome architect flashed her a charming smile that sent a thrill through her. They had been flirting effortlessly, each playful exchange causing a spark. Yet, as she glanced over at *Slow Dance* her thoughts went to Captain Reed, and she was revisited by a pang of disappointment. His indifference to her interactions with Morgan stung her a bit. He had given no indication that he cared. As she turned back to Morgan, she couldn't shake the nagging thought that she wished it was the captain sitting with her. The allure of the architect was undeniable, but her heart longed for the warmth and thrill that came from Reed's presence.

"Morning, Chef."

Sydney stepped into the galley, filling her Big Gulp–sized cup full of Jess's awesome coffee. Jess was ladling buckwheat batter into the waffle maker. "You know there's a McDonald's up the street, and I'm betting you can replace that cup. It looks like it's going to start leaking any minute."

Sydney reached for one of the sausage links and Jess swatted her hand away. Sydney leaned in close to Jess and whispered. "So, how was the architect? Not so good, judging by your mood."

Jess playfully pushed her away. "Well, two things: one, he couldn't get it up, and two, I think he tried to get his entire fist in my vaginal canal."

"Sounds gruesome, but you know that's a thing, right?"

"What's a thing?"

"Fisting. It's guys who want to crawl back into the womb but can only get a fist in."

Jess made a face. "Ugh. Maybe one day I'll attract a normal male before I forget how to have sex!"

Sydney grabbed a sausage and put the entire thing in her mouth.

"Bet you wished it was Captain Reed, and I am betting he went to bed wishing you'd make the first move. Honestly, what is it with you two? I bet the captain can still get it on."

Jess gave her a disapproving look. "I think I'm too old for him. He likes younger girls; didn't you see how he looked at the host's daughter on Palmerston?"

"Well, just be glad you don't have to put up with the weird sexual stuff of my generation."

"Like what?"

"Threesomes, or having sex with two guys at the same time."

Jess smiled. "I worked for the Woodstock Festival and lived through the generation of free love. Threesomes, sure, but never an orgy. Naked people writhing together like a mating ball of snakes is disgusting."

"What's disgusting?" asked Don entering the galley for his coffee.

"Never mind," said Jess. "You don't want to know."

Don shrugged. "Jess, do you ever make food that's normal? What's in that batter, dirt?"

"So how was Libby from Hawaii?" Sydney was leaning on the counter.

"Sad, really. Nice girl who came to see her friend Morgan to take her mind off breast cancer."

"How awful," said Sydney.

Jess handed Don some links and the syrup to Sydney.

"Take this up to the table and get out of my galley, both of you."

She mulled over her brief encounter with Morgan. It lasted all of twenty minutes before she excused herself and went back to the boat, sore and regretful.

Maybe Sydney was right about Captain Reed wanting her to make the first move. She dismissed the thought as ridiculous, having seen him move on a few women right in front of her. The captain puzzled her, and she reasoned he was still hesitant regarding any committed relationship. He obviously had no problem in Mexico paying for sex or allowing Lou to have her way with him. She had enough experience to know when men behaved like Captain Reed, it was to avoid any real intimacy. She wanted sex, the intimate kind, but she also didn't want commitment. A conundrum seemingly impossible to resolve. The whole matter tortured her. Morgan was so nice and good looking, and such an incredible disappointment. What was it about her that attracted weird, dysfunctional men?

Shaking it off, she went up on deck to enjoy her waffles.

Captain Reed was in the pilothouse looking at the manuals for *Slow Dance*.

"After breakfast, let's all go together to the immigration office and stop at the market. Don and I need to go to the port and inquire about shipping new battery banks here to American Samoa. There's no duty charged to import goods for American yachts. The battery banks are huge, and I haven't changed them in twenty years. After we place the order, Don will sail *Slow Dance* over to Western Samoa with Jess. There's a nice marina in Apia where the boat can stay for a month or so. I plan on flying out of here to Los Angeles. I need to take care of some business and see my doctors. Also, I want to make certain the batteries get shipped. Don will bring *Slow Dance* back here with his brother Zack and have the batteries installed. I'll fly back to the boat with Sydney, and then we sail to Tonga."

"What? Wait a minute, Sydney is leaving with you? I am sailing *alone* with Don to Western Samoa, and Don's brother is joining *Slow Dance*?" Jess was completely blindsided.

"Let's enjoy our breakfast," said Captain Reed, "and I will elaborate."

They gathered around the outside table and Captain Reed continued with his agenda. "Sydney is coming with me because she has a wedding to attend in Wisconsin. Jess, you have become more than a decent sailor and I have every confidence you will be a great help to Don in getting *Slow Dance* to Apia. It only takes twenty-four hours to sail there. Don can handle the boat just fine. Zack is very experienced and will be our new engineer."

Sydney wiped imaginary sweat from her forehead. "Whew, that is good news. The boat needs a grease monkey, and Don gets a new slave. I need to wash my hands for the next month to get the dirt out from under my fingernails."

Don gave Sydney a look. "We all know you're going home for one reason only, to see Fish Boy Marlin, who doesn't love you back because you *drink* like a fish."

Sydney looked like she might cry. "Shut up, Don. Watch out for this guy, if you tell him something personal, he will use it against you."

Jess put her arm around Sydney. "Don't trust anyone," she said, looking directly at Captain Reed. Her mind was racing after hearing the plan. He hadn't discussed any of it with her. Unable to speak, she sat, quietly fuming.

After breakfast, the group walked to McDonald's to have an hour of internet time and saw some stray dogs on the way. Jess shuddered at the sight of them. "We can never bring Trini off the boat, at least not up here to the street—and never at night. These dogs would tear her to bits."

The bus to immigration was so small, they had to duck down just to get to a seat.

Garlands of flowers hung from the rearview mirror and lively music was blasting from the radio. The Samoans were large people, and Jess wondered how they would possibly fit in the bus and in such tiny seats, but they managed. The people were incredibly friendly and overjoyed to see Americans from the mainland. Within minutes, everyone was conversing with them. At least five fellows were talking at once explaining all the best things to do on the island. Three shy teenage boys were asking Sydney about her dreads and the wooden rings that rimmed the large holes in her earlobes. The bus traveled along the western coast of the island where the sea flowed into small inlets, hugging sand beaches so white they looked like salt. Jess observed several women swimming in shorts and T-shirts where a huge sign read NO Swimming on Sundays. Captain Reed saw this as well and commented to Jess. "Cult plus time, equals religion." Jess nodded, but her thoughts were a million miles away.

After leaving immigration, Don and Captain Reed completed the arrangements for the batteries to be received by the port authority, and the group boarded a bus for the marina.

"We really need to find a laundromat." Jess was talking to Sydney.

"There is too much stuff to wash in our little washer and dryer. The manager at the McDonald's told me there's a place within walking distance from the boat."

"Okay," Captain Reed answered. "I will go with you. Don and Sydney can prepare the boat for departure. I also need to print out our tickets when we get back to the boat. We fly out the day after tomorrow."

Jess was upset she had been completely left out of Captain Reed's plans. Don and Sydney hadn't shared with her either. Why was she being told at the last minute? For the past eight months, Captain Reed shared his plans with her, asked her advice, and now she had been completely kept in the dark. She felt a sense of relief he was leaving. It would allow her time to herself, something she hadn't had for nearly a year.

"There is a place here we really should visit." Sydney was addressing Captain Reed.

"Where's that?"

"The boys on the bus said there is a woman named Tisa on the eastern side of the island who is the only woman to ever declare herself chief. She was the only child of a great chief who passed away, and he controlled a large piece of land running along the sea. Against tradition, she took over, ruled the village, and built a resort. Tisa also went to university in San Francisco before her father died. She sounds awesome and I thought it would be cool to visit her place. It's called Tisa's Barefoot Bar."

Captain Reed thought about it for a minute. "Sure, we can all go tomorrow."

After lunch, Jess loaded several plastic bags full of clothes and bedding into the dock cart then headed to the laundromat with Captain Reed.

"I've never been inside a laundromat." Captain Reed was feeding coins into the slots of six washing machines.

"Why am I not surprised. I bet you brought your dirty clothes home after every adventure for your mother to wash."

Captain Reed put his hands in the air. "Jess, you know me too well."

Jess decided not to mention her exclusion from his plans, afraid she might yell at him. Instead, she found a magazine, settled in a chair, and waited for the wash cycle to finish. When the machines stopped, she went to find the captain for more coins. He was outside speaking to an attractive young Chinese woman.

"I see you found a new friend."

"Yeah, but she only speaks Chinese, and I can't flirt with her."

"Hmm, use body language," she said, trying not to show her aversion to his womanizing behavior. "I need coins for the dryer," she suddenly snapped.

Captain Reed handed her a roll of coins and she went inside to place a few in each of the dryers.

The only reason Captain Reed could engage for so long with someone he couldn't understand was because she was an attractive female, and the only reason the woman engaged with Captain Reed was because she was—more than likely—a working girl.

Jess folded the clothes and loaded them into the cart. Unable to hide her annoyance, she interrupted the nonverbal communicators.

"Sorry to pull you away; we are done here—at least I am."

Captain Reed gave the woman his number. "I'll see you at seven."

Disgusted, Jess rolled her eyes as the woman walked away. "How can you make a date with a woman who doesn't understand one word coming out of your mouth?"

He started pushing the cart down the street toward the marina. "By the way, how was the evening with the architect?"

Irritated, she decided to abandon any romantic feelings she may have harbored for the captain and openly express herself.

"Disappointing." She proceeded to tell him about the fisting, how she left Morgan after twenty minutes, how she felt like a magnet for strange men, and how she had never been able to have an orgasm on a one-night stand. She told him she needed to have a connection to experience sexual pleasure. She told him about a woman she worked with who was bisexual and desired her until an opportunity arose when the woman seduced her. Jess recounted the entire experience in detail and how it was one of the most erotic and pleasurable experiences in her life, and that she was quite possibly bisexual. Unable to stop herself, she went too far, the rant was in response to the anger she was currently feeling toward him. Captain Reed was listening intently to her, and when she finally fell silent, he stopped pushing the cart and turned to her.

"You continuously surprise me," he said. "If I wasn't afraid of ruining you, I'd keep you for myself, and I do want to keep you."

His words hung heavy in the air. They had ventured into similar territory in previous conversation. Jess felt a mix of confusion, hope, and fear swirling within. Could she trust him to truly see her, to understand her, to keep her safe? A wave of embarrassment washed over her. She had borne herself in a moment of upset, shown her vulnerability, and now she felt exposed and raw.

"Do you care at all about my feelings? I am trying hard to understand why you pull me in and push me away at the same time. I am trying hard not to like you so much."

His light mood turned serious. "You are very important and valuable to me, Jess. Please accept my inadequate attempt to explain why we should remain good friends. I respect you, something other women never get from me. You're lovely and intelligent. You're honest, strong, and authentic. Your mind is clear, and you can penetrate to the truth without confusion, something that makes me uncomfortable. I love your freedom of thought—how your mind is bound to nothing other than your own compass. We both have gone down the path of gaining, losing, and regaining. Jess, you give me hope, something I haven't considered for quite some time, but trust me when I say, I am a horrible boyfriend and a worse husband."

And probably a fantastic lover, she thought.

The captain continued, "Although what you just shared is intriguing," he cautioned, "let's keep this between us, or you may find Don or Sydney in your bed!"

Her laugh was a nervous and uncomfortable expression of what she had shared with Captain Reed.

The captain's words cast Jess into an emotional abyss, a bottomless chasm of ultra-confusing thoughts and emotions. She needed to pull herself together; he wanted to be friends. She spent every waking moment with him for the past eight months and she needed time away from him to reclaim herself. She needed to stop thinking about loving him and start loving herself. She reminded herself why she boarded *Slow Dance* in the first place. Captain Reed spoke the truth; he would ruin her, give her more of the same disappointments and heartache. Jess wasn't fully aware yet, but she was learning to claim her power and the day would come when they would meet on her terms.

As they neared the marina, Jess took the cart from him. "Why didn't you talk to me about your plans to leave me alone with Don? It's pretty shitty, and I am pissed no one consulted me or whether I was okay with it. You can't treat me like that. I am part of the crew, and you left me out of discussions that directly affect me." She was pushing the cart vigorously, puffing between her words, when Captain Reed pulled the cart to a halt.

"I am sorry," he said gently, "but my reasoning is that I know you so well. If I had shared the plan with you sooner, you would have thought about it until you were in a full-blown panic. I promise the trip will be smooth and Don is more than capable. Our rough trip to Rarotonga and the unfortunate injury to Peter scared you. *Slow Dance*'s mechanical problems are solved, and you can feel safe. I asked Don and Sydney not to tell you. I wanted to wait until just before I was leaving so you didn't have time to think about it too much. We all need you, and I hope you will forgive me. Do you forgive me?"

Captain Reed screwed up his face like he was about to cry.

"Push the damn cart already, you are forgiven."

She was beginning to think he really did know her better than she realized.

After an early dinner, Captain Reed showered and dressed for his date. Don and Jess greeted him in the pilothouse.

"You sure about this, Captain?" Don asked. "This woman might be luring you for devious reasons."

"I hope so," he answered.

"Don't bring a lot of cash in your wallet."

"Don't worry about me, Don. Remember, I've been here before."

"Like a century ago," said Jess. "Things may have changed since then, so be careful.

"Do you want me to tag along?" Don asked.

Captain Reed shook his head side to side. "Three's a crowd, unless it's all girls and they're naked."

Jess sighed and thought, *The man is irredeemable, so why do I like him so much?*

It was after midnight, and Jess was growing concerned. Why the hell did she worry so much about him? He was a grown man. He got himself into these situations and he could get himself out.

She was just about to wake Don when she heard the captain come aboard.

"Oh, Mom, were you waiting up for me?"

"Well, I was getting worried. Did you get what you were looking for?" she asked sarcastically.

"No," he answered. "She took me to her place, which was a room with a mat on the floor and a sheet covering the door. There were Chinese guys smoking opium pipes and other young Chinese girls."

"Huh," Jess huffed, "a brothel as expected. Hopefully, you haven't contracted an STD."

"I wanted to leave, so we left, and she took me to a bar run by rough-looking characters. I was tired by that point, so I split."

"Sounds like you were taken to the underbelly of the island. No wild dogs attacked you on the way back?"

"Nope, made it safe and sound."

Jess didn't want any further details. "You're such a shit. Now I understand how you killed your wife."

Captain Reed's gaze softened as he looked at Jess, a flicker of something unreadable in his eyes. "Angie was a good woman, and she deserved better than what I could give her. We had five wonderful years, then everything went to hell. Her cigarette habit, breast cancer, and inability to tell me how she felt, it all drove a wedge between us. She'd rather run off to her friends and cry her eyes out than confront the problem directly with me. Truth is, I sailed away many times to escape my wife, my family, and my unhealthy lifestyle."

Jess and Captain Reed stood there, locked in a silent exchange of emotions. The pilothouse seemed to hold its breath, the future uncertain but brimming with possibilities.

30

The Barefoot Bar

July 2024
Pago Pago, American Samoa

In the morning, Don opted to stay on the boat while Captain Reed, Sydney, and Jess boarded a bus for Tisa's Barefoot Bar. The eastern side of the island was even more lush than the western side. With only a few other passengers, the bus left Pago Pago and traveled along a remote stretch of highway near Alega on the island of Tutuila. Sudden glimpses of blue water peaked through dense clusters of palm trees as they made their way to Tisa's place. Finally, after forty-five minutes, they exited the bus and found themselves on a deserted stretch of road surrounded by jungle.

"This can't be right," said Sydney.

"Look, over there." Jess was pointing to a sign covered in vines that read THIS WAY TO TISA'S BAREFOOT BAR. They followed the sand path through a gate where a second sign announced they had found the bar.

"If you weren't looking for this place, you would never find it," Captain Reed said and walked out toward the beach. "There's no sign of life. The place is totally forgettable and remarkable all at the same time."

"Hey, there's a treehouse on the beach," said Sydney as she walked over to a bar situated under a large, thatched roof. Faded sports flags from colleges around the world hung randomly from the ceiling over a wooden bar. On the walls hung an assortment of international license plates and multiple posters for the local beer, Vailima. The barstools were cheap, and the bar was entirely open to the sea. They were chilling at the bar listening to the soft rhythm of the waves, when suddenly, a Bob Marley song came blasting out of the stereo system and a woman came walking toward them at a fast pace, while fastening a sarong around her body.

Jess asked, "You open?"

The woman responded, "Well, it depends."

Sydney slid off the wobbly bar stool. "Hell, you got to be Tisa, and we three salty sailors need beer."

Tisa smiled. "In that case, go sit out on the deck there by the water, and I will bring beer and a menu."

Tisa delivered the beers and poured herself a glass of white wine from the bottle she carried for herself. Pulling one of the plastic chairs up to their table, they engaged in some conversation. It was like meeting up with an old friend. Between sips of wine, Tisa chatted about her life, her travels, and the joy of a simple life by the sea. Tisa was not only a chief but an advocate for creating a conservation sanctuary in the surrounding bay. She led the charge to push for ecotourism on the island and was host to the annual Tisa's Tattoo Festival, held at her offbeat resort.

"How is the snorkeling on the reef?" Captain Reed picked up the bag he had brought along containing his fins and snorkel.

"Excellent, but the current is strong, so I suggest only going in if you consider yourself a strong swimmer."

Captain Reed gave Tisa a wink. "Jess, will you join me to make sure I don't drown out there? If you're not still mad at me, that is."

Reluctantly, Jess joined him to walk down the beach to find a good access point to the reef.

"Don't worry about Captain Shark Bait," said Sydney as Tisa watched him and Jess depart. "He practically has webbed feet."

The women laughed and Tisa poured herself more wine.

Jess sat on the soft sand watching the captain as he removed his shirt and sandals. After he unpacked his snorkel and long flippers for reef diving, he stood up and turned to her.

"Now, you are going to save me if I have trouble out there, right?"

Taking her hat off, Jess replied, "You need saving all right, and in so many ways."

He nodded agreement at her remark and entered the sea. She watched as he swam toward the reef and disappeared underwater. Moving into the shade of a banyan tree, she closed her eyes and attempted to analyze her feelings about him. She believed his womanizing was a defense mechanism to avoid any real intimacy or commitment. He did it with her, too. Sometimes interested and flirty, and other times aloof and disinterested, his attention elsewhere.

Jess felt good about herself and the way she looked. Her skin was nicely tanned, and her hair was now past her shoulders, highlighted by the sun. Pulling sails and coiling lines had toned her muscles and built up her confidence. She felt disappointed Captain Reed didn't notice her the way he noticed other women. Her feelings toward him were making her a victim—and that was the last thing she was going to allow. She would remain open and willing to take a lover when the opportunity arose.

Her encounter with the architect was a lesson to not settle for the men in her limited surroundings, and although Don exuded sex appeal, he was the kind of man who saw women as objects. Not that Don had a shred of interest in her. As she confessed to Captain Reed, sex without a connection left her unfulfilled.

Jess was trying to spot the captain out on the reef when he emerged a distance down the beach, pale and exhausted.

Walking toward her and breathing heavily, he remarked, "She wasn't kidding about the current. Geez, I nearly did drown out there."

He plopped down by Jess and laid back to catch his breath. "I need more than a beer; I hope Tisa has some decent tequila . . ."

After Captain Reed recovered, they walked back to Tisa's place in silence.

Tisa went to the bar and returned with a bottle of Don Julio, 1942.

"My God, woman, where did you get this? I am in trouble now," said Captain Reed.

The three sailors and Tisa enjoyed each other's company until the sun nearly set and Tisa announced she had to get ready for the evening Umu Feast held at her bar every Wednesday. "In a few hours," she explained, "many people will arrive for our traditional Samoan dining experience."

Jess leaned forward in interest. "What do you serve?"

"Well, the fish, chicken, and taro are cooked in an oven powered by hot rocks called *umu*. There is Kale Moa, which is like chicken curry, Sapa Sui, much like Chinese chop suey, and Palusami, made with corned beef and the leaves of the taro plant. Oka I'a is raw tuna in lemon juice and coconut cream—basically our version of Mexican ceviche. Soon the bar will be filled with tourists from the cruise ship and hotels. You should stay for the food and the party."

Captain Reed stood up and stretched his tall, lanky body. "Honey, you lost me at tourists. I am sure the food is wonderful, but I am drunk and in need of my bed. Is it possible to get a taxi?"

Tisa put her arm around Captain Reed. "Not only is it possible, but at this very moment one is outside waiting to take you back to your ship."

Captain Reed kissed Tisa's hand. "Madam, you are simply wonderful."

Tisa gave him a playful slap. "My cousin waits here every Wednesday with his taxi to take drunks like you back to Pago Pago; go now, you rogue, and take the pretty girls with you!"

Don was finishing preparations for *Slow Dance* to leave port when they arrived back at the boat. Trinidad was dancing in circles when she saw Jess.

"You look like you had a good time."

Captain Reed nodded his head as he passed Don. "Got my butt kicked by Don Julio, so I am straight to bed."

"Good fun, hey? You ladies care to join this hardworking sailor for a beer at the local bar up the hill?"

Jess yawned. "No thanks, I am not far behind Captain Reed," she said, descending the stairs to her cabin, Trini at her heels.

"I'm game, boat boy, let's be on our way," Sydney said, leaving with Don to the local bar.

Sometime around midnight, Jess was awakened by Don and Sydney giggling as they stumbled into the pilothouse. Since she had reclaimed her old cabin across from Don's, she opened her door a crack and saw Don with his hand over Sydney's mouth to quiet her giggling. Jess saw Don push Sydney into his cabin and close the door. She heard them getting it on and thought to herself, *This is going to cause trouble.* She lay awake thinking about Captain Reed wanting to keep their relationship at a friendship level, and she began to understand why.

The following morning Jess was in the pilothouse printing out boarding passes, when she saw Sydney sneak out of Don's cabin.

Don and the captain were on deck with their coffee, discussing a plan for replacing the battery banks, when Captain Reed suddenly stuck his head in the pilothouse.

"How about some breakfast for a couple of hungry sailors?"

"How does a veggie omelet sound?"

"Fantastic," the captain replied. Jess went to the galley and took out the eggs, cheese, and assorted vegetables necessary to prepare the omelet.

Sydney arrived and headed straight for the coffee pot. Filling her cup to the brim, she attempted to exit the galley when Jess put her arm across the doorway, preventing her escape.

"So, what's with you and Don? I saw you come back to the boat last night, drunk and rowdy. You woke me up, and I saw Don pull you into his cabin without your shirt. Granted, it's none of my business, and he is very sexy, adorably flirty, and a giant among players. A good lover when he wants to be, yes?"

Sydney looked down at her cup. "Like you saw, I was drunk, and like you know, when I get drunk, I do some stupid things. I am nervous about seeing Marlin. We're going to our friend's wedding together. I can't get over him no matter how hard I try. Love sucks. Leaving men in every port is much more fun."

Jess removed her arm from the doorway. "Yes, but last night's lover will not be left in port. What happened with Marlin?" Jess hadn't seen this serious side of Sydney.

"I was young and fell in love because we were into all the same things except beer. We hiked and camped, swam in the lake, made love under the stars . . . we even bought a little sailboat to sail around on Lake Superior. We had the same friends, the same ambitions, same likes—but one dislike. What he didn't like was drinking. He was really uptight when I partied with our friends. I think one of his parents was an alcoholic, and that's probably where his dislike of drinking came from. I am not one to be controlled."

"Oh really, I couldn't tell," Jess answered sarcastically. "You're seeing him again, so maybe things will be different. He's had some time to miss you."

Sydney topped off her coffee. "I am trying not to have any expectations, that way I won't be disappointed."

Jess returned to chopping the vegetables. "How'd you get so wise?"

That afternoon, Captain Reed and Sydney boarded a plane for Los Angeles and Jess was left with Don, Trinidad, a head full of thoughts, and a gut full of feelings.

"What could go wrong?"

She didn't even want to think about the possibilities.

31

Fa'a Samoa

August 2024
Apia, Western Samoa

Jess was at the helm with Don, who was thumbing through one of Sydney's Lonely Planet books. "Samoan culture is deeply rooted in Polynesian traditions with a heavy focus on family, community, and respect for the environment. *Fa'a* translated means "the Samoan Way," and a Fiafia in Samoa is an event where tribes gather for a fun evening of food, music, and dancing, accompanied by awesome displays of sword twirling and fire dancing. Western Samoa was as different as night and day from American Samoa."

"Interesting," said Jess. She pointed to the coastline. "It's so beautiful."

As *Slow Dance* was approaching Apia on the island of Upolu, Jess marveled at the lush tropical rainforest, stunning beaches, and rugged volcanic terrain. Smoke rose from small interior villages, and fishing boats dotted the seascape.

"Good thing we're coming in during daylight," she said. "Best to use the chart, Don. The channel is wide, and it should be easy to see the breakers between the reef on either side. The markers port/starboard look unreliable."

Don nodded his acknowledgment. "Captain Reed was right; you've turned into a decent sailor."

Jess lifted the receiver of the radio. "Why thank you, Captain Don, I am a good student, especially when my life is at stake. I must admit I was nervous about sailing here with just the two of us, but it was easy breezy. Plus, I get the master cabin all to myself, and I deserve it."

Don nodded agreement. "You sure do!"

Jess was on the radio announcing their arrival as Don drove the boat cautiously into the marina. Jess requested some dock handlers to assist with the lines and a dinghy from the marina to guide *Slow Dance* to their slip. Trinidad was running up and down the deck barking at the approaching dinghy.

"Trinidad, shut up! You're a yappy little shit," Don shouted.

Don handed Jess the yellow quarantine flag to send up the mast.

"You hurt Miss T's feelings when you yell at her. It's not going to make her stop barking. She's a good watchdog."

"Watchdog? That's bloody hilarious! What is she going to warn us about, darling? Fish approaching?"

Jess gave the ungroomed pedigree a pat on the head. "Don't listen to him, Trinidad, he's joking."

"One day, I'll chuck her overboard."

Jess fastened the yellow quarantine flag to the line and hoisted it up the mast. Don joined her.

"We must stay on the boat until the authorities come to us: Ministry of Health, and Quarantine first. Afterwards we drop the Q flag, raise the Samoan flag and finish on shore at Customs and Immigration."

"I hope Trini can get off the boat," said Jess. "It will be great to be in a nice marina for a while."

Don added, "I'm happy to be on shore power and give the generators a break. American Samoa doesn't compare with Western Samoa. This marina looks clean, and the water is clear." Don was looking over the side of the boat. "I can clean the bottom while we're here, or better yet, hire someone to do it. They have twenty-four-seven guards at the entrance gate, so we probably need an ID to get in and out."

Jess was looking at the boats in the marina when she recognized a few of the vessels.

"Hey, I see a few familiar cruisers. That smaller boat, *Nikkia*, belongs to the older couple from San Diego sailing around the world with their daughter Cody. They were aboard *Slow Dance* in Nuku Hiva."

Don looked to where she was pointing. "Younger daughter did you say? How young?" Jess gave Don a look.

Two stout Samoan officials arrived at the boat wearing sarongs, pressed shirts, and neckties too tight for their thick necks. They stood waiting at the dock, clipboards in hands, until Don invited them aboard, where Jess had assembled the necessary documents for their inspection. The men looked over *Slow Dance*'s previous ports of call and proceeded to inspect the boat. Don led the way, answering questions as they looked in bilges, freezers, and storage spaces. Jess had placed Trinidad in the master-cabin bathroom to avoid any potential problem of transporting an animal. Unfortunately, Don opened the door during the inspection and Trinidad popped out wagging her little two-inch tail. Shocked at the sight of the wooly pedigree, the officer commented, "My God, you have a sheep on board!"

Don's smile was more of a grimace when he returned on deck with the men and the poodle. Jess explained that Trinidad was a pure breed mini gray poodle in need of a haircut and not a sheep, although she looked very sheeplike. She handed Trinidad's papers to the men, which included her vaccination record. The men studied the documents carefully and, nodding their heads, they spoke in their native tongue about the dog-sheep. Giving Trinidad's head a pat, one of the men addressed Don: "You may bring Miss Trinidad on the island, but be careful in the night. There are wild dogs."

After clearing in with Customs and Immigration, the two sailors along with Trinidad went to explore the town. Apia was where most of the island's population lived, with its collection of small shops, street vendors, and food markets. Most of the bars and restaurants were located closer to the marina. Nearly every Samoan they passed on the street halted and stared in amazement at Trinidad.

"You sure know how to draw attention to yourself, Trinidad." Don gave the poodle a chin rub. He turned to Jess. "You ready for a beer?"

Jess nodded and they opted for a restaurant just across from the marina where Don returned with two beers and a menu.

"According to this brochure, there are some pretty nice restaurants in town." Jess was looking through a tourist guide she had picked up at immigration.

"Well, this place has a great bar, a pool table, and it's near the boat." Don set the beer on the table. "You up for a game after we order some grub?"

"Okay, but don't hustle me, pool shark. Let me win just a little and maybe teach me how to bank."

Don smiled. "My brother will be here tomorrow and then we will show these Samoan boys how to play the game."

A local man who had been watching Don and Jess interrupted their game, asking if he could challenge Don to a match. Don, of course, smugly agreed and proceeded to sink all the balls on his turn. Don liked beating the competition and it showed. Before he could humiliate the poor fellow in a rematch the food arrived at their table.

"The bartender informed me every Wednesday the bar hosts an open tournament, singles and doubles. My brother will be here tomorrow, and we'll beat the sarongs off them, maybe even win some money, whatever money is called here."

"Don't be so sure; and the money here is called tala."

Don ordered another beer, ignoring the food. Jess hadn't seen him this enthusiastic about anything except women. The prospect of a pool tournament had him fired up.

"What a gorgeous morning! I love this Apia marina, and I get the feeling we are going to have some me time."

Jess addressed Don as they enjoyed their breakfast on deck. "After Captain Reed and Sydney return to the boat, we need to be somewhere safe for typhoon season. Probably Fiji."

Don took a bite of his scrambled eggs, and taking out his iPhone, he showed Jess an app called Open Oceans. "I can install this on the main computer in the pilothouse and enlarge the charts. The program is amazingly accurate with up-to-date maps and weather forecasts. I showed it to Captain Reed, and he wants me to install it while we're here."

Jess examined the program's features on Don's phone. "Wow, that's cool. Cruising has improved greatly since Captain Reed started sailing, and I like the idea of being able to outrun a storm." Jess was grateful for Don's knowledge of modern technology and how to implement it on *Slow Dance*. It made her feel safe. She knew people were neither all bad nor all good, and she was determined to focus on Don's good points as opposed to his faults. This she would do without ever letting her guard down.

Jess's thoughts were becoming uncluttered. She gave herself permission to let the past go and embrace the present. Captain Reed's absence allowed her time to sort out and digest the last eight months of her life. She was looking forward to creating a few adventures on her own. When she asked Captain Reed about Sophia, he had been honest, saying he was going to spend time with her while he was in Los Angeles. She asked him if he was in love with her and he replied with a curt "No," but maybe he was just protecting her feelings. Somewhere inside the man, there seemed to be a conscience.

When Zack arrived in Apia, Jess noticed he was nothing like his brother. Zack was shy, self-effacing, with polite qualities that immediately endeared him to Jess. It was clear that Don, the eldest brother, looked after Zack. Don had confided in Jess about their troubled family history: their father was often too drunk to notice them, except when it was time for a beating.

Their mother's second marriage had brought them a decent stepfather, providing some stability. Don left Johannesburg at sixteen to seek adventures at sea, and Zack left South Africa at the age of nine to live on his mother and stepfather's boat in Manaus, Brazil. They supported themselves by offering charters on the Amazon River, where Zack often watched local children swimming in the river, begging to join them and always being told no because the river water contained dreadful bacteria. One afternoon, while his mother napped, Zack jumped into the shallow water to join the native children for an hour of fun that nearly cost him his life. He spent the next year in a Brazilian hospital due to contracting schistosomiasis and viral hepatitis. Zack rarely removed his shirt because of the deep pockmarks on his back, a testament to the pain he endured from infected lesions.

The first few days on *Slow Dance*, Zack familiarized himself with the engine, generators, and watermakers that were nonoperational—another sign that Captain Reed had taken *Slow Dance* to sea unprepared. It was late August, and Jess was delighted to find out she and Zack had birthdays one day apart. Jess decided they should have a dock party to celebrate, and she invited a few of the other boats to join.

Jess prepared a double-layer chocolate cake for the birthday celebration and although the party was a small, informal get-together, familiar faces made for a fun night. Don exchanged future sail plans with the other cruisers headed to Tonga and then Fiji to wait out the hurricane season. Tate, Nikki, and daughter Cody were also headed to Fiji to do the same. The men discussed possible routes to Fiji, weather windows, and open-water conditions. Jess, meanwhile, was making new friends with a man named Oscar and his girlfriend Carly, a nurse visiting from Seattle. The couple planned on taking the ferry from Apia to the island of Savai'i, the largest and highest island in the Samoan chain, and invited Jess to come along, who agreed if she could bring Trinidad. They said yes, so it was turning out to be a pretty good fifty-eighth birthday.

Savai'i consisted of six political districts. Each district was made up of villages that had strong traditional ties with one another. History, land, and kinship connected them. The island was the largest shield volcano in the South Pacific. A shield volcano is named for its low profile, resembling a warrior's shield lying on the ground. The largest contiguous rainforest in the South Pacific was also located on the island. This rainforest was dotted with more than one hundred volcanic craters and contained most of Samoa's native species.

Oscar and Carly turned out to be worthy adventure companions, never making Jess feel like a third wheel. The three spent ten days together, climbing mountain trails, swimming in deep pools under waterfalls, kayaking to smaller islands, feasting with the natives, and hiking over long swaying bridges one hundred feet over the forest floor.

Everywhere they went, Trinidad went with them, and the villagers never ceased wanting to stroke her curly fur. Most nights they slept in a beach fale, a small, thatched hut with three single beds on a sandy floor. On the morning of their last day, Jess was pulling up the covers on her cot when an enormous, saucer-sized black spider jumped out from under them with some type of giant brown seed in its mandibles. Jess was relieved to not be sleeping in the hut another night. She hated spiders. Joining Oscar and Carly for breakfast, she was relating her horrific spider story when Oscar picked Trini up and began combing through her fur.

"That was no seed in the spider's grip, but most likely a large bloated female tick. These islands are infested with them but don't worry, they are brown tropical ticks and carry no diseases. The males breed with the female, and she attaches herself in a good hiding place until it's time to give birth to literally thousands of little ticks. The males die off or are easily picked off."

Jess looked like she was about to be sick. "I thought this whole time I was getting the ticks off her, but it was only the dead males, while the bloated female was hiding somewhere?"

Oscar put Trini down on the sand. "You need to check around her anus and inside the folds of her ears. That's their favorite hiding spot."

Jess made a face. "How do you know so much about ticks? Do you have a dog on board your boat?"

"No dog," said Oscar. "I am a veterinarian."

The ferry arrived back to Apia and Jess was anxious to get back to *Slow Dance*. When she arrived at the boat, the boys were drinking beer with a new friend named Wade from Arkansas, a boat boy tending to a ten-million-dollar vessel berthed in the Apia marina.

Cody, the young girl from the sailboat *Nikkia*, was also aboard strumming guitars with Wade, who was, surprisingly, a very good musician.

Don took Jess's backpack as she boarded the boat.

"How was it? Did you get to have a threesome?"

Jess gave him a disapproving look. "That's quite a mind you've got there, always thinking from your pants. Ask me about the islanders, the culture, the rainforest."

"Nah," said Don, "the island people are fat and ugly."

Cody stopped strumming her guitar. "Not true, dude. Get your butt out here at five in the morning to see the tribal longboat guys rowing and grunting. Twenty in a boat, all buff and good-looking."

"Oh wow," said Jess. "I am glad to be back!"

Don lifted his shirt and pointed to his ripped stomach. "This is hot, and I am going to kill those guys for waking me up every morning except Sunday with their grunting."

Cody and Wade began playing and harmonizing to Bob Marley's "Redemption Song" and Jess went to grab her flute.

The next morning Jess was awakened by Don shouting for help. Wrapping a sarong around her, she came out to see what all the fuss was about. Don was in his aft cabin holding up the mattress showing Zack thousands of baby ticks crawling everywhere.

"I am going to kill that mutt."

Jess picked Trini up, carrying her to the top deck, and Don and Zack followed as she began to explain to them about the brown ticks and how after the huge, bloated female crawled off Trinidad in Savai'i, she thought that was the end of it.

"Fuck me," said Don. "The entire boat is infested. We're going to have to contact Captain Reed and get off the boat so it can be fumigated."

Jess handed the poodle to Zack. "I'll email him and let him know I'm using some petty cash to hire a fumigator and rent us a few rooms at a resort. It should only take a couple days."

Zack held Trini at arm's length. "Well, Miss Trinidad, I have just the thing for you: my electric shaver. I won't be needing it, and we are going to get all that hair off you along with all those nasty ticks. No one will think you're a sheep when I am done shearing you."

Jess found a splendid resort where they could hang out until the boat was fumigated, and as promised, Zack shaved Trinidad bald except for a mohawk on top of her head. She looked ridiculous, but she was tick-free for the first time in many months.

After a pleasant dinner, Jess, Don, and Zack sat relaxing by the pool when Oscar and Carly dropped by the resort to invite them to join them on a hike to an incredible place called "the Trench." Don invited Cody and Jake to come along as well.

Carly positioned herself on the arm of Don's chair. "The Trench is the most spectacular thing on this island, and we don't want to miss it. Be sure and pack snorkel and flippers."

Jess was trying not to notice how flirtatious Carly was toward Don, and if it perturbed Oscar, he didn't show it. How did Don do it? He was a babe magnet.

The To Sua ocean trench was a large sinkhole surrounded by lush, tropical vegetation, including palm trees and other plants. The hole was filled with crystal-clear saltwater, connected to the ocean through underwater tunnels and channels. To access the water, visitors must climb down a long ladder, which leads to a small platform where they can swim. Jess had never seen anything so awesome, and despite her fear of heights she made the climb down the steep fifty- foot ladder to the platform. Unpacking her snorkel and fins, she jumped into the water for a swim, and as she was coming up for air Zack swam up to her.

"Hey, come check this out, we can swim through the tunnels full of water, floating up to the top of the cave where there is an inch or so of space, grab a breath, and dive back down and swim through to the sea. Come on, it's so cool."

Jess gave him a horrified look. "I don't think so; caves are not my thing, and especially when they're underwater. Have fun and don't die, because we need you in the engine room. Besides, I'm climbing back up to Trini; she's barking her head off up there and the way she looks after her hair cut, someone's liable to think she's rabid and shoot her."

Jess carefully climbed the ladder out of the Trench, being sure not to look down. Trini stopped her barking as soon as she saw Jess emerge from the sinkhole. Don and some local boys, apparently endowed with an overload of testosterone, were judging the running distance necessary to jump into the Trench. Jess shook her head. "Really, Don? Is that a good idea? Are you too impatient to climb down?"

Ignoring her, Don took a flying leap into the crystalline water and Jess closed her eyes to his poor choice. A few moments later Don was waving and calling up to her.

"Don't worry, Mom, I am alive!"

Jess ignored him. She found his act of bravado unappealing.

After the group finished their swim, they spread out on blankets at the top of the Trench and Don handed out cold beers and a joint.

"Where did you get that?" asked Jess.

"From those Americans over there." He pointed to a group of young men getting ready to descend into the Trench.

"They're here on the island with about a hundred crew shooting an episode of an American reality show called *Survivor*. They're a bunch of stupid people competing for one million dollars to survive in the wild with no assistance, and just a few miles away there are hundreds of people eating, drinking, fucking, and filming them. The crew has good weed."

Cody took the joint from Don. "I've heard of that show; it's super popular in America."

32

Maka

August 2024
Apia, Western Samoa

Jess took a deep breath, inhaling the salty air, and let a smile break across her face as she watched the new day awaken over the Apia marina. An overwhelming sense of tranquility washed over her as the sun rose in a cascade of colors across the horizon. For the first time in eight months, she was on her own, savoring the freedom that came from Captain Reed's return to America. The gentle morning breeze mirrored her inner calm, opposite to the whirlwind of activity that had defined her days. This moment was hers; she reveled in the anticipation of exploring and reconnecting with herself.

Nearly every evening, Jess joined Don, Zack, Wade, and Cody for dinner, drinks, and pool tournaments at the Blue Whale across from the marina. From all the display of affection, it was apparent Cody had become Don's playmate. Jess didn't care because it didn't concern her. She was free, her only responsibility was the once-a-week boat polishing, and Don wasn't pressuring her because having a girlfriend greatly tempered his mood.

It was one of those evenings when a sensuous soft breeze gently caresses your senses, and Jess was reveling in the feeling of her new carefree spirit. She had agreed to join the others for an evening at the Blue Whale, where she spotted a young, handsome Samoan man sipping a beer and watching

Don obliterate anyone who challenged him and Zack for the doubles pool tournament. The local boy was wearing shorts, and she could see his legs were completely tattooed with black and white tribal designs. Her curiosity got the best of her, so she approached him, but before she got a word out, he spoke first. "Your crew members are very good at the game of pool."

"Yes, excellent. How did you know we were from a boat?"

The young man smiled. "The Blue Whale has been a gathering place for seamen over the past one hundred years, maybe longer. I am Maka, and you are?" He took her hand and gave it a firm handshake.

"I am Jess, chef on yacht *Slow Dance*. I hope I am not being offensive or intrusive, but I couldn't help but notice the tattoos on your legs. I've been around town and have not seen this on other Samoans. Is it cultural?"

"Yes, in Samoa, it is our tradition of applying the family *pe'a* for men, and *malu* for women. *Tatau* is inking done by hand with a fishbone—a tradition passed down for over two thousand years. The skill of the artist, or *tufuga*, learns the craft over many years as an apprentice to his father."

Jess found this fascinating. "Women have this done as well?"

Maka was looking intently at Jess, and she thought he was even more handsome.

"Yes, for women the meaning is protection and shelter, for men, it is a rite of passage, courage, respect, honor, community and pride. Every individual *tatau* tells the person's story, so copying any of these designs is disrespectful, because that is considered stealing the person's story. Not every Samoan embraces the old ways nor are they strong enough to endure the pain."

Jess was thinking about Don's comment regarding how ugly the Samoans were, and she couldn't disagree more.

"Can I see all of your tattoos?"

He lifted an eyebrow. "Not unless I remove my shorts."

Jess conjured an image of Maka without pants. "Sorry, it's just so interesting, your culture, I mean."

Maka touched her hand. "Can I buy you a beer?"

"Yes, but only if you tell me more about your customs and tattoos."

Maka was from a prominent family on the island. He was not married and according to his traditions—corrupted by missionaries—premarital sex was not okay. Maka followed many tribal traditions, but his tattooed body was by far the most intense. He told Jess his tattoos ran from his abdomen to his knees, and included his buttock, groin, and pubic area. The tattooing process began when he turned twenty-one, and he was required to abstain from meat, alcohol, sugar, and sex, even if married. If any man or woman could not withstand the agony and withdrew from the process, they wore a *tatau* around their navel area symbolizing shame. During the long agonizing days, the grandmother took care of the grandchild, feeding them, bringing water, and applying natural medicines to abate the pain and assist in their healing.

Maka shared his stories as they watched Don's challengers get defeated one after another.

"We don't get many tourists here, and the sailors show little interest in our culture—other than drinking in the bars and seeking to steal our *tatau*."

"What exactly is a *tatau*," she asked, "and how is it stolen from you?"

"As I said, a *tatau* represents our family's tribal tattoo; it is our story. For decades, white foreigners have come here, seeking to copy these tribal designs. And again, to copy them is to steal the family story, a story they know nothing about. I like that you show so much interest in our way of life."

Jess finished her beer. "In the past, wherever I traveled, I always had a curiosity for the people, their culture, and the food, of course. I wasn't just passing through. I've learned that people are basically the same everywhere. They love their families and want their basic needs met."

"You are a wise woman, chef from *Slow Dance* yacht. If you are free tomorrow, there are some interesting places I would like to show you on my island, if you agree, of course."

Jess made a face. "It doesn't involve swimming in caves or looking into volcanos, does it?"

Maka smiled. "No, it is the home of Robert Louis Stevenson, who lived on our island and wrote his famous book *Treasure Island*. Then on to the monument of King Malietoa, who long ago ended the custom of cannibalism."

Jess could hardly believe it . . . Robert Louis Stevenson, *Treasure Island*, surely there was meaning to this. It was too much of a coincidence.

"This is amazing, Maka. *Treasure Island* is a very special book to me, and yes, I am free tomorrow."

His smile made her stomach flutter. "I will tell you all about it when we stop for lunch." He stood up. "May I walk you to the marina?"

"Of course, thank you."

Jess was enjoying Maka's attention. She was acutely aware of their age difference but saw no harm in letting a local boy show her his island, especially the home of Robert Louis Stevenson.

Maka walked Jess to the gates of the marina and took her hands in his. "Ten o'clock?"

"Perfect," she replied.

He watched her as she walked down the pier toward *Slow Dance*.

Don and Zack returned to the boat, with Cody, to find Jess on deck with Trinidad.

She was deep in thought when Don interrupted her. "Good evening. Who was the local boy I saw you cozying up to? Best be careful he doesn't eat you, darling. In a bad way that is." Don was amused by his joke. "These natives only recently gave up cannibalism, you know."

Jess wasn't amused. Maka had more class in his little pinky than Don had in his entire body.

"Ha. Don't be ridiculous. His name is Maka, and cannibalism was abolished centuries ago."

Don gave Jess a pat on her back. "Well, it's about time you get yourself a good shagging, so good on you."

Then he disappeared below with Cody, and Zack sat down with Jess.

"Don't pay attention to him, he can be a real ass. Maka looked like a nice guy, and not everyone is out to get laid. Don wouldn't know real love if it fell on his dumb head."

"You're right about that; he's a top player among players. I am off on an outing with Maka in the morning. He's going to show me some neat stuff on the island. You okay to make your own breakfast?"

"I never eat breakfast, just coffee, and Don has beer for breakfast."

At ten sharp, Maka arrived at the front gates of the marina. He was riding a Harley, which surprised Jess.

"Good morning, do you know how to ride on a motorcycle?"

"I sure do," she said as she climbed behind Maka and tucked her hair under the passenger helmet.

"Okay, first stop is the home of Robert Louis Stevenson."

The author's former home was perfectly restored back to its glory days with some of Stevenson's work and family memorabilia on display. Maka held her hand—which she thought was very sweet—as they toured the museum estate, now supported by donations from around the world. They strolled through the lush gardens, coming to rest on a bench under a huge sprawling Banyan tree.

Maka put his arm around Jess. "I come here often," he told her. "My ancestors lived and worked here for the author, from 1888 until he died in 1894. He was not in good health. The Samoans had deep respect for him. He is buried at one of our most sacred spots on top of Mount Vaea overlooking the sea."

Jess sighed. "My mother died when I was a very young girl. Before she was too sick to speak, I would lie with her, and she would read to me. My favorite book was *Treasure Island*. I made her read it many times while she still could. Bringing me here has been profoundly moving. It brings back the best of my memories."

Maka ran his thumb down her face. "That is very sad. To have no mother is unthinkable. Did your grandmother guide you?"

"My grandmother Rose was a strong woman, but she was a woman of few words. I can't recall her teaching me anything except how to sew. She was raised in a wagon in the 1800s in upstate New York. When she was sixteen, she worked as a maid at the estate of a wealthy doctor. He had one son, Charles, who fell deeply in love with my grandmother. His father forbade them to see each other, but Charles married Rose, and his father disowned his only son. Despite the hardship, my grandparents owned land and several houses. My father's parents died before I met them."

Maka listened with interest. "Who were your ancestors?" he asked.

Jess shrugged. "It doesn't work in American culture like Samoan culture. All I know is I am Scottish, English, Irish, and Dutch."

Maka raised his eyebrows. "So many voices to speak with. Your mind must be very busy!"

Jess felt herself smile. She found him charming.

After the Robert Louis Stevenson estate, Maka drove to a two-story monument dedicated to the first king who abolished cannibalism on the islands. Standing under the huge statue of a man holding a younger man in his arms, Maka relayed the tale of King Malietoa.

"It was a shameful custom practiced by my ancestors throughout the islands. The villagers would send their young men to be feasted upon by the king. This was considered a great honor and sacrifice. One day, a young man was wrapped in palm leaves, having been prepared for the fire; he was crying that he did not want to die. The king's son took pity on the man and exchanged places with him. When they brought the boy to the king, he saw that it was his very own son. Crying out in horror, he asked why his son was wrapped to be sacrificed. His son replied, 'Why should the young men of the village be any different than your own son? It would honor me to be sacrificed like so many others.' Right then, the king declared that from that day forth, his people would eat fish and never feast on human flesh."

Jess was listening to Maka tell the story, watching his body movements and paying particular attention to his mouth, which she thought was very sensuous.

"That's quite a story."

"It is," Maka replied. Turning to Jess then, he asked, "May I kiss you?"

Jess didn't know how to respond, and before she could answer, his mouth was on hers, and she was kissing him back.

33

Survivor 24

August 2024
Apia, Western Samoa

In the soft glow of the late morning sun pouring into the portholes, Jess felt a rush of exhilaration coursing through her body. After a tangle of emotions tied to the captain—his enigmatic nature always leaving her in a haze of uncertainty—she let herself connect with Maka, whose warmth and charm had captivated her. As they lay together, Jess felt a sense of liberation she hadn't experienced in years. Despite their age difference, there was a beautiful innocence to their encounter, and for the first time in a long while Jess truly felt seen and cherished. The weight of past feelings for the captain faded away, replaced by the tender afterglow of shared intimacy. Jess opened to love in a way she thought was lost to her. This lovely romantic experience had reignited a spark within her, reminding her of the joy that comes from embracing life's unexpected pleasures.

"Jess, there are two producers out here who want to discuss chartering *Slow Dance* for the TV show *Survivor*."

Don was knocking on the cabin door. Jess fashioned her sarong into a dress and went to meet the men who were waiting on deck. The men introduced themselves, explaining they were filming episode twenty-four in Western Samoa.

One of the producers addressed Jess. "Some of our crew met Captain Don at the Trench, and when we learned what a fabulous sailing yacht you have, we were so excited. We desperately need an awesome reward for the winners of the show's next challenge. As you know, there's not much to work with on this island, except beautiful natural wonders; yet the contestants don't want more nature, they want creature comforts and food!"

"There are beautiful resorts here," said Jess. "Why not pamper them at a luxury resort as their reward?"

The producer continued, "Any reward must be carefully monitored so no cheating takes place. A reward at a resort would be impossible to control, whereas your boat could be easily staged and monitored. We need to ensure the contestants do not hide any extra food or take any outside items like a knife, fishing lines, a lighter, or anything useful to help them survive."

"Makes sense," Jess replied. "We will have to discuss the potential charter with our owner and get back to you."

"What is the timing and how long would you need to charter the boat?" Don asked. "And, where on the island do you need the boat anchored for this gig?"

"Not far from where the ferry comes in," one of the producers said. "Maybe three miles that way." The man gestured to his left.

"Well, that's bloody useless," Don replied. "Let's do this when we get more details from you. We can take you in our dinghy up the coast, so you can show me exactly where *Slow Dance* would anchor."

The men shook Don's hand after exchanging emails and telephone numbers.

"Oh yeah," said Jess. "Don't you want a tour of *Slow Dance*?"

Don grimaced at Jess and whispered, "Everything presentable down there? All the whips and chains put away?"

"Ha ha, very funny."

Just then Maka came up from the cabin.

"I have to get home before my father sends the cousins out looking for me." He gave Jess a kiss as Don disappeared into the pilothouse where the TV producers were waiting for their tour.

Don possessed many talents, but negotiating a Hollywood deal was not one of them, so Captain Reed asked Jess to act as a liaison between himself and the producers. Captain Reed phoned from Los Angeles after receiving the email about the potential charter and Don had the speaker of his iPhone turned up. "Understand, Don, if they want *Slow Dance*, they can pay for her. It's not every day you come across a boat like *Slow Dance* in that part of the world. They're darn lucky she's there to save their show."

Don shook his head. "That's a huge amount of money, mate, for twenty-four hours."

Captain Reed sounded annoyed. "She's worth every penny. I emailed Jess the contract, and she has their banking information for the deposit. As soon as the deposit clears, they can start filming. Based on the contract I signed, three girls who won the reward are to spend the night aboard *Slow Dance*."

Don perked up at the mention of three girls.

Captain Reed continued, "Our chef will prepare a dinner for the three contestants while you guys tend to the boat. The film crew, along with the host, will be interviewing the girls during their meal. First, they are allowed to shower and put on clean pajamas, then Jess will wash their clothes. All the drawers and the medicine cabinet in the master cabin need to be completely emptied. The film crew will provide shampoo and conditioner that have no labels. All three girls are to sleep in the master cabin together. There will be a twenty-four-hour security guard to make sure no one comes out or goes into the girls' cabin. Oh, and no photographs."

Jess handed to Don the signed contract Captain Reed had emailed.

"Fuel and use of our dinghy?" Don asked.

"All included in that huge charter fee you were commenting on."

"What about me?" asked Jess.

"What about you?" Captain Reed answered in a snarky tone.

"My chef skills are required to prepare these girls a feast as well as wash their clothes."

"You're a chef, aren't you?" he asked.

"Yes, but this is catering and laundry."

Captain Reed sounded impatient. "You will get bonus pay, in cash, when I get back to the boat. Good luck, and let me know how it goes," he finished and hung up.

Jess thought the captain was curt, bordering on rude. He was probably with Sophia.

Jess was wearing her white chef coat with the double rows of round black buttons, and a green bandana held her hair to keep it out of the food. The girls had requested steak, mashed potatoes, asparagus, a mixed green salad, and cheesecake topped with fresh strawberries. Zack accompanied Jess into town to procure the ingredients for the girls' feast.

The following afternoon, Don and Zack transported the three girls to *Slow Dance*, along with the film crew and their colossal amount of equipment. The host was the last to arrive as a helicopter flew overhead filming *Slow Dance* from the air. The three lucky contestants looked pale, listless, and exhausted when they boarded *Slow Dance*. The shower and fresh clothes restored them to life. The girls lounged on the bow of *Slow Dance* for a photo shoot, and afterward were seated on the outside deck for the excessively lavish meal Jess had prepared.

When the food arrived, they were transformed into giddy, chatty besties on a tropical vacation. Jess was instructed to carry each course down the portside of the boat and place it in front of the girls. The camera followed Jess every time she delivered a dish to the contestants, and every time they gasped dramatically in gleeful delight. The host sat across from them asking questions and inquiring what future strategies they were devising to win the game. After the cheesecake was consumed, the interview concluded, and the lights, cameramen, and action were taken off the boat. The three contestants were escorted to their cabin after a pat-down to see if they were hiding food or silverware. The security guard posted himself in the pilothouse where he could keep an eye on their cabin door.

Jess was cleaning up in the galley when Don and Zack returned with the dinghy.

"Any leftovers?" asked Zack.

"A little," said Jess. "Those poor girls were starving, and their clothing was disgusting. I had to wash it four times to remove the smell of campfire smoke. I would think if you were going to be in the jungle, you would wear something useful, like water-resistant pants that unzip into shorts. These chicks have Daisy Duke shorts, little halter tops, and rubber flip-flops."

Zack was stuffing a piece of filet mignon into his mouth. "That's the point. They want sexy girls so people watch the show. Did you see the helicopter flying over the boat today?"

"No, but I sure heard it. I was stuck down here in the galley. You know, galley slave.

Captain Reed sounded excited there were three gorgeous girls sleeping in his bed."

Don tipped his head to one side. "We won't tell him who else was in his bed while he was gone," he said, and he gave Jess a wink. She hadn't thought about how Captain Reed might react to her taking a lover to his bed.

It had been a week since Jess spoke to Maka, but when *Slow Dance* returned to the marina there was a letter waiting for her. It was an invitation to join him at his grandmother's home for dinner. The letter read, "You can't say no. Pick you up Wednesday at 4 o'clock."

Jess felt apprehensive about meeting his family. She had only spent one night with him and meeting them seemed weird in every way. She was certain they would kill her if they suspected she had sex with him. Major taboo. She was disappointed in herself for sleeping with him, but dang, she missed having a man pay attention to her, and pay attention to her he sure did. It also disturbed her that she was twenty years older than Maka, and in a few short weeks she would be sailing away forever. The memory of his gentle and sensuous lovemaking erased any regrets.

As promised, Maka arrived at four.

"Hop on and hold on tight," he told her.

After a bumpy ride over muddy trails Maka brought the bike to a stop. He opened the side pouch and pulled out a basket of food and a bottle of red wine. Maka took Jess's hand, leading her down a path that ended in a magical place where a waterfall cascaded over a limestone cliff into a deep pool surrounded by lush jungle. The pool flowed into a meandering river making its way down the mountainside through green fields and palm forests. Maka spread out a blanket, opened the wine, and handed her a glass.

"This is a very special place for me, and I wanted to share it with you. This is where I come to talk to my ancestors, to think, and to make serious decisions for my life."

Jess was taken completely by surprise. "Is your grandmother about to spring up from the water?"

He gave Jess a mischievous look. "I wanted to surprise you, and of course I wouldn't bring an older American woman to meet my family. They would not approve and kill us both!"

She smiled and touched his hand. "Thank you for sharing this with me, it's breathtaking."

"In Samoan culture, whichever spouse dies first, they are buried on the family land, but aboveground in a crypt. This is so every family celebration can be shared with them. When the other spouse dies, the bones of the first are taken apart and polished, then placed in a sacred cloth to be buried with their mate. Now both are together forever, sharing in all the family celebrations. This is how we are in love and death."

"Are you planning on killing me?"

"Certainly not." Maka laughed. "I am planning on loving you one last time."

Jess was suddenly guilty. She didn't belong here with him and felt as if she were leading Maka astray by causing him to break his vows and traditions. Changing the subject she asked, "So, what did you bring in that basket of yours?"

He began unpacking the food. "Palusami, which is baked coconut cream cooked inside coconut leaves. Oka is raw fish in coconut cream with lime, chili, and onions; and this, this is chicken cooked in the *umu* oven."

"It looks delicious, and I love learning about new foods almost as much as I love eating them."

Maka laughed and handed Jess a Palusami.

After they had eaten, Maka stood up and suggested they have a swim. Jess watched him as he removed his shorts and T-shirt, admiring his muscular form and the tribal tattoos that covered his manly body. He was beautiful. She contemplated the distance between their worlds, knowing after this evening she would never see him again. How strange her culture must seem to him.

Maka was never allowed into the marina unless she or Don were with him. To the white people, he was simply an uncomfortable unknown.

"Come, let's have a swim!"

Jess removed her clothes down to her panties, and Maka stood admiring her. He picked her up with his strong arms and tossed her over his shoulder. Holding her tightly, he jumped into the crystal-clear water of the pool. She was giggling at his playfulness. The water was surprisingly warm as they held onto each other, their lips meeting in a passionate kiss.

The sun was setting as Jess and Maka climbed out of the pool. Maka picked up the blanket and wrapped it around them. He led her up the hill to a small clearing in the palm trees. After spreading the blanket on the soft earth, they lay down.

Maka pulled her into his arms. "When you look up through the trees, you see all the people who have gone from this life and are now stars," he said. Turning to Jess, he ran his fingers along her cheek and brushed his lips across hers. "I will tell you a famous Samoan love story about two lovers from warring tribes, forbidden to be together. They risked their lives to meet here, in this place, every full moon. They swam naked by the light of the moon and loved each other through the night. One night, his lover failed to come. It was later revealed that her father had married her to the son of a chief on a distant island in exchange for keeping the peace between the tribes. The boy never married, and every moon he would come to this place to mourn the loss of his love. There is even a song about this story."

Maka began to sing the sad ballad of lost love, and Jess was surprised at what a lovely voice he had. The song was their song, much like the lovers in the story, circumstances not allowing anything but this perfect moment together. She was beginning to understand that love was in oneself. If you look for love to be given to you by another person, you will never find it. Love is your own responsibility; it starts with you.

Bathed only in moonlight, and filled with desire, they released all their passions to one another.

It was late when the Harley pulled up in front of the marina. Jess climbed off the bike, and Maka followed. They stood embracing, looking into each other's eyes. She tried to imprint his face in her mind so she could recall the memory. Jess began to speak, but Maka put his fingers to her lips. He took her face into his hands and kissed her forehead. Then he climbed onto the motorcycle and was gone.

34

The Return

August 2024
American Samoa

Jess stirred awake, her heart heavy with a bittersweet ache. Last night with Maka had been a beautiful escape, a moment of pure connection, something necessary for her to let go and immerse herself in the lovemaking. She was grateful for the lesson Maka taught her about love and self-acceptance. She reflected on how their short time together helped her embrace the parts of herself she long neglected, igniting a spark of confidence and joy. But now, the reality settled in; their paths would never cross again, but the impact of their connection would remain a part of her journey. Jess dislodged any sad thoughts, showered, dressed, and joined the South African brothers on deck.

"Good morning, Chef, and good morning to you, too, Miss T." Zack was pouring himself a cup of coffee, and Trini was wagging her little tail as she moved in and out from between his legs.

"She really loves you, Zack. That's saying something, because Trinidad doesn't care for most men except Captain Reed. Wait until you see her humping his arm. You'll pee yourself laughing. He is the only one she does that to."

"No way," Zack exclaimed. "I can't wait to see that. Miss T, you naughty little girl."

Don stepped into the galley and interrupted the conversation. "Morning, mates. Happy to have our cook back, all sexed up with a smile on her face." Don put his arm around Jess. "I swear you are becoming a true sailor."

Jess took his arm away and grimaced. "Shut up. I am as old as your mother, and you shouldn't be speaking to me that way."

"Okay," Don said, "point taken. Now to serious business. The batteries arrived in Pago Pago, so we are leaving here in two days. I arranged for two mechanics to swap out the old batteries. Captain Reed and Sydney fly back to Pago Pago in two days."

Zack was making a pouty face as he picked up Trini.

"I hope we don't have to dock in that horrid place for very long, Miss T. I've heard there are packs of savage dogs wandering about." Zack was a sweet, happy-go-lucky kind of guy, and although he hadn't been on *Slow Dance* very long, Jess was picking up on the dynamics between him and his brother. On more than one occasion Jess overheard Don speak to Zack in a condescending tone because like their father, Don imagined it would toughen Zack up, the way their father toughened him up.

The next few days were spent preparing *Slow Dance* for the sea, and on their final evening in Apia, Cody and Wade joined them for one of Jess's fabulous dinners, playing their guitars after the meal. It was a pleasant evening with good food and music. Jess was surprised that Don was still hanging out with Cody, but then, not many yachts docked in Apia, limiting the potential pool of available females. Jess was in the pilothouse when she saw Cody slip off the boat with a squeeze and a pat on the butt from Don. Jess heard her say she wasn't sure where they might meet up and guessed maybe Fiji.

It only took one day to sail the forty miles from Apia to Pago Pago. The same boats and sailors were still tied to the concrete wall. Greetings were exchanged, and Zack was introduced to the group. After securing *Slow Dance*, everyone gathered around in folding chairs to hear Don's stories about Western Samoa and the *Survivor* TV shoot on the boat. Jess baked off some Brie toasts, and the crusty treats made the dock smell like a French restaurant. Grace contributed homemade hummus with crackers and cut vegetables. Morgan put beer on ice, and Jess stayed busy in her galley, retiring early to avoid Morgan.

The days that followed were all work and no play. Jess was surprised by the size of the batteries being replaced and the enormous effort it took to switch them out. Two stout Samoan men, weighing close to five hundred pounds each, arrived at the boat with the replacement bank of batteries. The twelve batteries, each weighing over two hundred pounds and standing four feet tall, were no easy task to replace. She had no comprehension of where these batteries belonged or how the large men were going to maneuver around the engine room to replace them.

Removing and installing them took the entire day. Don regained her respect as she watched him oversee the operation. He may not have a head for business but more than made up for it with his ability to give orders.

While Jess was busy polishing teak and getting the inside of the boat ready for Captain Reed's return, Don washed the boat down and polished the outside. Zack organized the toolbox in the engine room and, as directed by Don, painted the engine-room trim dark blue from its original white. Don wanted to surprise Captain Reed and earn his praise, but Jess knew Captain Reed would not care about the color of the trim. What Captain Reed cared about was improved maintenance and organized boat parts in the bilges. It was clear to Jess that Don focused on all the wrong things, consistently evading her suggestions that *Slow Dance* needed the bilges cleaned out and boat parts inventoried and organized. He spent too much of his time in Apia, drinking and playing pool at the Blue Whale. It was apparent to Jess that Don was missing something underneath his exterior layers of confidence. Thanks to "Mr. Shit," Jess had firsthand experience.

Travelers were exiting the terminal at Pago Pago International Airport, and Jess was looking for Captain Reed and Sydney. Suddenly, she saw Sydney pushing a huge cart containing several large boxes and suitcases.

"Gosh almighty, what did you bring back with you?" Jess put her arms around Sydney and gave her a big hug.

"What about me?" said Captain Reed, holding his arms out. Jess gave him an uneasy embrace. She was experiencing a mix of emotions on his return. The last time she spoke with him, he was distant and cold.

"Don borrowed a truck from one of the Samoan guys who replaced those ginormous batteries, and good thing, because you have a lot of stuff. What's in those boxes anyway?"

"Three collapsible bikes for the boat," said Sydney. "We can use them to get around the marinas and villages."

Don and Zack greeted them at the ramp, along with Trinidad, who was wiggling and barking excitedly.

"You must be Zack," said Captain Reed extending his hand.

"Yes sir, it's nice to finally meet you. It's a very fine vessel you have, and thank you for having me aboard."

Trinidad ran to greet the captain, dancing in circles around him.

"Oh my God, T," said Sydney, "what have they done to you? Honestly, though, I kind of like the mohawk. I think we should dye it pink."

Zack was officially introduced to Sydney before taking the heavy cart from her. He was placing the boxes and suitcases into the back of truck when Don opened the cooler and pulled out a couple beers. He opened them with his lighter and handed one to Captain Reed, who promptly refused it.

"What's this?" the captain asked.

"It's a family tradition with us," said Don. "Whenever we fly home our mum or dad meets us at the airport with cold brews."

Zack was chuckling as he opened a beer and lit a cigarette. Jess could see Captain Reed's mood turn dark.

"Sounds like your family is a bunch of alcoholics." He turned to Zack. "Put that cigarette out. Didn't Don tell you about smoking on the boat or anywhere near me?"

Zack tossed the cigarette on the ground and stomped it out. He dumped the rest of his beer and put the bottle back in the cooler.

"I think it's a great family tradition," said Sydney as she opened one of the beers and chugged it down. *That's Sydney*, thought Jess, *always lighting up the situation.*

The other cruisers welcomed Captain Reed and Sydney back to the dock and the guys gave Zack a hand with unloading and unpackaging the bikes. Captain Reed was eager to look at the new batteries and headed straight to the engine room with Don, while Sydney and Jess unpacked the spare boat parts brought from California.

"How was your trip home?" Jess asked.

"Kind of a bust," said Sydney. "Mutual friends of ours got married, so Marlin and I went to the wedding together. It was outside by a lake, and everyone camped out that night."

"Sounds nice," said Jess. "So, did you rekindle your flame?"

"It was going swell before the attack of food poisoning set in. Everyone who ate the chicken pasta salad spent the night pooping and puking in the woods. Not exactly romantic. I saw him a few times while I was there, but he made it clear we are no more."

Jess put her hand on Sydney's shoulder. "I am sorry, but you're like a cat. You'll land on your feet."

Sydney made a meowing sound. "I got even with him by having a threesome with his best friend Grant and his girlfriend Lilly."

"Goodness," said Jess.

"I also went to a nudist resort in Palm Springs with Captain Reed. Bunch of black guys followed me around because of my dreads and big booty."

Jess was surprised to hear this, and although she was curious to know more, she didn't show it.

Don and Captain Reed were coming up from the engine room when Don asked the captain how he liked the dark blue trim. Jess could tell by his expression Don was going to be disappointed.

"The batteries were a tough job, but after twenty-five years, they were due to be replaced. Good job on that, Don, but blue is my least favorite color, and I want you to repaint the trim white. Next time, ask me first."

Don closed the engine-room door. "Right, gotcha," he said, and he got off the boat to help Zack assemble the collapsible bikes.

"Gee, Dad, you were a little hard on him, don't you think?" Sydney was holding up a box of fuel filters for the 6-71 Detroit diesel engine. "Where do these go?" she asked Captain Reed.

"Fuck if I know. In a bilge somewhere—ask Don and the engineer. Hopefully, they have been organizing and maintaining the boat in my absence."

Jess took a deep breath, knowing her perceptions were correct.

Captain Reed knew the boat was not organized, but he never discussed his expectations with Don. He relied on Don to be in charge and manage the details of the boat so he could be the wealthy yacht owner who flew back to a clean, well-maintained vessel. Don was a good sailor, and a lousy organizer. He was, on the other hand, very good at technology, and the Windguru program he downloaded onto *Slow Dance*'s navigation system greatly pleased Captain Reed. Jess was relieved to see the tension easing a bit between them. She wondered if he would ever find his perfect boat boy.

After a good night's sleep, Captain Reed's mood was much improved, and after Jess's fine breakfast of pancakes, sausages, papaya, fresh strawberries, real maple syrup, and her fabulous coffee, they all took turns riding the new bikes around the marina parking lot. Sydney put Trini in the basket on the front of her bike and peddled her around the lot. The other cruisers were amused at the sight of the little shaved poodle, ears blowing back, a curly mohawk atop her head.

After lunch, the captain called them all to the pilothouse.

"I've been looking over the charts with Don and decided to sail from here to Vava'u, Tonga. We must reach Fiji before typhoon season. I once sailed to Tongatapu, the capitol of Tonga, and met the head chief. He drove around in a big 1957 yellow Cadillac convertible. It was a fun time. I've decided to take that route. Come, have a look." Captain Reed gestured to the chart. "Tonga is a group of islands. Many of the smaller islands are uninhabited atolls less than seven hundred feet above sea level. We'll sail to Neiafu, and then into Vava'u and anchor here in this bay." He put his finger on the map by a small dot surrounded by blue. "It's time to get out of this shithole marina, kids."

As Jess listened to Captain Reed, she felt a rush of excitement filling her with a sense of freedom she hadn't felt before. She recalled her grandmother Rose's saying: "Everywhere I go, there I am." She finally understood what that meant. Wherever you travel, you are still you, and Jess was beginning to realize that real change came from within. Now, as she listened to the captain talk about their sail plan, her heart raced with anticipation. The thought of sailing on with him exploring unknown places stirred something deep within her. Her feelings for the captain remained complicated, but the prospect of discovering new horizons alongside him filled her with anticipation. She looked forward to the adventures that awaited both.

35

A.W.O.L.

August 2024
Vava'u, Tonga

Captain Reed was pointing to the billowing sails, attempting to explain wind direction to Jess.

"The wind is like a dance partner, always changing, always leading us in a different direction."

His voice was filled with the wisdom of someone who had spent a lifetime on the sea.

Placing his arm around her, he said, "You see how the sails catch the breeze from the portside? That means we're sailing close hauled, with the wind coming from the northeast."

Jess nodded thoughtfully, her eyes never leaving Captain Reed's face. There was a warmth between them, a connection beyond friendship or professional camaraderie, but neither dared to voice those unspoken feelings simmering beneath the surface. Jess had to admit she missed him. His quiet strength, his unwavering resolve in the face of the unpredictable sea. Neither made a move, each held back by fear and uncertainty, by the unspoken rules that governed their roles on *Slow Dance*.

Jess listened to the captain, but her thoughts were on her young Samoan lover. A wave of sadness washed over her as she wished she could open the captain's heart the way he had opened hers.

Captain Reed continued, "If the winds are high, we utilize the jib, because it's small and controls the amount of wind we want to take into the sail. If the wrong sail is up in fierce winds, you can lay the mast down on the surface of the water, and if that happens it's a real shit show. If *Slow Dance* catches a downward wind—and she will—the spinnaker sail goes up. A spinnaker is used to sail off the wind; in other words, it's set forward of the mainsail and balloons out, flying in front of the boat. The sail has a smooth round surface and is tight at the edges to hold its form when the wind fills it. It pulls the boat forward instead of pushing her from behind. You'll see when we put it out."

Jess was continually surprised at how much she had to learn about the wind and the sails. She was genuinely interested and totally confused. Moving to the rail, she looked down into the water. "Thank you for explaining the wind and sails. If I am going to be out in the open ocean, I should know about such things. I had no idea how much I would come to love it."

"Me too," said Captain Reed as he picked Trinidad up and put her on his lap. Moving away from his feelings, he changed the subject. "Trini, you are a sight for sore eyes, especially with this new haircut of yours."

When Sydney finished assisting Don and Zack with setting the sail she came over to where Captain Reed and Jess were sitting.

Captain Reed grinned at Sydney. "Beefcake, you have come a long way, baby."

Sydney put her head on Captain Reed's shoulder. "Thanks to you, O Captain, My Captain!"

Don and Zack joined them at the stern, and Don said, "I've been teaching her more hands-on style."

Captain Reed's expression revealed his disdain for Don's comment.

"Oh my," said Jess, "that could be interpreted in a few ways."

Captain Reed put his arm around Sydney. "Just remember, Don, you can have all the girls on shore you like, but the girls on my boat are mine."

Sydney pulled away from him "Now, now, boys, I am right here, and to be clear, I belong to only myself."

The captain's playful remark that "all the girls on my boat are mine" struck a nerve with Jess. Did something happen between the captain and Sydney when they went back to the U.S.? Jess dismissed the thought of Sydney having any sexual interest in the captain, and the captain had mentioned he was seeing Sophia when he returned to California. Still, the uncertainty gnawed at her, but Jess quickly masked her feelings with a practiced smile. She resolved to view the captain solely as a friend, pushing aside the flutter of emotions that threatened to surface.

The sail from Apia to Vava'u was almost uneventful until the 6-71 diesel engine quit running. Zack, Don, and Captain Reed spent several hours changing the engine's fuel filter, which took less time than locating a spare filter. It irritated Jess that the bins had not been organized. She considered organization a priority and especially crossing an ocean where locating things could mean life or death.

Vava'u proved a popular stop for sailors making their way to shelter from the typhoon season. It proved difficult getting *Slow Dance* through the fjord-like Ava Pulepulekai channel inland to the capital city of Neiafu. Captain Reed stood at the helm maneuvering the boat in between the small islands, coral outcrops that rose ten meters from the sea floor, and unmarked rocks. The charts were inaccurate, but a good sailor trusts his eyes more, so Zack stood at the bow with a handheld radio communicating any obstacles they needed to avoid.

Sydney joined Captain Reed and Jess at the outside helm. "Captain Cook knew about these islands but avoided them," she said, "because the protective natives in Ha'apai tricked him by telling him there was no harbor. Spain claimed the islands, but once the whalers discovered Vava'u, it was game over. It's the season right now to swim with the humpbacks. This is their playground."

Don gave Sydney an annoyed look. "Did you find a restaurant place mat or something, or do you have an internet connection already?"

"No, Captain Sexy," Sydney countered. "I enjoy reading the history of this planet as opposed to all the *Game of Thrones* fantasy books on a Kindle. This is living history. It doesn't lay dead in books."

Don ignored her.

Slow Dance passed by numerous uninhabited islands. They were beautiful, wild, and untamed. Jess was thinking of Maka and sighed. "It is said these islands were created by the God Maui, who reached into the sea with a magic hook and pulled Vava'u to the surface."

Don shook his head. "Bloody great, a history buff and a mistress of myth." His mood was turning sourer by the day.

Slow Dance anchored offshore from Neiafu, and once the boat was settled, Jess went below to make lunch while Zack and Don lowered the dinghy into the water. Don instructed his brother to check all the fluids in the main engine and make a list of any belts, filters, or fluids they might need. He asked Captain Reed's permission to go ashore and investigate the town for a supermarket and marine store.

Captain Reed handed Don a radio. "Keep it on channel 12 so we can stay connected and see about internet and SIM cards for our cell phones while you're there."

"Can I come?" asked Sydney.

"No, I need some me time," answered Don, as he climbed into the dinghy and prepared to set out for the town. Jess prepared pasta pomodoro for lunch, along with a green salad and garlic bread made from the last of the French bread in the freezer. Captain Reed lay on the outside couch with Trinidad for a nap, and Zack went to the engine room to prepare an inventory of any mechanical items needed for their continued passage to the Fijian islands.

Sydney and Jess were sitting forward on the deck finishing a fine bottle of Merlot when Captain Reed asked if there was any word from Don. It had been over four hours since he left the boat. Late afternoon faded into early evening and no matter how many times the captain hailed Don on the radio, there was no response.

After ten o'clock there was still no word from him. Zack seemed to be the only one unconcerned.

"Don't worry, Don is most likely drunk and passed out or with some girl," commented Zack.

Sydney looked disgusted. "Well, good for him—except he has the dinghy, and we're all stranded on the boat unable to get to shore. It's especially messed up that he's ghosting the owner."

Captain Reed remained unusually calm considering the circumstances. "I am going to bed, and judging by Zack's comments, this isn't the first time Don has been MIA, so I wouldn't worry. If he doesn't come back tomorrow, I'll call to the port captain."

It was nearly noon the next day before Don returned to *Slow Dance* looking disheveled and hungover. He tossed the line up to Zack, who assisted in securing the dinghy to the yacht. Captain Reed, Jess, and Sydney were all sitting on the outside couches when Don sheepishly sat down across from Captain Reed.

"Sorry, mate, but I needed that. Started with a few brews and then there was this gorgeous redhead hitting on me . . . you know how it is . . . sorry."

Captain Reed calmly answered, "Yes, son, I know how it is—but *never* take my dinghy, turn off your radio, and disappear, leaving me stranded. We all needed a little shore time yesterday and it was totally irresponsible and selfish of you, not to mention worrisome."

Don stood up, offering no further apology for his actions. "I need a shower and some coffee. If you'll excuse me . . ."

"I bet," said Sydney angrily. "That's it?! A slap on the wrist?" She huffed. "My punishment was so much worse after I jumped on the cruise ship."

36

The Billy Goat Tavern

September 2024
Vava'u, Tonga

Slow Dance anchored in the Port of Refuge in Neiafu, a well-known harbor for yachts and sailboats and the second-largest city in the sixty-one islands of Vava'u in the nation of Tonga. Many of the islands were uninhabited, surrounded by pristine waters and white beaches, perfect for swimming, snorkeling, and diving. With a population of nearly four thousand, the town of Neiafu was a cluster of brightly painted houses mixed in with bars, restaurants, and decent supermarkets. Adjacent to the Port of Refuge, the deepwater part of the harbor was the center of tourism with many larger visiting yachts, stopping over on route to Fiji and New Zealand. *The Pinta* was sailing the same route as *Slow Dance*, and she was anchored in the same bay, which made Sydney happy. She was in love with the beautifully restored, tall wooden ship, built in Denmark between 1886 and 1909. Don and Zack discovered a little restaurant and bar owned by two Americans and suggested they all go there for lunch and a game of darts. The bar also had a television broadcasting the rugby game, another reason the two brothers wanted to go.

Zack held the dinghy for Sydney as she climbed down the ladder into the boat. Captain Reed informed them he and Jess were not going to join them. Don started the engine, and Captain Reed waved them off. "Have fun and don't do anything I wouldn't do, and if you do, name it after me."

"You hungry, Captain?"

"Yes, how about you?"

"Famished," she answered. "I'll go make your favorite."

"What could that be? Honestly, you spoil me. Bring a bottle of wine up with lunch, a nice red."

Jess made a couple of tuna melts with avocado and topped each with red onion. There were no chips on the islands, so she substituted sliced cucumber. Carrying a tray to the outside table, she placed the sandwiches down, along with two wineglasses and a bottle of pinot noir.

"Looks great. I missed your cooking while I was gone."

"I'm sure you did, and I enjoyed not cooking while you were away—except for the starving contestants of the *Survivor* reality show."

Captain Reed opened the wine and poured two glasses. "You didn't cook for the guys?"

"Don primarily eats beer, and Zack goes out for hamburgers practically every day."

"What did you do with yourself all day?"

"Well, I went to the island of Savai'i for ten days, with two new friends. It was my birthday present to myself. Trini tagged along and that's where I discovered she was infested with ticks.

"Right, glad I wasn't here for that."

Trinidad perked up when she heard her name and jumped up on the sofa next to the captain.

"Poor Trini"—he gave the pooch a pat—"that haircut. Angie's rolling over in her grave. She was so particular about Trinidad's grooming."

Jess sipped the wine. "I also made a Samoan friend named Maka. He showed me the island, took me to the estate of Robert Louis Stevenson, and taught me about his culture and his tribal tattoos. He was quite a bit younger, and I took him as a lover."

She waited for his reaction. Captain Reed crossed his legs and began intertwining his fingers as if contemplating his response.

"It was bound to happen; look at you. I hardly recognized you when I saw you at the airport. Sailing has transformed you, both mentally and physically. It has a way of doing that to a person. I am relieved it wasn't Don, because then I would have to kick him off the boat."

Jess choked on her sip of wine. "Oh no, never. Besides being an ass, he's a womanizer like you, except you're wiser and much more experienced."

Captain Reed lifted his glass in a gesture of toasting. "Why thank you."

She poured them more wine. "So, how did it go with Sophia?"

Captain Reed uncrossed his legs and thought before answering.

"I was busy, but we did spend some time in the desert. I also spent a few nights at her condo in Marina del Rey. Her place in the desert is hers, but the condo belongs to her husband, and he spends his time there when he's in Los Angeles. To be honest, I hated sleeping in that bed with her. I didn't like sleeping where he slept. It felt weird, like I could smell him."

Jess wondered if the captain would smell Maka in his bed. "Any other pretty girls let you have your way with them?"

He put his empty glass on the table. "Any more of this wine and I am going to chase you around the boat."

Jess brushed off his comment, but the tension between them was undeniable.

In the morning Don and Zack needed to go to town and look for parts for the watermakers. Sydney and Jess went along to shop for new clothes, taking Trini with them. Captain Reed remained onboard to watch over the boat, and Don and Zack asked the girls to meet them at the same bar for lunch and a round of darts.

"So, what did you buy?" Zack was poking through the bags Sydney and Jess placed on the table.

Sydney opened her bag, pulling out a trendy floral-print backless sundress. It was knee-length, white with red flowers.

"Wow. You're going to look smashing in that. What's the occasion?"

Sydney shrugged. "I don't know yet, but in case some handsome sailor in Fiji asks me out, I'll be prepared."

Jess opened her bag and showed Zack her new bikini. It was dark blue and crocheted. She also showed him the jewelry she bought, an imitation diamond bezel necklace, and an anklet made from small seashells.

"I haven't bought a bikini in a long time because I gained weight and was too self-conscious to wear one."

Sydney picked up the top and held it to her chest. "Not anymore, Jess. You're going to rock this thing."

Jess put the necklace around her neck. "I can't believe they had this in such a remote place! It looks real."

The bar was a charming, cozy little slice of American Southern hospitality called the Billy Goat Tavern. Billy and his wife were partners in the bar with their fellow American friend, Foster, a handsome man in his forties. They all lived together in a huge plantation house rented from a local family. Billy and his wife had two children, aged six and nine. Foster lost his wife a few years earlier to a sudden illness and his friend Billy convinced him to travel to Vava'u, Tonga, and buy a restaurant. In addition to the tavern, Foster owned a bed and breakfast that catered to backpackers. Jess learned this information while taking a tour of the kitchen with Foster.

After ordering lunch and a bowl of water for Trinidad, they chose teams for a game of darts, Don, Zack, and Billy against Foster, Jess, and Sydney. It just so happened Jess was very good at darts. Don fancied himself good at any sport, so after losing for the second time, he said,

"I didn't know they had redneck dart sharks in New York."

Foster was looking at Jess, and she felt his lingering stare must be apparent to the entire room.

Jess replied to Don's comment, "There was nothing to do on snowy days except play darts in the basement with my older brothers."

It was nearly midnight when they all climbed into the dinghy and headed back to *Slow Dance*. Don was driving and Sydney was sitting next to him. Sydney pointed two fingers at her eyes and then at Jess and began singing some Marvin Gay lyrics—"When I get that *feeeelin'*, that . . . *sex*ual feeeelin'"—Jess understanding that she was referencing Foster's obvious interest in the chef of *Slow Dance*.

Foster had made Jess feel uneasy, in fact, but she decided not to overthink the situation and just take it as a compliment.

Surprisingly, Captain Reed was still awake when they returned. After securing the dinghy on the platform, Don and Zack followed Sydney into the pilothouse.

Captain Reed looked upset, and Jess asked, "What's wrong?"

Swallowing hard, he replied, "The engine is completely dead. It won't start and I tried everything."

Don opened the engine room door. "Zack and I will have a look. Start her up when I tell you to."

After several unsuccessful attempts to start the engine, Don and Zack returned to the pilothouse and sat on the couches with the others.

"Zack and I will check around town tomorrow to see what kind of repairs this town can handle. We're in a good port for marine mechanics, and I know they have a marine center one bay over. Let's get some sleep, and in the morning, we'll find a mechanic straight away."

Don gave Captain Reed's shoulder a squeeze. "It will get handled, mate, no worries."

Don and Zack headed off to their cabins, but Sydney and Jess remained with Captain Reed.

Sydney tried to reassure him. "Don't worry."

He replied, "Ignorance is bliss. The harsh truth is the French mechanic who completed the repairs in Marina Taina screwed up the engine somehow. I had a sick feeling this would happen, and the worst part is, typhoon season is coming. We only have a few months to get out of here to a safe harbor." His statement weighed heavily on Jess.

The next few days, Don searched for a marine mechanic but had zero luck finding anyone who worked on 6-71 Detroit diesel engines. Zack opted to stay down in the engine room with the technical manuals, trying to locate the problem. After several continuous days in the engine room, he excitedly rushed up on deck and presented Captain Reed with a metal rod from the engine.

"Here's the problem," he said, pointing to a spot of the rod that was shearing off fine pieces of metal. "Looks like it was not properly fitted into the shaft after the water was flushed out of the engine."

Captain Reed shook his head. "Bastard! When Don gets back, we need to contact the marine center in Long Beach California and see if we can get the part shipped ASAP."

After numerous emails and phone calls to both the U.S. and Australia, it was determined the damaged rod was a part on the 6-71 engine that never had to be replaced, so there was no replacement part.

Don and Zack continued the search for a mechanic but spent more time drinking beer than searching. Sydney was frequently in town with Rose and her son Dylan from the *Pinta*, and Captain Reed spent the day driving around the island in the dinghy, inquiring if any other captains knew a diesel mechanic on the island. Jess remained with Captain Reed searching for a solution to their serious problem via the internet. The captain rooted himself in the engine room, poring through his repair manuals. The man was like a dog with a bone. Each passing day he became sullener and more withdrawn, and Jess was becoming depressed by his incorrigible mood. She needed space from the situation to center her thoughts.

Overwhelmed and troubled, Jess decided to take Sydney up on her offer to have a night off. She needed a change of scene and went with Sydney to the tavern for pizza and beer. Foster's flirtations were heartfelt, but Jess couldn't bring herself to be more involved with him beyond conversation. On this evening Foster invited Jess and Sydney along with the crew from *Slow Dance* to a barbecue being held on one of the small outer islands. The gathering was hosted by another American and his family living in Tonga.

Slow Dance anchored in Vava'u for ten days, and Captain Reed barely left the boat. The morning after her outing with Sydney, Jess found him mopping the deck.

"There's a barbecue and bonfire tonight on a small island where an American couple live with their kids. They're hosting a late Fourth of July party. Everyone from *Pinta* is going, and the boys from the bar are good friends with this guy, 'cause they're all American. Don and Zack are coming for sure, and you can't say no. We will figure something out; have faith. It's been less than two weeks." Jess had never seen Captain Reed so despondent. "Have faith that something will turn things around."

He answered her with disdain. "Faith is a fairytale made up for religious crowd control. I feel like I've been sitting in this bay for a year already. Maybe I should be making a dream board or something . . ."

Jess stood up and put her hands on her hips. "We are getting you off this boat, so go shower and put some clothes on that aren't covered in grease."

Sydney came over and helped pull him to his feet. "Jess is right. Shower off that mood and smell and come with us."

He stood up. "Okay, okay, you win," he said, begrudgingly making his way below to clean up.

Don and Zack were building a huge bonfire when Captain Reed drove the dinghy to the accessible part of the shore, where Sydney and Jess jumped out. Folding chairs surrounded the firepit and a wooden fence, covered in beautiful yellow flowers, was set back from the beach. The gate was open, and Jess could see a Dutch colonial house painted blue with white plantation shutters. A woman came out from the house with a platter of chicken and headed to the barbecue table at the end of the fence. After wiping her hand on her apron, she extended it to Jess.

"Hi, my name is Shelby, and the guy at the barbecue is my husband, James. Where in the world do y'all hail from?"

Jess took her hand. "We sailed from the Cook Islands to Tonga, but originally we set sail from Los Angeles, California; and where in the world does that accent of yours come from?"

"We're from Alabama."

Jess smiled. "And what in the five seas brings you and your family to Tonga?"

"That's a long story, honey; now come help me carry out the potato salad, coleslaw, and baked beans."

Jess was feeling a bit homesick after eating the delicious American barbecue. As the sky darkened, Zack and Don lit their awesome fire and Jess took a chair pulling it next to Captain Reed, who wasn't hungry and remained entrenched in his cloudy mood. They were watching the fire grow larger with each new log that Zack tossed on, when the captain leaned toward Jess.

"So, where is lover boy?"

Jess felt his anxiety. "His name is Foster."

"What kind of name is Foster?" Captain Reed snarled. "Did his parents name him after their favorite beer or something?"

"Foster is working and joining us later—and he's not my boyfriend. I am sorry you feel abandoned, but honestly, you haven't been pleasant to be around. I know something will happen to resolve the problem with the boat."

"Yes, and maybe we should chant to keep the typhoons away," Captain Reed answered sarcastically.

Sydney interrupted them by placing a large yellow flower behind each of their ears, then climbed a nearby tree and sat on one of its branches to watch the fire.

The men were standing around the fire drinking beer and talking when Don and their host, James, excitedly walked over to Captain Reed.

"You are not going to believe this," said Don. "This is James. He is from Alabama, and he has been a Detroit diesel mechanic for thirty years—both in the military and in Detroit. He moved to Tonga with his family to work on diesel engines in container ships on route to Australia. His shop is right here on his property!"

Captain Reed stood up, stupefied, and vigorously shook James's hand.

"Do you think you can help us?" asked the captain.

In his thick Southern accent James replied, "I think I just might," and gave a wink.

James took the metal rod to his machine shop, reshaping it, and placed it in the engine. After three days, *Slow Dance* was running good as new. Finding James was a miracle. The area in the engine room where James had to work required someone small enough to crawl under low-hanging pipes in the bilge to access the motor. It had taken Zack several days of struggling to remove the pipe, and James a mere hour to replace it.

Captain Reed believed the boat was finished and they would all be flying out of Vava'u. Jess wondered if he considered what she and Sydney said about having faith. Either way, she was happy to see the captain returning to his jovial self.

Slow Dance had been restored, along with the happiness of her crew. Jess placed a pot of coffee, cream, and sugar on the chart table along with freshly baked pineapple scones. "Ah, this looks delicious—*ouch*, hot," Captain Reed said, trying to handle one of the warm scones.

"Now that we have a sail plan in place," the captain said a moment later over a mouthful of Jess's pastry, "may I suggest we take a day or two and explore a few of these deserted islands before sailing on to Fiji." He didn't seem to be asking anyone's opinion.

37

Swimming with Whales

September 2024
Vava'u Islands, Tonga

Don was a certified PADI Pro and agreed to teach Sydney how to scuba. Jess, on the other hand, wanted no part of being weighed down under the sea. Sky diving, spelunking, and deep-sea diving crossed off her list long ago.

Don drove the dinghy into a lagoon of crystal-blue water. As Don maneuvered the boat toward the beach, Trinidad began her habit of whining as the dinghy approached the shore. The whimpering made Don crazy, and, on this occasion, he picked the little pooch up and tossed her into the water. Trini swam to the sand, shook herself off, and proceeded to run wildly up and down the length of the beach.

"See, she liked it. Look how happy she is," Don said as he climbed out of the boat.

"She acts like a real dog," commented Captain Reed, waving a stick at Trinidad, who grabbed it in her mouth, growling and tugging until the captain let go. Shaking it fiercely, she charged down the beach.

After lunch, Don readied the diving equipment and began teaching Sydney the basics.

Don led Sydney into the bay with just the regulator to start, and Jess joined them for a swim.

"My God, Sydney," Jess said, "you look like Bob Marley and an octopus produced offspring."

Zack was standing at the shore snapping photos while Captain Reed lay on a blanket under a palm tree. It was a perfect lazy afternoon. Sydney and Don finished their lesson, but Jess opted to remain languishing in the warm water of the lagoon.

After a time, Jess noticed Captain Reed and Sydney had disappeared. The bay was so calm she decided to swim out around to the next bay. Just past the tree line, she saw Captain Reed and Sydney swimming naked. They hadn't seen her because they were playfully splashing one another. Jess felt too awkward to join them, opting instead to swim back to the beach.

Zack was snapping photos of Jess and Trini rolling in the sand when Captain Reed and Sydney returned.

"What is this, a photo shoot? You look like sugar cookies," Sydney said.

Jess wondered if something had taken place between the captain and Sydney on their trip back to the States. Sydney had mentioned a nude resort, but it seemed unlikely they were more than just friends. Jess was posing in the surf for Zack, her tan, lean body glistening with sand, her dark, wet hair tangled around her shoulders. She saw the captain looking at her, but he quickly looked away when she caught his gaze.

The captain clapped his hands. "Let's be on our way. But first, you all need to wash the sand off or it will be all over the dinghy."

Don and Zack pushed the boat effortlessly off the sand so the others could jump in. Jess was holding Trini knee-deep in the water trying to rinse the sand off.

"Rinse her good," said Don. "Ticks were bad enough. We don't want bloody sand fleas infesting the boat."

Jess tossed the pup into the dinghy. "No worries, nothing sticks to her now, because she's bald."

Zack picked the little pooch up and kissed her nose. "Miss T, you're becoming a good little mate." He put Trinidad on the seat next to him. "I am told there are a lot of awesome cave dives near here. Any of you sailors up for a dive tomorrow morning?"

Jess made a face. "Will there be sharks?"

Enjoying her morning coffee on deck, Jess felt the promise of another beautiful day in paradise. Knees pulled up to her chest, she watched the world come alive around her. The tranquility of the bay and the beauty of the natural surroundings created a sense of peace and serenity that was truly magical. After breakfast, Don, Zack, Sydney, and Jess headed for Swallows Cave. Captain Reed stayed aboard *Slow Dance* with James to do a final check on the engine.

It was one of those mornings where you can't tell where the water ends and the sky begins. The ocean was calm as a lake when Don stopped the engine. Jess volunteered to stay with the dinghy while the others readied their tanks, masks, and fins, before flipping backwards into the water.

"It's more a snorkeling spot," said Zack, "but great for beginner scuba," and he winked at Sydney. A short time later Sydney emerged from the water.

"Back so soon?" Jess helped her remove her tank. "Honestly, Sydney, the thought of going under the sea, weighted, and breathing through a mask makes me crazy. I like to observe from above with a snorkel and fins."

Sydney was squeezing the seawater out of her dreadlocks. "It's not so bad. You should face your fear, woman, it's magical down there."

"What are those brown streaks floating over the water? It wasn't there an hour ago. Looks like sewage but it can't be." Jess pointed near the cave.

"It's seaweed, kelp," said Sydney. "It's filled with gas and floats because of pneumatocysts."

"Because of what?"

"It floats on the surface to get the sunlight."

Jess shook her head. "You're smarter than you look!"

Zack surfaced about ten feet from the boat and began swimming toward them.

Unfortunately, Don surfaced closer to the boat, in the middle of the brown kelp floating on the surface, and he began pushing it away as he swam to the boat.

"Watch out, Don," Sydney called in alarm, "a dive boat went by and dumped its black water."

Don immediately pulled off his mask and vomited into the water. Sydney doubled over with hysterical laughter. They were all still laughing when Don climbed into the boat looking very pissed.

"It's brown kelp, but it sure looks like poop." Sydney was trying to make up to Don, but he wasn't having it. He started the engine and pulled away so abruptly the others were hurled to the back of the dinghy. Jess was glad she decided to leave Trinidad on *Slow Dance* with the captain.

Suddenly, Don slowed the engine and pointed to a group of whales swimming some fifty feet in front of the boat.

"Every year the humpback whales migrate three thousand miles from their feeding ground in Antarctica to the remote kingdom of Tonga," said Sydney. "They are here to mate and give birth in these warm waters. Tonga is one of the only places in the world you can get in the water with these animals unsupervised. Hand me a snorkel, Jess, I am going in."

Zack already had his mask on and was pulling on his flippers. "Me too!"

"Be careful," said Don, "they're huge beasts."

Jess turned to Don. "Not going in?"

"You know I hate fish. Question is, are you going in, mountain girl?"

Don irritated Jess on so many levels. "Hand me a snorkel from the locker," she snapped. "I decided I am going in after all, because how many people get to be in this place, at this moment, and swim with whales? Besides, they're just large mammals, like the cows on the farm."

Don gave her a hand into the water. "Don't get too close. You're a newbie when it comes to the ocean and Cappy will never forgive us if we lose his cook."

Jess spit in her mask and rubbed it over the glass. Her long fins held her at the surface as she fit the mask tightly on her face and placed the breathing bit into her mouth. Trembling, she began swimming toward the whales. Jess had been close to whales a few times but that was in a boat. One time, going from Puerto Vallarta to the island of Jalapa, she sat watching a whale sunning himself on the surface, but this was something totally different. She was in the open ocean, wearing only a bathing suit, flippers, and a snorkel. She was betting most people who swim with whales go with a seasoned guide and have some kind of preparation. What was she trying to prove and to whom and for what reason? Don was right, she was a novice, and suddenly she felt extremely vulnerable and frightened.

At that moment, she felt a tug on her fin. It was Sydney pulling her backward and motioning to a huge male swimming toward the surface. Jess watched as if in slow motion as the majestic animal breached high above the surface. The force of his return caused the two women to bob like corks in his temporary wake. Sydney held onto Jess until the turbulence passed.

Sydney pulled her mask off. "Oh my God, how cool was that!"

Jess removed her mask. "Amazing—but what if he landed on us? We'd be dead."

Sydney replaced her mask. "They won't. You're with me, and I got this. Just follow me and do what I do."

Jess was trying to get up enough saliva and courage to ready her mask. She told herself,

I am fearless, I am fearless, I am fearless.

Empowered by her thoughts, Jess followed Sydney as she dove under the surface to get a closer look at a mother and her newborn calf. Jess's heart raced with excitement at the sight of the mother whale and her calf swimming elegantly beneath the surface. The massive creatures moved with such grace and power, their movements a mesmerizing dance. As Jess drew closer, she could see the intricate patterns and textures on the whale's skin, marveling at the mottled shades of gray that shimmered in the sunlight.

They were amazingly close as they watched the interactions of the mother and her baby. Jess was swimming alongside the mother whale when she heard her whale song, a hauntingly beautiful sound. Jess thought the song told a story of love, connection, and the mysteries of the deep ocean. She felt something stirring in her primal soul as the whale's song vibrated through her being, leaving her profoundly moved by the experience. Zack and Sydney swam up to her and the three removed their masks.

"That was so awesome," said Zack.

Jess added, "Made me cry."

"Right?" said Sydney. "Like your first orgasm."

Jess shook her head. "How do you come out with such things? Did you hear the whale sounds? Remember the *Star Trek* movie where Kirk and Spock go back in time to capture some whales and repopulate the earth's oceans?"

Sydney started swimming toward the dinghy. She turned on her back kicking her fins,

"What's *Star Trek*?" she asked. Then she laughed. "Just messing with you."

Don steadied the dinghy as Sydney handed her flippers up to Captain Reed, who was waiting for them on deck.

"Cappy, it was so awesome. Thank you for bringing me along on your adventure. Have you ever been in the water with whales?"

"No," he replied, "but I've seen plenty of whales and did plenty of diving but never got close to them in the water," and he turned to Don and Zack who were rinsing the snorkels with fresh water to remove the salt.

"Don, can you flush the engine on the dinghy? It needs to be flushed."

"Yeah, sure, but can it wait until morning? There's an important rugby game tonight. South Africa's playing France. We were all going over to the Billy Goat Tavern to watch. I know you're not one for sports, but there are darts and good beer. Can't say much for the ladies of Tonga—all stout, religious, and for the most part, unattractive."

Captain Reed smiled. "Good thing. I wouldn't want you to desert ship again, 'cause then I'd have to fire you. I want to leave tomorrow after breakfast, so enjoy this last night in Tonga."

38

Self-Actualization

September 2024
Vava'u Islands, Tonga

The tavern was buzzing with activity. There were familiar faces, along with a group of six young attractive women from Europe. They had just arrived on the island to swim with whales and Captain Reed didn't waste any time introducing himself, buying them drinks, and charming them with his sea stories and quick wit. *Nothing like a group of pretty women to bring out his charms*, thought Jess.

The soccer game was about to begin, and people were securing their spot in front of the television. Don and Zack were up front, and Sydney abandoned Captain Reed to flirt with the cute island boy from Rose's boat, the *Pinta*. Jess found Foster in the kitchen giving the staff tips on making pizza. No matter how many times he demonstrated the process, they never seemed to get it right. He was wearing an apron and showing one of the girls how much sauce to put on the pizza. Jess watched him from the doorway, admiring his muscular frame and curly brown hair pulled back into a ponytail.

"You put the sauce first, then the toppings, and finally *this* much cheese."

Foster opened his hand to show the girl before putting it on the pizza. He hadn't seen Jess when she came into the kitchen.

"Why don't you take photos of the steps for each menu item and place the information in a kitchen recipe book?" she said. "You can also put a scale in here and make them weigh the portions."

Foster turned around and greeted her with a big smile.

"If only you were here to straighten this place out, Chef. With your expertise, the Billy Goat would be the talk of the town." He removed his apron and took Jess's hand. "I've been waiting for you; come on, I have a surprise."

Jess noticed the workers blush as if they knew there would be "a little something-something" between them. The crowd inside the bar was loud and rowdy as Foster and Jess escaped out the back door.

Foster had arranged a beautiful candlelit dinner at one of the nicer restaurants in town. Seated on a garden patio overlooking the sea, Foster's easy laughter and engaging conversation drew her in, making her almost forget about the captain. As Jess sat across from Foster, the soft glow of the candlelight flickering between them, she felt a sense of warmth and excitement envelop her. The serene backdrop for their dinner amplified the romantic atmosphere. Jess found herself captivated by Foster's genuine interest in her stories. As they shared anecdotes and exchanged shy smiles, Jess felt a spark she had not anticipated.

Foster took a deep breath, and his expression turned serious. "I want to share something with you, Jess," he began, his voice steady yet tinged with vulnerability.

Foster proceeded to speak of his late wife, and how her sudden passing left him shattered and adrift.

"For two years, I've been living in a fog." He looked deep into Jess's eyes. "But being here with you, it's like you are waking something inside me that I thought was lost."

As he shared his heart, Jess felt a surge of empathy and attraction, realizing the weight of his past and the courage it took to open up. She wondered if Captain Reed was capable of such openness.

Jess's thoughts remained on the captain. She wished he looked at her the way Foster was looking at her now. She knew he cared for her as more than just a friend, but he purposefully gave amorous attention to random women. He had his reasons for fending her off, but was she making herself indispensable to him at the expense of compromising what she wanted? Was she falling back into her old pattern of being absorbed by yet another selfish man?

Foster reached across the table and put his hand over hers. "You looked far away just then. You okay?"

She put her other hand on top of his and said, "Let's go."

They spent the night at Foster's hotel finding pleasure in each other's arms. He was a sweet man with warm ways, but her mind was on Captain Reed. In the morning, they were awakened by a knock on the door. Foster was needed at the front desk.

"Yes, I'll come in a few minutes." He rolled over and pulled Jess close. "So, how do you feel this morning, Chef?"

Jess stretched, propped herself up on her elbow, and replied, "If it got any better, there would be two of me!"

Foster pulled on pants and a shirt. Turning to her, he said, "Don't go anywhere. I am not finished with you."

After a few minutes, Foster returned to the room wearing a strange expression.

"Your captain is at the front desk asking if you're here. He looks upset. Is there something I should know, or didn't you have permission to jump ship for the night?"

She sat on the edge of the bed. "I didn't bother to tell anyone where I was going. Things were so spontaneous. He's probably upset because he was worried, and the crew was worried. Somehow, he tracked me down."

Foster sat down next to her. "I told him he should wait for you at the coffee shop next door. I hope that was cool. Listen, I more than like you. I am crazy about you." He stood up then and pulled Jess to her feet and wrapped his arms around her. "It's lonely here in the middle of the Pacific Ocean. We'd be such a great team running the business together. Your talents are wasted on that boat, and you told me your captain has no clear plan of where he's going or where he may end up. Hopefully, not at the bottom of the sea. I've heard rumors regarding the safety of the boat. I don't care that you have sons and that you're older than me. We can have a great life here, together. I have enough money, and we can fly back to the States whenever we want."

Jess was feeling completely overwhelmed. Her mind was spinning like a top as she tried to process what Foster had just said.

"You're a wonderful man, Foster. Can we talk about this later? Right now, I must go deal with my boss. Then I need some time to think about everything. Literally everything." She dressed quickly and went to find Captain Reed.

As Jess walked toward the coffee shop, she conjured up a vision of life on Vava'u, and the thought of staying on the island wasn't appealing. It was much more exciting sailing across oceans to places unknown. Captain Reed was fascinating, mysterious, intelligent, adventuresome, funny, inappropriate, sad—and sexy as hell. She admitted it was the captain she was thinking about when Foster made love to her. But the captain didn't reciprocate her feelings. She spotted him at the café and reminded herself this chapter was about her relationship with herself.

She wasn't on this adventure to find a man.

Captain Reed was seated at an outside table, legs crossed, sipping an espresso.

"Morning. I ordered you a cappuccino and a cinnamon roll."

The waitress delivered the coffee to Jess along with the poor attempt at a cinnamon roll.

"You disappeared last night. Sydney told me you went off with Foster, but I didn't expect you to not come back to the boat."

She took a sip of her cappuccino. "I'm surprised you noticed, considering that you were occupied with several young girls when I left. Do I detect some jealousy?"

Captain Reed chose his words carefully. "I was amusing myself. You should know that by now."

"Yes," she answered. "I've witnessed how much women amuse you. I had a fantastic time. I need a man who likes my mind and finds me attractive, sexy, and desirable."

"You are also those things to me. Every day it becomes more difficult to keep my hands off you. We have had this discussion. I don't want to lose you, and I will lose you if we move past friendship. I am not ready for a commitment, and you are a woman who deserves commitment. You deserve a man who loves you in every way, not a man with as many faults as I possess. You don't need to get tangled up in another broken relationship. This Foster guy seems like a good man, but I hope he hasn't persuaded you to stay here."

"Not yet anyway," Jess replied, her voice breaking slightly as she digested what the captain had revealed about his feelings for her.

He stood up and put money on the table. "*Slow Dance* is running, thanks to James from Alabama—and a great deal of luck. You were right. Thank you for attempting to keep me positive when I was at an all-time low. I didn't think the boat would ever move again."

"You know what luck stands for, don't you?" she asked.

"No," he said.

"Living Under Correct Knowledge."

"Good one. We pull up anchor at fifteen hundred to make our way to Fiji. I hope you choose wisely."

Jess ordered a second cappuccino and sat alone with her thoughts about what the captain had said. When Foster spoke to her about staying with him on the island, she knew immediately that was never going to happen. It was absurd that Foster would think she would give up her life to stay with him after one night of passion. She knew all too well from her past mistakes how things turn out when you jump too quickly into a relationship. Her relationships were with men who only saw the value she added to *their* lives. She never thought about what she wanted, only what they wanted. She made their life better while hers became worse. Captain Reed once told her all relationships are contracts between two people. Each person has something of equal value to enhance their partner's life. Love between two people can mean different things at different times: honesty, support, mutual respect, communication, and intimacy. Captain Reed had just openly admitted his feelings for her. She was not as naive as he imagined her to be. He had shown her who he was: a man in love with the sea, a man who lets the wind take him, a man who enjoys teaching others about sailing. She was coming to terms with her choices, past and present. She was learning that wisdom often comes with an emotional cost. She finished her coffee and went to find Foster, because leaving without saying goodbye would not be kind.

Fijian Islands

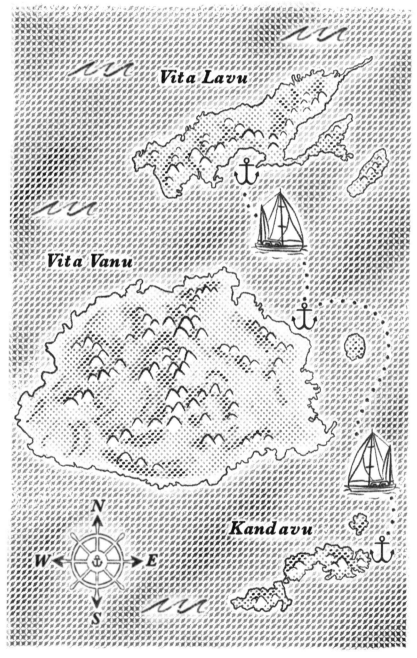

39

Vinaka Vaka Levu (Thank You Very Much)

October 2024
Denarau Island, Viti Levu, Fiji

"Fiji is an archipelago of three hundred islands in Melanesia, part of Oceania in the South Pacific. The two major islands, Viti Levu and Vanua Levu, are about eleven hundred nautical miles from New Zealand. Most Fijians live on the coast of Viti Levu in the capital city of Suva, or in smaller urban centers such as Nadi or Lautoka. Nandi is a tourist destination and Lautoka is known for its sugarcane industry." Sydney was reading from one of the Lonely Planet books she brought back from the States. "I am ready for some tourist action."

The sail from Vava'u to Fiji's capitol city of Suva was uneventful but for a few hours of rough seas when *Slow Dance* neared the coast. Captain Reed was in the pilothouse familiarizing himself with the Open Oceans program Don had downloaded on the main computer.

"What do you think of the program?"

Jess, having finished her work in the galley, was in the pilothouse looking over Captain Reed's shoulder. Gently taking her hand, Captain Reed placed her index finger on the icon of a little red boat on the computer screen that followed a red dotted line depicting their course.

Leaning close to him, she said, "That's amazing, and the chart also shows the depth and any objects in the water that we should avoid, like reef and rocks. I love this. It makes me feel a whole lot safer."

Captain Reed put his arm around Jess and gave her a squeeze. "Indeed it does, and I need my little *cookie* to feel safe, otherwise she may jump ship."

Jess shook her head and pulled away from him. "Cookie? That name somehow makes me feel subservient."

The captain put his hands up. "I assure you it is meant in the fondest of ways. If you don't like it, say the word and I'll never call you that again."

"Let me think about it," Jess answered.

Captain Reed turned his attention to settling *Slow Dance* in the port of Suva.

"Jess, can you call the port authority while Don puts up the yellow quarantine flag?"

Captain Reed expertly eased *Slow Dance* into the narrow slip at the Royal Suva Yacht Club, which looked old and outdated. It took several hours for passports and ship documents to be verified. The quarantine master informed Captain Reed that Trinidad would not be allowed off the boat. Hoping to persuade the official, Jess presented Trinidad's vaccination paperwork.

The quarantine master carefully looked through the poodle's record book, commenting, "Very nice dog. I believe to come onto the islands is possible for your dog; however, you must give a deposit of fifteen hundred U.S. dollars to the Administration of Health. Then you may take your nice dog off the boat. The deposit will cover any problems that might arise during your stay. When you clear out of Fiji, we will return the deposit. Cash, of course."

Captain Reed went below and returned with the money. When the man went to take it, the captain held onto it, making him tug hard before he let it go.

"You are writing me a receipt for the cash, right?"

The man chuckled, tucked the cash in his shirt pocket and exited the boat.

"Never going to see that money," said Captain Reed.

Sydney was outraged. "Why didn't you make him write you a receipt? That's a lot of dough he just extorted from you!"

"You will learn, Sydney, the farther we sail into less-traveled parts of the world, the larger the bribes become. That was nothing compared to my sailing into Columbia."

The Royal Suva Yacht Club was old and outdated inside, as well. There was a pool table and a bar, so the South African brothers were content. Captain Reed chose an outside table, and Sydney and Jess ordered some Chinese food off the menu.

"They're slow with the drinks around here." Sydney looked for the waitress.

Don and Zack joined their table just as the food and drinks arrived.

Sated and relaxed, Captain Reed pushed away from the table. "I'm eager to get *Slow Dance* to the marina at Denarau Island, so I'd like to shove off from here first thing in the morning. Sailing close to the coastline should temper the rough ride, and once she rounds the tip of the island, the sea will be calm and flat."

Fiji's tourism was centered on Denarau Island. A well-manicured strip of land with big-name hotels, golf courses, and a boardwalk of fancy shops and bustling eateries. Kiosks lining the waterfront offered dive excursions, dinner cruises, snorkeling trips, sleep-aboard ferries, deep-sea fishing, and surf trips to the island of Taveuni. Denarau Marina was well maintained, exceptionally secure, and offered many professional marine services, including haul-out. *Slow Dance* was just big enough to qualify for the VIP dock, and the port captain placed her in a slip next to the luxury boats, including the superyacht *Noble House*, which neighbored them in the portside slip. The luxury boat was leased for two hundred and fifty thousand a week.

Jess loved everything about Denarau and the marina. It was a hectic, bustling mixture of tourists, Fijians, Chinese, dark-skinned Tamils from Southern India, and cruisers from around the world. There were a lot of Australians and New Zealanders living and enterprising on the island. Captain Reed rented a car for long-term use and took Jess with him for a bit of exploring. They drove to the town of Nandi, where they discovered a butcher shop with prime cuts of meats from Australia. Another shop offered European cheeses and fine prosecco from Italy. The owner of the cheese shop was a lively Italian, who hosted dinner parties for eight guests every Wednesday, and his event was so popular that reservations were made weeks in advance.

Nandi's population consisted primarily of Tamil people who worked at the resorts and restaurants along the boardwalk.

Captain Reed was driving through Nadi when Jess pointed excitedly and said, "Hey, there's a Dravidian temple like the ones I visited in Southern India."

The captain slowed down to have a peek at the temple and replied, "They brought the Indian Tamils here to work in the sugarcane fields and promised to send them home with money in their pockets but never did. I'll bet most of these people have never seen India. They integrated themselves with Fijians, but it's nice to see they maintained their culture. There's probably some great Indian food here . . . are you hungry?"

"I am always hungry for Indian food," answered Jess. "Can we stop at the temple first and have a look? It brings back memories for me."

Captain Reed turned the car around and headed to the temple. Jess was required to cover up with a sarong handed to her by the sentinel at the front gates. Wrapping the colorful, mirrored cloth to hide her shorts she took the captain's hand to lead him inside. They lit incense and sat on the floor to admire the frescos that adorned the temple ceiling and walls.

Captain Reed gazed up at the ceiling. "I have never been to India, but if the women are as beautiful as these paintings, maybe I should go."

Jess rolled her eyes. "The paintings tell a story from the Bhagavad Gita."

"What?" Captain Reed looked confused.

"The Gita is one of the most famous pieces of Hindu literature. It is one of the most important ancient texts in the world. It's basically a conversation between Prince Arjuna and Krishna, a mortal incarnation of the god Vishnu. Arjuna is worried about a battle for succession. Those paintings up there are of Radha." Jess pointed to an area of the ceiling. "Krishna enchants the world, but Radha enchants even him."

Captain Reed looked up at the ceiling. "Who wouldn't be enchanted by such a beauty? I do believe your wanderlust and pursuit of adventure may be greater than mine."

Jess gave him a side smirk. "I doubt that."

Captain Reed and Jess left the temple in search of some Indian food. Driving through the town, they found the choice of Indian restaurants all offered a mixture of North and South Indian cuisine.

They settled on the Indigo Indian Asian Restaurant. The captain fumbled with the menu before turning to Jess. "You're going to have to help me out, because I am clueless."

The air was filled with the scent of Indian spice combined with sautéed onions and garlic.

"I hope it's as good as it smells," said the captain.

Jess replied, "It's good to try new foods. You may like it."

Jess ordered the tandoori chicken, several curries, a biryani rice dish, and some roti.

By the end of the meal Captain Reed was filled with a newfound appreciation for Indian food.

Lazy days followed with Captain Reed and Jess walking Trinidad along the island's garden path to grab coffee and a croissant at one of the numerous resorts on the island. On occasion they rode the bikes for several miles over a dirt road to the local beach, with Trinidad trotting alongside the bikes. Seeing Captain Reed riding the portable bike was amusing to Jess. His legs were too long and when he peddled, his knees came nearly to his chin. She got a kick out of the gnarly sea captain looking silly. The road ended at a place where they could park the bikes and walk down to the beach.

One afternoon at the beach, while the captain enjoyed a swim with Trinidad, Jess relaxed on her beach towel, having removed her shorts and tank top to sunbathe in her new blue crocheted bikini. Captain Reed was holding Trini out of the water and her little legs were still moving in a dog-paddle motion.

"Hey Jess, look at Trini." Glancing up and seeing her in her blue bikini, he couldn't take his eyes off her as she walked into the water to join him.

"I am going to fly back to Los Angeles. I thought of bringing you with me because it's been a while since you've seen your sons. Unfortunately, I need you to stay with the boat. I don't trust Don to handle the finances, but I do trust you. Don does great with driving the boat, but he's not good with business."

Jess swam over to him. "I agree. *Slow Dance* needs significant repairs, and we will need at least three bids from contractors. I will tell Don to send you the best bid for approval. He should also ask around for reviews of the contractors. You're spending twenty thousand a month . . . and that seems excessive to me. Don thinks buying a case of beer for the workers will get him a better price. Honestly, the boy drives me mad. You're so astute at so many things, I can't believe you give him free rein to spend your money, or should I say waste your money."

Captain Reed was treading water. "I don't need another heart attack. That's why I'm putting you in charge of the petty-cash fund—and please review any bids before you send them to me for approval. I'll only be gone for a month. My cousin Sheldon, his friend Miles, and girlfriend, Paige, want to come back with me for a sail around Fiji. They heard I have a fabulous chef, but wait until they meet you!" He playfully splashed her. "Great bikini. Are you going to miss me?"

She swam away toward the beach with Trini and then said, "You know you can't live without me, Captain Reed."

Jess was thinking about Captain Reed's reaction as she walked into the water, his lingering gaze on her. The interaction made her acutely aware of the chemistry simmering just beneath the surface, a sense of possibility in the warm tropical air.

40

Beachcomber Island

October 2024
Fijian Islands

Captain Reed was preparing for his return trip to Los Angeles when Sydney had a suggestion.

"Before you head out, Captain, I think it would be fun if you took Jess and me to Beachcomber Island. I'm told it's beautiful and the island is full of younger tourists who go there for great snorkeling and live bands at night. It's supposed to be quite the party. It will take us less than forty-five minutes to get there in the dinghy. I scoped it out."

Captain Reed went to the charts and quickly located the island Sydney was referring to.

"Great idea, Sydney. I need to let loose before my trip back to Los Angeles. Let's go tomorrow."

The following afternoon Captain Reed, along with Sydney and Jess, climbed into the dinghy and headed to the backpacker paradise filled with young, international travelers sleeping in dormitories, or pooling funds with friends to rent a hut. Sydney jumped off the dinghy into the soft white sand to hold the line until Captain Reed could secure it to the shore. A man from the resort asked if they were checking in and assured the captain his very nice dinghy would be safely looked after. Sydney pulled on her backpack and removed a bag from the dinghy locker. "Refreshments," she said and smiled.

"I've reserved a luxury bungalow with two bedrooms," said Captain Reed. "Let's check in and see what this place is all about."

The woman at the front desk gave the captain a curious lifted-eyebrow look as she handed him the keys. She had short, kinky black hair, and when she smiled Jess saw she was missing a front tooth.

"Bula," she said, which meant both hello and thank you in Fijian, "you be careful not to hurt yourself, Papa." She winked. "Breakfast for everyone at ten, lunch noontime, and dinner at six, all buffet style. The bar is open always and tonight we have a band at the sandbar."

"Fijians are like adult seven-year-olds," said Sydney. She flopped on the king bed in her part of the bungalow. "I'll mix up a couple of drinks to carry with us while we have a look around."

Beachcomber Island was small and picturesque, a paradise in the middle of the Mamanuca Islands. Cast Away, the island featured in the Tom Hanks movie by the same name, was within sight of Beachcomber. It was the kind of place that was easy to get to and hard to leave. It took fifteen minutes to walk around the island and less time to walk from one side to the other. Encircled by a broad white sand beach, the interior of the island was a lush jungle of palm trees, rock-lined paths leading to thatch huts, community bathrooms and showers, and a few luxury bungalows. In the middle of the island stood an enormous thatched-roof open-air dining area consisting of twenty long wooden tables with bench seating. The buffet line was an L-shape with plates positioned at one end to indicate the beginning of the chow line. Across from the dining hall was a tiki bar, a raised stage area, and more wooden tables and benches. The entire area was covered in an elaborate roof made of palm-leaf thatch tied together with coconut rope and raised to a high peak much like a tepee. They followed the paths through the island, passing by the dorm-style accommodations where bathing suits, wetsuits, and towels hung on makeshift clotheslines. The smell of cooking smoke filled the air, and the sound of a bell signaled that dinner was being served.

Sydney returned to the dining table after placing her plate in the dirty-dish cart. "The food wasn't as bad as I imagined it would be. I saw a sign by the office where they post the activities for the day. Scuba, snorkel, kayak, swim with sharks, or just lie on the beach with a beer and a book."

Two girls wearing scant bikinis sat down at their table and Captain Reed immediately started chatting them up. He was asking where they were from and what brought them to this island.

"We're from Tasmania," said the girl. "We came here because you know, this is a crazy-fun place, and Tasmania is dull."

They both giggled, and Captain Reed replied. "Sex, drugs, and rock 'n' roll, baby!"

Sydney stood up and put her arms around him. "My grandfather is reminiscing, but be warned, he is not harmless."

"Ah, very funny, Sydney," the captain replied.

One of the Tasmanian beauties lowered her voice. "Be careful with your drinks. A guy told us people put drugs in them."

"What kind of drugs?" asked Sydney.

"The date-rape kind, or shrooms."

"Any Ecstasy?" asked Captain Reed.

"Don't mind our friend here," said Jess. "If he says anything shockingly inappropriate it's because he is shockingly inappropriate."

The girls looked baffled. "What's that?"

"It's when a person can't control what they say and often blurts out their lecherous thoughts. Okay, Captain, let's go have a rest before the band starts."

Captain Reed got up from the table and with Sydney on one arm, Jess on the other, he turned around and called back to the girls, "Save me a dance."

Rested and showered, drinks in hand, Captain Reed, Sydney, and Jess headed to the Tiki Bar. The band was playing a Red Hot Chili Peppers song, and people were dancing in the sand.

Sydney put her drink down on the table and did the same with Jess's. Swaying her hips, she led Jess to where a crowd was gathered around a handsome young man dancing on his hands. Meanwhile, the captain found the Tasmanian girls, bought them drinks, and invited them to come sailing.

By three in the morning, the three sailors were having great difficulty locating their bungalow. They circled the island at least four times and walked the interior twice. Everything was amusing to them, and they could not stop laughing. Amazingly, they walked every path in the interior without encountering another living soul. Eventually spotting the luxury bungalow and moving toward it, they happened upon a large cement pool of water.

"Look, it's a jacuzzi; let's get in." Jess started climbing in.

"No, no—naked, we must be naked." Captain Reed was removing his Tommy Bahama T-shirt, shorts, and Calvin Klein underwear, when Sydney stopped him.

"We are on to you, Captain. First you get us naked and then you try for a threesome."

Jess was already in the cement tub with her shorts and tank top still on. "Is that what happened when he convinced you to go to the nudist resort?" she asked.

Sydney shook her head. "No, he couldn't get into the place without a girl. It was my first time at a nudist resort, but not my first time being naked with friends. It turned out to be a swinger's club, with a pool, a huge hot tub, and a bunch of gross naked people doing gross stuff to each other."

Sydney joined Jess in the water. "It's not hot. Look for the On switch, Cappy."

Captain Reed, still in his Calvin Kleins and unable to locate any controls, plopped down in the pool with them.

They sat in the water looking up at the stars when Jess asked them, "Did you two get it on?"

Sydney laughed. "Me and Gramps? No way. He apologized, and we bolted out of there."

Captain Reed put his arm around Jess. "I love a nice naked beach, but not with swingers. The place advertised as a 'clothes optional' resort, and

I had no idea. After a pause he said, "You realize we've been dosed with a drug."

Sydney started laughing. "I don't feel a thing," she said and slid underwater.

Whatever it was, Jess thought it must have been a truth-serum drug, because it made it easy to communicate what she was thinking.

Sydney resurfaced laughing. "How could you even think that? He's old enough to be my—"

"Don't say it," Captain Reed stopped her. "You'll hurt me deeply."

Jess began splashing them when suddenly a security guard appeared near the pool.

"What are you doing in the dive-training pool at four in the morning?"

"Shrooming, I think," said Captain Reed, and with that the women couldn't contain their laughter.

"This is not allowed," the guard said. "Please go to your room."

"What's not allowed?" asked the captain.

"Both," answered the man. "Now you must go!"

The guard waved his hat at them to shoo them away. Climbing out, laughing hysterically, they scurried off like naughty children.

Once inside their bungalow, Captain Reed shut the drapes, removed his wet clothes, and dried himself off with a towel. He then walked over to the king-size bed, jumped in, and curled up under the covers, patting the mattress for Jess to join him.

Jess pulled on a dry T-shirt and underwear and crawled in next to him. The mushroom high made her want to seduce him. Her desire for him was overwhelming, but with Sydney in the next room, she suppressed the urge. His back was to her, and she could tell from his breathing he had already fallen asleep. Jess lay next to him, eyes closed, imagining what it would be like to make love with him.

Breakfast and lunch came and went before Jess opened her eyes sometime in the late afternoon. Captain Reed and Sydney were already out of the bungalow. Jess pulled the curtains open to let the sunlight in. She brushed her teeth and put on the blue bikini with a cover-up. Then she grabbed the beach bag and towel provided by the resort and headed to the canteen with hopes there would still be coffee.

Sydney was at the Tiki Bar pouring boxed milk into a cup.

"Top o' the morning to ya, lassie," Jess greeted. "How's the coffee?"

Sydney made a gagging sound. "Like it was made ten hours ago, and this is what's left in the bottom of the urn."

"In that case, I'll have mine with a few shots of Baileys."

Sydney headed to the bar with Jess. "Darn good idea, Chef."

The bartender handed Sydney two coffees and four shots of Baileys.

"Where is everyone?" asked Jess. Sydney dumped three of the shots into her coffee along with more boxed milk.

"The beautiful people are either still sleeping, sunning their flawless bodies on the beach, or taking a sex nap. Our captain is on the beach with a gorgeous mother and daughter and frankly, I can't tell which is which. They're sunbathing topless with him. I joined them for a bit, but they're bimbos, and all these creepy Korean guys kept kayaking two feet away to stare at the mom and daughter's fake boobs."

Jess smiled. "Did Captain Don Juan invite the mom and daughter to the boat yet?" Jess surprised herself at how the captain's behavior amused her.

Sydney poured the last shot of Baileys into her coffee. "By the time we leave Beachfucker Island, Captain Reed should have a harem of female guests, and you'll be cooking for them."

Jess set her cup down on the table. "And you will be making their beds and leaving a chocolate on the pillow."

"Not a chance. You spend so much time with him, I think of you as a couple. A couple of what, I don't know. What's the real deal between you two?"

Jess shrugged. "I'm not sure what it is between us. I would take it further with him, but he wants to keep me as a friend. Friendship and adventure, that's all there is right now."

Sydney pursed her lips. "I call total bullshit on that. I see the way he looks at you. What do you like about him that makes you want to stick around?"

Jess thought for a moment.

"He's fascinating. He marches to his own drum, is a bit of an enigma. And sexy. I began this adventure because I needed to heal, to learn to live again, and turns out, it's the same for the captain, but for totally different reasons. It's a slow process. He wanted to sail back to Tahiti, but his wife was sick. He stayed until her last breath, and that was a very difficult thing for him to do. He's been running away or running to something; I don't know which. He needs his boat, a sail plan, and the wind to carry him. That type of adventurous life sounds good to me, too. I think we make a good couple, but he doesn't see it."

Sydney gulped down her coffee. "Right now, he only sees big fake boobs. Maybe one day he'll want to be part of a unit. Come on, let's swim."

As predicted, Captain Reed invited several of the Beachcomber women to dinner on *Slow Dance*, but the only takers were the mother-and-daughter duo. Jess prepared chicken piccata with garlic mashed potatoes, green salad, and long beans.

When the two women arrived on the dock, Don told the captain, "Nice job."

After introductions, the women sat at the outside table with Captain Reed and the brothers, while Sydney and Jess tended to the meal, plating food and pouring wine. While the men listened attentively to the women, Jess found their conversation boring. The mother was going on about how exfoliating your skin with beach sand rubs away your tan, while her young daughter flirted with Don. Holding up a pair of flippers left on deck, the daughter asked Don how they worked when you put them on your feet. She was leaning over him with her perfect boobies in his face. Don grabbed the end of the fins and moved them in a back-and-forth motion, "You kick your feet with the fins on, like this."

Sydney and Jess exchanged an "oh my God" expression, and Sydney said, "Did you know that if you don't plug a light bulb into the empty socket within two hours electricity leaks out into the atmosphere and can cause brain tumors?"

"Yeah, it's for real. I know," answered the girl. "Like holding your cell to your ear."

Jess looked over at Captain Reed, who smiled and gave his shoulders a shrug. A voice was heard calling up from the dock. "Hey mate, permission to come aboard?"

The engineer and bosun from *Noble House* were asking permission to come aboard.

"Yeah, come join the party," said Don. The men were handsome Australians same as the mom and daughter, and it didn't take long before the intruders invited the ladies for a tour of their majestic yacht.

"They basically hijacked your bimbos because their boat is bigger," announced Sydney, who was standing by the captain.

"Easy come, easy go," said Captain Reed. "And speaking of going, I am going to bed. Thanks for the delicious dinner, Jess. Goodnight."

"I didn't realize anyone could be that out of it," said Zack.

Sydney laughed. "Just kick your feet."

Don put his plate on the counter. "Her looks made up for the rest."

Jess handed Zack a dish towel. "The *Noble House* boys don't seem to mind."

"Oh, for God's sake," said Don, "this is the yachting world, everyone's shagging everyone."

When Don wasn't pretending to work on the boat, he was at Carlo's, a popular bar and restaurant; and when Sydney completed her chores for the day, she hung out with different island boys, assisting them with turning their kinky hair into dreadlocks. Don complained daily to Captain Reed regarding Sydney's lack of interest in being part of the crew, and Captain Reed was listening.

He called a meeting to settle the boat before his departure to Los Angeles.

"Don, I want you to get me bids on repairs for the watermakers, generator, and a new Webasto water heater. The timing is important because if we need parts, I can bring them back with me from Los Angeles. Jess will be the pursuer and maintain a petty-cash wallet for your smaller purchases.

You will bring her the receipts so she can reconcile the purse each week for my bookkeeper. Your pay continues to go direct deposit into your accounts. Zack, please service the Hundested Propeller. It probably needs grease and an expert to inspect the entire shaft. See if you can locate one here in Denarau. Sydney, I want you to organize the small spare parts in the boxes under the pilothouse cushions. I am reachable by phone and email. Any questions?"

When Captain Reed left for the airport, Jess felt different this time regarding his leaving. In Samoa, she had been happy and relieved to have time to herself. Now, she missed him almost immediately. She busied herself by taking command of the boat, managing the purse, and reviewing the bids Don brought to her. Don made his own schedule for meetings with contractors and took time off the boat the entire day visiting marine stores to look for parts. The truth about Don was that he was lazy and didn't like to work. He liked to delegate, and Jess saw how this negatively impacted any crew that came aboard while he was in charge. Zack carried the workload, and the dynamic between the brothers bordered on disturbing. Others saw Zack as the weaker brother with low confidence, but Jess saw it the other way around. Zack was always there to catch his big brother when he fell, and she imagined Don fell a lot.

The weeks wore on while repairs took place and *Slow Dance* received parts for the watermakers ordered from Australia. The boat was finally getting the attention she deserved. Jess's evenings were spent eating and drinking with new acquaintances and fellow cruisers from The *Pinta* and *Nikkia*. Carlo's provided live music on weekends, and the *Slow Dance* crew gathered with other yacht crews as well as locals to listen to the live bands. Sydney became infatuated with Phil, a didgeridoo player whose dreadlocks were longer than hers and soon, he began spending time on the boat. After the workday, there were fun nights on the dock playing music, swapping stories, and drinking wine.

On one such evening, Bruno, the Italian chef from *Noble House*, asked Jess if she would like a tour of his galley, and she eagerly accepted his invitation. The majestic yacht was awe-inspiring. At the midship stood a winding staircase leading to the upper deck's swimming pool and jacuzzi. A baby grand piano stood in the majestic sitting room where spectacular crystal chandeliers hung overhead. The staterooms were breathtaking, but the galley was jaw-droppingly incredible. Jess spent most of the tour there, admiring the refrigeration, stovetops, Japanese knives, and French cookware.

"Thank you, Chef Bruno, for the tour."

"You're most welcome. It's not all that glamorous—you saw the small crew quarters—and believe me, we have mechanical, refrigeration, and navigation issues like any other boat, except on a larger scale."

As grand as it was, Jess was happy to be on *Slow Dance* as opposed to the luxurious super yacht. She had more freedom. The crews on the big boats lived in cramped quarters, some so ridiculously frugal that the stews had to share a cabin with the boat boys. They had demanding, rigid work schedules, inappropriate relationships that caused drama, and incompetent captains that often bullied them. Jess imagined this was the reason they partied so hard in port—the long periods of confinement, lack of any personal space, and living on top of other crew members they disliked. She thought about the good money she could make cooking on a super yacht, but truth be told, it seemed like a bleak and stressful existence.

41

The Uprising Music Festival

October 2024
Viti Levu, Fiji

"Roti, fresh roti," the old one-eyed Indian woman called out as she made her rounds.

Jess was on deck buying the breakfast roti from the woman who came around the marina each morning to sell her delicious flatbreads. Sydney snatched one from Jess, unwrapped it, and practically stuffed the entire thing in her mouth. Don and Zack arrived on the upper deck carrying cups of coffee.

"Go figure," said Don. "We have super-tight security, and that ole crone is in here every morning selling roti. I am going to find out how she's pulling it off because it isn't from handing out sexual favors."

Don turned his attention to Sydney. "Jesus, Rasta girl, you're like a dog who swallows food whole without chewing."

Sydney gave Don her best barking-dog imitation, and Trinidad began barking as well.

"Okay, okay Miss T, calm yourself," said Sydney. "By the way, we are all invited by Phil, the digeridoo player from Carlo's—and my new infatuation—to drive up this weekend for the Uprising Music Festival. It's a big deal here on the island; lots of people attend. There will be beer, hot chicks, marijuana, and you two Africans might even get lucky, which would hopefully improve your temperament."

Don chuckled. "Sounds like a blast—and what makes you think we haven't been getting laid?"

Sydney grabbed another roti. "I am out of here before I get into trouble."

Zack was feeding Trini a piece of his roti. "Sydney, you were born trouble."

On Saturday morning, they loaded blankets, pillows, the beer cooler, sandwiches, and Trinidad into the rental car and headed for the music festival a few hours away in Pacific Harbor. The event was held on the outside lawn of a resort. The stage was front and center with food and beverage booths lining the edges of the lawn. Don parked the car and carried the blankets and cooler to the lawn where they staked out a space in front of the stage. There were people lounging, children running around with balloons, and dogs stopping to say hello. Jess hadn't noticed the others vanish nor did she care; she was feeling ultra-relaxed lying on the blanket with Trini, sipping her beer and watching people have a great time. The last rays of the sun were fading when Sydney came back with several women carrying varied instruments. A blond handed Jess a lit joint and she took a puff.

"I haven't had any of that in a while. Are you four beauties going to perform?"

"Yes, darling," answered a petite redhead in a heavy Australian accent as she removed her saxophone from its case. Don and Zack arrived with two women also from Down Under, and Jess couldn't help but notice Don's infatuation with the tall, slender, raven-haired beauty named Emma. The all-girl band assembled on the stage, and when they began to play not a single person was sitting; everyone was dancing. Jess danced with what seemed like a hundred different people. She danced with girls, guys, couples, kids, Sydney, pretty Emma, Trinidad, and the other dogs that loved to dance. She danced until her legs refused to cooperate. She danced until the final song and the emcee declared intermission.

During the break Don checked for rooms at the resort and was told there were not any available. The manager informed him the only rooms were miles away in the town, so they were on their own. When the last band finished, Jess dragged blankets and a pillow to a chaise lounge by the resort pool where she and Trini spent the night in relative comfort.

In the morning, Jess and Trinidad went inside the resort where she found coffee and her fellow crewmates.

"Morning. Did everyone sleep okay?"

Sydney was wrapping her dreads up in her Bob Marley headscarf. "I slept in a tent with some random guy. I couldn't find Phil. The guy kept poking me with what I wanted to believe was a stick, but I know it was his dick. Ugh!"

"Zack and I got lucky," Don chimed in. "Emma let us crash on the floor of her hotel room."

"You slept, no shagging?" asked Sydney.

"No," Don answered indignantly, "Emma is a remarkable girl. A big shot with a marketing firm selling tourism in Fiji."

Sydney finished taming her hair into the scarf. "Did she tell you she's been engaged to some guy for eleven years? She has a big rock on her hand—or did she remove it before you saw it?"

Don's mood turned dark with the news Sydney delivered about Emma.

Phil, who had been searching for Sydney, found them in the café and asked if they would give him a lift back to the surf resort where he worked.

"Sure," answered Don, "it's on our way."

The sun was high overhead when they piled in the car with Trini sitting up front with Zack. Eventually, they turned off the main road and for the next fifteen miles drove on dirt roads through lush jungle, the road climbing to cresting mountaintops with amazing island views, and back down again onto the jungle road that led to the bohemian seaside resort. Upon arrival they learned that Phil didn't just work there; he owned the place.

"I am so impressed," said Sydney. "I thought you were just another cute, starving didgeridoo player."

Phil gave Sydney a peck on her cheek. "My first love is surfing; the music is just for fun. Laurie, my manager, is going to get you all settled in nice bungalows, my treat. Stay until tomorrow, I insist." Phil put his arms around Sydney. "Pretty please, stay a night with me."

Sydney made a face like she was thinking about it.

"Okay, but only one night."

Don was eyeing Laurie, a beautiful, brown-skinned woman from his homeland in Cape Town, who was ignoring him.

"Okay," said Don, "sounds like fun, and no one will miss us back at the marina."

Jess took Trini for a walk along the beach before going back to rest in the cute bungalow she had been provided by Phil. The sun was gone and the stars were out when she and Trinidad joined the other guests for a delicious meal of parrotfish, chicken, and potatoes all roasted in the ground, along with green salad, and mango ice cream for dessert.

After dinner, the travelers and sailors gathered on the large veranda where several of the guests were playing guitars, including one American woman from Nashville. There were various types of hand drums, maracas, bells, and rhythmic gourds to choose from, and of course Phil played his didgeridoo. Zack built one of his awesome fires and the group gathered round talking and playing music until the stars were fading in the light. Jess felt alive, happy, grateful to the universe. She thought about her twenty-something self in Boulder, Colorado, surrounded by music, nature, and creative, free-spirited individuals—some of whom had since become famous. On this night she was feeling twenty-five, not fifty-eight. Thirty-five pounds of chub— and a hundred pounds of worry—gone.

42

Carlo

October 2024
Denarau Island, Fiji

At first light Jess hurried on deck to watch as the sky transformed into a palette of vibrant colors. She embraced the tranquility of the morning as she sat on the sofa with Trini's head in her lap. Listening to the gentle waves lapping at the side of the boat, she was thinking what a truly magical experience her life had become.

When the morning colors began to fade, Jess went down to her galley to make coffee. She needed to begin preparing the aft cabins for Captain Reed's guests arriving in one week's time. Sydney was putting minimal effort into her assigned duties, and tensions were building between her and Don. He barked orders at Sydney rather than assigning a daily plan. Jess, having managed people most of her life, was acutely aware of Don's shortcomings. She knew he would never be a successful captain for more reasons than his lack of management skills. There was an awkwardness between him and Sydney since their night of drunken sex in American Samoa. Sydney confided in Jess that she knew Don was a player, and he had played her. She said Don had sex with her because she was available, and she resented him for pretending he cared about her. Jess tried to comfort her but knew she had a right to be angry. She had shared her

278

feelings about Marlin with Don, and he used the information against her. "I'm mad at him and mad at myself," she told Jess. "I should have known better."

They spent several days getting the cabins prepared for the guests, and when Saturday night came around, Sydney asked Jess if she wanted to go to Carlo's to listen to some live music. Phil was playing his digeridoo in the band, and Sydney insisted Jess come out for a bit of fun.

Jess was sitting with Sydney and Zack at a table near the band when someone gently touched the back of her neck. She turned to see a handsome, dark-skinned, fiftyish man, who leaned in to gently put his lips ever so lightly on hers, then took her hand, kissed it, and with a smile, retreated into the crowd. Zack and Sydney had witnessed the man's behavior and were smiling devilishly. Jess knew her expression had to be one of disbelief.

"Who was that guy?" she asked.

Sydney chuckled. "That was the infamous Carlo!"

Monday morning during breakfast, Don had asked Jess to join him later in the day for a meeting with a potential contractor. It was late afternoon, and the meeting took place at Carlo's. Don drank several beers while he and the contractor discussed the technical aspects of the job along with his estimate for parts and labor. Jess was disgusted by Don's lack of professionalism and requested he bring her the written bid for review. Excusing herself from the meeting, she rose to leave, and someone pulled her chair out for her. It was Carlo.

"These fellows look like they are boring you. Could I interest you in a drive around the golf course?"

"Maybe . . ." she replied.

"Please excuse my rude behavior. I am Carlo, the owner of this fine establishment. And you are?"

Jess answered, "Right, you're the stranger who took the liberty to attempt a kiss on this unsuspecting cook."

Carlo smiled coyly as he extended his arm to her. "Yes, and for that please accept my apology. Will you do me the pleasure of taking a tour of our magnificent golf course?"

Taking Carlo's arm she answered, "How can a girl resist such a charming fellow as yourself?"

Carlo walked her to his golf cart parked nearby. It was a warm afternoon, and the breeze felt lovely on her moist skin as they drove along the designated pathways.

"This course has hosted some of the world's most famous tournaments," he said. "Fiji has been a popular place for golf since the Scots started hitting balls."

Jess chuckled at his comment. "I've played a bit, but honestly, I enjoy driving the cart more than hitting the ball."

Carlo nodded. "We could have a game sometime, if you'd like."

Jess thought to herself, *This man is beyond charming*. He was wearing a white, loose-fitted, short-sleeved shirt, tucked into white tailored trousers, with a black belt. On his head, he wore a white Panama hat. His skin was the color of caramel, smooth and unblemished. He was a very attractive, charismatic man.

"Would you be my guest and share a glass of wine with me? I would like to get to know you better."

She answered with a polite "Yes," both intrigued and cautious.

Carlo drove the cart up a long driveway lined with palm trees, stopping in front of a luxurious property. The house seemed to merge out of the surrounding landscape. Jess thought he was taking her back to his restaurant, but he had brought her to his residence.

As if reading her thoughts, Carlo said, "You are safe, and in the company of a gentleman. Let me share my home with you. It is a great escape from the noise."

There were large potted trees inside, outside, and around the pool. A waterfall spilled over rocks into the swimming pool located amid a bamboo forest.

"Come into the kitchen while I open some wine."

Carlo took her hand and led her into the house. The living room was 1930s Kreiss rattan furniture arranged on a seagrass woven rug. It was beautiful. The man had exceptional taste.

Carlo opened a bottle of red wine and poured two glasses. "The Australians produce the finest Shiraz. Come sit with me by the pool."

She followed him outside and sat in one of the cushioned chairs.

"I am half Fijian and half Chinese. I was educated in Australia where the Chinese are looked down upon, much like the aboriginals. I married a New Zealand woman, and we opened the restaurant here thirty years ago. We raised two children, and then she left because I am not an easy person to live with or work for."

Jess listened, amazed that he openly revealed so much about himself to a total stranger he had just met.

"You are very accomplished, and your achievements couldn't have come easy under the circumstances of prejudice," she told him. "Your restaurant is the most popular one on Denarau, and judging by your home, you've done well for yourself and your children."

Carlo stood up and filled her glass with more wine. "Success comes with a cost. My business is very demanding. You are a chef, so you would know. Now tell me more about that."

Jess shared her restaurant experience along with snippets of her life, keeping the conversation cordial.

As the afternoon turned into early evening, Carlo looked at his watch.

"Oh, look at the time. Thank you for a lovely afternoon. I must return to the restaurant for the dinner hour. Will you join me for dinner on Friday, say, eight o' clock? Don't say no."

He let her off at the marina gate with a simple wave. There was something simultaneously warm and cold about Carlo, and she was surmising he must be lonely judging by the intimate details he shared about himself.

Don was on deck when Jess returned to the boat.

"How was your afternoon, love?"

She waved him off. "It's not what you think. We had some wine and conversation—not that it's any of your business," she teased.

Jess had dinner with Carlo on Friday evening at his restaurant. He ordered her the fresh catch, and she reluctantly tasted his quail. After dinner, they moved to a table of rowdy Australians who were regular customers. Carlo introduced her, and she got the distinct feeling he was showing her off to his buddies. She didn't like it. After the second bottle of wine, Jess thanked Carlo for a nice evening. He was obviously disappointed it had been only dinner and conversation and begrudgingly said goodnight.

Captain Reed's email arrived saying he would return in two days with his guests. He requested Don make a sail plan to spend two weeks in the Yasawa Islands and make certain *Slow Dance* had enough fuel for the dinghy during the duration of the trip. Jess stayed occupied with provisioning the boat so she could avoid Carlo. Don and Zack prepared the dive and snorkeling equipment as well as the kayaks. The crew would need to change cabins to make room for the visitors, so they began relocating their personal items. Don and Zack would bunk in the crew cabin, Sydney would take the forward cabin at the bow, and Jess would be with Captain Reed in the master. The thought of being in his cabin again was much more exciting than another dinner with Carlo. She set to work preparing menus for Captain Reed's guests. She was looking forward to his return.

43

Cousin Sheldon

October 2024
Port Denarau Marina, Fiji

Captain Reed arrived at the boat by taxi, along with Sheldon, Sheldon's friend Miles, and his girlfriend Paige. Zack carried the luggage to their respective cabins while Jess and Sydney offered refreshments of coconut fruit salad, shrimp cocktail, garlic toast, and several bottles of chilled prosecco.

"Oh, I don't drink. What else do you have?" Paige, a plump blond with a pretty face, was dressed in a tracksuit that made her look out of place for the tropical climate.

Miles was twenty years older than Paige, with a sprinkling of gray in his black hair, a nice smile, and a decent physique for his age. Sheldon didn't look anything like Jess imagined from Captain Reed's stories. He was short in stature, balding, but exuded youthful arrogance.

Unpacked, well-fed, and rested, the guests settled in on *Slow Dance*. Captain Reed was reviewing the sail plan with Don, Sheldon, and Miles, while Jess was in the galley with Sydney preparing the evening meal. Sydney attempted to assist Jess in some way but ended up feeding carrots to Trini.

"Good grief, you're useless. Didn't your mom teach you anything about the kitchen?"

Sydney put a piece of carrot in her mouth. "Yeah, how to eat and besides, I'm Gen X and we don't want to be in the kitchen, or have kids, or get married. I am nervous about this trip. I am not a good servant, *as you know*, and these are fancy people. I am going to mess up. I don't know how to wait on people."

Jess patted her head. "I'll train you, grasshopper. I am excellent at training cats, so I know I can train you. Now scoot. You too, Miss T."

Slow Dance sailed northwest of the main island toward the Yasawa Island group. They were blessed with perfect weather. There were twenty islands and atolls in the archipelago, gorgeous islands with dramatic peaks, sun-drenched beaches, and turquoise lagoons. A collection of boutique resorts and homestay backpacker huts were tucked back in the jungle behind the beaches. Ferries, catamarans, and seaplanes carried tourists to the remote islands. Water taxis were also available to carry passengers from one resort island to another.

Sydney was looking at the chart with Sheldon and the captain. "You know, these particular islands were virtually undiscovered until the 1980s."

"And now they're crawling with tourists," said Sheldon sarcastically.

Captain Reed put his finger on the chart. "No tourists here. Look at all the secluded bays we can anchor in and have the whole place to ourselves. The boys can build a fire on the sand tonight, and Jess will serve dinner on the beach."

"Now you're talking," said Sheldon. "And I am going to indulge in the fine scotch I know you keep on hand just for me, coz."

Don and Zack demonstrated their flawless guest service skills by keeping the dinghy clean and well-stocked with beer, water, beach towels, snorkeling gear, extra hats, and sunscreen.

Soon *Slow Dance* anchored inside the beautiful and famous Blue Lagoon, and as promised, the guys built a roaring beach fire. Around the firepit, they placed folding chairs on top of bamboo mats. Jess set a beautiful, portable table with help from Sydney, and Don began to ferry the guests from *Slow Dance* to the beach.

"This is delicious," said Miles. "What is it exactly?"

"Kokoda, the Fijian version of ceviche, made with coconut milk, coriander, onion, spring onion, and raw fish, of course."

"What's the main course?" Sheldon placed his appetizer dish on the table.

"Nearly ready," said Jess as she walked over to the hot coals and turned over the fish she was grilling. "Sea bass prepared with fresh chilis, lime, cilantro, and sea salt, served with roasted red potatoes, and rourou, a Fijian dish made with taro leaves resembling spinach."

"What about this cake here?" asked Sheldon.

"Cassava cake."

Sheldon raised his eyebrows. "Wow, coz, I had no idea you had it so good."

Jess noticed Paige's plate was virtually empty except for the vegetable she was pushing around with her fork while making a face.

Captain Reed noticed as well. "Not hungry?" he asked.

"I am a vegetarian, and I am gluten sensitive, so I must eat very clean and organic. I am surprised Miles is eating any of this. Miles, you know you're going to have a stomachache later."

Sydney gave Jess one of her looks.

"You can't eat the potatoes or spinach?" asked Captain Reed before looking at Jess. "Jess, can make you vegetables, honey? No one knew you had dietary restrictions," he said, turning back to Paige.

"In case you weren't aware," Paige answered contemptuously, "things have changed over the past twenty years, and women don't like being referred to as honey, sweetie, or any other words that demean them."

Captain Reed made a long face. "In my generation, it was meant as an endearing phrase, but I take it back."

Sheldon, who was standing by the fire with Miles, spoke up. "I have just the thing for stomachaches and irritabilities."

To their amazement, Sheldon pulled out a rolled joint and lit the end. "Oh, for goodness' sake, Sheldon," Paige said. "You know Miles and I don't do drugs."

Miles took the joint from Sheldon and put his arm around Paige.

"We're in Fiji, hon. Let's get stoned with the natives."

He put the joint to Paige's lips, and she took a little puff without inhaling. "Where in the world did this come from? I hope you weren't smuggling this, Miles, or you, Sheldon."

Sheldon took the joint.

"Last time Miles smuggled weed, he didn't tell me, and we got arrested crossing the border out of Mexico."

"No, we didn't smuggle it, Paige," Sheldon assured her. "Miles bought it from Carlo, the guy who owns a popular restaurant in the marina. Don introduced us when we asked where to change money. Carlo gave us a great exchange rate on our U.S. dollars to Fijian dollars. He said he was helping us out because of the cook."

Jess pretended she hadn't heard the remark and started cutting the cake.

Miles attempted to hand the joint to Captain Reed.

"No thanks, I never smoke, anything, ever."

Sheldon took the joint from Miles. "He liked the white powder, but didn't we all back in the eighties. Hopefully, you gave that up, coz."

Captain Reed gave his cousin a derisive look. "It was the eighties, and I owned the Palace Discotheque. Powder was everywhere. Yes, I did give it up, right before my triple bypass surgery."

"I think we all had our time in the barrel during the eighties," Miles said.

Paige glared at him. "You . . . never told me you used cocaine."

"I need to keep some things secret, baby doll. Familiarity breeds contempt."

Paige gave him a scornful look and moved over by the fire.

It was becoming embers while Don helped Jess place dirty dishes into a basket.

Speaking in a low voice, Don said, "That bird is going to need a lot more than marijuana to loosen her up."

Jess put the last of the plates into the basket. "A crowbar is more like it."

Captain Reed walked over to them. "When we get back to the marina, I need to see if Carlo will change some dollars for me. I imagine he wants U.S. dollars to convert into Australian dollars. The exchange rate is good right now. And what's the deal with you and Carlo? What are you two exchanging?"

"He's a new friend."

Jess felt a flutter in her stomach because he might be a bit jealous.

He's jealous but doesn't want to be a couple?

Ironic, Jess thought, how sailors spend their lives tying knots, and this sailor wants nothing to do with getting knotted up with someone.

Was it still too soon after his wife's death? Or would he be this way forever? And why was she waiting for him to decide? She wasn't Cinderella waiting for the Prince to choose a fair maiden.

She continued to ponder their awkward attraction. She saw his cracks and flaws and compared them to her own. She had failed at love, a few times, and she didn't want to make those same mistakes. She wondered how he saw her cracks and flaws. It's the differences that undo the knot of love; the similarities do not cause problems. Loving someone was loving all the small things, the way they sip their wine, their laugh, the way you read each other's mind, and the way you feel when you look into each other's eyes. Did they love one another? One thing was for sure. The day she interviewed for this gig, she had not been inclined to fall for Captain Reed.

Slow Dance had a pleasant and easy sail to the Yasawa Islands. They visited Tavewa, Likuliku Bay, Waya, Nacula, and the Blue Lagoon. Trinidad went with them on every outing, and the days they stayed aboard, Jess provided lavish meals, including vegan dishes for Miss Paige. Captain Reed and Paige had taken an instant dislike to each other, and Jess tried to placate the situation with food. Paige remained in yoga pants most days, but with Miles's coaxing, ventured into the clear, cool waters of the South Pacific for some snorkeling, wearing a long-sleeved O'Neill shirt and board shorts. Paige was fair skinned, and Jess assumed she needed to protect herself from the Fijian sun.

Jess stood at the edge of the deck, the warm tropical sun kissing her skin as she adjusted her sexy blue bikini. It was another stunning morning in the Yasawa Islands, where the vibrant colors of the morning matched the azure waters of the Blue Lagoon. Feeling playful, Jess caught a glimpse of the captain and his cousin Sheldon already splashing in the shimmering sea. Carrying her customary giant cup of coffee, Sydney appeared on deck, where she encountered Jess and Paige, who was reading a book on the outside sofa.

"Another perfect day," Sydney said to Jess. "Did you sleep well?

Jess tossed her towel over the rail. "I sleep like a baby with the rocking motion of the boat."

Paige put her book down. "Actually, it's difficult to sleep in the cabin assigned to us because of the putrid stench of sewage that permeates the entire cabin."

"Ugh, that's awful," said Sydney. "I'll talk to Don and Captain Reed. Why didn't you say something sooner?"

Paige shrugged. "I didn't think it could be fixed."

"I'll speak to him as soon as he gets out from his swim," said Sydney.

Paige gestured toward the stern. "Yes, he's in the water with Sheldon and his cook appears to be joining them."

Jess's enthusiasm was dampened by Miss Yoga Pants, her arms crossed over her chest, her expression a mixture of disapproval and disdain regarding Jess's swim attire.

Sipping her coffee, Sydney rolled her eyes at Paige's uptight attitude and after giving off a low long whistle, said, "Wow, Jess, you look great in that suit."

Jess was determined not to let Paige ruin her fun. She was determined to never let anyone make her feel less than. With that thought, she jumped off the platform into the delicious sea surrounded by paradise, ready to embrace every moment of her new life.

Paige retreated to the salon when the three swimmers climbed onto the boat, seemingly disgusted by something as simple as an early morning swim. Captain Reed rinsed off with the fresh-water hose and then held it for Jess while she rinsed the salt from her hair. Sheldon was watching as she wrapped a towel around herself.

"I am off to make some breakfast," Jess said, but stopping in the pilot-house to dry her hair, she overheard the captain and Sheldon talking.

"I like her more than Sophia," Sheldon said. "Does she know about her?"

Jess stopped drying her hair to hear more clearly.

"She knows," Captain Reed said.

"So," Sheldon pressed on, "she sleeps in your cabin sometimes and on deck other nights?"

"She slept in my cabin before we left L.A., because of my broken arm. I couldn't do anything, let alone have sex."

"Yeah, I remember. You were a mess, in more ways than one. Your arm is healed, so, what's the story?" Sheldon's tone was playful.

"It's complicated. I am not ready for a committed relationship."

"Were you ever ready?"

"I guess not."

"I think you will go well together," said Sheldon. "You have the same vibe. I'll leave it at that."

"Thanks for your two cents, I'll take it under advisement."

Jess stood in the pilothouse, a few steps away, her heart sinking as she overheard the captain about his reluctance to commit. Their chemistry was undeniable, but hearing him say he wasn't relationship material sent a wave of uncertainty crashing over her. A mix of frustration and longing surged within her. She wanted to believe they could be more than just friends. Would she ever be more than a passing moment in the captain's life? Reminding herself she was out for adventure and self-discovery; she pushed her thoughts about Captain Reed to the back of her mind and went to the gally to prepare breakfast.

Captain Reed was still wearing his bathing suit when they gathered around the outside table. Jess delivered a breakfast of warm, flaky croissants, a veggie frittata, sliced mango with fresh coconut, butter, raspberry jam, scrambled tofu, and noni juice to please Paige. Paige neither complained nor showed gratitude.

Miles turned to Captain Reed. "By the way, could someone fix the smell in our cabin?"

44

The Situationship

October 2024
The Yasawa Islands, Fiji

"You're looking relaxed," said Jess as she cleared the breakfast from the outside table.

Captain Reed was lounging on the sofa with Trini, and as Jess picked up the plates, he took her wrist. "Please stay for a bit. Sit. We haven't had a chance to just chill and talk. You have been working hard to keep our guests happy, especially that Paige."

Jess sighed and sat at the end of the sofa. "My customer service skills came in handy. It wasn't all work and no play; we've had a lot of fun off the boat snorkeling, swimming, and dining at the resorts. It gave me a break from being your galley slave." She had decided to lock her heart up and keep it light and carefree with Captain Reed.

He chuckled at her comment.

Jess added, "You could be nicer to Paige; she's not so bad. She's an artist. She showed me some of her paintings, and they're quite good. She's not the beachy type. She's more of the yoga, meditation type."

Captain Reed nodded agreement. "You're right. I could have been nicer, but you must admit she doesn't like me either. Thinks I'm a misogynistic, anti-feminist man-pig. Good thing she didn't see Miles checking out the girls at the resorts whenever she went to the restroom or stayed on the boat."

Jess sniggered. "I noticed that, too. She's obviously his caregiver, making sure he takes his pills and checks his blood pressure. . . . Do you think they have sex?"

"Knowing Miles, I'd say yes, they still make love, and he takes care of her financially, so it works for them. Now, tell me about Carlo?"

The captain's inquiry caught Jess totally off guard, and she took a beat to gather her thoughts. "I had dinner with him one night at his restaurant and spent an afternoon drinking wine by the pool at his house. He has a fabulous home off the golf course."

"And . . . ?" asked the captain with a raised eyebrow.

Jess suddenly felt guilty even though she knew it was absurd.

"What specifically do you want to know? How much I like him?" Jess stood up. "He's handsome, charming, warm, cold, and too busy for a relationship—much like you."

Captain Reed gently pulled Jess back to a seated position. Turning to her and looking serious, he said, "I have never been completely truthful with anyone until you, Jess. It's very unsettling."

Mustering courage, he continued, his voice tinged with vulnerability. "You have a way of letting me be me without judgments. I feel accepted in a way I never thought possible by a woman. I cherish our friendship and the connection we have. I love having you aboard, Jess, and I have come to care for you in a way that goes beyond friendship. I don't want to lose what we have by pursuing something more." The captain seemed to be feeling the weight of his words, unsure how Jess would respond. "I needed you to know how special you are, regardless of what the future holds."

In that moment unfolding between them, Jess's thoughts became a storm of unspoken emotions and fears. Before she could answer, Sheldon came on deck holding a second cup of coffee.

That evening, Jess served several of her homemade pizzas with a mixed salad and a choice of pinot noir or chilled chardonnay. The dessert, a raspberry tiramisu made from scratch, took most of her day to prepare. Cooking was her meditation when her mind needed clearing.

Sydney was about to pour herself another glass of wine when Jess observed Don motioning with his eyes toward Miles's empty glass. Taking the hint, Sydney filled Miles's glass to the rim, making it impossible for him to take a sip without spilling it. Jess watched Don give Captain Reed a disgusted look.

Sydney got up and stood over Don, draping her white napkin over her arm. She put the other arm behind her back and spoke in a fake British accent.

"Excuse me, sir, are you through? May I take your plate?"

Don handed her his plate, clearly not amused. Taking his plate and a few others, Sydney followed Jess to the galley.

"Don has it in for me," Sydney complained. "I bet I get eighty-sixed as soon as we get back to the marina. You see it, I know."

Jess did see it coming. *Slow Dance* would be in Fiji for several more months, and much of that time would be on the dock. Captain Reed needed Don and Zack but had no reason to keep Sydney on his payroll. She had joined *Slow Dance* for the experience, and after proving her worth to the captain, Sydney ended up as paid crew.

Slow Dance would be sailing back to Denarau, and Jess was looking forward to some downtime. Sydney had been little help when it came to tidying up the guest cabins. She had no interest in changing out the towels and bedding or folding guest laundry. During their outings, Sydney would often disappear with other young people partying at the resorts. Don and Zack spent a few nights off the boat when the guests retired early, asking permission from Captain Reed to do so.

The final evening in the Yasawa Islands, everyone retired to their cabins after dinner. Finishing up in the galley, Jess decided to go on deck and observe the night sky. She didn't see the captain sitting on the couch until Trini came over wagging her tail.

He joined her at the rail. "Beautiful night."

"Yes, beautiful."

At that moment, the sky erupted in a spectacular meteor shower. They stood together at the rail as flickers of light streaked across the night sky, fading back into the darkness. Jess felt uneasy as she had yet to respond to the captain's true feelings toward her.

Captain Reed broke the silence.

"It's been great having Sheldon aboard. He's quite impressed by you. He said we're good together, and I suppose he should know. He's been married to his wife Robin for forty years, maybe more. What do you think?"

Deciding to no longer avoid the conversation, Jess turned to him. "I think becoming a couple can be a loss of control. Your life is affected by someone's body language, mood, or their favorite food. It's thrilling, but not everyone looks at love the same. What do you think?"

He turned his gaze toward the sea. "I think love takes time. It never turned out well for me, but I did learn what not to do. I believe we learn to love ourselves before we can love another."

"I believe that, too," she said. "Sailing with you has been life-altering for me. It's been a long time since I had a feeling of belonging somewhere. Every day we sail on to a new adventure, it becomes clearer to me what I want for my future. When I had lunch with Kari— before joining the boat—she told me to be careful of you. She told me to stand up for myself. She warned me you would use me up if I didn't have boundaries. She told me I was a lot like her, a giver, and that was exactly what you looked for in a woman, so you could take advantage, because you are selfish. I assured her that wouldn't happen."

Captain Reed was staring at her. "You *are* like Kari: kind, caring, giving, but so much more."

Jess turned to look at him. "True, I am those things, but the difference between me and Kari is, she wore her heart on her sleeve, and my heart is safely tucked away and beating just for me," she lied. "Kari was looking for Mr. Right. I am looking for me."

Captain Reed pursed his lips. "Carlo doesn't make your heart flutter?"

"No," she said. "I've been looking for some fluttering, but it didn't happen with him, not in any part of my body."

She suddenly felt a fluttering, and the captain was the reason.

"You constantly surprise me, Jess. You're not the same woman who came aboard my boat a year ago."

As gentle waves rocked *Slow Dance* under the starlit sky, Jess stood before the captain, her heart racing with emotion. She had listened to Captain Reed confess his deeper feelings for her, and she was a mix of surprise and trepidation. Jess took a deep breath, her eyes meeting his.

"Your words touch me in a way I didn't think possible. The moments we've shared on the boat, the lessons you've taught me about the sea and the sails, are experiences I hold dear. I never imagined my feelings could evolve into something more. Hell, I didn't like you much at the beginning of this journey. We have been moving toward each other the way a hurricane moves toward land, constantly changing direction with various degrees of intensity."

Jess's hands began to fidget nervously as she took a step closer to the captain.

"I care for you deeply," he said, "and I don't want to lose the bond we have formed. But at the same time, the idea of exploring these feelings is appealing."

With their hearts laid bare and their emotions exposed, the captain and Jess stood looking into each other's eyes, silently communicating the depths of their feelings and the uncertainty of what the future may hold.

45

Farewell

November 2024
Port Denarau Marina, Fiji

Sydney was at the bow with Jess, watching Don maneuver *Slow Dance* into their slip at the marina.

"It's amazing how many places we have sailed to over the past year," said Sydney. "Geography is good knowledge to have if you're solving a crossword, but not always easy to experience in real life."

"You sound like you're already gone, Sydney."

"I am not kidding myself, and it's okay. I miss my family and my life back in Wisconsin.

It's been the adventure of a lifetime, something to tell my kids about—if I have any."

After the boat was settled, Captain Reed, Sheldon, and Jess ventured over to Carlo's to see if Carlo would exchange Captain Reed's U.S. dollars for Fijian dollars.

"May as well have lunch," Captain Reed said. "I hope Carlo is here so I can change my dollars."

Captain Reed and Sheldon sat at one of the outside tables and Jess was hoping Carlo wouldn't show up. Carlo was at the restaurant, and he ventured from the office when he saw Jess, immediately walking over to their table.

Carlo shook hands with Sheldon and Captain Reed, giving them each a firm handshake. Turning his attention to Jess, he addressed her in an overly familiar manner.

"It is so lovely to see you're back. How were the islands?"

"Very beautiful," she answered. "Have you sailed to the Yasawas, Carlo?"

"Yes," he answered. "I would love to take you to the Blue Lagoon—when you're available, and if Captain Reed will allow you time off."

The captain abruptly answered, "I've already taken her to the Blue Lagoon."

Jess was acutely aware of his discomfort.

"Sheldon tells me you offer a good rate for changing U.S. dollars. How much do you need to change?" Carlo asked.

Captain Reed replied, "Do you have an office where we can talk?"

"Yes, this way. Meanwhile, lunch is on the house and let me send a bottle of your cook's favorite Australian Shiraz to the table."

Frowning at Carlo's knowledge of Jess's favorite wine, Captain Reed disappeared with him into his office.

"Carlo's very smooth, Jess," Sheldon said. ". . . You realize my coz is jealous, right?"

"Why should he be?" she answered.

"Because he cares for you but is too stupid to act on it. Thinks he'll break your heart, and you'll jump ship."

Jess shook her head. "I care for him as well, and you would think after all this time together, he would know I am not as naive and delicate as he thinks. I am just as apprehensive about entangling myself as he is. I've told him, we don't have to be monogamous, just honest. I think I love the boat more than I love him," she said. "So, there's that."

Sheldon was about to comment when the waitress arrived with two bottles of wine and four glasses. Captain Reed and Carlo returned to the table, and the waitress poured the wine.

They ordered lunch, and Jess sat listening, amused at the bantering between Captain Reed and Carlo. After several glasses of wine, the captain referred to Carlo as a lackey, and Carlo was calling Captain Reed a "poofda," meaning he was gay.

Sheldon, Captain Reed, and Carlo became engaged in a discussion regarding money.

They finished their meal and were well into the second bottle of wine when Captain Reed and Sheldon got into a heated debate about the haves and have-nots of the world. Carlo leaned over and asked Jess if she would like to see the baby quail that were hatching off his office in the courtyard. They got up from the table and he led her to a room with an incubator. Jess was looking at some adult birds in cages.

"They're so cute. You're raising them for the menu? I couldn't eat one, they're too pretty."

Carlo put his arm around her. "See here . . . it's the incubator to hatch the eggs."

Bending down, Jess placed her face close to the glass for a better look. Carlo was next to her as they peered into the glass, and when she stood up, he put his arms around her, pressing his body into hers and burying his head against her shoulder. Jess felt herself stiffen as he attempted to kiss her neck. At that moment, Captain Reed walked in and pulled Carlo away from her.

"What is this? I can't have my cook fraternizing with the money changer. It's inappropriate."

Carlo released her and stepped back away from the captain.

"Your cook hasn't mentioned that you are a couple."

"That's because we're not."

Carlo raised his eyebrows in surprise. "Then what is your objection to me giving her a kiss?"

Captain Reed stood there, unable to answer, and Jess hurried back to the table to join Sheldon.

"Are they duking it out over you?" he said with a laugh and poured Jess more wine.

"Honestly, I had dinner with Carlo a few times, but it was just dinner. He was always a gentleman until today. Captain Reed triggered his alpha male."

"No," said Sheldon, "you did!"

Carlo and Captain Reed eventually returned to the table, and Jess wished she had been a fly on the wall to hear what was said between the two men. She was happy the captain intervened before Carlo kissed her. Their juvenile competition amused her. Maybe Carlo had created a situation that would prompt the captain to act on his feelings toward her.

After lunch Captain Reed, Jess, and Sheldon returned to *Slow Dance* to find Miles and Paige handing their bags to Zack, who placed them in the trunk of a taxi. Miles waved at Sheldon and said, "Better get your gear, buddy. We have a plane to catch."

Paige was on deck and Jess asked her if she had any good photos she might like to share on her blog.

Paige replied in a snarky voice. "I already packed my camera away and I am not getting it out."

Sydney gave Jess a pretend horrified look as Paige exited *Slow Dance*.

"Man, that chick is uptight. Someone needs to tell her it's okay to have fun. I need a beer after dealing with Ms. Yoga Pants."—and with that, Sydney disappeared below deck.

Jess stood on the dock with Captain Reed, Don, and Zack to say good-bye to their guests.

Captain Reed gave Sheldon a bear hug. "I am gonna miss you, coz. Give my best to Robin. See you on the backside."

Three days after Captain Reed's guests left, Don and Captain Reed sat Jess down and informed her Sydney was off the boat. It came as no surprise.

"Where is Sydney now?"

Don waved her question off. "I don't know, but she needs to pack because her flight out of here is early tomorrow morning."

Jess found Sydney sipping a beer at Carlo's. Trinidad was on her lap keeping her company.

"Hey girl, Don of the Dead just informed me you are, in fact, fired."

Sydney wiped the foam from her lips. "It's cool, I am happy to be going home. This has been one hell of an adventure, but honestly, I hate the tropics. I have itchy bumps on my skin and the humidity doesn't do much for the rest of me. After buying a place back home and repairing my little twenty-foot boat, I may join an expedition ship to Alaska. That's more my type of gig."

Jess pulled up a chair and ordered a beer. Trinidad's entire back end was gyrating wildly with excitement as Jess reached for her. She jumped off Sydney's lap and onto Jess for face licks.

"Jeez, Miss T, it's only been, like, five minutes since you saw her! This mutt loves you, Jess. I am going to miss you, T. You're the best little sailor dog I've ever met, and although I am a cat person, you rock. I am also going to miss you and Captain Shark Bait. It's sure been a wild ride. A box full of fun memories."

Jess moved her chair closer to Sydney. "You know, I am a bit psychic, and I can assure you, we will see you down the road somewhere, sometime." Jess laid her head on Sydney's shoulder. "I am sure going to miss you, Cat Mop."

46

Companionate Love

November 2024
Port Denarau Marina, Fiji

With the guests gone and Sydney terminated, *Slow Dance* settled into an organized routine. Over Jess's breakfast, Don updated Captain Reed daily on boat business, and contractors came aboard to discuss their scope of work, while Zack handled general maintenance in the engine room. Jess decided the time was right to take on the overwhelming task of organizing the storage bins beneath the bilges. Sydney had accomplished sorting the screws, fasteners, and bolts in the small lockers under the pilothouse cushions; however, important boat parts had been haphazardly placed into unlabeled bins. Inventorying the contents of each bin, and grouping similar items, she listed them on an Excel spreadsheet. Jess insisted the captain sit with her while she emptied each bin, requesting he identify any unfamiliar items. Don had been monopolizing his time, so Jess devised a way for them to be together, her main motivation for organizing the bins, along with her desire to keep a tight ship.

"I can see why my crew over the years have never wanted to attack this job."

Captain Reed was sitting in the salon, and Jess was holding up items from one of the storage bins. "That's packing wadding," he explained. "It keeps seawater from leaking into the bilge where the Hundested shaft passes through the boat to the prop."

Jess placed the package on one of her piles. "Isn't this great? Now, when you call for a fuel filter in the middle of night—in turbulent seas—we can refer to the list on the computer and locate it immediately. There are eight filters in bin number two, and they're easy to grab."

The captain gave her one of his sexy smiles. "I should make you captain. *Slow Dance* has never been so organized. The watermakers are working, and we have a new water heater."

Jess's mood turned serious. "The boat has been under repair since we left Mexico. We made it to Fiji, and you probably risked my life along with the others."

Captain Reed shrugged. "It would take a lot to put this girl down, and once I get her to Thailand, she's getting a complete refit and a new teak deck. Teak is cheaper there, and they do fantastic work."

Jess lifted her eyebrows in surprise. "Thailand?"

"Why not?" he answered. "Once *Slow Dance* is refit, she will go wherever the wind takes us."

Jess noticed his choice of pronoun—*us* rather than *me*.

"When I get back, we sail to the Kadavu Islands to test all the sails, radar equipment, and mechanical systems."

"When you get back? Where are you going?"

"To L.A. for a couple of weeks. You know, business and doctors."

Captain Reed had been somber since the incident at Carlo's, and although they spent most of the day together, their conversations were light. Jess was disappointed he would be leaving again so soon and felt they were moving further apart instead of closer together. It also troubled her that he made the decision to sail to Thailand without discussing it with her, as was his usual way. She pushed the thought from her mind. The stories about Thai women were infamous. Men who went to Thailand tended to never come back.

As if sensing her uncertainty, Captain Reed said, "I know you're up for sailing on, and I could never make it to Thailand without you."

Jess felt that familiar flutter in her stomach.

"Am I interrupting?" Don was standing on the steps to the salon.

"No," said Captain Reed.

Don came in and sat on the sofa. "I think we all need some R 'n' R. Maybe we take the boat over to Malolo Island to test the new watermakers and have some fun? I wanted to ask you if my friend Emma could join us for the trip. She's in Denarau doing a training and can get a few days off to come along."

"Sounds reasonable. When do you want to go?"

"Saturday."

Saturday arrived, and Emma joined *Slow Dance* for the sail to Malolo Island. Captain Reed seemed happy to get away from all the organizing tasks and get back on the water. The two-hour trip to the island was superb, with just enough wind to sail without the engine.

After dropping anchor, Don and Zack lowered the dinghy for the ride over to the local beach bar. Emma climbed down gracefully into the dinghy. She was wearing a red-string bikini that complemented her raven hair. Emma was an animated and vivacious beauty, and Jess could see why Don was smitten.

The local beach bar was situated on a small islet surrounded by the blue waters of Fiji. Trinidad was on Emma's lap and Don was petting her—which was unusual. A Fijian band played popular songs, and Captain Reed moved to a stool next to Jess. Putting his arm around her, he asked, "Something to drink? And don't say Australian Shiraz."

She felt her butterflies coming back.

"How about a mai tai?"

"Perfect." He ordered two from the bartender and handed one to Jess. She noticed his behavior had morphed from cool to warm. What was going on with him? He was aloof and reserved, and now he had his arm around her. The man was driving her crazy.

The band was playing Michael Jackson's "Billie Jean," and Zack was dancing with two women in the sandpit.

"I love this song," said Emma before pulling Don to his feet for a dance.

The band was taking requests, and because of the excellent female vocalist, Jess requested "Dreams" by Fleetwood Mac. Captain Reed ordered them two more drinks, and she began to sing along. He was listening, and he was looking at her.

"You have a nice voice." Captain Reed got up then and asked the band if they knew the Al Green song "Let's Stay Together."

When the song began, he walked over to Jess, took her by the hand, and led her to the sandpit. Placing his arms around her, he drew her close for the *Slow Dance*. Jess's butterflies were replaced by pure desire. What Captain Reed couldn't express he was telling her with the words in the song.

He held her close, swaying in place to the music, and she could feel his breath on her neck. She never wanted the song to end. Was he finally going to act on his feelings? She hoped so.

Every day at precisely four in the afternoon, a long sandbar rose from the sea with the outgoing tide. From a distance, people appeared to be walking on water.

Leaving the bar, Don was driving the dinghy toward *Slow Dance*, when Emma asked, "Can we go have a look? It's so brilliant!"

Two small tour boats were leaving as Don guided the dinghy onto the sandbar, securing the line with a stake in the sand. Emma was running up and down the sand strip, frolicking in the surf, and Trini was running alongside her, barking and leaping into the air. Zack took snorkel masks out of the locker and handed one to Jess and the other to Emma. He took his unfinished sandwich from the bar and handed it to the women.

"You could feed this to the fish. There must be a thousand species here."

Jess was amazed at the number of fish the sandbar attracted, some of which were nipping at her hands. Suddenly, she spotted a huge purple jellyfish floating on the current.

"Hey, anyone ever see a purple jellyfish? There's one over here."

Emma waded over to Jess and put her face in the water to see where the gelatinous wad of stinging misery was floating.

"Got it." She held up the jellyfish in her hand.

"Are you mad?" Jess was horrified.

Emma laughed and handed the purple blob to Don. "Not the stinging kind," said Emma,

"We have them all over these waters."

Jess ran to the dinghy to fetch her camera so she could snap a photo of Emma holding up the jellyfish.

The tide was coming in and the sandbar began to disappear under the surface of the water. Climbing into the dinghy they headed back to *Slow Dance*. Captain Reed was climbing onto the boat when Emma and Jess, along with Trinidad, jumped in the water for a swim. Don tied the dinghy to the side of *Slow Dance* so the girls could sit on the platform and Trinidad could take a break from treading water.

Captain Reed was sitting on the sofa at the stern of the yacht looking down at the girls, who were enjoying their swim in the sea. He was looking at Jess in her blue bikini, and this time he had no intention of ignoring the passion he felt. He wanted to stop pushing her away. There was only this moment, and he didn't want to think, he wanted to act.

Don lowered the kayak, and a few water toys, before jumping into the water to join Emma.

"Hand me a towel, Zack," Jess requested. "I'm getting out."

Before Zack could bring a towel, Captain Reed held out his hand and helped Jess climb onto the boat. Taking the towel from him, she felt the tension as he touched her hand.

"Thank you for the hand up and a fun afternoon."

"The afternoon is not over yet." His words sent a shiver down her spine.

"I am going to shower off the salt." Her anticipation of what might happen next overwhelmed her.

Jess was in the shower, eyes closed, head filled with erotic thoughts, when the captain opened the shower door and joined her. She felt his hands on her back as he turned her to him, and opening her eyes, she held his gaze. He moved his hands from her back to her bare shoulders and then down onto her bare breasts. As he bent down to cover her nipple with his mouth, she put her hands on the back of his neck. His tongue flicked over her nipple until it responded with arousal. He pulled her naked body against his, and she felt his arousal. She teased his lips with a slow sensuous kiss, touching her tongue lightly to his. Their breath deepened, and she began to moan when he placed his hand between her thighs. Her muscles began to clench at the soft strokes from his fingers. All the desire she felt for him burst like a dam when he covered her mouth with his. All thoughts of the captain not desiring her were abolished by the passion and urgency with which he drew her to him.

Some moments later, he led her out of the shower, wrapping her in a towel before drying himself. Sitting on the sofa in his owner's suite, he pulled her onto his lap.

Reaching between her legs, she guided him inside her and slowly began rocking back and forth. He let her determine the rhythm and he matched it as his mouth moved from one of her erect nipples to the other. She pulled his head away from her breasts and kissed him. He put his hands under her butt to pull her further onto him, and she separated her mouth from his as she threw her head back.

"Oh, God, Cliff."

With her hands on his face, they were looking at each other as she sped up her hips. He waited for her mouth to open, and eyes to close, as she orgasmed on top of him. It was then he reciprocated the pleasure, gasping as he buried his head into her wet hair.

The morning light was streaming through the portholes when Jess awakened with Captain Reed's arms around her. When he stirred slightly, Trini jumped on the bed to begin her morning ritual of licking his ear. Wiping his saturated earlobe, he made a face. "Okay, Trini, enough." Coming awake, he propped himself up on his elbow acknowledging Jess. "Good morning," he said studying her face. "I don't want—"

Before he could finish, she said, "If there's no expectations, then there won't be disappointments. We shouldn't overthink this. Just enjoy.

Like alcoholics, let's take it one day at a time. Now, how about some coffee, sailor?"

Captain Reed stretched and placing his hands behind his head, he lay contemplating what she had said.

On the upper deck Jess was surprised to find Cody playing guitar. Zack was tapping rhythm on hand drums, and Emma was singing harmony to Cody's song.

"Hey Cody, how'd you get here?" Jess gave her a hug. "Last time I saw you and your parents we were in Samoa."

"We just arrived from New Zealand, and my dad decided to anchor here at Malolo before going into the Denarau marina. I was super stoked when I saw *Slow Dance*. Always a party with you guys."

Captain Reed arrived on deck not surprised to see Cody, as he expected sailors to cross paths multiple times as they followed the trade winds. Fiji was a well-known hiding place from fierce tropical storms that raged across the Pacific Ocean.

Jess was observing Don to see if he was unnerved by Cody arriving unexpectedly. If he was, she couldn't tell by his actions.

Cliff put his arm around Jess. "Can you make a pot of coffee, please?"

Her body was still tingling, and she wanted more. Their night together was better than she imagined, but she was going to hold true to her words. "No expectations, and one day a time."

47

Sophia

November 2024
Malolo Island, Fiji

When morning coffee and breakfast concluded, Jess and the captain spent the day charting possible sailing routes to Thailand and walking Trini on the sandbar at low tide. Throughout the day their desire was rekindled as both anxiously desired a repeat of their previous night together.

After dinner, Cliff and Jess were cozying up on the outside sofa enjoying conversation with Emma and Cody when Don asked the women if they wanted to watch a movie in the saloon.

Jess was enjoying her glass of wine when the captain blurted out, "I think love doesn't necessarily restrict one's freedom," but before he finished his thoughts, she took the wineglass from him and set it on the table.

Straddling him with her hands on the sides of his face, she drew him to her and kissed him. Her hands moved to the inside of his shirt to rub his chest, and one moved further down to stroke him through his shorts. He gently bit her lower lip as he moaned from the pleasure. Her heart rate and breathing increased as he slipped his hands under her shirt and whispered, "Will you sleep with me tonight?"

Jess's arousal was so intense she simply nodded yes.

"Let's go below before we get caught."

She followed him to the cabin.

"Trinidad, you can come in later," the captain said to his trailing companion, then closed the door.

They stood facing each other as she unbuttoned his shirt. She put her fingers inside the waistband of his shorts to push them down. As he kicked them away, she moved to put her mouth on his erection.

"No babe, you'll make me come too fast." Turning her so she faced away from him, he undressed her slowly. Cupping her breasts from behind, he kissed each shoulder and then moved her toward the bed. Laying her down, he kissed her mouth, then between her breasts, and then lingered at her stomach. The suspense was driving her crazy. Moving down between her legs, he used his warm breath to heat her clitoris and ran his fingers along both sides to further stimulate her arousal. Up and down, he stroked her until she put her hands in his hair, her body tensing as he moved his fingers inside her. Her hips were writhing as she reached for the orgasm. She cried out, "Oh, Cliff—" The waves of her climax were so intense she felt tears forming in her eyes.

She took a beat to let her body settle as he used her stomach as a pillow. When he felt her relax, he moved up and rolled her on her side. Lifting her top leg slightly, he gently entered her.

She arched her back as he moved slowly in and out.

"I'm close." She pushed back against him to let him know it was okay, and he came inside of her. He held her close, and she closed her eyes, wondering if this was real. They lay silent in each other's arms until they fell asleep.

In the morning, Cody returned to her parent's boat and agreed to take Emma to Denarau so she could catch her flight back to Australia. Jess was in the galley when Don entered for coffee. She was curious about Emma and Cody spending the night on the boat and decided to ask Don about it.

"How did you manage the situation when Cody turned up unexpectedly and Emma was on the boat? They looked like they were getting along just fine."

Don gave her a wicked smile. "Simple, we had a threesome. And judging by the sounds coming from Captain Reed's cabin, you two were having a time of it yourselves."

She swatted him with her dish towel. "You're a total rogue. How do you get women to do such things."

"Easy. Just look at me."

Jess had to admit, Don was hot standing there shirtless in the galley.

Cliff set the autopilot for Denarau, and then he and Jess sat with Trinidad in the captain's chair at the outside helm. He put his arm around her and said, "I could get used this."

There was so much she wanted to say, but reminded herself: no expectations, no disappointments. One thing was certain. She loved him and the mind-blowing sex. She couldn't define it because it was undefinable. At this time, he was happy and content, and so was she. Any conversation regarding them as a couple could wait.

Arriving at the marina and settled into their slip, Cliff was at the computer checking his emails when the port captain hailed *Slow Dance* on the radio. Jess was in the galley preparing lunch when Don came in looking troubled.

"What is it?" she asked.

"Captain Reed wants you to come up to the pilothouse. He received a call from the gate. Sophia is here."

Jess felt a knot forming in her stomach as she climbed the steps to the pilothouse. Cliff was standing at the chart table when Jess entered the pilothouse. As their eyes met, she felt her heart race. By the expression on Cliff's face, Jess could see his anxiety rising as he realized Sophia was waiting at the gate.

Cliff took a deep breath, and she could tell he knew he had to be honest.

"I need to talk to you," he said, his voice steady yet filled with emotion. "What we shared, Jess, was real, and it's everything I need and want. I don't want to hide from my feelings anymore. But Sophia is about to arrive at the boat expecting something different. I never loved her, Jess. She's married and that made it safe; I never led her to think our trysts were anything more than just that, an occasional hookup. My plan was to fly back to Los

Angeles, pick up the part for *Slow Dance*, see my doctor, and fly back. I intended to break it off with her. I need to be honest with Sophia, even if it hurts her. No matter what happens next, I want you to know—"

He was cut off by Sophia calling up from the dock. "Cliff, darling, didn't they call to let you know I was waiting? The dock boys are wheeling down my luggage."

Zack met the dock boys and carried Sophia's bags aboard the boat, opting to leave them on deck in the event the captain sent her straight back to the airport. He and Jess were still standing in the pilothouse when Sophia stepped onto the boat. Trotting up to the captain, she put her arms around his neck, planting a kiss on either cheek before releasing him.

"Surprise," she giggled. "It's my birthday tomorrow, so this trip is extra special. Oh, hello, Jess. I brought some specialty food for Trinidad and a few things that need to be refrigerated."

Without responding, Jess retreated to the galley, and as she descended the steps, she heard Cliff offering to take Sophia out to lunch. Jess sighed with relief, knowing she would not have to make lunch for Sophia and the captain. She couldn't even think of him as Cliff anymore. He was the captain, and she'd do what he paid her for.

After they left, Don asked Jess to grab a few beers and come up top. Jess opened two and joined him on deck.

"So, now what?" she asked him.

Don shifted nervously as he looked at Jess. "The captain wants you to clear out your gear from the master cabin and make up the bed with the nice sheets for Sophia. Since it's her birthday, he wants to go easy on her, so she doesn't have a nervous breakdown."

"Unbelievable," she snapped, furious. "What did Captain Reed have to say about her coming? Can't he take the part and send her right back on another plane? He's a coward! He couldn't tell me that himself, so he asked you to do it?"

Don put his arm around her. "Sorry. Men can be real shits."

Right, and you should know, she thought, tears welling up as she retreated to her cabin. Lying on the bed, her limbs heavy, she felt a paralysis sweeping over her, a numbness as if she were dead. It felt like a murder had been committed. The murder of everything she had shared with the captain. Trini began scratching at the door and, regaining her ability to move, she opened the door to let her in. Trini jumped on the bed approaching Jess with soft, comforting nudges, her warm presence serving as a source of solace and companionship. Curling up beside Jess and resting her head on her lap, she showered Jess with licks and nuzzles, providing her comfort in her own unique way.

After her crying jag, Jess removed all traces of herself from Cliff's cabin and left with Trini for a long walk along the tree-lined path that led to the resorts. Stopping at one of the numerous garden bars, she ordered coffee and sat with her thoughts. No expectations, no disappointments, was one thing, but cowardice was something else. The situation was almost comical if she chose to view it from a different perspective. She was determined not to show Cliff her anger or disappointment. Calming her emotions, she admitted she had accepted him for who he was, imperfections and all. Everyone struggles with past experiences that shape their actions. Jess knew her worth, and she would never again define herself solely through a relationship with a man. Her stability and warmth were a haven in Cliff's turbulent world, and she would not allow herself to be pulled into his chaotic emotional dysfunction. She would set boundaries: physical, verbal, psychological, and emotional. She took Trini from her lap and finished her coffee.

When Jess returned to the boat, Cliff was waiting for her on deck.

"Jess, I—" And before he got another word out, she shrugged him off.

"No worries, deal with the situation whichever way you need to, and if you have something important to say to me, you can tell Don to tell me."

He stood helpless like a man who just took a bullet to the chest.

That afternoon, Captain Reed made a sail plan with Don to take Sophia sailing to the northern island of Vanua Levu, and Jess headed up to Carlo's for an early dinner.

48

Conundrum

November 2024
Port Denarau Marina, Fiji

Don asked Cody if she would accompany *Slow Dance* on their seven-day sail north—to help Jess entertain Sophia—and she agreed. While the captain was at lunch with Sophia, Jess had prepared his cabin for Sophia. She pulled out the fine white sheets that had been washed and pressed at the cleaners for any special occasion. She scrubbed the bathroom, fluffed up the pillows, and made room in the closet for Sophia's designer sundresses and thousand-dollar T-shirts. *What kind of idiot sleeps with the boss and then prepares for his girlfriend to stay over?* Jess found herself thinking. When she had done enough prepping for Cliff's concubine, she went to speak to *Noble House*'s chef about a dock party he was planning.

When Cliff and Sophia returned from lunch, Jess wanted to believe he had told Sophia she must return to Los Angeles, but instead, the captain introduced her to the crew.

"This is Don, his brother Zack, Cody, and of course you know Jess."

Cliff shot Jess a brief, rueful look.

Don shook Sophia's hand. "Welcome aboard. Zack and I delivered your bags to your cabin."

Jess cringed when the captain reintroduced her to Sophia. Why was he moving forward with a plan to take Sophia cruising for a week? Was he stringing her along waiting for the right moment to let her down easy? It was, after all, her birthday, and in the captain's defense, he did not know she was coming. He probably didn't want to be unnecessarily cruel. Jess's thoughts and emotions were in a tumult. She needed to calm down. The captain most likely had a plan to extradite himself from his conundrum.

Cody offered to assist Sophia with unpacking. After their exit, the captain said, "Sophia unpacked the part she brought for the engine. Let's go down to the engine room and make some assessments."

Don and Zack followed Cliff below to the engine room, and Jess retreated to the galley to prepare some small sandwiches to accompany her raspberry iced tea.

An hour later, Cody was serving Sophia and the captain on the top deck while Jess remained in the galley with her thoughts. On one hand, she reasoned, Cliff was unaware Sophia was already en route to Fiji. On the other hand, the way he decided to inform her was insensitive. She thought she knew him; they had opened to each other on so many levels. She now questioned everything she thought she knew about him. At this point, it was better to backpedal than continue down a road of heartache.

Jess spent the rest of the afternoon reading in her cabin, relieved when Cliff announced he was taking Sophia to Carlo's for dinner. Cody, Don, and Zack, along with Jess and Trini, also headed up to Carlo's for a beer. The hostess seated them four tables away from Cliff and Sophia. Jess was watching the captain interact with Sophia and didn't see Carlo approach the table.

"Hello, beautiful, where have you been?" He put his arm around her and greeted the others. Carlo gestured toward Cliff's table. Sophia was leaning in close to him, touching her hand to his.

"Your captain has excellent taste in women. Please introduce me." Before she could object, Carlo moved Jess reluctantly from her chair and walked her over to Cliff's table.

"Good evening, Captain Reed. Who is this enchantress?" Carlo took Sophia's hand and kissed it. "Good evening, I am Carlo, the owner of the restaurant."

Sophia left her hand lingering in Carlo's, enjoying the attention.

"Lovely to make your acquaintance, Carlo. Our dinner is excellent, and the view is spectacular."

Cliff looked annoyed, and Jess ignored them all. Two nights prior, she was having awesome sex with the captain, and now he was dining with his lover Sophia. She wanted to return to her cabin and avoid everyone, especially the captain.

An employee from the kitchen called for Carlo and he politely excused himself from the table. He walked Jess back to her staring crewmates.

Cody leaned over to Jess. "I didn't think people your age still had sex and relationship drama. Why not go for the younger guy?"

Don laughed. "You mean to tell me that after sailing on your parents' small boat, you never heard them shag?"

"Oh yuck, probably—change the subject."

Jess gulped down the remainder of her beer and stood up from the table. "I bid you sailors good night. I have an early morning food prep for the dock party tomorrow and an Italian torte to bake in honor of the cheater's birthday."

"I am sorry, Jess." Don sounded genuinely concerned.

Jess began to walk toward the boat docks, and as she passed by the captain's table, she heard Sophia say, "Are you listening? You seem distant." Then she heard the captain reply, "Let's just enjoy the dinner and the moonlight. You should know by now: I am not a very good conversationalist."

Coward, Jess thought as she quickened her pace toward the dock.

Jess was in her cabin when she heard Cliff return to the boat with Sophia. They were sitting on the outside sofa, and Jess could hear their conversation through her open porthole.

"What islands do you have planned for us? Do you think we can be under way in two days? I have my friend Mike watching the dogs and the house. It's been difficult dealing with my aging parents, so I can't stay away for any extended time. I hope I haven't blindsided you, Cliff. You seem upset. Are you angry with me for showing up to surprise you?"

"I am glad you're here," he started, clearly trying to maintain a calm demeanor. "But there's something important we need to talk about."

"What's wrong?"

"I don't want to hurt you, Sophia, but I think it best if we end things here. I planned on telling you this when I returned to Los Angeles to pick up the part for *Slow Dance*. I care about you, but I need to be true to myself. I hope you understand."

As he spoke, Jess imagined how difficult it must be, but he knew it was the right thing to do. Cliff had shared with her that in his past he had been a womanizer, a cheater, chasing fleeting pleasure and avoiding any real commitment. Jess felt the bonds he formed with her were deeper than he had ever experienced.

"Jesus, Cliff, you never gave any indication that you lost interest in me. I've embarrassed myself by coming here to surprise you. Apparently, you're more selfish than I thought. It's obvious you only want me on your terms. Well, I am here, and you are going to take me sailing. It's the least you can do after I flew here with your boat part." Sophia stood up from the table, wiping tears from her eyes. "I am going to the cabin to take a bath, and I am locking you out." Jess heard Sophia come down to Cliff's cabin, as well as Cliff leaving the boat.

An hour later Jess was brooding in her cabin with Trini when Sophia knocked on her door.

"Sorry to disturb you, but could you please help me with the plug to the bath? I can't seem to get it to hold water, and Don said you would know how to fix the issue." Jess took a deep breath and tried to eliminate all thoughts of Sophia naked in the tub.

"Of course, be right there." Jess reluctantly entered the cabin, thinking how two days ago, she had made passionate love with Cliff on the sofa, the bed, and the bathroom counter. She effortlessly plugged the drain.

"Thank you, dear," said Sophia as if speaking to one of her servants, and she closed the door.

Jess bristled when Sophia referred to her as "dear," but was determined to keep her dignity, remain detached, and above all, not play the victim. Cliff was noticeably absent from the boat, and judging by Sophia's attitude it appeared as if she felt confident she could lure him back into bed.

Jess retreated to her cabin with Trini. Pulling off her clothes, she crawled under the covers wondering if the captain had any intention of sending Sophia back to Los Angeles.

49

The Solutionist

November 2024
Port Denarau Marina, Fiji

To Jess's relief, Cliff and Sophia were off the boat early for some sightseeing, and she busied herself in the galley preparing some of her signature dishes for the evening dock party. Jess spent the day there searching for inner peace amidst the chaos of her current situation.

The sun was setting as Cody and Jess carried out the dishes Jess had prepared for the dock party, placing them on the table with the other delicious foods prepared by Chef Bruno of *Noble House*. Zack and the bosun from the super yacht positioned folding chairs along the dock, and Don loaded beer and wine into a large metal ice tub as sailors from around the world gathered on the dock to celebrate the sailing life.

Jess circulated through the crowd, chatting with everyone, receiving numerous compliments on her Southwestern black bean, roasted corn, and grilled shrimp salad. She ignored the captain and Sophia, only briefly looking over at them to notice the captain watching her. She was talking to a woman when one of Carlo's employees arrived and handed Jess a note. It was an invitation from Carlo to join him for the evening. The note felt like Cliff's knotted rope: the rope had been tossed out, and if she caught the line, it would save her from drowning. Tucking the note in her pocket, she left the party to freshen up and change. She was fastening her black lace bra when Cliff opened her cabin door. Trini rushed in, jumped on the bed, her little tail wagging wildly.

"Oh, Miss T, I know, I know, Captain Reed's girlfriend has been keeping us apart. I am happy to see you, too!"

The captain followed Trinidad into Jess's cabin and closed the door. "You look nice."

Jess took a step back from him. "Um, I'm standing here in my underwear, in case you hadn't noticed. Is there something you need before I go out?"

His expression was that of a man in acute distress, his tension filling the cabin. "Yes, I noticed; and are you going to see Carlo?"

Jess pulled her dress over her head. "Yes, I am going to see Carlo."

Cliff took a beat and then moved toward her. "I think I am really, actually in love for the first time. With you, Jess."

Jess sighed. "You think, or you know? And if you are, you have a bizarre way of showing it. I'm going out for a fun night. . . . Did you think I was going to hang around and change your sheets? I love you, I do, but I am not going to be treated the way you're treating me right now. It seems you haven't confronted Sophia by the looks of things and have no intention of canceling our sail plan to the north." Jess did not want to reveal that she had overheard Cliff's conversation with Sophia. "No worries, I was warned, no expectations, no disappointments." *Let him suffer a bit*, she thought.

Cliff stepped closer to Jess. "Yes, you have every right to be upset, but let me explain. Sophia was on her way, and I told her after dinner—"

Jess put her hand over his mouth to stop him. "What's done is done, and it can't be undone. I have a date waiting for me."

She slipped her feet into her sandals.

"Even your feet are pretty. Jess, let me explain, please."

Sophia could be heard on the deck, calling for him.

"You best go back to Sophia," she told him. "I'll be back on the boat early to prepare coffee and breakfast."

Jess handed over the poodle. "You stay home tonight, Trini, Sophia needs you more than I do. I get the feeling she's the next one to be on the receiving end from Captain Lover Boy."

Exiting the boat, Jess blinked back the tears welling up in her eyes. She lifted her chin and walked the dock toward one of the hotels on the strip. She had no intention of spending her evening fending off Carlo's advances. She simply wanted to be away from the boat to get her thoughts and feelings under control.

Returning early morning from her supposed night with Carlo, Jess showered, went to the galley, and busied herself by brewing coffee, slicing fresh fruit, and proofing some of the croissants she kept handy in the freezer. Cody poked her head through the small sliding glass window in the pilothouse that looked down into the galley.

"The lovebirds are awake and on deck requesting coffee."

Jess readied a tray with cups, cream, sugar, and two French presses of her delicious coffee. "Cody, please come down and take the tray up to the table."

Cody fetched the tray and informed Jess she had already placed a tablecloth and napkins on the table. She also used the fancy napkin rings, which impressed Jess. Cody was going to be a tremendous help and an excellent buffer for the upcoming sail to the northern islands. A good helper, Cody also had a wicked sense of humor, which Jess found comforting. She missed Sydney, and Cody was turning into a kind of replacement child.

Returning to the galley for the tray of sliced fruit, Cody said, "Sophia's dressed like she's doing a photo shoot for *Nautical Magazine*. What are we going to do with her if the seas come up?"

Cody had gone around the Cape of Good Hope and the Horn. She had more sea miles than Don. "If we get in the soup, we're going to have to take care of her, you know, chuck her overboard."

Jess suppressed a laugh. "Now, now. Take these croissants up there while they're still warm, and the butter and jam, too."

Cody took the tray from Jess and added, "By the way, Captain Reed looks miserable."

Jess poured herself a cup of coffee, contemplating what Cody had said regarding Cliff. She decided to make an appearance and see for herself; she wasn't about to hide from him.

In fact, she wanted to present herself as carefree and happy.

"Good morning, Sophia." Jess's greeting was overly cheerful. "Did you sleep well?"

Sophia was buttering a croissant and judging by the expression on her face, she was not happy either.

"Yes, thank you. Sleep is all there is to do because the boat isn't going anywhere," she said. "Thank you for breakfast, the croissants were exceptional. Don't bother with lunch for me though; I am going shopping at the marina."

The dissent between Sophia and Cliff was apparent, and Jess wondered what had transpired between them during the night. Nothing physical, she hoped. Perhaps he had told her after all that she needed to go home. Finishing the Italian torte for Sophia's birthday was going to be so much easier now.

Later in the afternoon, Jess was putting the finishing touches on Sophia's cake when Cody joined her in the galley, a rascally expression on her face.

"I have a feeling Sophia isn't going to be eating that delicious torte," Cody said with raised eyebrows as she pinched a few of the almonds Jess had in a bowl and sprinkled them over Jess's sultana-and-ricotta creation.

Jess dusted the top of the cake with some powdered sugar. "Why? Have you heard something?"

"Plenty," said Cody. "I was polishing in the pilothouse, and those two were having it out on deck. Sophia just got back from shopping, and Captain Reed was waiting for her. I heard him say, 'What makes you think I had any plans to marry you after you were divorced? We both agreed this was a casual thing.'"

Jess couldn't help grinning. This was better than she'd hoped for.

"Then Sophia started going off on him. At that point I made a beeline to the galley."

Before Cody could elaborate further, Sophia burst into the galley crying. "What's wrong, Sophia?" Cody gave Jess a wide-eyed "yikes" look.

Jess could only imagine what Cliff said to cause Sophia to dissolve into such a state. She handed Sophia a dish towel, and Sophia soaked up her tears at the corners of her eyes, sobbing as she spoke.

"He told me to change my attitude or get the fuck off his boat. He invited me to go sailing, and we've been sitting on the dock for days. He told me he was ending our relationship. I feel like a complete fool to ever imagine the man had one romantic bone in his body. I am humiliated." Sophia turned to Jess. "Will you help me pack right now and get to a hotel here on Denarau? I can call for a driver."

"Of course," answered Jess. She felt sympathy for Sophia but had to admit she was happy the woman was leaving.

"I'll help as well," said Cody, and both Cody and Jess dropped everything to help Sophia exit *Slow Dance*.

50

Voluntary Separation

Sophia had one hand on the car door and the other on Jess's arm. The predicament was beyond awkward, but Jess succumbed when she saw the anguished look on Sophia's face, agreeing to lend assistance until she booked her return flight and was safe in one of the luxury hotels on the island. After inquiring at the three most exclusive resorts, Sophia booked a room with a view and a bathtub. Once the bags were in the room, the fiddly situation heightened when Sophia persuaded Jess to stay for dinner. The woman did not want to be alone and most likely wanted to vent about Captain Reed's atrocious behavior, especially after she flew so far to surprise him.

Though Jess was trying to muster sympathy, she felt sorrier for herself than Sophia. Without looking at the menu, she ordered the same dish as Sophia and, as predicted, listened as she prattled on about Cliff's horrible behavior. Jess was inclined to agree without saying it aloud. It amazed Jess how Sophia kept a mental list of every grievance, and she wanted to vent that list to her.

"We took a cruise in Italy—which I mostly paid for—and he fell asleep at the opera in Teatro dell'Opera di Roma. So embarrassing. During the cruise, he openly flirted with the single woman seated at our table. When the boat was in Puerto Vallarta, I took him to the Ritz Carlton, and he blew his nose in the cloth napkin at the table! Talk about uncouth. My therapist is going to be so proud of me for cutting and running from this mess of a guy. I refuse to be a number on his list of women."

Jess had been listening to Sophia, and when her rant was over, she asked, "What did you see in him, and why would you jeopardize your marriage for a mess of a guy?"

Sophia leaned over the table. "My husband and his children have tortured me for nine years. I have one year remaining, and then I can divorce him and receive half the assets. Cliff, for all his faults, is a very charming and sexy man. He was my neighbor, and he chased me after his wife died. His wife knew he would try for me the minute she was gone."

Jess nodded. "Yes, Captain Reed told me that story."

"He did?" Sophia looked surprised.

"Yes, his wife told him she would rather he sleep with a thousand women than the same woman a thousand times."

Sophia was tending to her tearful eyes. "I feel for that poor woman . . . married to him all those years. Cliff must consider you a good friend. He never shared anything with me."

Jess thought, *If only you knew.*

"Can you stay the night with me? The sofa pulls out into a bed, or you can sleep with me. The bed is huge."

Jess imagined the look on Cliff's face if she didn't return until the morning, telling him she spent the night in Sophia's bed. The thought rather amused her. He had been distressed when she climbed into the car with Sophia. Staying the night was tempting, but her desire to get away from Sophia was more powerful than payback. He brought all this unpleasantness on himself.

"I am sorry, Sophia, but I can't stay. If the part for the engine is installed and working, the boat sails early in the morning. Your flight is tomorrow, you'll be fine. You're strong," she lied.

"Find a nice man at your tennis club and stay clear of messy guys."

Jess finished the tasteless meal, emptied her glass of Veuve Clicquot, and pushed her chair away from the table. She offered her hand, but Sophia stood up from the table and gave her a hug.

"Good advice. Be safe, and thank you."

Jess decided to walk back to the marina along the tree-lined path near the water. The tropical air felt heavy, like her heart and mind. Her disappointment had subsided, and she was left with questions. Jess thought about what she shared with the captain. You can't fake that bond; it went beyond the sex; their connection was what made the sex so incredible. She loved so many things about him, despite his transgression, which no denying, was a doozy. She wanted to stay on the boat and keep sailing. Could he ever be faithful to one woman? No expectations, no disappointments, she reminded herself. She allowed Cliff to be himself without any thought of changing him, and he allowed her total freedom to be who she was. The relationship was unique, and she was determined to remain open to whatever came next. She was curious how Cliff could be strong enough to face turbulent seas, but rendered impotent when faced with an emotional conflict . . .

It was late when Jess boarded *Slow Dance*. The boat was dark and silent as she headed to her cabin. Trini unexpectedly came running out of the darkness.

"So, am I the biggest shit on earth?"

Jess hadn't seen the captain sitting on the sofa in the pilothouse.

"Well, Sophia sure thinks you are a huge shit, and I'm inclined to agree." His legs were crossed, and he was doing that thing with his hands. "You were gone a long time, I was worried."

Jess sat on the sofa across from him. "Sophia invited me to have dinner, and I had to listen to every horrible thing you've ever done to her. It went on for some time until the drama wore on me. It was hard—mustering sympathy for a woman cheating on her husband. She said she fell for you because you're charming, sexy, and exciting—nothing like the men at her tennis club."

Cliff moved close to Jess. "I didn't touch her once. I couldn't after what we shared in Malolo. Sophia hates me. But do you?"

"Maybe," she lied. He moved closer, and she stood up. "I can smell her perfume on you. Like I said, I am worn out from the drama, and this"—she gestured toward him then herself—"feels like it could be a huge mistake."

"I am sorry. I can't believe I let it get this far. My plan was to get the part and, well, you know, I told you my plan to end it with her. I had no idea she was flying here to surprise me."

Jess looked down, not wanting to look into his eyes. "Sorry doesn't change what just happened, Cliff. You shouldn't have let her come here like that."

Cliff turned to face her. "I know, I should have been honest from the start. I didn't want to crush her, but I ended up hurting both of you. I didn't know what to do, and having Don tell you to prepare our cabin for her was the worst part of it all."

Jess felt tears build up behind her eyes, her voice trembling. "But you did hurt me. You made me feel like I was in the shadows, like you needed me to hide. I don't want to feel like the second choice, Cliff. You love me, but . . . you let her stay for days. It felt so disrespectful. I won't put my heart on the line if you're not ready to fight for it."

"I am ready, Jess," he said. "I want to be with you. No more hiding, no more games. Just you and me moving forward."

Jess held his gaze. "I want that, Cliff, I really do. But it's going to take some time. I need to know I can trust you."

Cliff reached for her hand. "I'll give you all the time you need. I want you to know how much you mean to me. You're my choice, and my chance."

Cliff sat down on the sofa, head in hands.

"You slept with Carlo."

Jess sat down next to him. "Honestly, I didn't even see Carlo. I stayed at a hotel that night. I could have had sex with him, but I chose not to—because I didn't want to follow one mistake with another."

He looked up at her. "I am woefully inept when it comes to expressing my feelings, and I have never been in love, except with the sea. I have been in lust and intense infatuation with women, but I never wanted them with me the way I want you. I love you. I do—"

She cut him off. "Love manifests in many ways. Support, respect, honesty, passion. Sailing with you is incredible, making love with you takes my breath away, but what's not incredible is being made a fool of and taken for granted. These are triggers for me, and as I said, I refuse to be a victim. I have a lot to think about, and I am emotionally exhausted, so good night. I am locking my cabin door, so don't get any ideas. Leave me be, please."

Trinidad jumped up on the bed as soon as she entered her cabin. Locking the door, she removed her clothes and climbed into bed. He said he hadn't touched Sophia, and she believed him. Good that Cliff thought she had sex with Carlo. He deserved to suffer a bit emotionally after being so careless with her feelings.

But he had been vulnerable, sensitive, and truly distressed, a side of him she had not seen.

Curling up with her thoughts and the little poodle, she fell asleep, dreaming of white sails and blue water.

51

Quietude

A light breeze whispered through the portholes as Jess opened her eyes.

"Good morning, Trinidad. I bet you need to pee." Jess gave Trini's head a rub and got dressed. Opening her door, she saw Cliff sitting up in bed, and he motioned for her to come into his cabin.

Trinidad raced in, wagging her tail. Cliff patted the mattress, and the pooch leaped up licking his ear. Jess found this very sweet, and she wondered if Cliff enjoyed it or simply tolerated the puppy's love. She tended to think the latter.

Cliff turned to Jess. "I need to go sailing."

Jess also wanted to go sailing. They both needed to clear their minds and their hearts.

"Are we still sailing to the north, as planned?" Jess didn't want to bring up Sophia.

"No," he said. "Meet me in the pilothouse. I'm gonna grab some pants and brush my teeth."

In the pilothouse, Cliff motioned her to the computer where a chart of the Fijian islands was displayed. "We're going South, to the Kadavu island chain, remote and uncrowded—an untouched Eden as I recall. I got blown off there in Port Washington, my first landfall after sailing out of New Zealand."

Don entered the pilothouse with his morning coffee and came over to have a look at the charts. "Let me load up the Windguru application on the computer monitor. We're not safe from cyclones outside of Viti Levu."

Cliff ran his finger along the map. "Here, here, and here, all hiding places from storms. It's summer in this hemisphere, and it's rare that Fiji gets any direct hits. Plus, the stronger the wind, the better the sailing."

For the next few days, Cliff occupied himself preparing *Slow Dance* for departure, while Jess busied herself provisioning the boat for their sail to Kadavu. He wanted to talk to her. He wanted her to forgive him, and he wanted her back, but he recognized they both needed space.

52

The Swede, the Irish Girl, and the Fly Fisherman

December 2024
Port Denarau Marina, Fiji

Denarau Island was a diverse gathering place for tourists, backpackers, and yachting enthusiasts from around the world. Don was spending time with a European couple he met at Carlo's, a Swede named Anders and his Irish girlfriend Maeve. The couple arrived in Fiji after they replied to a post seeking sailing crew. However, arriving in Fiji to meet the owner they discovered his boat was unseaworthy, and he took to drinking a bit too much. Don decided to approach Cliff and discuss the possibility of bringing the couple aboard. He explained the situation to the captain and a bit about their backgrounds.

"Anders is an exceptional sailor. If you're interested, I can bring them round this afternoon so you can meet them."

Cliff only nodded. When Don left the pilothouse, Cliff asked Jess to be at the meeting.

"You're a much better judge of character than I am. Sizing up a couple of hippy backpackers won't be difficult for you."

That afternoon, Don arrived at the boat with the young couple. Anders was a stocky, handsome lad with a serious demeanor. Maeve was a stunning redhead, had a thick Irish accent, and also a guitar. Jess liked her immediately.

Concluding the meeting, Cliff shook hands and said he would get back after he talked it over with Don. Once they were off the boat Don asked for their thoughts.

"Anders knows his way around the sails," the captain said, "and he's done varnish and deck work. His girl doesn't know anything about boats, but she could learn." Cliff turned to Jess. "What do you think?"

"Being a musician, she would provide entertainment. But seriously, she seems capable of anything she sets her mind to, so I am betting I can train her to polish teak and clean toilets. Think of the fun beach fires with live music."

Cliff smiled, something he hadn't done in days.

Don asked, "When should we bring them aboard, and at what wage?"

Cliff thought for a moment. "They get the nice aft cabin with the bunk across from Jess's cabin, and I will pay them seven hundred dollars on the first of every month."

Don nodded in approval. "They should be happy with that. They are literally sleeping in a cardboard box on the broken boat. I am sure they will want to come aboard sooner than later, which is great, because Zack and I need help. And I'm sure Jess would love a hand with the polishing."

"Yes," Jess admitted, "the extra hand will be great since I have two more mouths to feed."

Cliff added, "Let them know they are coming aboard on a trial basis, so in case it doesn't work out, we're covered."

"It will be nice to have the extra hands for the sail to Kadavu," Don answered.

Over the next few days, Anders and Maeve proved to be good shipmates and a tremendous help in preparing *Slow Dance* to sail south.

After a few days aboard, Anders approached Cliff and Jess with a request.

"My best friend, Victor, is on his way here from Wyoming. He was supposed to sail with us. Victor makes his money taking clients fly fishing in the summer months."

Jess chimed in, "Like the movie, *A River Runs Through It?*"

Anders grinned. "Honestly, he looks just like Brad Pitt. He was planning to sail with us for a few weeks."

Captain Reed looked up from the chart he had been studying. "Okay, Victor can bunk with Zack in the crew cabin. The more the merrier."

Two days later, Victor arrived to Fiji bringing an aura of perpetual joy that engulfed *Slow Dance*. Jess noted Cliff especially liked his ready-for-anything attitude that more than likely reminded him of his younger self. As the new crew settled onto the boat, the heaviness that hung in the air vanished, replaced by the lightness of youthful exuberance. Cliff's mood lightened, and his enthusiasm was renewed by the young newcomers. Jess felt the energy on *Slow Dance* was alive with the promise of adventure, excitement, and a touch of rebellion, as they sailed out of Denarau toward Kadavu.

53

The Convergence Zone

December 2024
Kadavu Islands, Fiji

"The Kadavu Islands are three main islands surrounded by a group of smaller islands; see them here on the map."

The men were looking at the chart with Cliff, along with Jess.

"This is Galoa, and here is Ono—I think that was my first landfall after sailing from New Zealand. I was headed for Los Angeles but got blown off course near Fiji. I dropped anchor right about here." Cliff pointed to an inlet on the map. "Within five minutes, dugout boats carrying villagers circled my boat."

Victor was wide-eyed, thoroughly enjoying the captain's story. "Whoa. What did you do?"

The captain scratched his head. "Well, we took the dinghy down and followed the natives to the beach. Turns out, they had never seen white people. They were so excited; the chief held a huge feast prepared in our honor, complete with a kava ceremony. We had showers from a bucket, and later found out the village was low on fresh water. We felt so honored they would allow us to use their water."

The fly fisherman's elbows were on the chart table, chin resting on his hands. "Wow, I hope it's still authentic when we get there. What's kava?"

Jess made a face. "It's a root the Fijians pound into a fine powder. The powder is wrapped in cloth and then steeped in water until it turns into a brown liquid. Primarily, the men partake in the kava ceremony; sitting in a circle, they pass the bowl around. Terrible stuff, makes your mouth numb. Also makes you sleepy."

"I'd be up for drinking some," answered Victor. "Hey Captain, can we hook up the fishing poles to see what's swimming around down there?"

Cliff gave Jess a wink and gestured to Victor. "Sure, kid. Come up on deck and check out my lures."

Jess was on deck with Maeve watching Don and Zack prepare the sails for some weather ahead. Her attention diverted to Cliff, who was teaching the young man from Wyoming how to tie a sailor's knot. Cliff knelt beside the boy, his strong hands deftly demonstrating how to tie the knot. Jess felt a warmth in her chest, a sense of connection to this moment—a simple act of teaching but imbued with the kind of patience and care that spoke volumes. It was a beautiful morning, but it was the scene unfolding before her that truly captivated her heart. There was something deeply touching about the bond forming between Cliff and the boy, a shared experience that felt timeless. Memories of her own childhood flooded back, days spent learning and exploring in the kitchen with her father's guiding hands teaching her the ropes—both literally and metaphorically.

Suddenly, the fishing pole portside began to spin its reel. Trinidad began running up and down the deck barking. Cliff sprang into action. Victor began reeling in the fish while Cliff went for the gaffing hook and a five-gallon bucket.

"Easy. Pull him closer so I can hook him," shouted the captain.

Cliff was shirtless leaning over the rail with the gaffing pole. "Got him! A large dorado."

Jess snapped photos of Victor holding the fish, and afterwards the crew gathered around to watch the captain masterfully filet their catch. All except Don, who hated fish and poop.

Jess rinsed the filets and placed them on ice. She knew cooking the fish would have to wait until they got through the upcoming squalls. Returning to the upper deck, she watched Cliff and crew readying the sails for the oncoming weather. As the sky turned gunmetal gray, Cliff moved amongst the younger men, loosening sail ties, reefing the main, and putting out the spinnaker sail to increase the speed of the boat. She saw his joy. She saw his excitement rise as the winds increased and the seas came up. He loved sailing. He loved the ocean, and she loved it too.

The engines were off and *Slow Dance* was heeling over portside, gliding effortlessly across the tops of the waves. The seas kept the boat on an endless race as the winds screeched.

Jess was in awe of the magnificent vessel's performance in the hands of true sailors. The South African brothers and Anders worked in unspoken harmony. Utilizing the storm, the sailors harnessed the wind and pushed the boat to an impressive speed of fifteen knots.

Cliff moved to the outside helm to hold their heading manually; he had turned off the autopilot and charts. He was sailing without the engine, without any assistance from modern gadgets; he was sailing by instinct, and he was in his element. *Slow Dance* was not digging in the trench, or taking water over her bow, but instead, she was riding along the side of the waves. At times it seemed as if the mast would lie down on the water. The rush of the wind was intoxicating. Jess and Maeve were on the outside sofa using their feet to wedge themselves between the sofa and the table. They held Trinidad tightly between them to keep her safe.

"Bring it on!" Victor was at the stern holding onto the flagpole with one hand. The wind tore at his shirt and his blond hair blew wildly across his face. Jess feared the wind would take him at any moment.

Maeve called out to him, "You look like Lieutenant Dan in *Forrest Gump!*"

Several hours later, the sea calmed, and the sky cleared. A rainbow arched across the horizon as the boys furloughed the headsails and let out the main. Jess went below to think about supper, her heart still pounding from the sheer thrill of sailing through the squall. She felt like a real sailor.

To Jess's delight, Maeve joined her to lend a hand in the galley. "How will you prepare the fish?" she asked.

Jess was just about to answer when Anders called down from the top of the stairs.

"We anchor in thirty minutes, and Don and Zack are planning a beach fire. They're pulling out a grill to cook the fish."

Jess asked one of the guys to bring the coolers to the galley. Maeve gathered plates and utensils while Zack loaded the folding chairs and straw mats into the dinghy. Jess knew Don wouldn't forget the alcohol, so no need to ask.

When the anchor settled, they assembled everything they'd need for the beach and Victor carried the cooler to the upper deck. Jess followed carrying a container of fresh sliced mango for dessert.

Victor plopped the cooler down and reached his hands toward the sky. "My God, I am in paradise."

Don looked at him with an annoyed expression. "We're on a small island in the Astrolabe Reef area, an amazing place, yes, and also treacherous as hell. All these islands are surrounded by reef; one wrong move and you're finished, mate."

Zack pressed the control to lower the dinghy into the water. Cliff maneuvered the dinghy near the ladder and Jess climbed in with the crew. Zack handed Trini down to Maeve before climbing down.

"Come, Miss T, I've got you."

The evening proved magical. The sky was filled with a million stars and once again, Zack built one of his amazing campfires. Cliff was discussing sailing with Victor. "I spent one hundred thousand miles under sail. I was born at the wrong time, kid. I was meant to be on the wooden ships in the 1700s, sailing by celestial navigation, tossing a knotted line in the sea to determine depth. Those were times of raw adventure."

Jess was watching how his face lit up in the firelight. She pictured him dressed like a seventeenth-century sailor, and it suited him.

Anders was going for seconds of Jess's mahi. "This fish is amazing. What is the sauce? We have a wonderful chef."

"Thank you," replied Jess. "The fish is marinated in chili, cumin, fresh cilantro, fresh lime, and garlic. After grilling, it's topped with a fresh fruit salsa."

Anders was nodding his head. "Yes, and the salsa has a kick."

"It has a few fresh chilis," Jess answered. She noticed Anders enjoyed food as if it had been scarce all his life. He ate with gusto, which irritated Don, who was picky about food.

Maeve pulled out her guitar and began playing Bonnie Raitt's "I Can't Make You Love Me."

Jess felt Cliff's eyes on her. It was one of her favorite songs, but she was happy when it ended.

The fire died, and the music eventually ceased. It was time to clean up. Jess looked over toward Cliff and caught him staring at her. She knew that look; she had seen it before in Malolo.

The crew began packing up and Jess stood up to assist, but Cliff caught her hand.

"No, sit with me. We need to talk about what happened in Denarau. I've had a lot on my mind, and not just about the crew and the boat. I've spent most of my time on this trip with the boys in the pilothouse or on deck with the sails, so I need to clear the air. You said you needed to think about things, and I wonder what you've concluded."

Jess took the glass of wine from his hand and slowly sipped it.

"What was I supposed to be thinking about?"

She wanted to give him the space to explain himself. She had already laid out her boundaries, and she didn't want to risk sounding desperate.

Cliff took the wineglass back from her. "Listen, he began," his voice trembling slightly, "I never want to hurt you, Jess. I was a coward not to send Sophia away before she stepped foot on the boat, not after what we shared in Malolo." His face was illuminated in the moonlight as he sat staring into the embers. The gentle waves lapped at the shore, mirroring the turmoil within him. He set the wineglass in the sand and placed his hands on his knees as if he was going to stand up, but he didn't. Rather, he looked at Jess, his eyes conveying to her what he lacked in words as he spoke.

"Jess, I am not good with words . . . but I need you to know I've had time to reflect on my bad behavior, not only with Sophia, but other women as well. Do you think there is potential for redemption?"

Jess wondered how many women those pleading eyes had destroyed. Cliff continued,

"I love you, Jess." He reached out, taking her hand gently. "I've been miserable wondering if you would forgive my handling of the Sophia situation. I told her the first night at dinner I was ending it. I let her know I was going to tell her when I came back to L.A. for the boat part. I wanted to send her back as soon as she arrived, but I froze. I never flinch in a storm, but put me in front of a scorned woman, and I'm helpless. I handled it poorly, but when you left to see Carlo the tenson built up and I exploded. I wanted her gone. Sophia will probably never forgive me, but it's you I hope will forgive me. I never want to hurt you again. In the beginning you were a necessity—"

"A necessity . . . is that what I am?"

"Of course not. I can't imagine life without you. You make me feel things I thought I was incapable of, say things I never felt comfortable saying. Sleep with me tonight. I miss you next to me. I miss seeing you first thing in the morning."

He was so vulnerable and genuine, looking intently at her as he awaited her response. Jess felt her emotions bubbling to the surface, sensing hope mingling with uncertainty.

Don called from the dinghy asking if they were ready to shove off. Cliff called back, "No, we're going to enjoy the rest of the fire. Come back in an hour."

Cliff took Jess's hand and pulled her up from the chair. "How about a naked swim under the stars?" he said, beginning to remove his shirt. "Join me."

Making him wait, she took off her shorts, T-shirt, bra and panties and then followed him into the water. The sea was cool on her naked body as she walked on its soft, sandy bottom. Wrapping her arms around him, she softly kissed his lips. She was overcome with wanting him as she wrapped her legs around him. He playfully teased her with his tongue. With the buoyancy of the saltwater holding her up, she placed Cliff's hands on her hips. They stayed that way, connected and kissing until she shivered. Cliff carried her from the water to the straw mats where he covered her with his shirt as they lay in silence, holding each other and looking up at the stars.

As the new day filtered through the portholes of their cabin, Cliff spooned Jess, his arm wrapped around her body and his hand on her breast. She listened to his rhythmic breathing.

Trini sat patiently waiting to be invited onto the bed, and Jess shook her head to signal not yet. Jess knew nothing would be the same. Her sailing adventure with Captain Reed was forever changed. Now, he was Cliff, and she could not go back.

As soon as Cliff stirred awake, he hugged Jess tightly against his chest and began kissing her back. Trinidad jumped on the bed but lay still, sensing the moment.

"Miss T is just the sweetest thing." Jess had rolled over on her stomach and was looking at him.

Cliff snapped his fingers and Trini jumped off the bed. He then propped himself up on one elbow and looked down at Jess, who was smiling.

"Me too," she said.

"You too what?" he asked.

"Love you."

They climbed the steps out of the pilothouse to the upper deck, Trinidad trotting behind. Don was checking the outside helm when Anders and Victor carried up fresh coffee. Victor poured Cliff and Jess a cup and handed it to them.

Maeve shot Cliff a coy look. "You're in good form this morning, Captain."

Victor was smiling from ear to ear. "You two are such a great couple."

Don pursed his lips and raised one eyebrow. "No comment."

Zack looked at his brother. "Lighten up, bro."

Don took his coffee and walked away. Attempting to switch the mood, Anders asked, "What's the plan, Captain?"

"Let's sail outside the reef and do some diving and snorkeling. All in favor say *aye!*"

54

No Going Back

December 2024
The Great Astrolabe Reef, Kadavu, Fiji

Slow Dance anchored outside the vast and colorful Astrolabe Reef for a day of diving and snorkeling. Don opted to stay on board to ensure the yacht didn't drift onto the reef, and Zack finessed the dinghy to the perfect spot for jumping in near the fifty-foot coral wall. Victor, Maeve, and Anders were already in the water, as Cliff was adjusting a weight belt to Jess's waist.

"Trust me, this is better than scuba. It's surface-supplied diving; you have an umbilical cord to the surface."

Zack tapped the tank. "You'll be fine. I'll be watching over the tank."

Jess felt her anxiety levels rise. "I am uneasy about this. I'm not a water baby like the rest of you and would prefer to appreciate the beauty of the reef from the surface."

Cliff adjusted his tank and mask. "I've got you, and I am not going to let anything happen to you. Who'll feed me if you drown? We'll descend slowly to no more than twenty feet. Do you trust me?"

"Not really," she answered.

Cliff flipped backward into the water.

Placing the breathing mask over her face and pointing her flippers upward, Jess slid ungracefully off the dinghy into the sea.

Once she got her bearings, Cliff took her hand, and they slowly began descending the face of the reef. Almost immediately she panicked, pulling her hand away from his and kicking hard toward the surface, which was futile because the weight belt was holding her down. The fear of drowning overwhelmed her as she attempted to undo the belt.

Suddenly, she felt Cliff's arms around her. He was trying to calm her. He held her in place, and their flippers began to move in unison, creating a rhythm. Closing her eyes, she began to breathe normally, feeling weightless, thinking this must be what it felt like to float in space.

Cliff held her until her breathing completely normalized, and she began to relax. He pointed to the reef and for the first time, Jess focused on its beauty. The world was transformed into a breathtaking spectacle of colors and life. Her heart raced with anticipation as they descended farther, her eyes filled with wonder at the colorful wall of soft coral; she marveled at the multitude of colors—electric blues, fiery orange, and shimmering silvers. Sunlight filtered down in shafts, casting a magical glow over the reef and illuminating the intricate patterns of the coral formations.

Cliff took Jess's hand and touched it to a delicate sea fan, and a surge of emotion welled up inside her—a mix of awe, gratitude, and a profound connection to the natural world. Tears filled up behind her mask as she was struck by the fragility and resilience of this underwater ecosystem, far removed from the hectic surface world. In that moment, she felt a deep sense of peace and belonging. She had discovered a hidden place inside herself, a part that always longed for the tranquility and beauty of the ocean.

As the sunlight illuminated the brilliant colors surrounding her, she marveled at the copious species of tropical fish swirling around her in a kaleidoscope of hues. No wonder the captain wanted her to experience what he considered the most freeing sensation in the world.

As her fears dissipated, she completely surrendered, and after twenty minutes of exploration, the captain held her hand, returning her to the surface.

Cliff removed his mask, then assisted Jess in removing her weighted belt and breathing mask. Tossing it into the dinghy, he turned to her and saw that she was crying.

"You okay?"

She put her hands on his shoulders, their flippers keeping them afloat.

"Thank you. I had no idea how beautiful it would be . . . I'm so glad you didn't let me chicken out."

Offering his hand, Cliff helped Jess climb into the dinghy. He wrapped a towel around her to warm her as the other crew piled into the dinghy and Zack turned in the direction of *Slow Dance*.

That evening, Jess set the outdoor table with a white tablecloth, candles, fine china, and crystal wineglasses. She prepared the last of Victor's mahi-mahi, au gratin potatoes, and a freshly tossed salad. Maeve opened several bottles of pinot grigio and placed them on ice.

They anchored in the calm bay under a blanket of stars with a crescent new moon overhead, and the evening meal was filled with lively conversation and jovial camaraderie. Maeve entertained with her guitar and lovely vocals, and Victor provided light percussion on the hand drum. Jess snuggled up to Cliff. They had become a couple. The only one missing from the evening festivities was Don, who had retired to his cabin with a sandwich and a few beers after proclaiming how much he hated fish. His departing statement to Jess was a sarcastic comment regarding too much healthy food and not enough sausages.

In the morning, *Slow Dance* sailed toward the beach at Point Washington. Cliff scudded the boat along the reef to enter the deep inner lagoon. Jess could see the lighter turquoise hues of the inner shallow lagoon where he intended to anchor. His excitement showed as they lowered the dinghy and cast off toward the shore. Their cooler was packed with sandwiches, cold beer, and bottled water. Victor was bouncing on the edge of the dinghy, feet dangling in the water like an enthusiastic child, while Trinidad began her usual whining as the dinghy approached the beach. Unable to contain himself, Victor did a backflip into the water and Trini jumped in after him. The two young pups swam the short distance to the beach. Don and Zack secured the boat, and Anders carried the picnic to a shady spot under some coconut palms.

After a swim, they were enjoying their lunch when a large man in camouflage shorts and high-top leather boots came marching toward them.

"Yeah, mate, you can't be here. This is a private island. We're building a resort up that hill there."

Victor addressed him. "We were unaware, sir. Our captain made his first landfall here years ago, and now it's 2024. He has sailed his yacht from Los Angeles to this exact beach where he landed. It's amazing he sailed back here forty-five years later . . . don't you agree?"

Trinidad, who was covered in sand and seemed to understand the situation, instinctively started licking the man's leg above his heavy boot. Victor picked the little dog up before the man became annoyed by her affections. "He did it before GPS," he continued, "so incredible! Don't you agree?"

The man softened his stance. "Well, that's bonza, mate; stay for a bit on the beach, but don't go trekking up the hill."

The man turned and walked toward the hillside, his heavy feet laboring through the deep sand.

Cliff was about to speak when the loud sound of machinery interrupted him. Looking over, they saw a backhoe gouging into the island's hillside where the village once stood. Cliff's brow furrowed. He seemed lost in contemplation, and as he finally turned to Jess, his face was filled with disappointment. "The world is fading, Jess, beneath layers of concrete and technology. The modern world eventually finds its way everywhere."

Jess began to speak, her voice infused with excitement and wonder, painting vivid pictures of untouched islands and hidden wonders waiting to be explored.

"I've been doing some research and beyond Fiji there are some undeveloped places: Vanuatu, the Solomon Islands, Papua New Guinea, and seventeen thousand islands in Indonesia, including Bali. All of that before Thailand. There are land divers in Vanuatu on Pentecost Island. It's a tradition to celebrate the sweet potato festival. They are the original bungee jumpers, and their village women sing ancient tribal songs to call up sea turtles from the ocean."

As Jess described these incredible adventures, she could tell she had momentarily lifted the weight of his thoughts.

Cliff reached out and touched Jess's face. "Who knew my little cookie who was fearful of the sea would be up for such an adventure?"

Jess answered. "Who's afraid when there is an amazing captain at the helm of a magnificent ship?"

Captain Reed grabbed Jess, pulling her down on the blanket. Lying on top of her, he said, "Have I told you lately how wonderful you are?"

"No," she answered, "but you can show me later tonight."

55

Don of the Dead

December 2024
Viti Levu, Fiji

Cliff piloted *Slow Dance* into the slip at Denarau, and without issuing a single command, he watched his experienced crew dock the boat. Anders and Victor placed the inflated fenders on the docking side of the boat. Zack had the spring line, Don took the bow line, and the stern line was in Jess's hands as she manually pulled the yacht toward the dock.

Cliff turned off the engine and went to the rail to watch Jess. He had shown Jess how to use the stern line to manually pull *Slow Dance* to the dock. He explained how leveraging the vessel's physics makes the task of pulling the megaton boat an easy process.

That evening, Cliff treated everyone except Don to dinner at Carlo's restaurant. As they shared laughter and stories over their dinner the atmosphere was vibrant, filled with clinking glasses and the murmur of satisfied customers. Carlo watched the happy group from behind the counter, his once hopeful gaze darkening with a mix of envy and resignation, knowing he lost his chance with Jess.

Happy and a bit tipsy, Jess ventured to the ladies' room, where Carlo, who had been waiting silently in the shadows, caught her off guard. Jess gasped as she came face-to-face with him at the rear of the restaurant. His eyes were filled with frustration and disappointment.

"Carlo! You startled me."

Carlo took a step closer to Jess. "I can't help but feel a twinge of bitterness," he said. "I wish I could have been the one to take you on those adventures you dream of. I thought there was something special between us. I know you felt it too. I imagined sharing on a deeper level, Jess."

She felt trapped in the moment, the weight of Carlo's emotions pressing on her. She stood silently grappling with what to say. Carlo was staring at her, striving to maintain his composure. Panic rose as she realized she had no idea how to respond, and in a blur of instinct, she blurted out, "I have to pee," before darting into the safety of the ladies' room. The door shut behind her with a soft click, leaving Carlo standing there, as the lively sounds of the restaurant faded into an uncomfortable silence.

When Jess ventured out of the restroom, Carlo was gone.

Back at the table, Cliff had ordered several bottles of fine Australian wine and was proposing a toast.

"Here's to some of the best sailing on *Slow Dance* this captain has experienced in a long time, and a regretful farewell to our fly fisherman from Wyoming."

Victor stood up holding his glass in the air. "And here's to the best captain on the high seas. Thank you for welcoming me onto your amazing sailboat! I had the best time a cowboy could ever hope to have!"

The next morning, Victor boarded a plane to Wyoming, and Jess was sorry to see him go. She much preferred him to his Swedish friend.

Zack, Anders, and Maeve were on the bow sorting out the sails, and Cliff was on deck with Jess, enjoying a second cup of coffee. Don left *Slow Dance* the previous night after settling in the marina, and he hadn't been seen or heard from since.

Cliff took a banana from the fruit bowl centerpiece and broke a piece off for Trini. "I'm looking forward to sailing on with you, Jess. This last year has breathed new life into me. I wouldn't want to do any of this without you. One more quick trip back to Los Angeles to check in with my doctors, and when I return, we'll crew up and set sail for Vanuatu."

"I am looking forward to sailing on as well," said Jess, "but not with Don. I know he is experienced, but I am worried about him on such a long crossing. His attitude has not been the greatest, and his drinking is a valid concern."

Cliff nodded. "I haven't forgotten how he abandoned us on the boat in Vava'u. Don is confident but lazy, thinks on his feet but disorganized—and you're right. He drinks to the point it interferes with his job."

Jess added, "He hasn't tended to the dinghy or washed down the boat since we returned."

"True, he delegated that to Zack. We can't enjoy the journey if we feel insecure about our crew and our ship." There was a hint of respect in his tone as he acknowledged her concern. She could tell he appreciated that she referred to it as *our ship*. "*Slow Dance* is ready for a long voyage. The water-makers are functioning, generators, propeller shaft, refrigeration, ice makers all good, full water tanks and enough fuel to make it to Bali. Once we get to Phuket, Thailand, I am going to replace the teak deck, varnish inside and out, have new sails made, new rigging, and repaint the superstructure. I'll look to hire a project manager to oversee the work. I want this trip to be memorable for the right reasons."

Jess smiled, remembering all the captain's previous mishaps at sea. "This is a big port, Cliff, with lots of options, and I am confident we will find a replacement for Don and Zack."

He leaned over and gently kissed her cheek, a gesture that felt both warm and sincere. "What makes a girl like you fall for an old pirate like me? Do you have any idea how rare it is to find a live-aboard wife?"

Jess wondered if he had just made a Freudian slip when he said *wife*.

The Google yacht arrived in the marina bringing with it nineteen international crew members with a thirst for some raucous shore leave. The sun was setting, casting a warm glow over the ocean as Jess and Cliff strolled along the boardwalk in Denarau. They found a lively bar, where the sounds of laughter and clinking glasses filled the air, and Maeve suddenly appeared at the door motioning them to come in. "Join us for a pint?" she asked.

Entering the bar, Cliff and Jess joined the couple at their table. Jess was taking in the scene.

The bar was bustling with tourists, locals, and the crew from Yacht Google. At one corner of the bar stood a pool table with a crowd of spectators watching a game of doubles between none other than the African brothers and some poor, unsuspecting takers. Don was clad in a flashy Hawaiian shirt open to his navel and wearing a confident grin and bragging to the small crowd regarding his victories at the game of billiards. He chalked his cue, ready to show off, continuing to boast about how well-known he was for his skills, when across from Don stood his Irish crewmate, petite Maeve, with her fiery red hair and sly smile. She had gone over to observe the scene, sipping her Irish whiskey, and Cliff, Jess, and Anders followed.

Don racked the balls and called out, "Anyone want to challenge the champ?" Some in the crowd rolled their eyes at Don's arrogance.

With a twinkle in her eye, the Irish girl stepped forward. "I'll take you on."

The crowd was surprised that she was even interested in playing. Cliff put his hand on Maeve's shoulder. "You might want to reconsider."

Zack said, "In all fairness, Don, give Maeve a fighting chance, let her break."

The spectators began taking bets, with Anders laying odds on his girl and the others placing their bets on Don, the obvious choice to win.

Maeve broke, sinking a low ball.

Chalking her pool cue for the second shot, she was eyeing the table carefully when Zack began instructing her.

"Look, darling, your best shot is the five ball, and if you bank here"—he pointed to the spot—"you may have a chance to put it in the side pocket."

Maeve took a sip from her whiskey glass and set it down. "Okay, that could work. Let me try." She then proceeded to sink every ball on the table—calling each pocket first. The eight ball was the last one in for the win.

The group broke out in cheers. Don being the stubborn misogynistic man that he was, called it pure luck and challenged Maeve to several one-on-one rematches. If Maeve broke the set, Don never had the chance to sink one ball, as she called every pocket.

Everyone cheered, and Don earned the nickname "Don of the Dead," which greatly irritated him.

56

Malefactor

December 2024
Port Denarau Marina, Fiji

Jess was impressed.

"Where did you learn to play pool like that? You're a regular Minnesota Fats, girl."

Maeve smiled. "It's very cold in Cork, and many a night at the pub was spent playing pool. I was on the women's billiard team for five years and won myself a trophy or two."

Jess shook her head. "How about some whiskey? The look on Don's face when you beat the pants off him. Priceless!"

Jess recognized Don's attitude had noticeably soured, a sharp contrast to the vibrant environment around him. Anders and Maeve confided in Jess that they once admired Don's skills but were concerned at his current behavior. On more than one occasion Jess heard Don snap at the couple and Zack if they questioned his decisions or maintenance tasks. Ever since Maeve humiliated him at the pool table, Don was drinking more than usual, using the island's laid-back atmosphere as an excuse to avoid responsibility.

Cliff once had high hopes for Don, believing in his potential. But now, it seemed Don settled into complacency, ignoring routine checks and upkeep that were essential for any safe voyage. Jess watched Don's apathy grow, and with each passing day the gulf between him and Cliff grew wider. Don's reckless behavior left Jess wondering what the future held for the once promising young captain.

"I wish I could take you with me, Jess," Cliff said, his voice softening as Jess walked him to his gate at the Nadi airport. "It's going to be a long two weeks."

Jess felt herself smile. "I'll be a phone call away, and when you get back, we'll plan our sail to Thailand. It's so exciting."

"Just promise me you'll call if anything goes wrong," he insisted.

Jess put her arms around him. "Don't worry so much. Zack, Anders, and Maeve are still aboard and will keep everything in check until you get back. Go take care of your business. I've got this."

Cliff sighed. "As they say in Spanish, *Unico en su clase.* You're one of a kind. I am worried about the Mercury engine on the dinghy. I instructed Don to have it looked at, and if it's on its way out he needs to get me bids on replacing it. Zack is also aware, so stay on them, because we'll need to clear out of Fiji as soon as I return to make our weather window to Vanuatu."

Jess was concerned. "What about looking for another captain?"

"I can handle the navigation myself, but it would be more pleasant with a reliable crew. We can work on that when I return. Meanwhile, keep it under your hat for now. I don't want Don catching wind of it."

Jess sighed. "Don already senses his days are numbered."

Cliff nodded in acknowledgment. "If I can shorten my trip I will. It depends on if the boat parts ordered have come in to West Marine. "

Cliff's flight began to board, and he held Jess in a long embrace.

Reluctantly releasing him, Jess said jokingly, "Send me pictures of all the pretty girls you're flirting with."

Picking up his bag, Cliff kissed Jess, and as he was walking toward the gate, he called back to her, "Stay away from Carlo's!"

Jess returned to the marina the same time as Don, who appeared disheveled and hungover.

"I'd like to speak with you when you . . ." Jess hesitated. "When you feel up to it."

"Right mate, after a shower," Don answered her, his feet unsteady, before heading to his cabin.

The sun hung low over Denarau, casting a pinkish hue over *Slow Dance* as Don and Jess stood on the foredeck under the mast, the air thick with tension, a stark contrast to the sea breeze that usually brought calm. Don leaned against the railing, beer in hand, his eyes bloodshot, and his demeanor defiant. Jess remained poised, approaching Don with concern she knew probably showed on her face.

"Don," she began, her voice steady but gentle, "we need to talk about how things have been on board. Your behavior has me and the crew worried."

Don glanced at her, a sneer forming on his lips. "Worried? They should focus on their jobs."

"It's your job to lead them," she replied, maintaining composure. "Your disappearing for days and excessive drinking isn't just affecting you. It affects all of us."

"I don't need a lecture from you," he snapped. "You are no longer the cook, love. You're the owner's girl, and that never goes well for me. Always the owner's wife that gets me sacked. Just leave me be," he muttered, his defiance faltering.

"I'll be here, Don, if you want to talk. We used to get on well together," she said softly, turning away, leaving him to wrestle with his demons, uncertain what would come next. She hoped the situation would calm until Cliff returned.

Under the starlit sky of Denarau, *Slow Dance* rocked gently in the harbor, the soft lapping of waves barely masking the sounds of revelry coming from the boardwalk establishments. Cliff was gone less then twelve hours, and Jess missed him already. Don was going to be a problem, and she would need to go around him to Zack and Anders for repairs to the dinghy engine. If the motor was unfixable, she would search for a replacement with assistance from Zack and Anders.

Her thoughts settled, Jess retired to the captain's cabin with Trinidad for some much needed sleep.

Whatever Jess had been dreaming quickly faded into an unsettling reality as she felt hands pressing into her—calloused, hot, and pinning her down. The air heavy with the smell of salt and alcohol. Panic surged through her. *It can't be happening. Why isn't Trini barking?* The realization jolted her awake, her heart racing, and the nightmare loomed closer. Hands, uninvited and clumsy, stirred her from her sleep.

"Hey there," Don slurred, his voice thick, filling the dim cabin. "It's just us now."

Jess blinked in confusion, her mind struggling to process the scene. Horror washed over her as she fully comprehended the situation.

"What are you doing? Get away from me!" she exclaimed, her voice sharp with panic as she pushed Don off the bed with surprising strength, fury igniting in her expression.

"Come on, don't be like that," he mumbled.

"Leave now!" she yelled.

The confrontation escalated, their voices ringing through the cabin until he finally retreated, the weight of his drunken decisions cashing down on him like a wave.

The next afternoon, Jess found herself on the dock with Zack, discussing plans to evaluate the dinghy engine, when she spotted Don approaching. He looked disheveled and uneasy; a pounding headache evident on his face.

"Can we talk?" he asked, his voice hoarse and laced with panic. Jess could see the regret forming in his eyes, but her heart was still heavy with anger and disappointment.

"What do you want?" she snapped.

Don gave Zack a sheepish look. "Can you leave us?"

Zack glared at Don. "I heard everything last night," he said and retreated to the pilothouse.

"I am sorry," Don stammered, desperation creeping into his voice. "I didn't mean to—"

"Didn't mean to what?" she interrupted, crossing her arms. "Assault me? You think that's just a mistake?"

Don swallowed hard, the gravity of his actions sinking in.

"Please, Jess, don't tell anyone." His charm, once so potent, now felt like a distant memory.

Jess shook her head, her resolve unwavering. "This isn't just about you anymore. You lost my trust, Don. I am going to tell the captain because for all I know if I kept it a secret from him, you would tell him a different version, one where I willingly let you in my bed, and he would never believe me when I told him the truth."

As Jess walked away, she wondered if Don would ever realize the consequences of his reckless actions.

57

Sailing On

January 2025
Port Denarau Marina, Fiji

Jess dialed the country code, followed by Cliff's number.

"Hey, it's me. I hope everything is going well with the doctors. I need to talk to you about something important that happened. It's about Don."

"Baby! Is everything okay?" he asked, suddenly concerned.

Jess took a breath before speaking, knowing the weight of her words. "Last night Don got exceptionally loaded and in the middle of the night I woke up to him in our bed trying to remove my shorts. He was naked and reeked of alcohol. He was extremely apologetic when he sobered up, begging me not to say anything. Zack heard me yelling at him to get out of the cabin. I am sure Anders and Maeve heard it all as well."

Cliff was silent.

Jess continued, "I really hope you understand why I am telling you this. It's important to me that you know what happened. You need to think about what may happen next, especially when you return to the boat. We agreed Don must be replaced and he knows darn well you're going to sack him when you get back. He so much as said so."

Cliff's voice broke. "So, Don randomly jumped naked into your bed? Had you been out partying with him and the others?"

"No!" Jess's cheeks heated with anger, but she held firm. "I was not out partying, and no, I did nothing to lead Don to believe he was welcome in my bed. In fact, I had a stern conversation with him when I returned from the airport regarding his drinking and how it was affecting all of us on board. Your insinuation is disappointing, Cliff. The others can attest to what happened, and your attitude is the exact reason why I am telling you now, because if I remained silent, as Don wished, what would you think if when firing Don, he blurted out he was in my bed while you were gone? Would you believe me or him? I think we both know the answer to that. Without trust, there is zero hope of success in any relationship. As soon as you cheat, the trust is gone, everything is gone, and you should know."

Cliff took a moment to gather his thoughts, and when he spoke, his tone was filled with regret.

"I am sorry, Jess, for what I said. I shouldn't have implied you did something to encourage him. I do trust you completely, and I let my own insecurities get the better of me just then. Don deserves a pelting, but the guy is thirty years younger than me. The kid probably wants everything I have and decided to try a bite of my woman."

Jess cringed. "Jesus, I am old enough to be his mother."

Cliff whispered in the phone, "MILF."

"You're not funny," Jess said, still a bit annoyed.

"All kidding aside," Cliff said. "I want you to feel safe, in every way. I can take care of Don from here. Can you look immediately for two one-way tickets from Fiji to Johannesburg? Unfortunately, Fiji is one of the countries that follow maritime law, requiring me to fly Don and Zack to the country listed on their passport. Send me the reservation; I will pay with my credit card and email their tickets to them. I would like them gone before I arrive. It looks like all the boat parts are here, and I can cut my trip short. Can you deal with things for a bit longer?"

Jess answered, "Of course, and I have a lead on a Mercury four-stroke engine, brand-new, because the Honda is kaput." She could practically see Cliff smiling through the phone.

"That's my girl. I should make you captain."

Three days passed since Jess spoke with Cliff, having sent him the flight information for Don and Zack's return tickets to South Africa. Jess decided she should speak to Zack and Don rather than blindsiding them with plane tickets, creating an even more volatile scene. Don had been absent from *Slow Dance* for several days, but Zack was on deck this morning with Anders and Maeve. Trinidad, who had been sitting in Zack's lap, jumped to attention when she saw Jess.

"Good morning, all, and good morning to you, Miss T." Jess was aware they all went quiet when she came on deck. "Zack, can I have a word with you?"

Zack remained seated. "It's okay, Jess. Everyone knows what's going on. We got our ticket, and it sucks. Don and I want to fly to the British Virgin Islands to our mom and stepdad."

Jess felt genuine empathy. "I am sorry, Zack, but apparently Captain Reed had no choice but to fly you to the country of your passport."

Zack let out a huge sigh. "We fly out at five a.m. tomorrow morning, and I have no idea where Don is. We packed our gear yesterday, and he left."

"Will he make the flight?" Jess asked, concerned. "I can give you a lift to the airport."

Maeve chimed in. "Anders and I will take them, Jess."

Cliff arrived at *Slow Dance* relieved that Don and Zack had left the boat without further incident. He carried several suitcases containing spare parts for *Slow Dance*. Jess and Maeve were unpacking the suitcases, while Cliff and Anders studied the chart for the sail from Fiji to Vanuatu.

"Captain," Anders said. "I can handle *Slow Dance*. You saw me work the sails on our trip to Kadavu. My last two years of high school in Sweden were aboard the vessel *Gunilla*. Students work on the ship while taking classes. Graduation includes a rough sail to Tampa, Florida, in the U.S.A. My friend Erik graduated with me, and he is proficient in marine mechanics. He could join us in Port Vila, Vanuatu, if you buy his ticket and offer him a pay."

Cliff thought a moment. "That's an interesting prospect, and I'll think on it." Turning to Jess he said, "I just stepped on the boat, and the first thing I want to do is to take my girl out to dinner."

Cliff opted for the Thai restaurant along the waterfront. As the sun dipped below the horizon, casting a warm glow across the bay, he looked across the table at Jess.

"I wanted to say," he began, his voice full of emotion, "that I find your courage and determination inspiring." He reached for her hand. "The way you face challenges head on is admirable, Jess. I couldn't think of anyone I'd rather sail on with than you."

Jess felt a rush of gratitude. Their plan to sail to Thailand loomed ahead, a thrilling adventure that she hoped would bring them even closer.

"I was thinking," she said, "life is like a ladder. You must let go of one rung to reach up for the next one."

"As long as you don't fall off," he added with a grin. "It started with an accident. I didn't know the day you stepped onto my boat my life would change in so many wonderful ways."

Jess placed her hand on top of his. "Neither of us was in a peaceful place. I felt lost. I made a choice—against the advice of my sons and friends to board a sailboat and cross an ocean with strangers. Before this moment, I said yes to the wrong things and no to all the right things. Seems I had to lose everything to gain more than I could ever have imagined."

Reaching into his pocket Cliff took out five microchips and placed them in Jess's hand.

"Ocean charts for sailing from Fiji to Thailand, and maybe beyond if all goes well," he said.

"What about Anders's offer?" Jess asked.

Cliff took the microchips and placed them back in his pocket.

"It's five hundred miles to Port Vila. That's less than three days with a perfect weather window. You and I could do it alone, but I think it's a good plan to take him up on his offer. I need to think about his buddy Erik joining as our mechanic. I first want to see how the sail to Port Vila goes."

Jess nodded her approval.

Cliff paid the check and after pulling Jess's chair out, offered her his arm. Together they strolled along the boardwalk back to *Slow Dance.* Once aboard, he engulfed Jess in his arms.

"Come to the galley. There's this one thing I need your opinion on."

Jess followed Cliff below to the galley.

"What are you up to? You never come near the galley."

As they entered, Jess saw a dish towel tied with a ribbon lying on the counter.

"Something for the kitchen," he said.

"You're so silly."

Jess unwrapped the ribbon, and inside the dish towel was a wooden spoon.

"Just what I always wanted. Another wooden s—" Jess stopped as she saw the handle of the spoon had a pear-shaped diamond ring tied to it.

"Read the inscription inside," Cliff said.

Jess looked at the inscription, which read, "*Slow Dance with me.*"

Tears spilled down Jess's cheeks, a mix of joy and disbelief.

"I never thought . . . I mean, I hoped, but . . ."

She looked up at him, her heart racing. "Of course, yes! A thousand times yes!"

With that, Cliff slipped the ring onto her finger. The galley, once a place of work and practicality, transformed into a sanctuary of their dreams. Jess reached out, pulling him close.

"Now, about that spoon," she teased, holding it up. "What's it for? Cooking up more surprises?"

He grinned, that familiar spark lighting up his eyes.

"Well, there's always somethin' cookin' in this galley, but this one's for us. A symbol of our adventures to come. We'll share meals together, share stories, and laugh over burnt toast—because you know I can't cook to save my life. I'd be dead without you, Jess."

Jess answered him, "No worries, you will always be my captain, and I will always be your cookie."

"Except," he said, "you know more about sailing than I know about cooking. A lot more."

"Captain, my captain," she said with mock seriousness. "Are you afraid I'll mutiny?"

"I wouldn't put it past you," he said, holding her close and letting out one of those big barking laughs she loved.

They stepped onto the deck, the ocean breeze wrapping around them. The moon hung low in the sky, casting silver beams over the water, and the stars twinkled above like a thousand tiny candles lighting their path.

Acknowledgments

Writing a book is not a solitary endeavor, even though it may seem that way. I would like to extend my heartfelt gratitude to everyone who contributed to the creation of *The Captain's Cook*. This journey has been both challenging and rewarding, and I could not have done it without the support of many incredible individuals.

I am profoundly grateful to:

- ⚓ My friends, who offered their time to read drafts, provide feedback, and inspire me with their own creativity and passion. You have all been a source of motivation and your insights have significantly enriched this book.

- ⚓ My Palm Springs Writers Guild, I am indebted to your unwavering encouragement and belief in my vision.

- ⚓ Brown Books Publishing Group editor Ben Davidoff, whose thoughtful suggestions helped me refine my narrative, and to Bonnie Hill, who helped elevate my writing to new heights.

- ⚓ Ranee Alison Spina for taking a ball of clay and shaping it into chapters, and to my artist Conner Erb for turning pictures in my mind into remarkable illustrations.

⚓ The community of writers and readers, whose passion and dedication to literature continue to inspire me. Your companionship and shared love for the written word fueled my enthusiasm throughout this journey.

⚓ My readers for embarking on this journey with me. Your passion for stories fuels my creativity, and I hope *The Captain's Cook* brings you as much joy as it brought me.

This book is a testament to all the wonderful people who have supported and believed in me.

About the Author

Victoria Vanransom's extensive travels and rich experiences in the culinary world are reflected in *The Captain's Cook*. Asian culture profoundly shaped her culinary philosophy because she had the unique opportunity to learn directly from native women. Sharing time in the kitchen taught her about their cuisines, spices, and time-honored cooking techniques. These immersive experiences have given her a deep appreciation for the cultural significance of food and the stories it tells.

A graduate of culinary school, Victoria spent years honing her skills. In 1977, she joined The Good Earth Restaurant in Boulder, Colorado, and spent twelve years developing recipes and opening new locations. Victoria owned her own restaurant in Encinitas, California, for four years, and in 1997, she was back to corporate life as Executive Chef for a Palm Springs Marriott property. When her heart longed to see the ocean again, she moved to Malibu where she catered to private clients.

In addition to her culinary expertise, Victoria is an accomplished sailor, having logged over 150,000 sea miles as a chef aboard sailboats. Her journey at sea began in 2010, where her love for the ocean and culinary arts converged. Cooking at sea has allowed her to adapt to the challenges of limited resources while still creating flavorful, satisfying meals that reflect her diverse background.

Ms. Vanransom is an avid reader of fiction, nonfiction and current events. She lives in California with her whiskered writing assistants Cleo, Juji, and Piper.

Connect:

www.CaptainsCookNovel.com
Facebook: Author Victoria Vanransom
Instagram: @Captains_Cook_Novel

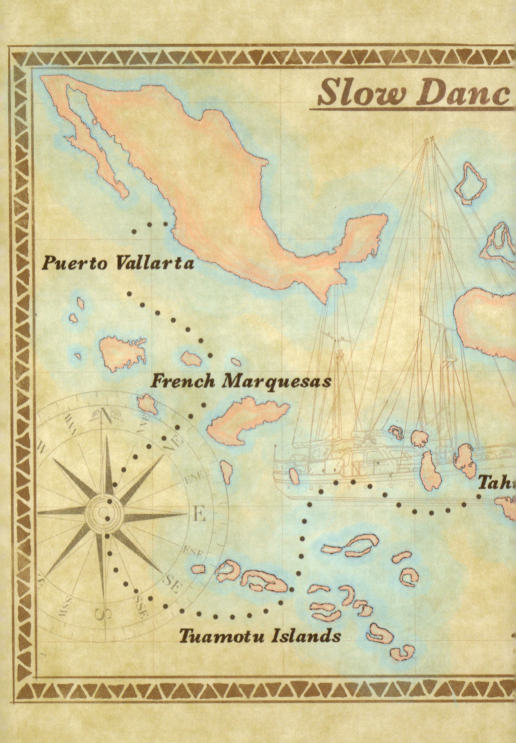